Praise for the novels of #1 *New York Times* bestselling author Debbie Macomber

"No one pens a Christmas story like Macomber."
—*RT Book Reviews*

"Macomber is a master storyteller, and [*The Christmas Basket*] is a testament to her lively skills... A warm and loving novel that is destined to quickly become a Christmas favorite."
—*Times Record News*

"Macomber is a skilled storyteller."
—*Publishers Weekly*

"Debbie Macomber tells women's stories in a way no one else does."
—*BookPage*

Praise for the novels of bestselling author Sheila Roberts

"Sheila Roberts makes me laugh. I read her books and come away inspired, hopeful and happy."
—#1 *New York Times* bestselling author Debbie Macomber

"[Sheila Roberts is] renowned for her stocking-stuffer tales."
—*Publishers Weekly*

"Quirky characters, snappy dialogue and sexy chemistry all combine to keep you laughing, as well as shedding a few tears, as you turn the pages."
—*RT Book Reviews* on *Merry Ex-Mas*

"You'll fall in love with both the town and the characters. Put this one on your reading list."
—*Fresh Ficton* on *Christmas on Candy Cane Lane*

Dear Friend,

Merry Christmas! I'm pleased that my holiday story *The Christmas Basket* is being published with *Merry Ex-Mas* by Sheila Roberts, a friend, almost neighbor and one of my favorite writers.

The Christmas Basket won a RITA® Award, which is the Romance Writers of America's highest award for excellence in writing. That's especially gratifying because it was chosen by my peers.

The holidays are a special time with our children and grandchildren, and our friends. It's a time of gathering together, building memories, sharing laughter and fun. My wish is that these two stories will be part of your holiday enjoyment.

Debbie Macomber

PS: I'd love to hear from you! You can reach me through my website (debbiemacomber.com) or via Facebook. Or you can write me at PO Box 1458, Port Orchard, WA 98366.

DEBBIE MACOMBER

SHEILA ROBERTS

Because It's Christmas

MIRA

MIRA

Recycling programs for this product may not exist in your area.

ISBN-13: 978-0-7783-1917-7

Because It's Christmas

Copyright © 2016 by Harlequin Books S.A.

The publisher acknowledges the copyright holders of the individual works as follows:

The Christmas Basket
Copyright © 2002 by Debbie Macomber

Merry Ex-Mas
Copyright © 2012 by Sheila Rabe

For questions and comments about the quality of this book, please contact us at CustomerService@Harlequin.com.

www.MIRABooks.com

Printed in U.S.A.

CONTENTS

THE CHRISTMAS BASKET

Debbie Macomber

Also by Debbie Macomber

To
Laurie and Jaxon Macomber
and
in memory of our son Dale

NOELLE MCDOWELL'S JOURNAL

December 1

I did it. I broke down and actually booked the flight to Rose. I have a ticket for December 18—Dallas to San Francisco to Portland and then the commuter flight to Rose.

All my excuses are used up. I always figured there was no going back, and yet that's exactly what I'm doing. I'm going home when I swore I never would. Not after what happened... Not after Thom Sutton betrayed me. I know, I know, I've always been dramatic. I can't help that—it's part of my nature.

When I was a teenager I made this vow never to return. I spoke it in the heat of passion, and no one believed me. For that matter, I didn't believe me, not really. But it proved to be so easy to stay away.... I hardly had to invent excuses. While I was in college I had an opportunity to travel to Europe two years in a row. Then in my junior year I had a summer job and was a bridesmaid in a Christmas wedding. And when my senior year rolled around, I was working as an intern for the software company, and it was impossible to get time off. After that... well, it was just simpler to stay away. Without meaning to, my family made it convenient. I didn't need to visit them; they seemed willing enough to come to Dallas.

All of that is about to end. I'm prepared to face my past. I joined Weight Watchers. If I happen to see Thom Sutton, I want him to know exactly what he's missing. I've already lost five of the ten pounds I need to get rid of, and by next week he'll hardly recognize me—if we even run into each other. We won't, of course, but just on the offchance, I plan to be prepared.

Good ol' Thom Sutton. I wonder what he's doing now. Naturally I could ask, but no one dares mention the name Sutton to my family. It's the Hatfields and McCoys or the Montagues and Capulets all over again. Except that it's our mothers who started this ridiculous feud.

If I really wanted to know about Thom, I could ask Megan or Stephanie. They're the only two girls out of my entire high school class who still live in Rose. But I wouldn't do that. Inquiring about Thom would only invite questions from them about what happened between the two of us. As far as I'm concerned, the fewer people who know, the better.

He's bound to be married, anyway. Good. I want him to be happy.

No, I don't.

If I can't be honest in my journal, then I shouldn't keep one. Okay, I admit it—what I really want is for him to have suffered guilt and regret all these years. He should have pined for me. His life should be a bleak series of endless days filled with haunting memories of me. It's what he deserves.

On a brighter note, I'm thrilled for Kristen. I'll return home, help her plan her wedding, hold my head high and pray that Thom Sutton has the opportunity to see me from afar, gorgeous and thin. Then I want him to agonize over all the might-have-beens.

One

It would be the wedding of the year. No—the wedding of the century.

Sarah McDowell intended to create the most exquisite event possible, a wedding worthy of *Vogue* magazine (or at least a two-page spread in the Rose, Oregon, *Gazette*). The entire town would talk about her daughter's wedding.

The foundation for Sarah's plans rested squarely on booking the Women's Century Club for the reception. It was why she'd maintained her association with the club after *that* woman had been granted membership. She was outraged that such a fine institution would lower itself to welcome the likes of Mary Sutton.

Sarah refused to dwell on the sordid details. She couldn't allow herself to get upset over something that had happened almost twenty years ago. Although it didn't hurt any to imagine Mary hearing—second-or third-hand, of course—about Kristen's wedding. As Sarah understood it, Mary's daughter had eloped. Eloped, mind you, with some riffraff hazelnut farmer. Sarah didn't know that for sure because it was her Christian duty not to gossip or think ill of others. However, sometimes information just happened to come one's way....

Pulling into the parking lot of the Women's Century Club, Sarah surveyed the grounds. Even this late in the year, the rose garden was breathtaking. Many of the carefully tended bushes still wore their blooms, and next June, when the wedding was scheduled, the garden would be stunning. The antique roses with their intoxicating scents and the more recent hybrids with their gorgeous shapes and colors would make a fitting backdrop for the beautiful bride and her handsome groom. It would be *perfect,* she thought with satisfaction. Absolutely perfect.

Sarah had stopped attending the Women's Century Club meetings three years ago. Well, there wasn't any need to obsess over the membership committee's sorry lapse in judgment. For many years Sarah had chaired that committee herself. The instant she stepped down, Mary Sutton had applied for membership to the prestigious club— and received it. Now the only social event Sarah participated in was the annual Christmas dance. Mary Sutton had robbed her of so much already, but Sarah wasn't letting her ruin that, too.

Sarah did continue to meet with other friends from the club and managed to keep up with the news. She understood that Mary had become quite active in the association. Fine. Good for her. It gave the woman something to write about in her column for the weekly *Rose Gazette.* Not that Sarah read "About Town." Someone had told her it was fairly popular, though. Which didn't bother her in the least. Mary was a good writer; Sarah would acknowledge that much. But then, what one lacked in certain areas was often compensated in others. And Mary was definitely lacking in the areas of generosity, fairness, ethics.... She could go on.

With a click of her key chain, Sarah locked her car and headed toward the large, two-story stone structure. There was a cold wind blowing in from the ocean, and she hurried up the steps of the large veranda that surrounded the house. A blast of warm air greeted her as she walked inside. Immediately in front of her was the curved stairway leading to the ballroom on the second floor. She could already picture Kristen moving elegantly down those stairs, her dress sweeping grandly behind her. Today, evergreen garlands were hung along the mahogany railing, with huge red velvet bows tied at regular intervals. Gigantic potted poinsettias lined both sides of the stairway. The effect was both festive and tasteful.

"Oh, how lovely," she said to Melody Darrington, the club's longtime secretary.

"Yes, we're very pleased with this year's Christmas decorations." Melody glanced up from her desk behind the half wall that overlooked the entry. The door to the office was open and Sarah heard the fax machine humming behind her. "Are you here to pick up your tickets for the Christmas dance?"

"I am," Sarah confirmed. "And I'd like to book the club for June seventh for a reception." She paused dramatically. "Kristen's getting married."

"Sarah, that's just wonderful!"

"Yes, Jake and I are pleased." This seriously understated her emotions. Kristen was the first of her three daughters to marry, and Sarah felt as if the wedding was the culmination of all her years as a caring, involved mother. She highly approved of Kristen's fiancé. Jonathan Clark was not only a charming and considerate young man, he held a promising position at an investment firm and had a degree in business. His parents were college professors who lived in Eugene; he was their only son. Whenever she'd spoken with Jonathan's mother, Louise Clark had sounded equally delighted.

Melody flipped the pages of the appointment book to June. "It's a good idea to book the club early."

Holding her breath, Sarah leaned over the half wall and stared down at the schedule. She relaxed the instant she saw that particular Saturday was free. The wedding date could remain unchanged.

"It looks like June seventh is open," Melody said.

"Fabulous." Sarah's cell phone rang, and she reached inside her purse to retrieve it. She sold real estate, but since entering her fifties, she'd scaled back her hours on the job. Jake, who was head of the X-ray department at Rose Hospital, enjoyed traveling. Sarah no longer had the energy to accompany Jake and also maintain her status as a top-selling agent. The number displayed on her phone was that of her husband's office. She'd call him back shortly. He was probably asking about the time of their eldest daughter's flight. Jake and Sarah were going to meet Noelle at the small commuter airport later in the day. What a joy it would be to have all three of their girls home for Christmas, not to mention Noelle's birthday, which was December twenty-fifth. This would be the first time in ten years that Noelle had returned to celebrate *anything* with her family. Sarah blamed Mary Sutton and her son for that, too.

"Should I give you a deposit now?" she asked, removing her checkbook.

"Since you're a member of the club, that won't be necessary."

"Great. Then that's settled and I can get busy with my day. I've got a couple of houses to show. Plus Jake and I are driving to the airport this afternoon to pick up Noelle. You remember our daughter Noelle, don't you?"

"Of course."

"She's living in Dallas these days, and has a high-powered job with one of the big computer companies." What Sarah didn't add was the Noelle had become a workaholic. Getting her twenty-eight-year-old daughter to take time off work was nearly impossible. Sarah and Jake made a point of visiting her once a year and sometimes twice, but this couldn't go on. Noelle had to get over her phobia about returning to Rose—and the risk of seeing Thom Sutton. Oh, yes, those Suttons had done a lot of damage to the McDowells.

With Kristen announcing her engagement and inviting the Clarks to share their Christmas festivities, Sarah had strongly urged Noelle to come home for the celebration. This was an important year for their family, and it was absolutely necessary that Noelle be there with them. After some back-and-forth discussion, she'd finally capitulated.

"Before you leave, there's something you should know," Melody said hesitantly. "There's been a rule change about members using the building."

"Yes?" Sarah tensed, anticipating a roadblock.

"The new rule states that only members who have completed a minimum of ten hours' community service approved by the club will be permitted to lease our facilities."

"But I'm an active part of our community already," Sarah complained. She provided plenty of services to others.

"I realize that. Unfortunately, the service project in question must be determined by the club and it must be completed by the end of December to qualify for the following year."

Sarah gaped at her. "Do you mean to say that in addition to everything else I'm doing in the next two weeks, I have to complete some club project?"

"You haven't been reading the newsletters, have you?" Melody asked, frowning.

Obviously not. Sarah refused to read about Mary Sutton, whose name seemed to appear in every issue these days.

"If you attended the meetings, you'd know it, too." Melody added insult to injury by pointing out Sarah's intentional absence.

Despite her irritation, Sarah managed a weak smile. "All right," she muttered. "What can I do?"

"Actually, you've come at an opportune moment. We need someone who's willing to pitch in on the Christmas baskets."

Sarah was trying to figure out how she could squeeze in one more task before the holidays. "Exactly what would that entail?"

"Oh, it'll be great fun. The ladies pooled the money they raised from the cookbook sale to buy gifts for these baskets. They've made up lists, and what you'd need to do is get everything on your list, arrange all the stuff inside the baskets and then deliver them to the Salvation Army by December twenty-third."

That didn't sound unreasonable. "I think I can do that."

"Wonderful." A smile lit up Melody's face. "The woman who's heading up the project will be grateful for some help."

"The woman?" That sounded better already. At least she wouldn't be stuck doing this alone.

"Mary Sutton."

Sarah felt as though Melody had punched her. "Excuse me. For a moment I thought you said *Mary Sutton.*"

"I did."

"I don't mean to be catty here, but Mary and I have... a history."

"I'm sure you'll be able to work something out. You're both adults."

Sarah was stunned by the woman's lack of sensitivity. She wanted to argue, to explain that this was unacceptable, but she couldn't think of exactly what to say.

"You did want the club for June seventh, didn't you?"

"Well, yes, of course, but—"

"Then be here tomorrow morning at ten to meet with Mary."

Numb and speechless, Sarah slowly turned and trudged toward the door.

"Sarah," Melody called. "Don't forget the dance tickets."

Dance. How could she think about the dance when she was being forced to confront a woman who detested her? The feeling might be mutual but that didn't make it any less awkward.

One across. A four-letter word for fragrant flower. Rose, naturally. Noelle McDowell penciled in the answer and moved to the next clue. A prickly feeling crawled up her spine and she raised her head. She disliked the short commuter flights. This one, out of Portland, carried twenty-four passengers. It saved having to rent a vehicle or asking her parents to make the long drive into the big city to pick her up.

The feeling persisted and she glanced over her shoulder. She instantly jerked back and slid down in her seat as far as the constraints of the seat belt allowed. It couldn't be. *No, please,* she muttered, closing her eyes. *Not Thom.* Not after all these years. Not now. But it was, it had to be. No one else would look at her with such complete, unadulterated antagonism. He had some nerve after what he'd done to her.

Long before she was ready, the pilot announced that the plane was preparing to land in Rose. On these flights, no carry-on bags were permitted, and Noelle hadn't taken anything more than her purse on board. Her magazines would normally go in her briefcase, but that didn't fit in the compact space beneath her seat, so the flight attendant had stowed it. She had a *Weight Watchers* magazine and a crossword puzzle book marked *EASY* in large letters across the top. She wasn't going to let Thom see her with either and stuffed them in the outside pocket of her purse, folding one magazine over the other.

Her pulse thundered like crazy. The man who'd broken her heart sat only two rows behind her, looking as sophisticated as if he'd stepped off the pages of *GQ.* He'd always been tall, dark and handsome—like a twenty-first-century Cary Grant. Classic features that were just rugged enough to be interesting and very, very masculine. Dark eyes, glossy dark hair. An impeccable sense of style. Surely he was married. But finding out would mean asking her sister or one of her friends who still lived in Rose. Coward that she was, Noelle didn't want to know. Okay, she did, but not if it meant having to ask.

The plane touched down and Noelle braced herself

against the jolt of the wheels bouncing on tarmac. As soon as they'd coasted to a stop, the Unfasten Seat Belt sign went off, and the people around her instantly leaped to their feet. Noelle took her time. Her hair was a fright. Up at three that morning to catch the 6:00 a.m. out of Dallas/Ft. Worth, she'd run a brush through the dark tangles, forgoing the usual routine of fussing with mousse. As a result, large ringlets fell like bedsprings about her face. Normally, her hair was shaped and controlled and coerced into gentle waves. But today she had the misfortune of looking like Shirley Temple in one of her 1930s movies—and in front of Thom Sutton, no less.

When it was her turn to leave her seat, she stood, looking staunchly ahead. If luck was with her, she could slip away unnoticed and pretend she hadn't seen him. Luck, however, was on vacation and the instant she stepped into the aisle, the handle of her purse caught on the seat arm. Both magazines popped out of the outside pocket and flew into the air, only to be caught by none other than Thom Sutton. The crossword puzzle magazine tumbled to the floor and he was left holding the *Weight Watchers* December issue. As his gaze slid over her, she immediately sucked in her stomach.

"I read it for the fiction," she announced, then added, "Don't I know you?" She tried to sound indifferent—and to look thin. "It's Tim, isn't it?" she asked, frowning as though she couldn't quite place him.

"Thom," he corrected. "Good to see you again, Nadine."

"Noelle," she said bitterly.

He glared at her until someone from the back of the line called, "Would you two mind having your reunion when you get off the plane?"

"Sorry," Thom said over his shoulder.

"I barely know this man." Noelle wanted her fellow passengers to hear the truth. "I once thought I did, but I was wrong," she explained, walking backward toward the exit.

"Whatever," the guy behind them said loudly.

"You're a fine one to talk," Thom said. His eyes were as dark and cold as those of the snowman they'd built in Lions' Park their senior year of high school—like glittering chips of coal.

"You have your nerve," she muttered, whirling around just in time to avoid crashing into the open cockpit. She smiled sweetly at the pilot. "Thank you for a most pleasant flight."

He returned the smile. "I hope you'll fly with us again."

"I will."

"Good to see you, Thom," the pilot said next.

Placing her hand on the railing of the steep stairs that led to the ground, Noelle did her best to keep her head high, her shoulders square—and her eyes front. The last thing she wanted to do was trip and make an even worse fool of herself by falling flat on her face.

She was shocked by a blast of cold air. After living in Texas for the last ten years, she'd forgotten how cold it could get in the Pacific Northwest. Her thin cashmere wrap was completely inadequate.

"One would think you'd know better than to wear a sweater here in December," Thom said, coming down the steps directly behind her.

"I forgot."

"If you came home more often, you'd have remembered."

"You keep track of my visits?" She scowled at him. A thick strand of curly hair slapped her in the face and she tossed it back with a jerk of her head. Unfortunately she nearly put out her neck in the process.

"No, I don't keep track of your visits. Frankly, I couldn't care less."

"That's fine by me." Having the last word was important, no matter how inane it was.

The luggage cart came around and she grabbed her briefcase from the top and made for the interior of the small airport. Her flight had landed early, which meant that her parents probably hadn't arrived yet. At least her luck was consistent—all bad. One thing was certain: the instant Thom caught sight of her mother and father, he'd make himself scarce.

He removed his own briefcase and started into the terminal less than two feet behind her. Because of his long legs, he quickly outdistanced her. Refusing to let him pass her, Noelle hurried ahead, practically trotting.

"Don't you think you're being a little silly?" he asked.

"About what?" She blinked, hoping to convey a look of innocence.

"Never mind." He smiled, which infuriated her further.

"No, I'm serious," she insisted. "What do you mean?"

He simply shook his head and turned toward the baggage claim area. They were the first passengers to get there. Noelle stood on one side of the conveyor belt and Thom on the other. He ignored her and she tried to pretend he'd never been born.

That proved to be impossible because ten years ago Thom Sutton had ripped her heart right out.

For most of their senior year of high school, Thom

and Noelle had been in love; they'd also managed to hide that fact from their parents. Sneaking out of her room at night, meeting him after school and passing notes to each other had worked quite effectively.

Then they'd argued about their mothers and the on-going feud between Sarah and Mary. They'd soon made up, however, realizing that what really mattered was their love. Because they were both eighteen and legally enti-tled to marry without parental consent, they'd decided to elope. It'd been Thom's suggestion. According to him, it was the only way they could get married, since the par-ents on both sides would oppose their wishes and try to put obstacles in their path. But once they were married, he said, they could bring their families together.

Noelle felt mortified now to remember how much she'd trusted Thom. But their whole "engagement" had turned out to be a ploy to humiliate and embarrass her. It seemed Thom was his mother's son, after all.

She'd been proud of her love for Thom, and before she left to meet him that fateful evening, she'd boldly an-nounced her intentions to her family. Her stomach twisted at the memory. Her parents were shocked as well as ap-palled; she and Thom had kept their secret well. Her mother had burst into tears, her father had shouted and her two younger sisters had wailed in protest. Undeterred, Noelle had marched out the door, suitcase in hand, to meet the man she loved. The man she'd defied her fam-ily to marry. Except that he didn't show up.

At first she'd assumed it was a misunderstanding— that she'd mistaken the agreed-upon time. Then, throwing caution to the wind, she'd phoned his house and asked to speak to him, only to learn that Thom had gone bowling.

He'd gone *bowling?* Apparently some friends from

school had phoned and off he'd gone, leaving her to wait in doubt and misery. The parking lot at the bowling alley confirmed his father's words. There was Thom's car—and inside the Bowlerama was Thom, carousing with his friends. Noelle had peered through the window and seen the waitress sitting on his lap and the other guys gathered around, joking and teasing. Before she went home, Noelle had placed a nasty note on his windshield, in which she described him as a scum-of-the-earth bastard. Their supposed elopement, their so-called love had all been a fraud, a cruel joke. She figured it was revenge what for her mother had done, losing Thom's grandmother's precious tea service. Not *losing* it, actually. She'd borrowed it to display at an open house for another real estate agent—and someone had taken it. That was how the feud started and it had escalated steadily after that.

To make matters worse, she'd had to return home in humiliation and admit that Thom had stood her up. Like the heroine of an old-fashioned melodrama, she'd been jilted, abandoned and forsaken.

For days she'd moped around the house, weeping and miserable. Thom hadn't phoned or contacted her again. It was difficult to believe he could be so heartless, but she had all the evidence she needed. She hadn't seen or talked to him since. For ten years she'd avoided returning to the scene of her shame.

The grinding sound of the conveyor belt gearing up broke Noelle from her reverie. Luggage started to roll out from the black hole behind the rubber curtain. Thom stepped forward, in a hurry to claim his suitcase and leave, or so it seemed. Noelle was no less eager to escape. She'd rather wait in the damp cold outside the terminal than stand five feet across from Thomas Sutton.

The very attractive Thomas Sutton. Even better-looking than he'd been ten years ago. Life just wasn't fair.

"I would've thought your wife would be here to pick you up," she said without looking at him. She shouldn't have spoken at all, but suddenly she had to know.

"Is that your unsubtle way of asking if I'm married?"

She ground her teeth. "Stood up any other girls in the last ten years?" she asked.

His eyes narrowed. "Don't do it, Noelle."

"You're the one who shouldn't have done it."

The man from the back of the plane waltzed past Noelle and reached for his suitcase. "Why don't you two just kiss and make up," he suggested, winking at Thom.

"I don't think so," Noelle said, sending Thom a contemptuous glare. She was astonished to see his anger, as though *he* had something to be angry about. *She* was the injured party here.

"On that I'll agree with you," Thom said. He caught hold of a suitcase and yanked it off the belt with enough force to topple a second suitcase. Without another word, he turned and walked out the door.

No sooner had he disappeared than the glass doors opened and in walked Noelle's parents.

Noelle's youngest sister held a special place in her heart. Carley Sue was an unexpected surprise, born when Noelle was fifteen and Kristen twelve. She'd only been three when Noelle left for college. Nevertheless, all three sisters remained close. Or as close as email, phone calls and the occasional visit to Dallas allowed.

Sitting on Noelle's bed, Carley rested her chin on one hand as Noelle unpacked her suitcase. "You don't mind that I have your old room, do you?" she asked anxiously.

"Heavens, no. It's only right that you do."

Some of the worry disappeared from Carley's eyes. "Are you really going to be home for two whole weeks?"

"I am." Noelle had tentatively planned a discounted cruise with a couple of friends. Instead, she was vacationing with her parents, planning her sister's wedding and trying not to think about Thom Sutton.

"You're going to the Christmas dance, aren't you?"

"Not if I can get out of it." Her mother was the one who insisted on these social outings, but Noelle would live the rest of her life content if she never attended another dance. They reminded her to much of those long-ago evenings with Thom....

"Mom says you're going."

Noelle sat down on the end of the bed and sighed. "I'll tell her I don't have anything to wear."

"Don't do that," Carley advised. "She'll buy you a pink dress. Mom loves pink. Not just any old pink, either, but something that looks exactly like Pepto-Bismol. She actually wanted Kristen to choose pink for her wedding colors." She grimaced. Reaching down for her feet, Carley curled her fingers over her bare toes and nodded vigorously. "You'd better come to the dance."

This was one of the reasons Noelle found excuse after excuse to stay away from Rose. Admittedly it wasn't the primary reason—Thom Sutton and his mother were responsible for that. But as much as she loved her family, she dreaded being dragged from one social event to the next. She could see her mother putting her on display—in Pepto-Bismol pink, according to Carley. If that wasn't bad enough, Sarah had an embarrassing tendency to speak as though Noelle wasn't in the room, bragging outrageously over every little accomplishment.

"Hey, you want to go to the movies tomorrow?" Noelle asked her sister.

Carley's eyes brightened. "Sure! I was hoping we'd get to do things together."

The doorbell chimed and Carley rolled onto her stomach. "That's Kristen. She's coming over without Jonathan tonight."

"You like Jonathan?" Noelle asked.

"Yeah." Carley grinned happily. "He danced with me once and no one asked him to or anything."

This was encouraging. Maybe he'd dance with her, too.

"Noelle!" Kristen called from the far end of the hallway. She burst into the room, full of energy and spirit. Instantly Noelle was wrapped in a tight embrace. "I can't believe you're here—oh, sis, it's so good to see you."

Noelle hugged her back. She missed the chats they used to have; discussions over the phone just weren't the same as hugs and smiles. "Guess who I ran into on the plane?" Noelle had been dying to talk about the chance encounter with Thom.

Some of the excitement faded from Kristen's eyes. "Don't tell me. Thom Sutton?"

Noelle nodded.

"Who's Thom Sutton?" Carley asked, glancing from one sister to the other.

"A guy I once dated."

"Were you lovers?"

"Carley!"

"Just curious." She shrugged as if this was information she was somehow entitled to.

"Where?" Kristen demanded.

"He was on the same flight as me."

"He still lives here, you know. He's some kind of executive for a mail-order company that's really taken off in the last few years. Apparently he does a lot of traveling."

"How'd you know that?" They'd always avoided the topic of Thom Sutton in their telephone and email communications.

"Jon told me about him. I think Thom might be one of his clients."

"Oh." Not only was Thom Sutton gorgeous, he was successful, too. "I suppose he's engaged to someone stunningly beautiful." That was to be expected.

"I hear—again from Jon—that he dates quite a bit, but there's no one serious."

Noelle shouldn't be pleased, but she couldn't help it. She didn't want to examine that reaction too closely.

"I want to know what happened," Carley demanded, rising to her knees. "I'm not a kid anymore. Tell me!"

"He was Noelle's high school sweetheart," Kirsten explained.

"The guy who left you at the altar?"

"Who told you that?" Noelle asked, although the answer was obvious. "And he didn't leave me at the altar." *Just being accurate,* she told herself. *I'm not defending him.*

"Mom told me 'cause she wants me to keep away from those Suttons. When I asked her why, she said you learned your lesson the hard way. She said a Sutton broke your heart and jilted you."

"There's more to it than that," Kristen told her.

"I want to know *everything*," Carley pleaded. "How can I hate them if I don't know what they did that was so awful?"

"You shouldn't hate anyone."

"I don't, not really, but if our family doesn't like their family, then I should know why."

"It's a long story."

Carley sat back on her heels. "That's what Mom said."

"God help me," Kristen murmured, covering her eyes with one hand. "Don't tell me I already sound like Mom. I didn't think this would happen until I turned thirty."

Noelle laughed, although she wasn't sure how funny it was, since she herself was only days from her twenty-ninth birthday.

"Did you love him terribly?" Carley asked with a far-away look in her eyes.

Noelle wasn't sure how to respond. She felt a distant and remembered pain but refused to let it take hold. "I thought I did."

"It was wildly romantic," Kristen added. "They were madly in love, but then they had a falling-out—"

"That's one way to put it," Noelle said, interrupting her sister. Thom had apparently fallen out of love with her. He'd certainly fallen out of their plans to elope.

"This is all so sad," Carley said with an exaggerated sigh.

"Our parents not getting along is what started this in the first place."

"At least you and Thom didn't kill yourselves, like Romeo and Juliet—"

"No." Noelle shook her head. "I've always been the sane, sensible sister. Remember?" But even as she spoke, she recognized her words for the lie they were. Staying away for ten years was a pretty extreme and hardly "sensible" reaction. Even she knew that. The fact was, though, something that had begun as a protest had simply become habit.

"Oh, sure," Kristen teased. "Very sensible. You work too hard, you don't date nearly enough and you avoid Rose as though we've got an epidemic of the plague."

"Guilty, guilty, not guilty." She wasn't *purposely* avoiding Rose, she told herself, at least not anymore and not to the extent that Kristen implied. Noelle's job was demanding and it was difficult to take off four or five days in a row.

"I've never met Thom, and already I don't like him," Carley announced. "Anyone who broke your heart is a dweeb. Besides, if he married you the way he said he would, you'd be living in Rose now and I could see you anytime I wanted."

"Well put, little sister," Kristen said. She shrugged off her coat, then joined Carley at the foot of the bed.

Noelle smiled at her two sisters and realized with a pang how much she missed them. Back in Texas it was all too easy to let work consume her life—to relegate these important relationships to fifteen-minute conversations on the phone.

"Look," Kristen said and stretched out her arm so Noelle could see her engagement ring. It was a solitaire diamond, virtually flawless, in a classic setting. A perfect choice for Kristen. "Jon and I shopped for weeks. He wanted the highest-quality stone for the best price." Her eyes softened as she studied the ring.

"It's beautiful," Noelle whispered, overcome for a moment by the sheer joy she saw in her sister's face.

"You'll be my maid of honor, won't you?"

"As long as I don't have to wear a dress the color of Pepto-Bismol."

"You're safe on that account."

"If you ask me to be the flower girl, I think I'll

scream," Carley muttered. "Why won't anyone believe me when I tell them I'm not a little kid anymore? I'm almost fourteen!"

"Not for ten months," Noelle reminded her.

"But, I'm *going* to be fourteen."

Kristen brushed the hair away from Carley's face. "Actually, I intended to ask you to be a bridesmaid."

"You did?" Carley shrieked with happiness. "Well, then, I'll tell you what I overheard Mom tell Dad." Her voice dropped to a whisper as she detailed a conversation between their parents regarding Christmas baskets.

"Mom's meeting with *Mrs. Sutton* tomorrow morning?" Noelle repeated incredulously.

"That's what she said. She didn't sound happy about it, either."

"I'll just bet she didn't."

"This should be interesting," Kristen murmured.

Yes, it should, Noelle silently agreed. *It should be very interesting, indeed.*

Noelle McDowell's
Journal

December 19
(2:00 a.m.)

So I saw him before I even got back to town. Of all the
flights I could've taken...

Seeing Thom after all these years was probably the
most humbling experience of my life, except for the last
time I was with him. Correction. Wasn't with him. Why
did this have to happen to me? Or did I bring it on myself
because of my obsession over seeing him again?

Okay, the thing to do is look at the positive aspect of
this. It's over. I saw him, it was worse than I could have
imagined, but now I don't need to worry about it anymore. Thom made it clear that he wasn't any happier to
see me than I was about running into him. At least the
feeling's mutual. Although I'm kind of confused by that,
since I'm the offended one. He jilted me. Unfortunately,
after this latest run-in, he doesn't have any reason to regret that. I behaved like an idiot.

On a brighter note—and I'm always looking for
brighter notes!—it's good to be home. I shouldn't have
stayed away for ten years. That was foolish and I'm sorry
about it. I walked all through the house, stopping in each

room. *After a while, I got all teary as I looked around. Nothing's really changed and yet everything's different. I didn't realize how much I've missed my home. Mom's got the house all decorated for Christmas, including those funny-looking cotton-ball snowmen I made at camp a thousand years ago. When I commented on that, she told me it was tradition. She puts them out every Christmas. She got all choked up and I did, too. We hugged, and I promised I'd never stay away this long again. And I won't.*

Carley Sue (she hates it when I use her middle name) is so much fun. Seeing her here, in her own space (even if it is my old room), is like discovering an entirely different side of her. She's freer, more relaxed, and so eager to share the camaraderie between me and Kristen.

Speaking of Kristen—she's on cloud nine. We sat up and talked for hours, and she told me all about meeting and falling in love with Jonathan. I'd heard it before, but the story felt brand-new as I listened to her tell it in person. It's so romantic, meeting her future husband in a flower shop when he's there to pick up a dozen red roses for another woman. I give him credit, though; Jonathan knew a real flower when he saw one. It was Kristen who walked out with those roses.

Carley warned me that Mom's going to be looking for company when she has to meet Mrs. Sutton in the morning. We've already thwarted her. We sisters have our ways....

Two

Sarah would have preferred a root canal to meeting with Mary Sutton. A root canal without anaesthetic.

Her husband lingered over his morning coffee before leaving for the hospital. "You're really stressed about this, aren't you?"

"Yes!" Sarah wasn't afraid to admit it. "The last time I spoke to Mary was the day she wrote that dreadful article about me in her column."

"You think that article was only about you," Jake said. "But it could've been about any real estate agent. Maybe even a bunch of different ones." His voice drifted off.

Sarah didn't understand why her husband was arguing when they both knew the entire dreadful piece titled *The Nightmare Real Estate Agent,* was directed solely at *her*. Although she hadn't committed any of sins Mary had described, she'd been guilty of the one crime Mary hadn't mentioned. Never once had she misrepresented a home or hidden a defect. Nor had she ever low-balled a client. But Sarah had borrowed something she couldn't return.

"Was that *before* or *after* you planted the *OPEN HOUSE* sign in her front yard?" Jake asked.

"Before, and she deserved it."

Her husband chuckled. "Go on, meet with her and don't for a moment let her know you're upset."

"You sound like a commercial for deodorant."

"Yes, dear." He kissed her cheek and headed out the door to work.

Tightening the belt of her housecoat, Sarah gazed out the front window as he drove away. *Meet with her...* Easy for him to say. He wasn't the one coming face-to-face with Mary after all these years.

Yawning, Noelle wandered into the kitchen and poured a cup of coffee. Sarah's spirits lifted immediately. It was so good to have her daughter home—and even better that she'd arrived at such an opportune moment. Noelle could act as a buffer between her and that demented newspaper writer who'd once been her friend. True, there was the business with the Sutton boy, but if nothing else, that unfortunate bit of history would distract them all from this current awkwardness. She felt a twinge of guilt at the idea of involving her daughter. Still, she needed reinforcements, and surely Noelle was long over her infatuation with Thom.

"Good morning, dear," Sarah said, mustering a cheerful greeting. "I was wondering if you'd like to come with me this morning." Try as she might, she couldn't keep the plea out of her voice.

Her daughter leaned against the kitchen counter, holding the mug with both hands. "I promised to take Carley shopping and to the movies."

"Oh. That won't be until later, will it?"

"Mom," Noelle said, sighing loudly. "I'm *not* going to let you use me as a buffer when you meet Mrs. Sutton."

"Who told you I was meeting..." She didn't bother to

finish the question, since the answer was obvious. Jake! Dumping the rest of her coffee down the sink, she reluctantly went to her room to dress. She'd be entering the lion's den alone, so she wanted to look her best.

"I don't think she's nearly the monster you make her out to be," Noelle called after her.

That her own daughter, her oldest child—the very one who'd been jilted by Thom Sutton—could say such a thing was beyond Sarah. As far as she was concerned, there was too much forgiveness going on here. And if Noelle thought Mary was so wonderful, then she should be willing to come along.

Didn't Noelle grasp the unpleasantness of this situation? Clearly not. Even Jake didn't take it seriously. He seemed to think this was some kind of joke! Well, she, for one, wasn't laughing.

Despite her bad feelings about the meeting with Mary Sutton, Sarah arrived at the Women's Century Club twenty minutes early. This was the way she'd planned it. As she recalled, Mary possessed a number of irritating habits, one of which was an inability to ever show up on time. Therefore, Sarah considered it advantageous to be early, as though that would highlight Mary's lack of responsibility and basic courtesy.

"Good morning, Melody," she said as she stepped briskly into the entry.

"Morning," came Melody's reply. The phone rang just then, and she reached for it, still standing in front of the copy machine.

While she waited, Sarah checked her appearance in the lobby restroom. She'd taken an inordinate amount of time with her makeup that morning. Her hair was impeccably styled, if she did say so herself, and her clothes looked both businesslike and feminine. Choosing the right outfit was of the utmost importance; in the end, after three complete changes, she'd chosen navy-blue wool slacks, a white cashmere sweater and a silk scarf with a pattern of holly and red berries.

Melody finished with the phone. "Sorry, it's crazy around here this morning. Everyone's getting ready for the dance."

Of course. In her dread, she'd nearly forgotten about the annual dance.

The door opened, and with a dramatic flair—all swirling scarves and large gestures—Mary Sutton entered the building. Did the woman think she was on stage, for heaven's sake? "Hello, Melody," she said, her voice light and breezy. Then—as if she'd only now noticed Sarah— she turned in her direction, frowned slightly and then acknowledged her with a curt nod.

"Good to see you, too," Sarah muttered.

"I'm here for the list. The Christmas basket list," Mary said, walking over to the half wall behind which Melody stood.

"That's why I'm here," Sarah said and forced herself into the space between Mary and the wall.

The two jockeyed for position, elbowing each other until Melody stared at them aghast. "What's *wrong* with you two?" she asked.

"As I explained earlier, we have a *history*," Sarah said, as though that should account for everything.

"A very long and *difficult* history," Mary added.

"You'll have to work together on this." Melody frowned at them both. "I'd hate to see these needy families deprived because you two can't get along." The phone rang again and Melody scooped up the receiver.

"You're impossible to work with," Mary said, practically shoving Sarah aside.

"I won't stand here and be insulted by the likes of you," Sarah insisted. Talk about impossible!

"This isn't going to work."

"You're telling me!" She was ready to walk out the door. But then she realized that was exactly what Mary wanted her to do. She'd been provoking Sarah from the moment she'd made that stagy entrance. This was a low, underhanded attempt to prevent her from holding Kristen's wedding reception at the club. Somehow Mary had found out about the wedding and hoped to thwart the McDowells' plans. That had to be it. But Sarah refused to let a Sutton—especially *this* Sutton—manipulate her.

"There are ways of doing what needs to be done without tripping over each other's feet," Sarah murmured, trying to sound conciliatory. She could only hope that Kristen truly appreciated the sacrifice she was making on her behalf. If it wasn't for the wedding, she wouldn't be caught dead working on a project with Mary Sutton, charity or not!

"What do you mean?"

"There *must* be a way." She personally didn't have any ideas, but perhaps the club secretary could think of something. "Melody?"

Another line rang, and Melody put the first caller on hold in order to answer the second. She placed her palm over the mouthpiece and said, "Why don't you two go talk this out in the lobby?" She waved them impatiently away. "I'll be with you as soon as I can."

Sarah took a few steps back, unwilling to voluntarily give up hard-won territory. This was more of a problem than she'd expected. For her part, she was willing to make the best of it, but she could already tell that Mary had her own agenda.

"The Christmas decorations are lovely this year, aren't they?" Sarah said, making an effort to start again. After all, she was stuck with the woman.

"Yes," came Mary's stilted reply. "I'm the chair of the decorating committee."

"Oh." She studied the staircase again and noticed a number of flaws apparent on closer inspection. Walking to the bottom step, she straightened a bow.

"Leave my bows alone!"

"A little possessive, are we?" Sarah murmured.

"You would be, too, if you'd spent twenty minutes making each of those velvet bows."

"I could have done it in ten."

"Next year, I'll let you." Then, as if she was bored with the subject, Mary said, "I understand Noelle's in town."

"Yes, and I'd appreciate if you'd keep your son away from her."

"My son!" Mary cried. "You don't need to worry about *that*. Thom learned his lesson as far as your daughter's concerned a long time ago."

"On the contrary, I believe your son broke my daughter's heart."

"Ladies!" Melody came out from behind the counter, shaking her head. "I thought we were discussing ways you two can work together to fill those Christmas baskets."

"I don't think I *can* work with her," Mary said, crossing her arms. She presented Sarah with a view of her back.

"Then divide the list," Melody suggested. "One of you can shop for the gifts and the other can buy the groceries. Arrange a day to meet and assemble the baskets, and then you'll be done with it."

Sarah didn't know why she hadn't thought of that earlier. It made perfect sense and would allow them to maintain a healthy distance from each other.

"Divide the list," Mary instructed with a dramatic wave of her hand.

"By all means, divide the list," Sarah said and mimicked Mary's gesture.

"All right," Melody said. She went back to her office, with the two women following, and slipped the list into the photocopier. The phone rang again, and she answered it, holding the receiver between her shoulder and ear. Melody retrieved the original and the copy, reached for the scissors and cut both lists in two. Still talking, she dropped the papers, then picked them up and handed half of the original list to Mary and half to Sarah. The copies of each woman's list went into a file on her desk.

Sarah glanced over her list and tucked it inside her purse. "When do you suggest we meet to assemble the baskets?"

"The twenty-third before noon. That way, we'll be able to drop them off at the Salvation Army in plenty of time. They'll distribute the baskets on Christmas Eve."

"Fine." That settled, Sarah charged out the door without a backward glance. This wasn't the best solution, but it was manageable. She'd do her share of the work, and she wasn't about to let anyone suggest otherwise.

"This is so cool," Carley said as they left the mall late Thursday afternoon, their arms loaded with bags and packages. Noelle smiled fondly at her youngest sister. That summer, Carley had spent two weeks with her in

Texas while their parents were on a cruise. She'd matured noticeably in the six months since then.

"Mom's not selling much real estate anymore," her sister told her as they climbed into the car. "I think she's bored with it, but she won't admit it."

"Really?"

"She's totally involved in Kristen's wedding. It's all she thinks about. She's read a whole bunch of books and magazine articles and has everything set in her mind. Just the other day, she said that what this town really needs is a wedding planner."

"And you think Mom would enjoy that?"

"Are you kidding?" Carley said. "She'd *love* it."

Their mother was extremely sociable, which was one of the reasons she was such a successful real estate agent, Noelle mused. Sarah knew nearly everyone in town and had wonderful connections. Perhaps Carley was right.

"The Admiral really hasn't changed," Noelle murmured. She'd spent a lot of time at the old downtown theater, back in high school. It was there, in the balcony, that Thom had first kissed her. To this day—as much as she wanted to forget it—she remembered the thrill of that kiss.

The Admiral was a classic theater built sixty years earlier. The screen was huge and the second-floor balcony held the plush loge seats—always Noelle's favorite place to sit.

They purchased the tickets, a large bucket of popcorn and drinks.

"Do you want to go up to the balcony?" Carley asked.

"Where else would we sit?" Noelle was already halfway up the winding staircase that led to the second floor. She went straight to the front row and plopped down on a cushioned seat. Carley plopped down beside her. The main feature was a Christmas release, an animated film starring the voices of Billy Crystal and Nathan Lane.

"I'm not a kid anymore, but I'm glad you wanted to see this movie, too," her sister confided.

Noelle placed the bucket of popcorn between them. "Thanks for giving me the excuse." She leaned forward and looked at the audience below. The theater was only half-full and she wondered if she'd recognize anyone.

"Oh, my goodness," she whispered. This couldn't be happening! Thom Sutton sat almost directly below her. If that wasn't bad enough, a blonde sat in the seat beside him and—to Noelle's disgust—had her hands all over him.

"What?" Carley demanded.

"It's Thom." Heaven help her, Noelle couldn't keep from watching. The blonde's hand lingered at the base of his neck; she was stroking his hair with all the tenderness of a longtime lover.

"Not Thom Sutton? The son of the enemy?" Carley asked.

Noelle nodded. Sad and shocking though it was, he obviously still had the power to hurt her. No, not hurt her—infuriate her!

Carley reached for a kernel of popcorn and tossed it down.

Noelle gasped, grabbing her sister's hand. The last thing she wanted was to call attention to the balcony. "Don't do that!"

"Why not? He jilted you and now he's here with another woman." She hurled another kernel in his direction.

Noelle glanced down and saw the blonde nibbling on his earlobe. That did it. She scooped out a handful of popcorn and threw it over the balcony railing. Noelle and her sister leaned back and smothered their giggles. A few minutes later, unable to resist, Noelle looked down again.

"Oh, no," Carley muttered under her breath as she sent a fresh shower of popcorn over the edge. She jerked back instantly.

"What?" Noelle asked.

"I think we're in trouble. He just turned around and looked up here and I don't think he's pleased."

Fine, the management could throw her out of the theater if he complained. Noelle didn't care.

"I want to know about you and him," Carley said. "I wasn't even born when his mom and our mom had their big fight."

Noelle was reluctant to describe all this old history, but she supposed her sister had a right to know. "Well, Mom had just started selling real estate and was making new friends. She claims Mary was jealous of those friends, especially one whose name was Cheryl. Cheryl had been working at the agency for a while and was kind of showing Mom the ropes. She was holding an open house and wanted something elegant to set off the dining room. Mom knew that Mary had this exquisite silver tea service—the perfect thing. But Mom also knew that if she asked Mary to lend it to Cheryl, Mrs. Sutton would turn her down. Instead, Mom asked to borrow it for herself, which was a fib."

Carley frowned. "So that's why Mrs. Sutton blamed Mom? Because Mom lied—I mean fibbed—and then the expensive silver tea service got stolen? Oh, I bet Mom was just sick about it."

"She felt awful. According to Mrs. Sutton, the tea service had belonged to her grandmother and was a family heirloom. It was irreplaceable."

"What did Mom do?"

"She called the police and offered a reward for its return, but the tea service didn't turn up. She went to every antiques store in the area, looking for something similar. Finally there was nothing more she could do. She tried to repair the damage to the friendship, but Mrs. Sutton was angry—and really, you can't blame her. She was hurt because Mom had misled her. They got into this big argument about it and everything escalated from there. Mrs. Sutton did some petty things and Mom retaliated. Next thing you know, a grudge developed that's gone on to this day."

"Retaliated?" Carley asked. "How?"

"When it became clear that Mrs. Sutton wasn't going to forgive and forget, Mom tried another tactic. She thought she'd be funny." Noelle smiled at the memory. "Mrs. Sutton got her hair cut, and Mom sent her flowers and a sympathy card. Then Mrs. Sutton ordered pizza with double anchovies and had it delivered to Mom. You know how Mom hates anchovies—and furthermore she had to pay for it." She shook her head. "It's sad, isn't it? That a good friendship should fall apart for such a silly reason."

"Yeah," Carley agreed. "They acted pretty childish."

"And my relationship with Thom was one of the casualties."

"When did you fall in love with him?" Carley wanted to know.

"We became good friends when we were kids. For a long time, our families got along really well. We often went on picnics and outings together. Thom and I were the closest in age, and we were constant companions—until the argument."

"What happened after the argument?"

"Mrs. Sutton sent Thom and his older sister to a private school, and I didn't see him again for about six years. He came back to public school when we were sophomores. We didn't have a lot in common anymore and hardly had anything to do with each other until we both were assigned to the same English class in our senior year."

"That was when you fell in love?" Carley's voice rose wistfully.

Noelle nodded, and the familiar pain tightened her stomach. "Apparently I fell harder than Thom."

Noelle carefully glanced down again. Talking about Thom and her romance—especially while she was sitting in this theater—brought up memories she'd prefer to forget. Why wouldn't the stupid movie start? It was two minutes past the scheduled time.

The boy who'd rung up the popcorn order marched down the side aisle toward Noelle and Carley. He wore a bored but determined look. "There's been a complaint from the people down below about you throwing popcorn," he said accusingly.

Noelle could feel the heat build up in her cheeks. "I'm sorry—that was, uh, an accident."

The kid's expression said he'd heard it all before. "Make sure it doesn't happen again, okay?"

"It won't," Noelle promised him.

"Sorry," Carley said in a small voice as the boy left.

"It was my fault. I encouraged you."

"But I started it."

"You think you're the one who invented throwing popcorn? Hey, I've got fifteen years on you."

"I want to fall in love one day, too," Carley said, leaning back in her seat, which rocked slightly.

"You will," Noelle said, hoping her sister had better luck in that department than she'd had.

The lights dimmed then and with a grand, sweeping motion the huge velvet curtains hanging over the screen slowly parted. Soon, they were watching previews for upcoming features. Noelle absently nibbled on popcorn and let her mind wander.

Thom had changed if the blonde down below was the type of woman he found attractive. That shouldn't surprise her, though. Time changed a lot of things in life. Some days, when she felt lonely and especially sorry for herself, she tried to imagine what would've happened if she *had* married Thom all those years ago. Getting married that young rarely worked out. They might've been divorced, she might've ended up a single mother, she might never have completed her education.... All kinds of difficult outcomes were possible. In all honesty, she told herself, it was for the best that they hadn't run off together.

Carley slid forward and peeked over the railing. Almost immediately she flopped back. "You wouldn't *believe* what they're doing now."

"Probably not."

"They're—"

Noelle gripped her sister's elbow. "I don't want to know."

Carley's eyes were huge. "You don't want me to tell you?"

"No."

Her sister stared at her in utter amazement. "You really don't care?"

Noelle shook her head. That wasn't the whole truth—or even part of it. But she didn't want to know if Thom had his arm around the blonde or if he was kissing her—or anything else. It was a lot less painful to keep her head buried in a popcorn bucket. Forget Weight Watchers. Sometimes fat grams were the only source of comfort.

"Are you going to confront him after the movie?" Carley asked excitedly.

Noelle snickered. "Hardly."

"Why not?"

"Just watch the movie," she advised.

Carley settled in her seat and and began to rock back and forth. Another time, the action might have annoyed Noelle, but just then she found it oddly comforting. She wanted a special someone to put his arm around her and gently rock her. To create a private world for the two of them, the way Thom had once done in this very theater, on this very balcony. He'd kissed her here and claimed her heart. It'd been a pivotal moment in their fledgling romance. From that point onward, they knew—or at least Noelle had known. She was in love and willing to make whatever sacrifices love demanded.

All too soon, the feature had ended and the lights came back on. "That was great," Carley announced.

Caught up in wistful memories, Noelle got to her feet, gathering her coat and purse. She took pains not to glance below, although her curiosity was almost overwhelming.

"We meet again," an all-too-familiar voice said from behind her.

"Thom?" She turned to see him two rows back, with a four-or five-year-old boy at his side.

Noelle's reaction was instantaneous. She looked below and discovered the blonde beauty with her male friend, who just happened *not* to be Thom Sutton. "I thought—"

"*You're* Thom?" Carley asked, glowering with righteous indignation.

"Don't tell me you're Carley," he returned, ignoring the girl's outrage. "My goodness, you've grown into a regular beauty."

Carley's anger died a quick death. "Do you really think so?"

"I sure do. Oh, this is my nephew Cameron."

"Hello, Cameron," Noelle said. "Did you enjoy the movie?"

The boy nodded. "Yeah, but the best part was when the man came up and told you not to throw any more popcorn. Uncle Thom said you got in trouble." The kid sounded far too smug for Noelle's liking.

So Thom had heard and seen the whole thing.

Oh, great.

Friday morning, Sarah dressed for her Christmas basket shopping adventure. She felt as though she was suiting up for an ordeal, some test or rite of passage. The hordes of shoppers were definitely going to try her patience; she'd finished her own shopping months ago and failed to see why people waited until the very last week. Well, the sooner she purchased the things on her half of the list, the better. With Christmas only five days away, she didn't have a minute to waste.

She wasn't getting any help from her family—not that she'd really expected it. Jake was at work, and Noelle was driving Carley to her friend's house and then meeting Kristen for lunch.

She was on her own.

Wanting to get the most for her buying dollar, Sarah drove to the biggest discount store in Rose. The Value-X parking lot was already filled. After driving around repeatedly, she finally found a space. She locked her car and hunched her shoulders against the wind as she hurried toward the building. The sound of the Salvation Army bell-ringer guided her to the front entrance. She paused long enough to stick a dollar bill in his bucket, then walked into the store.

Sarah grabbed a cart and used the booster seat to prop up her purse. The list was in the side pocket of her bag, and she searched for the paper as she walked. She hadn't gone more than a few feet from the entrance when she nearly collided with another woman obtaining a cart.

"I'm sorry," she said automatically. "I—" The words froze on her lips.

"I should've known anyone that rude must be you," Mary Sutton muttered sarcastically.

Although her heart was pounding, Sarah made a relatively dignified escape and steered the cart around Mary. With purpose filling every step, she pushed her cart toward the toy department. Her list was gifts, which meant Mary had the grocery half. Hmph. It didn't surprise her that Mary Sutton bought her family's Christmas gifts at a discount store—or that she waited until the last minute.

The first part of the list directed her to purchase gifts for two girls, ages six and seven. The younger girl had requested a doll. Having raised three daughters, Sarah knew that every little girl loved Barbie. This late in the season, she'd be fortunate to find the current Barbie.

Almost right away she saw that the supplies were depleted, just as she'd suspected. But one lone Firefighter

Barbie stood on the once-crowded shelf. Sarah reached for it at the precise moment someone else did.

"I believe I was first," she insisted. Far be it from her to allow some other person to deprive a poor little girl longing for a Barbie on Christmas morning.

"I believe you're wrong."

Mary Sutton. Sarah glared at her with such intensity that Mary must have realized she was not about to be dissuaded.

"Fine," Mary said after a moment and released her death grip on the Barbie.

"Thank you." Sarah could be gracious when called upon.

With her nose so high in the air she was in danger of hitting a light fixture, Mary stomped off in the opposite direction. Feeling satisfied with herself, Sarah studied the list again and noticed the name of a three-year-old boy. A small riding toy would do nicely, she decided and headed for that section of the department.

As she turned the corner she ran into Mary Sutton a third time. Mary stopped abruptly, her eyes narrowed. "Are you following me?" she demanded.

"Following *you?*" Sarah faked a short, derisive laugh. "You've got to be joking. I have no desire to be within ten feet of you."

"Then I suggest you vacate this aisle."

"You can't tell me where to shop or in what aisle!"

"Wanna bet?" Mary leaned forward and, intentionally or not, her cart rammed Sarah's.

Refusing to allow such an outrage to go unanswered, Sarah retaliated by banging her cart into Mary's.

Mary pulled back and hit her again, harder this time. Soon they were throwing stuffed French poodles at each other, hurling them off the shelves. A German shepherd sailed over Sarah's head. That was when she reached for the golden retriever, the largest of the stuffed animals.

"Ladies, ladies." A man in a red jacket hurried toward them, his arms outstretched. His name badge read Michael and identified him as the store manager.

"I'm so sorry, Michael," Sarah said, pretending to recognize him. "This little, uh, misunderstanding got completely out of hand."

"You're telling me!" Mary yelled.

"This woman is following me."

"Oh, puh-leeze." Mary groaned audibly. "This woman followed *me*."

"I don't think it's important to know who followed whom," the manager said in a conciliatory voice. "But we need to—"

"She took the last Barbie," Mary broke in, pointing an accusing finger at Sarah. "I got it first—the doll was *mine*. Any jury in the land would rule in my favor. But I kindly offered it to her."

"Kindly, nothing. I had that Barbie and you know it!"

"Ladies, please…" The manager stood between them in an effort to keep them apart.

"There's only so much of this I can take," Mary said, sounding close to tears. "I'm here—"

"It isn't important why you're here," Sarah interrupted. She wasn't about to let Mary Sutton come off looking like the injured party. The woman had purposely rammed her cart. "She assaulted me."

"I most certainly did not!"

"You should check the front of my cart for damage, and if there is any, I suggest that you, as manager, charge this woman," Sarah said.

Two security officers arrived then, dressed in blue uniforms.

"Officer, officer…"

Mary turned soft and gentle. "Thank you for coming."

"Oh, give me a break," Sarah muttered. "Is it within your power to arrest this woman?" she demanded.

"Ladies," the manager said, trying once more, it seemed, to appeal to their better natures. "This is the season of goodwill toward men—and women. Would it be possible for you to apologize to each other and go about your business?"

Mary crossed her arms and looked away.

Sarah gestured toward the other woman as if to say Mary's action spoke for itself. "I believe you have your answer."

"Then you leave me no choice," the manager said. "Officers, please escort these two ladies from the store."

"What?" Mary cried.

"I beg your pardon?" Sarah said, hands on hips. "What is this about?"

The larger of the two security guards answered. "You're being kicked out of the store."

Sarah's mouth fell open.

The only person more shocked was Mary Sutton. "You're evicting me from Value-X?"

"You heard the manager, lady," the second officer said. "Now, come this way."

"Could I pay for the Barbie doll first?" Sarah asked, clutching the package to her chest. "It's for a little girl and it's all she wants for Christmas."

"You should've thought of that before you threw the first poodle," the manager said.

"But—"

Dramatically, he pointed toward the front doors. "Out."

Mortified to the marrow of her bones, Sarah turned, taking her cart with her. One wheel was now loose and it squeaked and squealed. Just when she figured things couldn't get any worse, she discovered that a crowd had gathered in the aisle to witness her humiliation.

"Merry Christmas," she said with as much bravado as she could manage.

The officer at her side raised his hand. "We're asking that everyone return to their shopping. What happened here is over."

With her dignity intact but her pride in shreds, Sarah made her way to the parking lot, still accompanied by the officer.

She could see the "About Town" headline already. *Manager Expels Sarah McDowell From Value-X After Cat Fight*. Although technically, she supposed, it should be Dog Fight.

She had no doubt that Mary Sutton would use the power of the press to complete her embarrassment.

NOELLE MCDOWELL'S
JOURNAL

December 19
11:30 p.m.

I can't believe it! Even now, when it's long past time for bed, I'm wide-awake and so furious, any chance of falling asleep is impossible. I doubt if anyone could do a better job of looking like a world-class idiot. Right there in the theater, with my little sister at my side, I behaved like a juvenile.

I've worked hard to be a positive influence on Carley. I take my role as oldest sister very seriously. Then I go and pull a stunt like this. Adding insult to injury is the fact that I then had to face Thom, knowing he was completely aware of what a fool I'd made of myself.

Speaking of Thom...no, I don't want to think about him. First the airplane and now this! I'd sincerely hoped he'd be married with a passel of kids. I wanted him to be so completely out of the picture that I'd never need to think about him again. Instead—just my luck—he's single, eligible and drop-dead handsome. Life can be brutally unfair.

One good thing that came from all this is the long conversation I had with Carley after the movie. She's young and idealistic, much the same way I was at her age. We talked some more about Mom and Mrs. Sutton. It's really a very sad feud. I told her what good friends our two families used to be. The telling brought up a lot of memories. At one time, our families did everything together.

Thom was the first boy ever to kiss me. We were both sixteen. Wow! I still remember how good it felt. I don't remember what movie was playing and I doubt Thom does, either. That kiss was really something, even though we had no idea what we were doing. There was a purity to it, an innocence. His lips stayed on mine for mere seconds, but somehow we knew. I certainly did, and I thought Thom did, too.

It's funny how much it hurts to think about the way he deceived me. I try not to dwell on it. But I can't help myself, especially now....

Three

"I've never been so humiliated in my life!" Thom's mother sagged into the chair across from his desk as if she were experiencing a fainting spell. The back of her hand went to her forehead and she closed her eyes. "I'll never be able to look those people in the eye again," she wailed. "Never!"

"Mother, I'm sure no one recognized you," Thom said, hoping to calm her down before she caused a second scene by retelling the first. He hadn't really appreciated his mother's flair for drama until now. This was quite a performance, and he could only imagine the show she'd put on at the store.

"Of *course* I was recognized," Mary insisted, springing to life. "My picture's right there by my news column each and every week. Why, I could be fired from the newspaper once the editor gets wind of this." She swooned again and slumped back in the chair. "Where's your father, anyway? He should've known something like this was bound to happen. It seems every time I need him, he's conveniently in court." Greg Sutton was the senior partner in a local law firm.

Thom managed to hold back a smile. As far as he was concerned, his father possessed impeccable timing. Unfortunately, that meant his mother had sought solace from him.

"I'll sue Sarah McDowell," his mother said, as if she'd suddenly come to that decision. "Assault and besmirching my reputation and...and—"

"Mother," Thom pleaded. He stood and leaned forward, his hands on the edge of his desk. "Take a couple of deep breaths and try to calm down." Dragging a lawyer—most likely someone from his father's firm—into the middle of this feud would only complicate things.

"Do you believe it's remotely possible to calm down after this kind of humiliation?"

Perhaps she was right. "Why don't I take you to lunch and we can talk about it," Thom suggested. It was the Friday before Christmas and he could spare the time.

"The Rose Garden?" His mother raised pleading eyes to him. The Rose Garden was the most elegant dining room in town.

"If you like." It was more a "ladies who lunch" kind of place, but if that was what it took to make his mother listen to reason, then he'd go there.

"At least the day won't be completely ruined," she mumbled, opening her purse. "Let me put on some lipstick and I'll be ready to go." She took out her compact and gasped when she saw her reflection in the mirror.

"What?" Thom asked.

"My hair." Her fingers worked feverishly to repair the damage. "Why didn't you say something?"

Mainly because he hadn't been able to get a word in edgewise from the moment she'd stormed into his office. At first, Thom had assumed she'd been in some kind of accident. His mother had spoken so fast it was hard to understand what she was saying—other than the fact that she'd been kicked out of the Value-X because of Sarah McDowell.

"This must have happened when she hurled a French poodle at me."

"Mrs. McDowell threw a dog at you?" He gazed at her in horror.

"A stuffed one," she qualified. "It hit me on the head." Her hand went back to her hair, which she'd more or less managed to straighten.

Thom could picture the scene—two grown women acting like five-year-olds fighting in a schoolyard. Once again, he struggled to hide his amusement. His mother had tried to give him the impression that she was an innocent victim in all this, but he strongly suspected she'd played an equal role.

"I think I might be getting a bruise on my cheek," she said, peering closely into the small compact mirror. She lowered it and angled her face for him to get a better look.

"I don't see anything," he told her.

"Look harder," she said.

To appease her, he did but saw nothing. "Sorry," he said and reached for his overcoat. "Ready for lunch?"

"I'm starving," his mother told him. "You know how hungry I get when I'm angry."

He didn't, and felt this was information he could live without. The Rose Garden was only a block from his office, so they decided to walk. His mother chattered the whole way, reliving the incident and her outrage all over again, embellishing it in the retelling. Thom listened politely and wondered what Noelle would think when she heard *her* mother's version of the incident. He quickly pulled himself up. He didn't want to think about Noelle; that was something his self-esteem could do without.

As he'd expected, The Rose Garden bustled with activity. Christmas was only a few days away, and shoppers taking a welcome lunch break now filled the restaurant. Thom glanced about the room as they were waiting to be seated. He recognized a few associates, who acknowledged him with nods. Two women sitting by the window gave him an appreciative glance and he warmed to the attention. That was when he caught sight of another pair of women.

Noelle and her younger sister Kristen. Wouldn't you know it? He nearly groaned aloud. He hadn't seen or heard from her in ten years and yet in the last three days she seemed to turn up every place he went.

This wasn't good. In fact, if his mother were to see them, she might very well consider it her duty to create a scene and walk out of the restaurant. Worse yet, she might find it necessary to make some loud and slanderous comment about their mother. Staring in their direction was a dead giveaway, but for the life of him, he couldn't stop. Noelle. The years had matured her beauty. He'd been in love with her as a teenager and she'd become the greatest source of pain in his life. For a long time, he'd convinced himself that he hated her. Eventually he'd realized it wasn't true. If anything, he was as strongly drawn to her now as he had been back then. More so, and he detested his own weakness. The woman had damn near destroyed him. In spite of that, he couldn't look away.

"I can seat you now," the hostess said.

Thom hesitated.

"Thom," his mother said, nudging him, "we can be seated now."

"Yes, sorry." He could only hope it wouldn't be anywhere close to Noelle.

The hostess escorted them to a table by the window. He pulled out his mother's chair, making sure her back was to Noelle and Kristen. Unfortunately, that meant *he* was facing them. Kristen had her back to him, which left him with an excellent view of Noelle. She apparently noticed him for the first time because her fork froze halfway to her mouth. For the longest moment, she stared at him, then caught herself and averted her eyes.

"Do you see someone you know, dear?" his mother asked, scrutinizing the menu.

"Yes...no," he corrected. He lifted the rather large menu and pretended to read over the offerings. The strategy of entertaining his mother in order to get her mind off the events of that morning was about to backfire.

In the years since Noelle, Thom had been in several relationships, two of which had grown serious. Both times he'd come close to suggesting marriage and then panicked. It was little wonder after what Noelle had done to him, but he couldn't blame her entirely.

When the moment came to make a commitment, he couldn't. He simply couldn't. And he knew why—although the reason baffled and frustrated him. He didn't love either Caroline or Brenda with the same intensity he'd loved Noelle. Perhaps it was impossible to recapture the emotional passion of that youthful episode; he didn't know. What he did know was that the feelings he'd had for other women hadn't been enough. He'd found them attractive, enjoyed their company...but he needed more than that.

He needed what he'd had with Noelle.

As he thought about the scene at the theater, he started

to grin. It couldn't have worked out better had he planned it. Just thinking about her tossing popcorn at some poor, unsuspecting moviegoer's head was enough to keep him laughing for years. He'd listened in while she talked about their mothers—and about them. But the most priceless part of all was the astonished look on her face when she'd realized he was sitting right behind her and had heard every word.

"What is so amusing?" his mother asked.

"Oh, I was just thinking about something that happened recently."

"What? Trust me, after the morning I've had, I could use a good laugh."

Thom shook his head. "It'll lose something in the translation."

"Oh." She sounded disappointed, then sighed. "I do feel better. This was an excellent idea."

The waitress came by and his mother ordered a glass of wine. "For my nerves," she explained to the woman. "Ordinarily I don't drink during the day, but…well, suffice it to say I've had a very difficult morning."

"I understand," the waitress told her in a sympathetic voice. She glanced at Thom and gave him a small coy smile.

"What a nice young woman," his mother commented as the waitress walked off.

"I suppose so," he said with little interest. He looked up, straight into Noelle's steady gaze.

"Perhaps now isn't the right moment to broach the subject, but both your father and I think it's time you considered settling down."

She was right; the timing could be better. However, a little appeasement seemed in order. "I've been thinking the same thing myself," he said, forcing himself to focus on his mother.

"Really?" Her face lit up. "Is there someone special?"

"Not yet." Involuntarily he stared at Noelle again. As if against her will, her eyes met his and held. Then she looked away—but she quickly looked back.

Kristen turned around and glanced at him over her shoulder.

"Did you know Kristen McDowell is getting married?" his mother said.

Thom nearly choked on his glass of water. "Now that you mention it, I remember hearing something about that." It also explained why his mother had brought up the subject of his settling down. She didn't want Sarah Mc-Dowell to outdo her in the married children department.

"Now," his mother said, eagerly leaning forward, "tell me about your lady friend."

"What lady friend?"

"The one you're going to propose to."

"Propose?" He'd only proposed to one woman, the one watching him from two tables away. "I told you already—I'm not seeing anyone."

"You were never able to keep a secret from me, Thomas. I'm your mother."

He stared at her blankly, not knowing how to respond. "What makes you think I've met someone?"

"It isn't *think,* Thom, I know. I told your father, too. Ask him if you don't believe me. I noticed it the day you came home from your business trip to California. It was the sparkle in your eyes."

"California?" Thom tried to recall the trip. It had been a quick one, and strictly business. But on the return flight, he'd bumped into Noelle McDowell.

* * *

Noelle got home after lunch with Kristen to discover her mother sitting in the family room, stocking feet propped up on the ottoman. She leaned back against the sofa cushion and held an icepack to her forehead.

"Mom?" Noelle whispered. "Are you ill?"

"Thank goodness someone's finally home," her mother said, lowering the bag of ice.

"What's wrong?"

"Never in all your life could you guess the kind of morning I had." She clutched Noelle's arm as she spoke.

"What happened?"

Sarah closed her eyes. "I can't even tell you about it. I have never been more humiliated."

"Does this have something to do with Mrs. Sutton?"

Her mother's eyes sprang open in sheer terror. "You heard about it? Who told you?"

"Ah…"

"She's going to report it in the newspaper, I just know she is. I wouldn't put it past her to use her news column to smear my good name. It was *her* fault, you know. She followed me, and then purposely rammed her cart into mine. And that was only the beginning."

An ugly picture began to take shape in Noelle's mind. A Sutton/McDowell confrontation would explain the fierce looks Thom had sent her way during lunch. The fact that he'd showed up at The Rose Garden—with his mother in tow—was a coincidence she could have done without.

Kristen had invited her to lunch, and then after a few minutes of small talk, her sister had immediately turned to the subject that happened to be on Noelle's mind: Thom Sutton. Noelle had described the disaster at the movies the day before and reluctantly confessed her part. To her consternation, Kristen had thought the incident downright hilarious. Noelle, however, had yet to recover from the embarrassment of knowing that Thom had seen her resort to such childish behavior.

Now their mother had been involved in another confrontation with Mary Sutton. If her present state of mind was anything to go by, Sarah had come out of it badly. Judging by what Noelle had seen of Mrs. Sutton at the restaurant, *she* wasn't the least bit disturbed.

"The police took down our names and—"

"The *police?*"

"Value-X Security, but they wear those cute blue uniforms and look just like regular policemen."

"They took your names? What for?"

Her mother covered her face with both hands. "I can't talk about it."

The door off the garage opened and in walked Noelle's father. "Dad," she said, hoping to prepare him. "Something happened to Mom this morning."

"Oh, Jake…" Her mother languished in her seat as though she lacked the energy to even lift her head.

"Sarah?"

"Apparently Mom and Mrs. Sutton tangled with security at the Value-X this morning."

"We more than tangled," her mother insisted, her voice rising, "we were…banished. The officer who escorted me out told me I won't be allowed inside the store for three months." She bit her lip and swallowed a loud sob. "I don't know if I misunderstood him, but I think I might be permanently banned from all blue-light specials."

"No!" Her father feigned outrage.

"Jake, this is serious."

"Of course it is," he agreed. "I take it this is Mary's doing?"

Her mother's fist hit the sofa arm. "I swear to you she started it!"

"You don't need to tell me what happened," Jake said. "I can guess."

So could Noelle.

"From here on out, I absolutely refuse to be in the same room as that woman." She sat straighter, jaw firm, head back. "For years I've had to deal with her…her malice, and I won't put up with it anymore!"

Jake reached for Sarah's hand and gently patted it. "You're absolutely right—you shouldn't."

Her mother's eyes narrowed suspiciously. "How do you mean? Are you being sarcastic?"

"Of course not, dear," he said reassuringly. "But there's no need to rehash old history, is there?"

"No-o-o." Noelle heard her mother's hesitation.

"Not going to the Christmas dance will show Mary Sutton that she won't have you to kick around anymore."

As far as Noelle was concerned, missing the Century Club Christmas dance was far from a tragedy. The only reason she'd agreed to attend was to placate her mother. This mysterious incident at the Value-X was a blessing in disguise; it seemed her father saw it in the same light. She just hoped he hadn't overplayed his hand with that last ringing pronouncement.

"Who said anything about not going to the dance?" her mother demanded.

"You did." Her father turned to Noelle for agreement, which she offered with a solemn nod.

"Yes, Mom, you just said you won't be in the same room with that woman ever again."

"I did?"

"Yes, sweetheart," Noelle's father said. "And I agree wholeheartedly. Missing the dance is a small price to pay if it means protecting your peace of mind."

"We aren't going to the dance?" Carley asked, entering the room. She looked disappointed, but then Noelle's little sister was too young to understand what a lucky escape she'd just had.

"No," Jake said. "We're going to skip the dance this year, and perhaps every year from now on. We won't let Mary Sutton hurt your mother's feelings or her reputation again!"

"We're going," her mother insisted.

"But, sweetheart—"

"You're absolutely right, Jake, Mary Sutton's done enough to me. I refuse to allow her to ruin my Christmas—and Noelle's birthday—too. We're going to show up at the dance and hold our heads high. We have nothing to be ashamed of."

"But…" Her father cleared his throat. "What if Mary mentions the incident at the Value-X?" He lowered his voice, sounding as though that would be a horrible embarrassment to them all. Noelle had to give her father credit; he was good at this.

"She won't say a word," her mother said with complete confidence. "Mary wouldn't dare bring up the subject, seeing that she was tossed out on her ear, right along with me."

Her resolve clearly renewed, Sarah stood and placed her hands on her hips. Nothing would thwart her now. "We're attending the dance tomorrow night, and that's all there is to it."

Her father made a small protesting noise that echoed

Noelle's sentiments. She was stuck going to this dance when it was the very last thing she wanted.

Dressed in a floor-length pink formal that had once been worn by Kristen in high school, Noelle felt like last year's prom queen. Her enthusiasm for this dance was on a par with filing her income tax return.

"You look positively lovely," her mother told her as they headed out the door.

How Noelle looked had little to do with how she felt. Her father brought the car out of the garage and held open the doors for Noelle and Carley, then helped their mother into the front seat beside him.

"How did I get so lucky—escorting three beautiful women to the biggest dance of the year?"

"Clean living," Noelle's mother said with authority. "And a clear conscience." Noelle didn't know whether to laugh at that remark or shrug in bewilderment. Leaning forward in order to look out the front window, Sarah added, "I think it's going to snow."

Hearing "Jingle Bells" on the car radio, Noelle suspected her mother was being influenced by the words of the song.

"We're more prone to ice storms than snow this time of year," her father said mildly.

Noelle had forgotten about the treacherous storms, although she'd experienced a number of them during the years she'd lived in Rose. They created astonishing beauty—and terrible dangers.

"Kristen and Jonathan are meeting us at the dance, aren't they?" Carley asked.

"That's what she said," Noelle answered. Carley was dressed in a full-length pale blue dress with cap sleeves and she wore matching low-heeled shoes. She looked lovely and so mature it was all Noelle could do not to cry. Her baby sister was growing up.

"Do you think *she'll* be there?" her mother asked, lowering her voice.

"Mrs. Sutton's probably asking the same thing about you," Noelle said.

Her mother gave an exaggerated sigh. "I'll say one thing about Mary Sutton—she never did lack nerve."

The Century Club was festive, with Christmas music and evergreen swags and large red bows. The ballroom was on the second floor, the cloakroom, a bar and buffet on the first. Couples lingered on the wide staircase, chatting and sipping champagne.

Noelle glanced toward the upstairs, and her stomach tensed. Thom was there. She didn't need to see him to feel his presence. Why did he have to show up everywhere she did? Was this some kind of cosmic joke?

"Kristen!" her mother called. "Yoo hoo!" Anyone might think it'd been weeks since she'd last spoken to her daughter. "Hello, Jonathan." She hugged her soon-to-be son-in-law.

"Hi, Mom. Hi, Dad." Kristen paused in front of Carley, feigning shock. "This isn't my little sister, is it? It can't be."

Carley rolled her eyes, but couldn't hide her pleasure. "Of course it's me. Don't be ridiculous."

"Shall we go upstairs?" her mother suggested.

Noelle recognized the order disguised as a request. They were to mount the stairs on guard, as a family, in case they ran into the dreaded Mary Sutton.

Kristen cozied up to Noelle. "He's here," she whispered in her ear.

"I know."

"Who told you?"

"No one." She couldn't explain how she'd recognized Thom's presence. She just did. Like it or not.

The ballroom was crowded, and although this wasn't the kind of social activity Noelle would have attended on her own, she couldn't help getting caught up in the spirit of the evening. A six-piece orchestra was playing a waltz, the chandeliers glittered and she saw that it had indeed begun to snow; flakes drifted gently past the dark windows. On the polished dance floor, the women in their long shimmery gowns whirled around in the arms of their dashing partners. The scene reminded her of a Victorian Christmas card.

"Would you care to dance?" Jonathan asked.

Surprised, Noelle nodded. She'd only spoken once or twice to this man who was marrying her sister, and was anxious to know him better. "Thank you. That would be very nice."

Just as Noelle and Jonathan stepped onto the dance floor, Kristen's gaze met her fiancé's. Noelle could have sworn some unspoken message passed between them. She didn't have time to question her sister before Jonathan loosely wrapped her in his arms.

"I assume you heard what happened at the Value-X store," she said, searching for a subject of conversation.

"Did you have as much trouble not laughing as I did?"

"More," Noelle confessed with a grin.

"I've done business with the Suttons. They're good people."

"This feud between our mothers is ridiculous." Out of the corner of her eye, she noticed Kristen, who was dancing, too—her partner none other than Thom Sutton.

It didn't take a genius to put two and two together, especially when she noticed that Kristen was steering Thom in her direction. Noelle marveled at her sister's courage in asking Thom to dance with her. And of course she had. Thom would never have sought Kristen out, especially for a dance in the Women's Century Club Ballroom with both mothers present.

The two couples made their way toward the center of the polished floor. When they were side by side, Jonathan stopped.

"I believe you're dancing with the wrong partner," he said.

Noelle didn't need to look over her shoulder to guess Jonathan was speaking to Thom.

"I believe you're with the wrong woman," Noelle heard Kristen tell her partner.

Jonathan released Noelle, and Kristen stepped out of Thom's embrace and sailed into her fiancé's waiting arms, leaving Thom and Noelle standing alone in the middle of the crowded dance floor.

Slowly, dread dictating every move, Noelle turned and came face-to-face with Thom. He didn't look any happier than she felt at this sudden turn of events. "I didn't plan this," she said in clear, even tones.

His expression implied that he didn't consider her comment worthy of a response.

"Are you two going to dance or are you just going to stand there and stare at each other all night?" Jonathan asked.

Thom shrugged, implying that he could do this if he had to. Reluctantly Noelle stepped into his arms. She wasn't sure what to expect. Actually, she hadn't expected to feel anything, certainly not this immediate deluge of emotion. He kept her at arm's length and gazed into the distance.

To Noelle's horror, tears filled her eyes as all the old feelings came flooding back. She was about to turn and walk off the dance floor when his fingers dug into her upper arms.

"You're not running away from me again."

"Me?" she cried, furious at the accusation.

"Yes, you."

His words made no sense, she thought grimly, but said nothing. The dance would be over soon and she could leave him behind. Or try to. Kristen would answer for this.

No, she decided, she had only herself to blame. Over lunch, Noelle had confided in her sister. Kristen, being idealistic and in love, had plotted to bring Noelle and Thom back together. She didn't understand that reconciliation wasn't always possible.

"I'd like to ask you a question," she said when she could tolerate the silence no longer.

"Fine."

"Why'd you do it? Did you want revenge for your mother so badly it was worth using me to get it?"

He stopped dancing and frowned at her. "What?"

"You heard me." She couldn't keep the pain out of her voice.

He continued to frown, as if he still didn't understand the question.

"Don't give me that injured look," she said, clenching her jaw. "Too many years have passed for me to be taken in by that."

"You were the one who stood *me* up."

"Yeah, right," she said with a mocking laugh. "After I

made an idiot of myself in front of my parents, too. That must've given you a real kick."

"I don't know what you're talking about."

"Thom, I waited in that park for two miserable hours and you didn't show."

Not an inch separated them now as his icy glare cut into her. Dancing couples swirled around them, but Noelle was barely conscious of anyone else. For all she knew or cared, they were alone on the dance floor.

"I waited hours for you, too."

His lying to her now was almost more than she could stand. "I beg to differ," she said stiffly.

"Noelle, listen to me! I was there."

"You most certainly were not." Then, to prove that she wasn't going to accept a lie, no matter how convenient, she added, "You think I just waited around? I was sure something had gone wrong, sure there was some misunderstanding, so I phoned your home."

"I wasn't there because I was waiting for you!"

He persisted with the lie and that irritated her even more.

"You were gone, all right," she said, spitting out the words. "You were with your buddies bowling."

His eyes narrowed and he began to speak.

But the music stopped just then, which was all the excuse Noelle needed to get away from him. He reached for her hand and pulled her back. "We need to talk."

"No. It happened years ago. Some things are better left alone."

"Not this time," he insisted, unwilling to budge.

"What do you hope to accomplish by going through all of this now? It's too late." They'd gain nothing more than the pain of opening old wounds. Any discussion was futile. It'd been a mistake to let herself get drawn into this silly drama—just one very big mistake.

"I'm not hoping to accomplish one damn thing," he told her coldly.

"I didn't think so."

Thom released her hand. "Just a minute," he said as she turned from him.

Noelle hesitated.

"I *was* there. I stood there for two hours and waited. You were the one who never showed."

"That's not true!"

They stood glowering at each other, both refusing to give in. Noelle wasn't going to let him lie his way out of this, though—not after what his deception had cost her.

"Hey, you two, this is Christmas," someone called out.

The voice ended Noelle's resolve. Whatever had happened in the past didn't matter anymore. Certainly not after all these years.

"If you find comfort in believing a lie, then do so," he said, "but don't involve me." He walked away, his face hard and impassive.

Left alone in the middle of the dance floor, Noelle stared at him in amazement. Of all the nerve! He'd stopped her from leaving and now *he'd* taken off!

Picking up her skirt, she raced after him. "All right! You want to talk this out, then we will."

"When?" He continued walking, tossing the question over his shoulder.

With Christmas so close, her time was booked solid. "I...soon."

"Tonight."

"All right." She swallowed hard. "When and where?"

"After the dance. In the park, same place as before."

That seemed fitting, since it was where they were originally going to meet the day they'd planned to elope.

"What time is the dance over?"

"Midnight." He glanced at his watch. "So make it one."

"I'll be there."

He shot her a look. "That was what you said the *last* time."

NOELLE MCDOWELL'S
JOURNAL

December 21
5:00 p.m.

Everyone's getting ready for the big dance, but my head's still spinning and I've learned that it helps me sort through my emotions if I write everything down. I ran into Thom again. It's as though we're being drawn together, as though we're trapped in some magnetic field and are being pulled toward each other from opposite directions. I can tell he doesn't like it any better than I do.

It happened yesterday when I met Kristen for lunch at The Rose Garden. No sooner had our order arrived when in walked Thom and his mother.

Try as I might, I couldn't keep my eyes off him. He apparently suffered from the same malady. Every time I glanced up, he was staring at me—and frowning. His mother was with him and I could see that he was trying to keep her distracted so she wouldn't notice Kristen and me. I didn't completely understand why until we arrived home and discovered that Mom and Mrs. Sutton had had another run-in while shopping for the Christmas baskets. That must have been something to see, although I'm grateful I didn't!

After we left the restaurant, Kristen and I had a long

talk about Thom. I told her far more than I meant to. I don't think I've thought or talked this much about Thom in years, and I found myself experiencing all those pathetic emotions all over again. Kristen confessed that she's been hurt and upset with me for staying away, and now that I'm home, I can understand her disappointment. It's ironic, because after I told her how devastated I was when Thom and I broke up, she said she could understand why I'd stayed away. She even said she'd probably have done the same thing.

When I got back to the house, Mom was in quite a state. For a moment I thought she might have talked herself out of attending the dance, but our hopes were quickly dashed. Dad and I should've realized Mom has far too much pride to let Mary Sutton get the upper hand.

This Christmas-basket project is driving her nuts, but Mom's determined to make Kristen's wedding one this town will long remember, and she's willing to make whatever sacrifice is necessary. I do admire her determination.

It's time to get ready for the dance. Wouldn't you know it? Mom came up with a dress, and just as Carley predicted, it's pink. Pepto-Bismol pink. I can only hope Thom doesn't show up, but at the rate my luck is running...

Four

The rest of the Christmas dance passed in a blur for Noelle. She danced with a constant stream of attractive men. She greeted longtime family friends and socialized the evening away, but not once did she stop thinking about Thom. They were finally going to settle this. Only she wasn't a naive eighteen-year-old anymore and she wouldn't allow his lies to go unchallenged. Thom claimed he'd been waiting for her in the park, but she knew otherwise.

At the end of the evening, the families trooped down the wide sweeping staircase. Noelle, Carley and their mother waited while Jake stood in line to collect their coats. No more than three feet away from them was Mary Sutton, who also appeared to be waiting for her coat. Noelle had to hand it to the woman; she did a marvelous job of pretending not to see them.

"Good evening, Mrs. Sutton," Noelle greeted her, refusing to ignore Thom's mother.

Sarah's onetime friend opened and then closed her mouth, as if she didn't know how to respond.

"Noelle." Her mother elbowed her sharply in the ribs. "What's the matter with you?"

"Nothing. I'm greeting an old family friend."

"*Former* friend," her mother insisted. "We haven't been friends in almost twenty years."

"But you once were."

Her mother sighed wearily. "I was younger then, and I didn't have the discretion I have now. You see, back then I took friendship at face value. I trusted in good-will and forgiveness."

"Hello, Noelle," Mary Sutton said, moving closer. "I, too, was once young and I, too, believed in the power of friendship. But I was taught a painful lesson when the woman I assumed was my dearest friend lied and deceived me and entrusted a priceless family heirloom to another. But that was a very long time ago. Tell me," she said, turning a cold shoulder to Noelle's mother. "How are *you*?"

"Very well, thank you."

Her mother clasped Carley's arm and stepped back as though to protect her youngest daughter.

"You're looking lovely," Thom's mother said, and her eyes were kind.

"Thank you," Noelle said, although she could feel her mother's gaze burning into her back.

Mary Sutton lowered her voice. "I couldn't help overhearing your mother's comments just now about friendship. I probably should've stayed out of it—but I couldn't."

"It's so sad that the two of you have allowed this nonsense to go on for all these years."

"Let me assure you, my grandmother's tea service is not nonsense. It was all I had to remind me of her.

Your mother lied to me about using it, and then lost it forever." Her downcast eyes clearly said that the loss of her grandmother's legacy still caused her pain. "You're right, though. It's unfortunate this has dragged on as long as it has."

That sounded encouraging, and Noelle was ready to leap on what she considered a gesture of peace.

"However," Mrs. Sutton continued, "there are certain things no friendship can overcome, and I fear your mother has crossed that line too many times to count. Regrettably, our friendship is unsalvageable."

"But—"

"Another thing," Mrs. Sutton said, cutting Noelle off. "I saw you dancing with Thom this evening. You two were once sweet on each other, but you hurt him badly. I hope for both your sakes that you're not thinking of renewing your acquaintance."

"I… I…" Noelle faltered, not knowing how to answer.

Noelle's mother stepped forward. "I suggest your son stay away from our daughter."

"Mom, keep out of this, please," Noelle cried, afraid of what would happen if the two women started in on each other—particularly after the Value-X incident. This was the town's biggest social event of the year, and a scene was the last thing either family needed.

Mr. Sutton returned with the coats, and Noelle's father followed shortly afterward. The McDowells headed immediately for the parking lot, careful to avoid any and all Suttons. Everyone was silent on the drive home, but Noelle knew she'd upset her mother.

Fifteen minutes later as they walked into the house, she decided she should be the one to compromise. "Mom, I wish now that I hadn't spoken to Mrs. Sutton," she said quietly. And she meant it; she should have restricted her remarks to "Hello" and maybe "Merry Christmas."

"I do, too," her mother said. "I know your intentions were good, but it's best to leave things as they are. I tried for a long time to make up with her, but she refused to accept a replacement set and she refused my apology." Sadness crept into her voice. "Mary did make one good point, though."

Noelle mentally reviewed the conversation.

"She said it's a good idea for you to stay away from Thom, and she's right." She sighed, then briefly placed her palm against Noelle's cheek. Her eyes were warm with love. "The two of you have a history you can't escape."

"Mom, it isn't like that. We—"

"Sweetheart, listen please. I know you once had strong feelings for that young man, and it hurt me deeply."

"It hurt *you?*"

Her mother nodded. "Very much so, because I knew you'd be forced to make a choice between your family and Thom. I couldn't bear the thought of you married to him or sharing my grandchildren with Mary Sutton. You saw for yourself how she feels about me. There's no forgiveness in her. Really, is this the kind of woman you want in your life and the lives of your children? That's the history I mean." She kissed Noelle on the cheek and headed down the hallway to her room. "Good night now."

Noelle shut her eyes and sagged against the wall. She'd been just a moment away from explaining that she was going to meet Thom in order to talk things out. Her mother sounded as though she'd consider it a personal affront if Noelle so much as looked at him. It was like high school all over again.

The only thing left to do now was sneak out the same way she had as a teenager. She couldn't leave him waiting in the cold, that was unthinkable. Besides, this might be her one and only chance to sort out what had really happened, and she wasn't going to throw it away. She didn't intend any disrespect toward her mother or his, but she *had* to be there. If she didn't show up, she'd confirm every negative belief he already had about her.

Carley was in bed asleep as Noelle passed her room. She went in to drop a kiss on her sister's forehead, then softly closed the door. Noelle changed out of her party dress, choosing wool slacks and a thick sweater to wear to the park. Sitting on the edge of the bed, she waited for the minutes to tick past. With luck, her parents would be exhausted and both go directly to bed. Then Noelle could slip away undetected.

Finally the house was dark and quiet. The only illumination came from the flashing Christmas lights that decorated the roofline.

Opening her bedroom door, Noelle was horrified by the way it creaked. On tiptoe, she carefully, silently crept down the narrow corridor.

"Jake." Her mother was instantly awake. "I heard something."

"Go to sleep, honey."

"There's someone in the house," her mother insisted.

Noelle froze. She could hardly breathe. Just imagining what her mother would say was enough to paralyze her.

"Jake, I'm serious."

"I don't hear anything," her father mumbled.

"I did. We could all be murdered in our beds."

"Sarah, for the love of heaven."

"Think of the children."

Noelle nearly groaned aloud. She was trapped. She'd have to pass her parents' bedroom in order to steal back into her own. They were sure to see her. She couldn't go forward and she couldn't go back.

"All right, all right," her father muttered as he climbed out of bed.

"Take something with you," her mother hissed.

"Like what?"

"Here, take a wooden hanger."

"So I can hang him out to dry if I happen on a burglar?"

"Just do it, Jake."

"Yes, dear."

Noelle had made it safely into the kitchen by the time her father came upon her. "Dad," she whispered, hiding in the shadows, "it's me."

"Why didn't you say so?" he whispered back.

"I couldn't. I'm sneaking out of the house."

"This late? Where are you going?"

He wouldn't like the answer, but she refused to lie. "I'm meeting Thom Sutton in the park. We're going to talk."

Her father didn't say anything for a long moment. Then it sounded as if he was weeping.

Noelle felt dreadful. "Dad? I'm sorry if this upsets you."

"Upsets me?" he repeated. "I think it's hilarious."

"You…do?"

"Go ahead and meet your young man and talk all you want. This thing is between Sarah and Mary. Greg and I have been friends for years."

This was news to Noelle. "You're still friends?"

"Of course. He's the best golfing partner I ever had."

"You and Mr. Sutton are golf partners?" Noelle thought perhaps she'd slipped into another dimension.

"Shhh." Her father raised a finger to his lips. "Your mother doesn't know."

"Mom doesn't know." This was more unbelievable by the moment.

"Scoot," her father ordered, and reaching for the keys on the peg outside the garage door, he said, "Here, take my car. It's parked on the street."

Noelle clutched the set of keys and leaned forward to kiss his cheek. "Thanks, Dad."

He coughed loudly as she opened the back door. "You're hearing things, Sarah," he called out. "There's nothing." He gave her a small wave and turned back toward the hallway.

As soon as she was out the door, Noelle sprinted toward her dad's car. It took her a moment to figure out which key she needed and then another to adjust the mirror and the seat. When she glanced at her watch, she was shocked to see the time. It was already ten minutes past one.

Thom would assume she wasn't coming. He'd think she'd stood him up…when nothing could be further from the truth.

Thom expelled his breath into the cold, and it came out looking like the snort of a cartoon bull. An *angry* cartoon bull. That was exactly how he felt. Once again, he'd allowed his heart to rule his head and he'd fallen prey to Noelle McDowell.

He should have known better. Everything he'd learned about heartache, Noelle had taught him. And now, fool that he was, he'd set himself up to be taken again. Noelle

McDowell was untrustworthy. He knew it and yet he'd still risked disappointment and worse.

Slapping his hands against his upper arms to ward off the cold, he paced the area beneath the trees across from the pool at Lions' Park. This had been their special meeting place. It was here that Thom had kissed Noelle for the second time. Here, they'd met and talked and shared their secrets. Here, he'd first confessed his love.

A car door slammed in the distance. Probably the police coming to check out his vehicle, which was parked in a lot that was closed to the public at this time of night. He deserved to get a ticket for being enough of an idiot to trust Noelle.

He didn't know why he'd hung around as long as he had. Looking at his watch he saw that it was twenty after one. She'd kept him waiting nineteen minutes too long. Her non-appearance was all the proof he'd ever need.

"Thom… Thom!" Noelle called out as she ran across the lawn.

Angry and defiant, he stepped out from beneath the shadow of the fifty-foot cedar tree.

"Thank goodness you're still here," she cried and to her credit, she did sound relieved. She was breathless when she reached him. "I had to sneak out of the house."

"Sneak out? You're almost thirty years old!"

"I know, I know. Listen, I'm so sorry." She pushed back the sleeve of her coat and squinted at her watch. "You waited—I can't believe you stayed for twenty extra minutes. I prayed you would, but I wouldn't have blamed you if you'd left."

The anger that had burned in him moments earlier evaporated so fast it shocked him.

"When did they turn Walnut into a dead-end street?"

"Years ago." Of course she'd drive down the same street they'd used as teenagers. He'd forgotten the changes made over the last decade; it hadn't occurred to him that she wouldn't know. "You're here now."

"Yes…listen, I know I shouldn't do this, but I can't help myself." Having said that, she slipped her arms around his waist and hugged him hard. His own arms went around her, too, tentatively and then with greater strength.

Closing his eyes and savoring the feel of her was a mistake, the first of many he knew he'd be making. She smelled like Christmas, somehow, and her warmth wrapped itself around him.

"Why'd you do that?" he asked gruffly as she released him and took a step back. He was trying to hide how damn good it'd felt to hold her.

"It's the only way I could think of to thank you for staying, for believing in me enough to wait."

"I wasn't exactly enumerating your good points while I stood here freezing."

"I know, I wouldn't, either—I mean, well, you know what I mean."

He did.

Clearing off a space on the picnic table, Noelle climbed up and sat there just as she had when they were teenagers. "All right," she said, drawing in a deep breath. "Let's talk. Since you were the one to suggest we do this, you should go first."

So she'd become a take-charge sort of woman. That didn't surprise him. She'd displayed leadership qualities in high school, as well, serving on the student council and as president of the French Club. "All right, that's fair enough." She might be able to sit, but Thom couldn't. He had ten years of anger stored inside and that made it impossible to stand still for long. "We argued, remember?"

"Of course I do. The argument had to do with our mothers. You said something derogatory about mine and I defended her."

"As I recall, you had a less-than-flattering attitude toward *my* mother."

"But you were the first…" She paused. "None of that's important now. What we should be discussing is what happened afterward."

Once again she was right. "We made up, or so I thought."

"We made up because we refused to allow the ongoing feud between our mothers to come between us. Later that day, you wrote me a note and suggested we elope."

Her voice caught just a little. He wanted so badly to believe her. It was a struggle not to. "I loved you, Noelle."

She smiled, but he saw pain in her eyes and it shook him. For years he'd assumed that she'd used his love against him. That she'd stood him up just to hurt him. To humiliate him. He'd never really understood why. Was it vindication on behalf of her mother?

"We were going to confront our parents, remember?" Noelle said.

"Yes. I made a big stand, claiming how much I loved you and how I refused to let either of our mothers interfere in our lives. You should've heard me."

"I did, too!" she declared. "I spilled out my guts to them. Can you imagine how humiliating it was to have to go back and confess that you'd tricked me—that you'd jilted me?"

"Me!" he shouted. "You were the one—"

Noelle held up both hands and he let his anger fade. "Something happened. It must have." She pressed one hand to her heart. "I swear by all I consider holy that I've never lied to you."

"You're assuming I did?" he challenged.

"Yes. I mean no," she cried, confused now. "Something *did* happen, but what?"

"I don't know," he said. "I was here at three, just like I wrote you in the note."

She frowned, and he wondered if she was going to try to tell him she hadn't gotten his note. He knew otherwise because he'd personally seen Kristen hand it to her at school.

"The note said eight."

"Three," he insisted. Now it was his turn to look perplexed. "I wrote down three o'clock."

"The note said…" She brought her hand to her mouth. "No, I refuse to believe it."

"You think Kristen changed the time?"

"She wouldn't do that." She shook her head. "I know my sister, and she'd never hurt me like that."

"How do you explain the discrepancy then?"

"I have no idea." She squeezed her eyes shut. "I remember it vividly. You'd sent it to me after your math class."

His defenses were down. Time rolled back, and the events of that day were starting to focus in his mind. The fog of his pain dissipated. Finally he was able to look at the events with a clear head and an analytical eye.

"Kristen spilled soda on it," Noelle said thoughtfully. "Do you think that might have smudged the number?"

"It might explain part of it—but not the nasty note you left on my windshield."

She had the grace to blush at the reminder. "After waiting until after ten o'clock, I didn't know what to do.

It was pretty dark by then, and I couldn't believe you'd just abandon me. I was positive something must've happened, so I phoned your house."

He nodded, encouraging her to go on.

"Your father said you were out with your friends bowling. I went to the alley to see for myself." Her voice tightened. "Sure enough, you were in there, boozing it up with your buddies."

"Don't tell me you actually thought I was having a good time?"

"Looked like it to me."

"Noelle, I was practically crying in my beer. I felt… I felt as if I'd just learned about some tragedy that was going to change my whole life."

"Why didn't you call me? How could you believe I'd stand you up? If you loved me as much as you said, wouldn't you make some effort to find out what happened?"

"I did." To be fair, it'd taken him a day, but he had to know, had to discover how he could've been so mistaken about Noelle. "I waited until the following afternoon. Your mother answered the phone and said I'd already done enough damage. She hung up on me."

"She never told me," Noelle whispered. "She never said a word."

"Why would she?" Thom murmured. "Your mother assumed I'd done you wrong, just the way everyone else in your family did."

"I left that horrible note on your car and you still phoned me?"

He nodded.

"I can only imagine what you must have thought."

"And you," he said.

They both grew quiet.

"I'm so sorry, Thom," she finally said. "So very sorry."

"So am I." He was afraid to touch her, afraid of what would happen if she came into his arms.

Noelle brushed the hair back from her face and when he glanced at her, he saw tears glistening in her eyes.

"It all worked out for the best, though, don't you think?" he asked. He had to say *something*.

She nodded. Then after a moment she spoke in a voice so low he had to lean closer to hear. "Do you really believe that?"

"No." He reached for her then, crushing her in his arms, lifting her from the picnic table and holding her as if his very life depended on keeping her close to his heart.

His mouth found hers, and her lips were moist and soft, her body melting against his. Their kisses were filled with hunger and passion, with mingled joy and discovery. This sense of *rightness* was what had been missing from every relationship he'd had since his breakup with Noelle. Nothing had felt right with any other woman. He loved Noelle. He'd always loved her.

She buried her face in his shoulder and he kissed the top of her head. Her arms circled his neck and he ran his fingers through her hair, gathering it in his hands as he closed his eyes and let his emotions run free—from anger to joy. From joy to fear. From fear to relief.

"What happens now?" he asked. They didn't seem to have many options. Each had made a life without the other.

She didn't answer him for a long time, but he knew she'd heard the question.

"Noelle," he said as she raised her head. "What do we do now?"

She blinked back tears. "Do we have to decide this minute? Can't you just kiss me again?"

He smiled and lowered his mouth to hers. "I think that could be arranged."

Fresh from Sunday services—where she'd been inspired by a sermon on giving—Mary Sutton drove to the local Walmart store. She refused to show up the following day and not have the items on her list. No doubt Sarah McDowell assumed she'd arrive at the club empty-handed, but Mary fully intended to prove otherwise.

As soon as Greg had settled in front of the television set watching the Seahawks' play-off game, she was out the door. Shopping this close to Christmas went against every dictate of common sense. Usually she was the organized one. Christmas gifts had been purchased, wrapped and tucked away soon after Thanksgiving. But, with these six Christmas baskets, she had no choice. She had to resort to last-minute shopping.

The parking lot at Walmart was packed. Finding a space at the very rear of the lot, Mary trudged toward the busy store. She dreaded dealing with the mob of shoppers inside. On the off chance she might have a repeat of that horrible scene in Value-X, she surveyed the lot—looking up one row and down the next—in search of Sarah's vehicle. She sighed with relief when she didn't see the other woman's car.

List in hand, Mary grabbed a cart and headed straight for the toy section. She hoped the store would have Barbie dolls left on the shelf. She hated the thought of a single child being disappointed on Christmas morning. Fortunately, the shelves appeared to have been recently restocked.

Reaching for a Firefighter Barbie doll, she set it inside her basket. With a sense of accomplishment, she wheeled the cart around the corner to the riding toys. To her horror and dismay, she discovered Sarah McDowell reading the label on a toddler-sized car. This was her worst nightmare.

"No," she muttered, not realizing Sarah would hear her.

Her bitterest enemy turned and their eyes locked. "What are *you* doing here?" Sarah demanded.

"The same thing you are."

Sarah gripped her cart with both hands, as if she was prepared to engage in a second ramming session. Frankly, Mary had suffered all the humiliation she could stand and had no desire to go a second round.

"Can't you buy your grandson's gifts some other time?"

"How dare you tell me when I can or cannot shop." Mary couldn't believe the gall. She would shop when and where she pleased without any guidance from the likes of Sarah McDowell.

"Mary, hello."

Mary wanted to groan out loud. Janice Newhouse, the pastor's wife, was easing her cart toward them. "This must be Sarah McDowell. I've seen your photo on a real estate brochure." She smiled warmly at the woman who had caused Mary so much pain. "I'm Janice Newhouse."

"Hello." Sarah's return greeting was stiff.

"I've heard so much about you," Janice said, apparently oblivious to the tension between the two women.

"I'll just bet you have." Sarah said this as though to suggest that Mary was a gossipmonger, when nothing could be further from the truth. For years, she'd quietly refused to get drawn into any discussion involving Sarah. It wouldn't do either of them any good. The same could not be said for Sarah McDowell. She'd taken delight in blackballing Mary's membership in the Women's Century Club. She'd dragged Mary's name and reputation through the mud. Mary, on the other hand, had chosen the higher ground—with the exception, perhaps, of that newspaper column on the perfidy of real estate agents, and that certainly hadn't been a personal attack.

"I understand the Willis family bought their home through you," Janice said, making polite conversation.

"You know the Willises?"

"Yes, they're members of our church. So are Mary and her husband."

Sarah's expression was glacial. "Oh."

"Sarah and I are buying gifts for the charity baskets," Mary said.

"We divided the list and now we're each getting half," Sarah went on to explain. "Tomorrow we're assembling the baskets and taking them to Salvation Army headquarters."

That was much more than Janice needed to know, Mary thought irritably. Sarah was just showing off.

"That's wonderfully charitable of you both," Janice murmured.

"Thank you." Sarah added a pull toy to her basket.

Mary reached for one herself.

Next Sarah took down a board game; Mary took two. Sarah grabbed a skateboard.

"How generous you are," Janice commented, eyes widening as she observed their behavior. "Both of you appear to be very...zealous."

"I believe in giving back to the community," Mary said.

"As do I," Sarah insisted. By now her cart was so full she couldn't possibly cram anything else into it.

"Leave something for me to buy," Mary challenged, doing her best to keep the smile on her face from turning into a scowl.

"I'm the one who has the little girl who wants a Firefighter Barbie on my list," Sarah said, staring pointedly at the doll in Mary's cart.

"*I'm* the one with the gift list," Mary countered. "Besides, there are plenty of Barbie dolls."

"You aren't even supposed to be buying toys. That was *my* job." Sarah's eyes narrowed menacingly.

"Ladies, I don't think there's any reason to squabble here." Janice raised both hands in a calming gesture. "Let me look at your lists."

"Fine," Sarah snapped.

"Good idea," Mary added in a far more congenial tone. She opened her purse and dug out the list Melody Darrington had given her.

Janice examined both pages. She ran down Sarah's first and then Mary's. She frowned. "Here's the problem," she said, handing them back. "You have the same list."

"That's impossible," Mary protested.

"Let me see." Sarah snatched Mary's from her hand with such speed it was a wonder Mary didn't suffer a paper cut.

"That's what I think happened," Janice said. "You were accidentally given one list instead of two."

Sarah glanced over each page. "She's right."

Mary wanted to weep with frustration. "Do you mean to say we're actually working from the same list?" It made sense now that she thought about it. Melody had been so busy that morning, and the phone was ringing off the hook. It was no wonder the secretary had been distracted.

"You were supposed to pick up the grocery items," Mary said.

"I most certainly was not. That was *your* job."

If Sarah was trying to be obtuse and irritating, she was succeeding.

Janice glanced from one to the other. "Ladies, this is for the Christmas baskets, remember?"

Mary smiled benevolently at the pastor's wife, who was new to the area. Janice couldn't know. But then, a twenty-year-old feud wasn't something Mary was inclined to brag about.

"She's right," Sarah said again. "We're both behaving a bit childishly, don't you think?"

Mary was staying away from that question.

"I'll call Melody in the morning and pick up the second half of the list."

"No, you won't," Mary told her. "I'll do it."

"I said I would," Sarah said from between clenched teeth.

"You don't need to, I will."

"Would you ladies prefer that I do it?" Janice volunteered.

"No way," Sarah muttered.

"Thank you, but no," Mary said more politely.

Janice looked doubtful. "You're sure?"

"Yes."

"Yes." Sarah's voice blended with Mary's.

"All right, ladies, I'll leave you to your good works then."

Out of the corner of her eye, Mary watched Janice stroll away.

As soon as the pastor's wife was out of earshot, Sarah said, "You can pick up the list if you want." She made it sound as though she was making a big concession.

Naturally, she'd agree now. Mary sighed; this problem with the list complicated everything. "I'll need time to shop for the groceries."

"And your point is?"

"Shouldn't it be obvious?" Clearly it wasn't. "We'll need to meet on the morning of the twenty-fourth now."

"Christmas Eve?"

"Yes, the twenty-fourth is generally known as Christmas Eve," Mary told her a bit sarcastically.

"Fine. Let's meet at the club at nine and deliver the baskets to the Salvation Army from there."

"Fine."

"In the meantime," Sarah suggested, "let's do the sensible thing and divide up the toys on this list. Why don't I get the girls' stuff and you get the boys'?"

Wordlessly, they each returned half of their purchases. Mary hated to follow Sarah's lead, but for once the woman had come up with a reasonable idea. "I'll see you Tuesday morning at nine," she finally said.

Sarah gave a curt nod.

Mary wheeled her cart to the front of the store. All the cashiers were busy, so she found the shortest line and waited her turn. Not until a few moments later did she notice that Sarah stood in the line beside hers.

Mary took a magazine from the stand, leafed through it and tossed it into her cart.

Sarah placed two magazines in hers.

Mary decided to splurge and buy a candy bar. As she put it in the cart, she glanced at Sarah. The other woman grabbed one of every candy bar on the rack. Refusing to be outdone, Mary reached for two.

Sarah rolled her eyes and then emptied the entire container of candy into her cart.

Mary looked over and saw two men staring at them. A woman was whispering to her companion, pointing in her and Sarah's direction.

Once again, they'd managed to make spectacles of themselves.

Noelle McDowell's Journal

December 22

I just got back from church, and it was lovely to attend services with Mom and Dad and Carley. The music was stirring and brought back so many memories of Christmases spent in Rose. I wish I'd paid closer attention to the sermon, but my mind refused to remain focused on the pastor's message. All I could think about was Thom.

Now that we've talked, I think we've actually created more problems than we've solved. We're going to get together again later in the day, but that's not until one. We both realize we can't leave things as they are, yet neither one of us knows where to go from here.

Still, it's wonderful to know my faith in him was justified. That makes this decision even harder, though. I'm afraid I'm falling in love with him again — if I ever stopped!—but there are so many complications. In fact, I wonder if our best choice would be simply to call it quits. But I'm not sure we can, because we made a mistake last night. We kissed.

If we hadn't done that, I might've found the courage to shake Thom's hand, claim there were no hard feelings and walk away. But we did kiss and now…well, now we're in a quandary. I wish his kisses didn't affect me, but they do. Big-time. Oh boy, nothing's changed in that department. It's as if I was sixteen all over again, and frankly, that's a scary feeling.

I felt Thom's kisses all the way through me, from head to toe. Thom felt them, too, and I think he's just as confused as I am. Things got intense very quickly, and we both recognized we had to stop. Now it's decision time.

Thom withdrew from me, physically and emotionally, and I did from him, too. We both tried to play it cool— as if this was all very nice and it was good to clear the air. He acted as if we should just get on with our lives. I played along and was halfway back to the car when he stopped me. He wanted to know if we could meet at the mall today to talk again.

God help me, I jumped at the invitation. Maybe I should've been more nonchalant, but I couldn't do it. I was just happy for the chance to see him again.

Five

Shopping was the perfect excuse to get out of the house on Sunday afternoon, and Noelle used it. Her mother was gone, her father was absorbed in some televised football game and Carley was in her room checking *Buffy* web-sites on her computer.

"I'm going out for a while," Noelle said casually.

Her father's eyes didn't waver from the television screen. "Are you meeting Thom?"

"Ah…"

Her father raised his hand. "Say no more. What do you want me to tell your mother if she asks?"

"That I've gone shopping… We're meeting at the mall."

"That's all she needs to know."

Noelle kissed her father on the cheek. His eyes didn't leave the screen as he reached inside his pants pocket and handed her his car keys. "Why don't you take my car again?"

"Thanks, Dad."

"Don't mention it." Then her father did look away

from the television and his gaze sought hers. "You have feelings for this young man?"

Noelle nodded. It was the truth, much as she hated to acknowledge it, even to herself.

Her father nodded, too. "I was afraid of that."

His words lingered in Noelle's mind as she drove to the Rose Mall on the west side of town. She'd lived for this moment ever since she and Thom had parted the night before. They'd resolved what both had considered a deception, but so many questions were still unanswered. They needed time to think, to consider the consequences of becoming involved a second time. Nothing had changed between their families—or more specifically, their mothers—but other things *were* different. Noelle wasn't the naive eighteen-year-old she'd been ten years ago; neither was Thom.

It took a good twenty minutes to find a parking space, and the mall was equally crowded. Carolers dressed in Victorian costumes stood in front of the JCPenney store, cheerfully singing "Silver Bells." Noelle wished she could listen for a while, but fearing she might be late, she paused only a moment to take in the sights and the sounds of the holiday season.

She hurried through the overheated mall and found Thom at a table in the food court, just the way they'd agreed. He stood as she approached.

"I haven't kept you waiting, have I?" she asked.

"No, no. It occurred to me that with Christmas this close we might have trouble finding a table so I grabbed one early."

He'd always been thoughtful. As he put down his coffee and pulled out her chair, she shrugged out of her coat and threw it on the back of the seat. "Would you like to get some lunch?"

She shook her head. "You should have something, though." Her stomach had been upset all morning.

"Are you ill?"

"No—it's guilt." He might as well know. She'd been anxious since last night, since their first moonlit kiss... All through church services and afterward, she'd repeatedly told herself how ridiculous it was to sneak around behind her mother's back. Her father had apparently been doing it for years, but secretive actions truly bothered Noelle.

"Guilt?"

"I don't like being dishonest."

"Then tell your mother." Thom made it sound so easy, but he didn't need an excuse every time he stepped out the front door. He didn't even live at home, and he wasn't visiting his family for Christmas the way she was. He wasn't accountable to his parents for every minute spent outside their presence.

"Did you let your parents know we were meeting?" she asked.

He half grinned, looking sheepish. "No."

"That's what I thought."

"How about coffee?" he asked in an all-too-obvious effort to change the subject. "I could use a refill."

She gave a quick nod. She'd been counting the minutes until they could talk again. After their meeting in the park, she'd barely slept. She'd relived their conversation—and their kisses—over and over. It seemed a miracle that they'd finally learned what must have happened that day ten years ago. Truly a Christmas miracle. Now, if only their mothers would miraculously reconcile...

Thom left and returned a few minutes later with two steaming cups of coffee.

Noelle held her cup with both hands, letting the heat warm her palms. She hadn't felt chilled before, but she did now. "I—I don't know where to start."

"Why didn't you ever come home?" he asked bluntly. "Start by telling me that."

"It was just too painful to come back here. I made excuses at first and it got easier after a while. Plus, Mom and Dad and my sisters were always willing to visit Texas. It's beautiful in a way that's completely different from the Northwest. Oh, and the shopping is excellent."

He laughed. "Is there anyone special in your life?"

"I have a number of good friends."

"Male or female?"

She hesitated. "Female."

Thom visibly relaxed. "You don't date much, then?"

"Of course I date—I've gone out lots. Well, maybe not as much as I'd like, but I *was* engaged for a while. How about you?"

"I came close to getting engaged. Twice."

Without knowing a single detail, Noelle was instantly jealous. "Who?"

He seemed pleased by her reaction. He leaned back in his chair, stretched out his legs and crossed his ankles. "No one you know. Besides, I'm the one asking the questions here. You can drill me later."

"No way! In other words, you became some kind of ladies' man after you dumped me?"

His face suddenly grew serious and he reached across the table for her hand. "I didn't dump you, Noelle."

She'd meant to tease him but realized her remark was

insensitive—not to mention plain wrong. "I know. I apologize. Chalk it up to a bad choice of words."

Thom squeezed her hand. "Do you think that's what happened with our mothers?" he asked. "A bad choice of words?"

"How do you mean?"

"Think about it. Just now, you reverted to your old thought pattern—your assumption that you'd been betrayed. It wasn't until after you spoke that you remembered what had really happened."

He was right. The words had slipped out easily, thoughtlessly.

"Our mothers are probably behaving in the same way. After all these years, they're caught in this pattern of disparaging each other, and they can't break the habit."

Noelle wasn't sure she agreed with him. For one thing, she knew her mother had desperately tried to end the feud. Every attempt had been rebuffed. "I don't think it's a good idea to discuss our mothers."

"Why not?"

"Because we argue. You want to defend your mother and I want to defend mine, and the two of us end up fighting. Besides, weren't we talking about the women in your life after I left Rose?"

He chuckled. "You make it sound like there were hordes of them."

"There weren't?" She pretended to be shocked.

He shook his head. "Not really. Two I considered marrying and a few others I saw for a while. What about you?"

"You keep asking. All right, I was serious once. Paul was a computer programmer, and we both worked for the same company, developing new software. It was an exciting time in the business and we got caught up in the thrill of it all." Paul was actually very sweet and very brilliant, but their romance wasn't meant to be. Noelle had been the first to realize it. She'd ended their brief engagement, and they'd parted on good terms, remaining friends to this day. "After the launch of Curtains, our new operating system, well…it was curtains for our marriage plans, too," she said, smiling at her own feeble pun.

"Just one guy?" Thom asked.

"Don't sound so disappointed." Noelle had told him far more than necessary. He hadn't said a word about either of the women he'd loved.

"Listen, what I said earlier regarding our mothers— I wonder if—"

"I don't want to discuss our mothers, Thom."

"We can't avoid it forever."

"Maybe not," she agreed, "but does it have to be the first thing we talk about?"

"It's not," he argued.

"Look at us," she said. "I haven't been with you fifteen minutes and already we're both on the defensive. This isn't going to work." She was ready to give up and go home, but Thom stopped her.

"Okay, we'll leave our mothers out of the conversation."

Now it seemed neither one had anything to say.

"I kept waiting to hear that you were married," she said after a silence. "But I refused to ask. That's silly I suppose." It was like waiting for the dentist's drill; when it happened there'd be pain and she hadn't been in a hurry to experience it.

"I assumed you'd get married first," he said.

Noelle grinned, shaking her head. "There's something

else we need to talk about," she murmured. "What are we going to do now?" She began with the least palatable option—which was also the easiest. "I mean, we could shake hands and say it's great to have this cleared up, then just go back to our respective lives." She waited, watching for a response from him.

His face revealed none of his thoughts. "We could do that," he said. "Or..." He looked at her.

"Or we could renew our friendship."

Thom leaned back in his chair. "I like that option."

So did Noelle. "But, as you said, there's still the situation with our mothers." Now she was the one bringing it up, although she'd hoped to avoid any mention of their mothers' feud. It was futile, she realized. They *couldn't* avoid it, no matter how hard they tried.

"If your mother hadn't borrowed my great-grandmother's tea service," Thom began, "she—"

"My mother?" Noelle cried. "I agree she made a mistake, but she was the first to admit it. Your mother refused to forgive her, and that says a lot about the kind of person she is."

Thom's eyes were flinty with anger. "Don't paint *your* mother as the one who was wronged because—"

Noelle was unwilling to listen to any more. "Listen, Thom, this isn't going to solve anything. I think it'd be best if we dropped the subject entirely."

"That isn't the only thing you want to drop, is it?"

It was a question she didn't want to answer. A question that implied it would be best for all concerned if they simply walked away from each other right now. Their circumstances hadn't changed, not really; the business with their mothers would always be an obstacle between them. They could ignore it, but it would never disappear.

She stood and gathered her purse, pulled on her coat. This time Thom didn't try to stop her.

"So, you're walking away at the first sign of difficulty," he said.

"No. As a teenager my heart was open to you and your family, but I'm older now."

"What's that got to do with anything?" he demanded.

"This time, my eyes are open, too."

He looked as if he wanted to continue their argument. But she didn't have the heart for it. Obviously Thom didn't, either, because he let her go without another word.

"Help me carry everything in, Greg," Mary Sutton said as she stepped into the house. Her arms were loaded with plastic bags bursting at the seams.

Mary had never understood or appreciated football, and she didn't mind saying so. Her husband's gaze reluctantly left the television screen, where a bunch of men in tight pants and large helmets chased after an oddly shaped ball. As far as she was concerned, it was ridiculous the way they grunted and called out a few numbers now and then and groped their privates right on national television.

"Greg, are you going to help me or not?"

Her husband slowly stood up, his eyes still on the TV. "Honey, it's third down and inches."

He might as well be speaking Greek, but she wasn't going to argue with him. From the sudden reaction of the crowd, something had happened. Greg muttered, shaking his head in a disparaging manner. Mary pretended not to hear and walked back out to the car.

A moment later, he met her in the garage. "We're losing."

"Sorry, darling." She hoped she sounded sympathetic, but she didn't try very hard. Men and their football.

"What on earth did you buy?" he complained, lifting the last of the blue plastic bags from the car's trunk.

"Oh, various things," she said dismissively. "This Christmas basket project hasn't been a positive experience," she went on, following her husband into the house.

"Why not?"

Distressed and angry, she blurted out, "You won't believe this. Sarah McDowell was there!"

"At Walmart?" Even Greg sounded surprised. "Don't tell me we've lost our shopping privileges there, too?"

"Very funny." The incident at the Value-X would haunt her forever.

"So you got along better?"

"I wouldn't say that, but I did discover the problem. We had the same list."

"For the Christmas baskets?"

"Yes." Mary set her load on top of the kitchen counter.

The football game ended, and Greg reached for the remote control to turn off the television set. He opened the first sack and seemed pleasantly surprised to find a stash of candy bars. "For me?" he asked. Without waiting for her to respond, he peeled the wrapper halfway down a Baby Ruth bar and took a bite.

"You can have them all." She threw herself onto the sofa.

Her husband walked into the family room and sat down. "You'd better tell me exactly what happened."

"What makes you think anything did?"

Greg chortled. "I haven't been married to you all these years without knowing when something's bothering you."

"Oh, Greg," she moaned. "I behaved like such an idiot." She longed to cover her face with her hands.

"What went wrong this time?"

She shook her head, unwilling to reveal how low she'd sunk. One thing she'd discovered years ago was still true: Sarah McDowell brought out the very worst in her. It never failed. Mary became another person whenever Sarah was around—a person she didn't like.

"Do you want to talk about it?"

"No. I want to crawl into bed and hide my head in shame." The most embarrassing part of all was that the pastor's wife had seen the whole thing.

"Tomorrow morning, I need to go back to the club."

"For what?"

"I need the second half of the list."

"What's on the list?"

"I won't know until I see it, now will I?" She didn't mean to be short-tempered, but this afternoon hadn't been one of her best.

"I don't know if I want you driving. There's an ice storm forecast."

"Greg, I have to get that list. I told Sarah I'd take care of this. It's my responsibility."

"Then I'll drive you."

"You will?" Mary felt better already.

"Of course. Can't have you out on icy roads." Her husband finished off the candy bar and returned to the kitchen, where he rummaged through the bags on the counter. "You never did say why you bought all this candy."

Mary looked over at the ten plastic bags that lined her kitchen counter and shuddered. Half of them were filled with candy bars. "You don't want to know."

Greg didn't respond, but she caught him sneaking more Baby Ruth bars into his pockets and the sleeves of his sweater. He wasn't fooling her, but some things were best ignored.

On the other hand, certain things had to be faced. "Greg," she said thoughtfully. "I'm worried about Thom."

"Why?"

"Did you see him with Noelle last night? The two of them were dancing."

"Yes, dear, I saw them."

"Doesn't that concern you?" she asked.

"No." He added a couple of candy bars to his pants pockets, as though she wasn't going to see them protruding.

"Well, it should. Noelle is a sweet girl, but she's her mother's daughter. She's not to be trusted."

"Thom is an adult. He's fully capable of making his own decisions. My advice is to stay out of it."

Mary couldn't believe her husband would say such a thing to her. "You don't mean that! After what happened the last time—"

"You heard me. Stay out of it."

"But Thom is—"

Greg just shook his head. She wanted to say more but swallowed the words. Fathers weren't nearly as caring and concerned about matters of the heart; they lacked sensitivity. Greg hadn't spent time with Thomas the way she had that fateful summer ten years earlier. The McDowell girl had crushed him.

Her husband started toward the garage.

"Greg," she said.

"Yes, dear?"

"Put the candy bars back. I'm adding them to the charity baskets."

He muttered something under his breath, then said, "Yes, dear."

When Thom returned from the mall, he was suffering a full-blown case of the blues. His apartment had never seemed emptier. The small Christmas tree he'd purchased already decorated looked pitiful in the middle of his coffee table. Some Christmas this was turning out to be.

The light on his answering machine blinked, demanding his attention, and for half a heartbeat he thought it might be Noelle. But even as he pressed the Play button, he realized she wouldn't phone.

"Hey, Thom, this is Jonathan Clark," the message said. "Give me a call when you've got a moment."

Thom reached for the phone and punched in the number the investment broker had left. He knew Jonathan but didn't consider him a close friend. He was a business associate and Kristen McDowell's fiancé. This was the first time Jonathan had sought him out socially; Thom hoped it had something to do with Noelle.

After a brief conversation, they agreed to meet at a local pub. Jonathan didn't say why, but it didn't matter. The way Thom felt, he was grateful for any excuse to get out of the house. The walls were closing in around him. Some jovial guy-talk and loud music was exactly what he needed. Although Jonathan was about to marry into the other camp, Thom knew he'd be objective.

Jon was sitting at the bar nursing a dark ale when Thom joined him. The music in the background was Elvis Presley's "Blue Christmas"—appropriate under the circumstances. They exchanged pleasantries and then Jonathan got right to the point.

"I wanted to make sure there weren't any hard feelings about last night."

"You mean finagling it so I ended up dancing with Noelle? No problem."

"I didn't really want to do it, but Kristen seemed to think it was important."

Thom pulled out his wallet and paid for his beer when the bartender delivered it. "Like I said, it wasn't a big deal."

"So you and Kristen's sister were once an item?"

"Once."

"But no more?"

Thom took a deep swallow of the cold beer. "There's trouble between our families."

"Kristen told me about it."

"You're lucky, you know." Jonathan faced none of the challenges he did.

"Very," Jonathan agreed.

There was a pause, not an uncomfortable one. Jon seemed willing to discuss the situation further, but he wouldn't force it. He'd left it up to Thom.

"Noelle and I talked after the dance," he finally ventured.

Jonathan swiveled around on his stool in order to get a better look at Thom. "How'd it go?"

"Last night? Good." His blood warmed at the memory of their kisses. It'd taken every ounce of self-control he'd possessed to let her go. That was one of the reasons he'd suggested they meet at the mall today; it was neutral ground.

"Did you two work everything out?"

"We tried." He waited, half hoping Jonathan would question him about it. Jonathan didn't. Thom sighed, feeling a little discouraged. Now that he'd started, he wanted to talk. "I think we're both leery of getting involved a second time," he continued. "Her home's in Texas now and I live here."

"Right, got ya."

"But it's more than logistics." He tipped back the mug and took another swallow of beer. "We have…this situation. She wants to defend her mother. I want to defend mine."

"Only natural." Jonathan glanced at his watch.

Thom shut up. He had the feeling he was boring the other man. Perhaps he had someplace he needed to be.

Jonathan's next remark surprised him. "Kristen and I were making out our guest list and I put down your name. You'll come, won't you?"

"Sure," Thom answered almost flippantly, and then it occurred to him that if he accepted the invitation, he'd see Noelle again. He found himself eager for the opportunity. "Speaking of the wedding—" well, not really, but he didn't know how else to introduce the topic "—did Kristen ever mention her sister being involved with a guy named Paul?"

Jonathan considered it for a moment, then shook his head. "Not that I can remember. Why?"

"Just curious." And jealous. And worried. Noelle had said it was over between her and this Paul character, but Thom had to wonder. She seemed far too willing to walk away from their conversation this afternoon. Maybe the relationship with Paul wasn't as dead as she'd led him to believe.

"Paul," Jonathan repeated slowly. "Did she give you a surname?"

Thom shook his head.

The door to the pub opened, and Kristen McDowell walked inside. Jonathan glowed like a neon light, he was so pleased to see her. "Over here, sweetheart," he called, waving his hand.

Kristen walked to the bar and slipped her arm around her fiancé's waist. "Hello, Thom," she said as naturally as if they saw each other every day. "How's it going?"

"All right. I understand congratulations are in order."

Kristen smiled up at Jonathan and nodded.

Thom felt like an intruder. Reaching for his overcoat, he was getting ready to go when Kristen stopped him.

"There's no need to rush off."

He was about to pretend he had people to see, places to go, but then decided not to lie. "You sure?"

"Of course I'm sure."

Thom was eager to learn what he could about Noelle, so he lingered and ordered another beer. Jon did, too; Kristen had a glass of red wine.

Thom paid for the second round. The three of them sat on bar stools with Kristen in the middle, talking about Christmas plans for a few minutes. "She had me call you," Jonathan confessed suddenly.

Kristen elbowed her fiancé in the ribs. "You weren't supposed to tell him."

The second beer had loosened Thom's tongue. "She damn near knocked me off my feet when I first saw her."

"Kristen?" Jonathan asked, sounding worried.

"No, Noelle."

"Really?" This appeared to please Noelle's younger sister. "So you're still stuck on her, after all these years."

"Damned if I know," Thom muttered. He did know but he wasn't willing to admit it. "We decided it's not going to work."

"Why not?" Kristen sounded outraged.

"We met and talked this afternoon," Thom informed them both.

Jonathan frowned. "I thought you met last night after the dance."

"We did."

"So you've talked twice in the past twenty-four hours."

"Yeah, and like I said, we both realized there are too many complications."

Kristen raised her hand for the bartender. "We need another round."

"I think we've already done enough damage," Jonathan protested.

"Coffee here," she said, pointing at her fiancé. "Same as before over here." She made a sweeping gesture that included Thom.

The bartender did as requested. As soon as the wine and beer arrived, Kristen turned to face Thom. "I thought you loved my sister."

"I did once." He was still working on his second beer.

"But not now?"

Thom didn't want to answer her. Hell, the last time he'd admitted to loving Noelle he was just a kid. But he'd stood up to his parents and been willing to relinquish everything for Noelle. To say he'd loved her was an understatement. He'd been crazy about her.

"Well?" Kristen pressed. "Don't you have an answer?"

"I do," Thom said, picking up his beer. "I just don't happen to like it."

"What's that mean?" Jonathan asked Kristen.

"I think it means he still has feelings for Noelle." Then, as though she'd suddenly remembered, she said, "Hey! Her birthday's on Christmas Day, you know."

Like he needed a reminder. Not a Christmas passed that Thom forgot.

"She doesn't feel the same way about me," he murmured.

"Yeah, right," Kristen said, exaggerating the words. It took only two beers for him to bare his soul—and it was all for nothing because Noelle didn't love him anymore. It took only two beers to make him maudlin, he thought sourly.

"Yeah, right," Kristen said again.

"It's true," Thom argued. "Did you ask her?"

"Did you?" Kristen asked.

Noelle McDowell's
Journal

December 22
Afternoon

I blew it. I had the perfect chance to have a rational conversation with Thom. We had a chance to settle this once and for all without the angst and emotion. It didn't happen. Instead I let the opportunity slip through my fingers. Naturally I have a wealth of excuses, the first one being that I didn't sleep more than a couple of hours all night. This situation between Thom and me was on my mind and I couldn't seem to let it go. My feelings swung from happiness to dread and from joy to fear, and then the whole cycle repeated itself. I kept thinking about what I wanted to say when we saw each other again. Then I started worrying what would happen if he kissed me.

How is it that I can develop complicated software programs used all over the world, but when it comes to Thom Sutton I'm hopeless?

Mom's home from shopping, and when Carley asked if she'd gotten everything she needs for the Christmas baskets, it looked as if Mom was about to burst into tears. She said she had a headache, and went to bed. Apparently I wasn't the only one suffering from too little sleep.

I have a feeling that something happened with Mrs. Sutton again, which is bad news all the way around.

Kristen wasn't home when I tried to phone, although she hadn't said she was going out. I'd hoped to discuss this with her, get her perspective. She's heard just about everything else that's gone on between Thom and me since I arrived. I could use a sympathetic ear and some sisterly advice.

Everything fell into place so naturally between her and Jonathan, but it sure hasn't been that way with me. I actually considered talking to Carley, which is a sign of how desperate I'm beginning to feel.

I'm not going to see Thom again. We left the mall and nothing more was said. It's over, even though I don't want it to be. It was within my power to change things, and I didn't have the courage to do it. I could've run after him and begged him not to let our relationship end this way, not after we'd come so far. But I didn't, and I'm afraid this is something I'm going to regret for a long time to come.

Six

"You don't need to worry about the dishes," Sarah Mc-Dowell protested.

Noelle continued to load the dishwasher. "Mom, quit treating me like a guest in my own home." The menial task gave her something to do. Furthermore, she hoped it would help take her mind off her disastrous meeting with Thom at the mall. She'd reviewed their conversation a dozen times and wished so badly it had taken a different course. Their second attempt at a relationship had staggered to a halt before it had really begun, she thought with regret as she rinsed off the dinner plates and methodically set them inside the dishwasher.

"Thank you, dear. This is a real treat," her mother said, walking into the family room to join her dad.

Sarah had returned from her shopping trip in a subdued mood. Noelle didn't ply her with questions, mainly because she wasn't in a talkative mood herself. Even Carley Sue seemed to be avoiding the rest of the family. Except for dinner, her sister had spent most of the day in her room, first on her computer, and then wrapping Christmas presents.

As Noelle finished wiping the counters, her youngest sister entered the kitchen. Carley glanced into the family room, where her parents sat watching television. Their favorite courtroom drama was on, and they seemed to be absorbed in it.

"Wanna play a game of Yahtzee?" Noelle asked. It was one of Carley's favorites.

Her sister shook her head, then motioned for Noelle to come into her room. Carley nodded toward their parents, then pressed her finger to her lips.

"What's going on?" Noelle asked, drying her hands on a kitchen towel.

"Shh," Carley said, tiptoeing back toward her room.

"What?" Noelle asked impatiently.

Carley opened her bedroom door, grabbed Noelle's hand and pulled her into the bedroom. To her shock, Thom stood in the middle of the room, wearing his overcoat.

"Thom!"

"Shh," both Thom and Carley hissed at her.

"What are you *doing* here?" she whispered.

"When did you trade bedrooms with your sister?" he asked.

"A long time ago." She couldn't believe he was in her family's home. Years ago, he'd come to the house and tapped on her bedroom window, and she'd leaned out on the sill and they'd kissed. Amazingly, her parents hadn't heard—and the neighbors hadn't reported him. "Why are you here?"

"I came to see you."

Okay, that much was obvious. But she still didn't understand why he'd come.

"It was a bit of a surprise to bump into your little sister."

"I didn't mind," Carley said. "But he scared me like crazy when he knocked on the window."

"Sorry," Thom muttered.

"You said he broke your heart," Carley said, directing her remarks at Noelle. "We threw popcorn at him, remember? At least, we thought it was him, but then it wasn't."

Noelle didn't need any further reminders of that unfortunate incident. "I broke his heart, too. It was all a misunderstanding."

"Oh." Carley clasped her hands behind her back and leaned against the door, waiting. She was certainly in no hurry to leave and seemed immoderately interested in what Thom had to say.

Thom glanced at her sister, who refused to take the hint, and then said, "We need to talk."

"Now? Here?"

He nodded and touched her face in the gentlest way. "Listen, I'm sorry about this afternoon. We didn't even talk about what's most important—and that's you and me."

"I'm sorry, too." Unable to resist, Noelle slipped her arms around his waist and they clung to each other.

"This is *so-o-o* romantic," Carley whispered. "Why don't you two sit down and make yourselves comfortable. Can I get you anything to drink?"

Her little sister was as much of a hostess as their mother, Noelle thought with amusement. "No, but thanks."

Thom shrugged. "I should leave, but—"

"No, don't," Noelle pleaded with him. It might make more sense to meet Thom later, but she didn't want him out of her sight for another second.

Thom sat on the edge of the bed and Noelle sat beside him. He took both her hands in his. "I've been doing a lot of thinking about us."

"I have, too," she said hurriedly.

"I don't want it to end."

"Oh, Thom, I don't, either! Not the way it did this afternoon—and for all the wrong reasons." Noelle was acutely aware of her sister, listening in on their conversation, but she didn't care.

"Noelle, I know what I want, and that's you back in my life."

"Oh, Thom." She bit her lower lip, suddenly on the verge of tears.

Carley sighed again. "This is better than any movie I've ever seen."

Noelle ignored her. "What are we going to do about our families?" They couldn't pretend their relationship wouldn't cause problems.

"I've been thinking about that, but I'm just not sure." Thom stroked the side of her face, and his hand lingered there.

"Oh, this *is* difficult," Carley agreed.

Her little sister was absorbing every word. Had Carley left the room, Noelle was sure Thom would be kissing her by now. Then they'd be lost in the kissing and oblivious to anything else.

"Is there a solution for us? One that doesn't involve alienating our families. Or our mothers, at any rate." Thom didn't look optimistic.

"What about the tea service?" Noelle said, mulling over an idea. "You said there's no replacing it, but maybe if we found a similar one, your mother would be willing to accept it."

"I don't know," he said. "This wasn't just any tea service. It was a family heirloom that belonged to my great-grandmother. We'll never find one exactly like it."

"I know, but finding one even remotely similar would be a start toward rebuilding the relationship, don't you think?"

He didn't seem convinced. "Perhaps."

"Could you find out the style and type?"

Thom shook his head doubtfully. "I could try."

"Please, Thom. And see if there are any photos."

They hugged again and Noelle closed her eyes, savoring the feel of his strong arms around her, inhaling his clean, outdoorsy scent.

Everything had changed for her. The thought of returning to Texas and her life there held little appeal. For years, she'd stayed away from her hometown because it represented a past that had brought her grief, and now—now she knew this was where her future lay.

There was a knock on Carley's door.

Noelle and Thom flew apart and a look of panic came into Carley's eyes.

"The closet," Noelle whispered, quickly ushering Thom inside. No sooner had she shut the door than her little sister admitted their mother into the room.

Noelle figured they must look about as guilty as any two people could. Carley stared up at the bedroom ceiling and Noelle was tempted to hum a catchy Yuletide tune.

"I thought I'd turn in for the night," her mother said. She obviously hadn't noticed anything out of the ordinary.

"Good idea," Carley told her mother.

"You don't want to wear yourself out," Noelle added,

letting her arms swing at her sides. "With Christmas and all…"

Her mother gave them a soft smile. "It does my heart good to see the two of you together. You were like a second mother to Carley when she was a baby."

"Mom!" her little sister wailed.

"I always thought you'd have a house full of your own children one day," she said nostalgically. "Don't you remember how you used to play with all your dolls?"

Noelle wanted to groan, knowing that Thom was listening in on the conversation.

"You'd make a wonderful mother."

"Thank you, Mom," she said. "'Night now. See you in the morning."

"'Night." She stepped out the door.

Noelle sighed with relief and so did Carley. She was about to open the closet when her mother stuck her head back inside the room. "Noelle, do you have plans for the morning?"

"No, why?" she asked, her voice higher than normal.

"I might need some help."

"I'll be glad to do what I can."

"Thank you, sweetheart." And with that she was gone. For good this time.

After a moment, Thom opened the closet door and peered out. "Is it safe?"

"I think so."

"Do you want me to keep watch?" Carley asked. "You know, so you guys can have some privacy." She smiled at Thom. "He's been wanting to kiss you ever since you got here." She lowered her voice. "I think he's kinda cute."

"So do I," Noelle confessed. "And yes, some privacy would be greatly appreciated."

Carley winked at Thom. "I think I'll go out and see what Dad's doing."

The instant the door closed, Thom took her in his arms and lowered his mouth to hers. Noelle groaned softly, welcoming him. Together, they created warm, moist kisses, increasing in intensity and desire. Other than the brief episode in the park, it'd been years since they'd kissed like this. Yet his touch felt so familiar....

"It's always been you," he whispered.

She heard the desperation in his voice. "I know—it's always been you," she echoed.

He kissed her again with a hunger and a need that reflected her own.

"Oh, Thom, what are we going to do?"

"We're going to start with your suggestion and find a silver tea service," he said firmly. "Then we're going to give it to my mother and tell her it's time to mend fences."

"What if we *can't* find one?" She frowned. "Or what if we do and they still won't forgive each other?"

"You worry too much." He kissed the tip of her nose. "And you ask too many questions."

Sarah was sitting up in bed reading a brand-new and highly touted mystery when her husband entered their room.

"You've been quiet this evening," Jake commented as he unbuttoned his shirt.

"Have I?" She gazed at the novel, but her attention kept wandering. She'd read this paragraph at least six times and she couldn't remember what it said. Every word seemed to remind her of a friend she'd lost twenty years ago.

"You haven't been yourself since you got back from shopping."

Sarah decided to ignore his words. "I stopped in and said good-night to the girls before I went to bed. Isn't it nice that Noelle and Carley get along so well?"

"You're changing the subject," Jake said. "And not very subtly."

Sarah set aside the book. In her present frame of mind, she was doing the author and herself a disservice. She reached for the light, but instead of flicking it off, she fell back against her pillows.

"I ran into Mary this afternoon," she told her husband.

"Again?"

"Again," she confirmed. "This meeting didn't go much better than the one at Value-X."

"That bad?"

"Almost. I can't even begin to tell you how horribly the two of us behaved."

Jake chuckled, shaking his head. "Does this have anything to do with the two hundred or so candy bars I found in the back of the big freezer?"

"You saw?"

He nodded. "What is it with you two?"

"Oh, honey, I wish I knew. I *hate* this. I've always hated this animosity. It would've been over years ago if Mary had listened to reason."

Her husband didn't respond.

"Everything was perfectly fine until we were forced to work on this Christmas project. Until then, she ignored me and I ignored her."

"Ignored her, did you?" he asked mildly.

Sarah pretended not to hear his question. "I think Melody Darrington might have planned this." The scheme took shape in her mind. "Melody *must* have."

"Isn't she the club secretary?"

"You know Melody," Sarah snapped. "She's the cute blonde who sold me the tickets to the dance."

"I wasn't there when you picked up the tickets," Jake reminded her as he climbed into bed.

"But you know who I mean."

"If you say so."

"You do. Now listen, because I think I'm on to something here. Melody's the one who told me we couldn't rent the hall for Kristen's wedding unless I performed a community service for the club."

"Yes, I remember, and that's how you got involved in the Christmas basket thing."

"Melody's also the one who assigned me to that project," she went on. "There had to be dozens of other projects I could've done. Plus, she insisted I had to fulfill those hours this year. That makes no sense whatsoever."

"Why would Melody do anything like that?"

"How would I know?"

Her husband looked skeptical. "I think you might be jumping to conclusions here."

"Melody gave us half of the same list, too." Outrage simmered just below the surface as Sarah sorted through the facts. She tossed aside the covers and leaped out of bed. Hands on hips, she glared at her husband. Of course. It all added up. Melody definitely had a role in this, and Sarah didn't like it.

"Hey, I didn't do anything," Jake protested.

"I'm not saying you did." Still not satisfied, she started pacing the area at the foot of the bed. "This is the lowest, dirtiest trick anyone's ever played on me."

"Now, Sarah, you don't have any real proof."

"Of course I do! Why did Melody make a copy of that list, anyway? All she had to do was divide it."

"Sounds like an honest mistake to me. Didn't you tell me the office was hectic that morning? Melody was dealing with you, the phones and everything else when she gave you and Mary the lists."

"Yes, but that's no excuse for what happened."

"You're angrier with yourself than Melody."

Sarah knew the truth when she heard it. The outrage vanished as quickly as it had come, and she climbed back into bed, next to her husband.

For a long time neither spoke. Finally Jake turned on their bedside radio and they listened to "Silent Night" sung by a children's choir. Their pure, sweet voices almost brought tears to Sarah's eyes.

"In two days, it'll be Christmas," she said in a soft voice.

"And Noelle's birthday." Her husband smiled. "Remember our first year? We could barely afford a Christmas tree, let alone gifts. Yet you managed to give me the most incredible present of all, our Noelle."

"Remember the next Christmas, when I'd just found out I was pregnant with Kristen?" she said fondly. "Our gift to each other was a secondhand washer." In the early years of their marriage, they'd struggled to make ends meet. Yet in many ways, those had been the very best.

Jake smiled. "We were poor as church mice."

"But happy."

"Very happy," he agreed, sliding his arm around her shoulders. "I thought it was clever of you to knit Christmas stockings for the girls the year Noelle turned four. Or was it five?"

"I didn't knit them," Sarah said sadly. "Mary did."

"Mary?"

"Don't you remember? She knit all the kids' stockings, and I baked the cookies and we exchanged?"

"Ah, yes. You two had quite a barter system worked out."

"If we hadn't traded babysitting, none of us would've been able to afford an evening out." Once a month, they'd taken the girls over to their dearest friends' home for the night; Mary and Greg had done the same. It'd been a lifesaver in those early years. She and Jake had never been able to afford anything elaborate, but a night out, just the two of them, had been heaven. Mary and Greg had cherished their nights, as well.

"I miss her," Sarah admitted. "Even after all these years, I miss my friend."

"I know." Jake gently squeezed her shoulder.

"I'd give anything never to have borrowed the silver tea service."

"You were trying to help someone out."

"That's how it started, but I should've been honest with Mary. I should've told her the tea service wasn't for my open house, but for Cheryl's."

"Why didn't you?"

She'd had years to think about the answer to that question. "Because Mary didn't like Cheryl. I assumed she was jealous. Now… I don't know."

Sarah remembered the circumstances well. She'd recently begun selling real estate and Cheryl Carlson had given her suggestions and advice. Cheryl had wanted something to enhance the look of the dining room for her open house, and Sarah had volunteered to bring in the tea service. When she'd asked Mary, her friend had hesitated, but then agreed. Sarah had let Mary assume it was for her own open house.

"You were so upset when you found out the tea service had been stolen."

To this day her stomach knotted at the memory of having to face Mary and confess what had happened. Soon afterward, Cheryl had left the agency and hired on with another firm, and Sarah had lost touch with her.

"I'd always hoped that one day Mary would find it in her heart to forgive me."

"I did, too."

"I'm so sorry, sweetheart," Sarah whispered, resting her head against her husband's shoulder.

"Why are you apologizing to me?"

"Because you and Greg used to be good friends, too."

"Oh."

"Remember how you used to golf together."

"Yes."

"I wonder if Greg still plays."

"I see him out at the club every now and then," Jake told her.

"Does he speak to you?"

"Yes."

Sarah was comforted knowing that. "I'm glad."

"So am I," her husband said, then kissed her good-night.

On December twenty-third, Thom's office was running on a skeleton crew. His secretary was in for half a day and he immediately handed her the assignment of locating every antiques store in a hundred-mile radius.

He'd called his father before eight that morning. "Tell me what you know about Mom's old tea service."

"Tell you what I know?" he repeated. "It was stolen, remember?"

"I realize that," Thom said impatiently.

"What makes you ask?"

"I thought I'd buy her a replacement for Christmas."

"Don't you think you're leaving your shopping a little late?"

"Could be." Thom didn't feel comfortable sharing what this was really about, but he was going to do whatever he could to replace that damn tea service.

"I think we might have a picture of it somewhere."

Thom perked up.

"For years your mother looked for a replacement, you know. We hadn't actually taken a picture of the tea set, but it was in the background of another photograph."

Thom remembered now. His parents had the photo enlarged in order to get as much detail as possible.

"Do you still have the photograph? Or better yet, the enlargement?"

"I think it might be around here somewhere. I assume you need this ASAP."

"You got it."

"Well, I promised to drive your mother out to the Women's Century Club this morning and then to the grocery store. You're welcome to stop by the house and look."

"Where do you figure it might be?"

His father considered that for a moment. "Maybe the bottom drawer of my desk. There are a few old photographs there. That's my best suggestion."

"Anyplace else I should look?"

"Your mother's briefcase. Every once in a while she visits an antiques store, but for the most part she's given up hope. She's still got her name in with several of the bigger places. If anything even vaguely similar comes in, the stores promised to give her a call."

"Has she gotten many calls?"

"Only two in all these years," his father told him. "Both of them excited her so much she could barely sleep until she'd checked them out. They turned out to be completely the wrong style."

Thom didn't know if he'd have any better success, but he had to try.

"Good luck, son."

"Thanks, Dad."

As soon as he hung up, Thom called Noelle's cell phone. She answered right away.

"Morning," he said, warming to the sound of her voice. "I hope you're free to do a bit of investigating."

"I am. I canceled out on Mom—told her I was meeting an old friend."

"Did she ask any questions?"

"No, but I could tell she was disappointed. I do so hope we're successful."

"Me, too. Listen, I've got news." Thom told her about the old photograph and what his father had said earlier. He hoped it would encourage Noelle, but she seemed disheartened when she spoke again.

"If your parents searched all these years, what are the chances of us finding a replacement now?"

"We'll just keep working on it. I'm not giving up, and I'm guessing you feel the same way."

"I do—of course."

"Good. How soon before we can meet?"

"Fifteen minutes."

"I'll wait for you at my parents' place."

On his way out the door, Thom grabbed the list Martha, his secretary, had compiled and when he read it over, he knew why he paid this woman top dollar. Not only had she given him the name and address of every store in the entire state, she'd also listed their websites and any other internet information.

"Merry Christmas," he said, then gave her the rest of the day off with pay.

Noelle was already parked outside his parents' house when Thom arrived. She got out of her car and joined him as he pulled into the driveway.

"Hi," she said softly.

Thom leaned over and kissed her. "Hi." The key to the house was under a decorative rock. He unlocked the door and turned off the burglar alarm. Holding Noelle's hand, he led her into his parents' home.

Noelle stopped in the entryway and glanced around. It'd been many, many years since she'd walked into this house. It wasn't really familiar—everything had been redecorated and repainted since she was a little girl—but the place had a comfortable relaxed feel. Big furniture dominated the living room, hand-knit stockings hung on the fireplace and the mantel was decorated with holly. The scent of the fresh Christmas tree filled the air.

"Your mother has a wonderful eye for color and design," she commented, taking in the bright red bows on the tree and all the red ornaments.

Still holding her hand, Thom led her into his father's den. The oak rolltop desk sat in the corner, and Thom immediately started searching through the bottom drawer. He found the stack of photographs his father had mentioned and sorted through them with Noelle looking over his shoulder. She leaned against him, and he wondered if she realized how good it felt to have her pressed so close to him. Or how tempting it was to turn and kiss her…

"That's it," she cried triumphantly when he flipped past a black-and-white picture. She grabbed it before he had a chance to take a second look. Examining the print, she murmured, "It really was exquisite, wasn't it?" She passed it back to him.

"It *is* beautiful," he said, emphasizing the present tense. Thom wasn't sure why he insisted on being this optimistic about finding a replacement. He suspected that wanting it so badly had a lot to do with it.

Reaching into his coat pocket, he pulled out the list Martha had compiled for him.

"Now that we have a picture," Noelle said, "I'll go home and scan it into Carley's computer. Then I'll send it out to these addresses and see what comes back."

"Great. But before you do, I'll get a copy of this photograph and start contacting local dealers. They might be able to steer me in a different direction."

"Oh, Thom, it'd mean so much to me if we could bring our mothers back together."

They kissed, and it would've been the easiest thing in the world to become immersed in the wonder of having found each other again. Her mouth was warm, soft to the touch. She enticed him, fulfilled him and tempted him beyond any woman he'd ever known or loved. He didn't know much about her present life. They'd spoken very little of their accomplishments, their friends, their jobs. It wasn't necessary. Thom *knew* her. The girl he'd loved in high school had matured into a capable, beautiful and very desirable adult.

"It's hard to think about anything else when you kiss me," she whispered.

"It is for me, too."

Before leaving the Sutton home, Thom put everything back as it was, and remembered to reset the burglar alarm.

After making a photocopy at his office, Thom gave her the original, thinking that would scan best.

"I'll go back to the house now and plead with Carley to let me on the computer," she told him.

"Okay, and I'll see what a little old-fashioned footwork turns up."

Noelle started to get into her car, then paused. "What'll happen if we don't find a replacement before I return to Texas?"

Thom didn't want to think about that yet. "I don't know," he had to admit.

"Want to meet in the park at midnight?" she asked.

Thom chuckled. "I'm a little old to be sneaking around to meet my girlfriend."

"That didn't stop you from climbing in my bedroom window last night."

True, but his need to see her had overwhelmed his caution, not to mention his good sense.

"I love you, Noelle." There, he'd said it. He'd placed his heart in her hands, to accept or reject.

Tears glistened in her eyes. "I love you, too—I never stopped loving you."

"Even when you hated me?"

She laughed shakily. "Even then."

NOELLE MCDOWELL'S
JOURNAL

December 23
11:00 a.m.

I feel as if I'm on an emotional roller coaster. One moment I'm feeling as low as I can get, and the next I'm soaring into the clouds. Just now, I'm in the cloud phase. Thom found the picture of the tea set! We're determined to locate one as close to the original as possible. As I said to Thom, I'm hoping for a Christmas miracle. (I never knew I was such a romantic.) Normally I scoff at things like miracles, but that's what both Thom and I need. We've already had one miracle—we have each other back.

Before we parted this morning, Thom said he loved me. I love him, too. I've always loved Thom, and that's what made his deception—or what I believed was his deception—so terribly painful.

Now all we've got to do is keep our mothers out of the picture until we can replace the tea service. I know it's a challenging task, but we're up to it.

As of right now, we each have our assignments. Carley's using the computer for ten more minutes and then it's all mine. My job is to scan in the picture he found at his parents' house and send it to as many online antiques dealers as I can. Thom is off checking local deal-

ers and has some errands to run. We're going to meet up again later.

I had to cancel a lunch date with Kristen and Jonathan, but my sister understood. She's excited about Thom and me getting back together. Apparently she's had more of a hand in this than I realized. I really owe her.

Finding a tea service to replace the one that was stolen is turning out to be even harder than I expected—but we have to try. I believe in miracles. I was a doubter less than a week ago, but now I'm convinced.

Seven

"How many turkeys did you say we had to buy?"

"Six," Mary said, checking the list to make sure she was correct. December twenty-third, and the grocery store was a nightmare. The aisles were crowded, and many of the shelves needed restocking. The last thing Mary wanted to do was fight the Christmas rush, but that couldn't be helped. Next year, she'd leave the filling of these Christmas baskets to someone else.

"Get six bags of potatoes while you're at it," she told her husband as they rolled past a stack of ten-pound bags.

"Getting a little bossy, aren't you?" Greg muttered.

"Sorry, it's just that there are a hundred other things I'd rather be doing right now."

"Then you should've given the task to Sarah McDowell. Didn't you tell me she offered?"

Mary didn't want to hear the other woman's name. "I don't trust her to see that it's done properly."

"Don't you think you're being a little harsh?"

"No." That should be plain enough. The more she thought about her last encounter with Sarah McDowell, the more she realized how glad she'd be when they'd completed this project. "Being around Sarah has dredged up a whole slew of bad memories," she informed her husband.

Greg dutifully loaded sixty pounds of potatoes into the cart. As soon as he'd finished, Mary headed down the next aisle.

"My Christmas has been ruined," she said through gritted teeth.

"How's that?"

"Greg, don't be obtuse." She reached for several cans of evaporated milk and added them to the food piled high in their cart. "I've had to deal with *her.*"

"Yes, but—"

"Never mind," Mary said, cutting him off. She didn't expect Greg to understand. Her husband had never really grasped the sense of loss she'd felt when Sarah destroyed their friendship with her deception. The silver tea service was irreplaceable; so was the friendship its disappearance had shattered.

"Hello, Mary." Jean Cummings, a friend who edited the society page, pulled her cart alongside Mary's. "Merry Christmas, Greg."

Her husband had the look of a deer caught in the headlights. He no more knew who Jean was than he would a stranger, although he'd attended numerous social functions with the woman.

"You remember Jean, don't you?" she said, hoping to prompt his memory.

"Of course," he lied. "Good to see you again."

"It looks like you're feeding a big crowd," Jean said, surveying the contents of Mary's cart.

Mary didn't bother to explain about the Christmas baskets. "Is your family coming for the holidays?" she asked.

"Oh, yes, and yours, too, I imagine?"

"Of course." Mary was eager to get about her business. She didn't have time to dillydally. As soon as she was finished with the shopping, she could go back to planning her own family's Christmas dinner. Greg would need to order the fresh Dungeness crabs they always had on Christmas Eve; he could do that while they were here.

"Tell me," Jean said, leaning close to Mary and talking in a stage whisper. "Am I going to get the scoop on Thom?"

"Thom?" Mary didn't know what she was talking about.

"I saw him just now in Mendleson's."

It was well known that the jeweler specialized in engagement rings.

"Thom's one of the most eligible bachelors in town. I know plenty of hearts will be broken when he finally chooses a bride."

Mary was speechless. She'd had lunch with her son on Friday and although he'd hinted, he certainly hadn't said anything that suggested he was on the verge of proposing. She didn't even know who he was currently seeing.

"I'm sure Thom would prefer to do his own announcing," Greg said coolly, answering for Mary.

"Oh, drat," Jean muttered. "I was hoping you'd let the cat out of the bag."

"My lips are sealed," Mary said, recovering. "Have a wonderful Christmas."

"You, too." Jean pushed her cart past them.

As soon as the society page editor was out of earshot, Mary gripped her husband's forearm. "Has Thom spoken to you lately?"

"This morning," Greg told her. "But he didn't say anything about getting engaged."

"Who could it be?" Mary cried, aghast that she was so completely in the dark. As his mother, she should know these things.

"If he was serious about any woman, we'd know."

Mary wasn't buying it.

"Let's not leap to conclusions just because our son happened to walk into a certain jewelry store. I'm sure there's a perfectly logical reason Thom was in Mendleson's and I'll bet it hasn't got a thing to do with buying an engagement ring."

"This is all Sarah's fault," she murmured.

Her husband looked at her as though she were speaking in a foreign language.

"I mean it, Greg. I've been so preoccupied with the whole mess Sarah's created about these baskets, I haven't had time to pay attention to my son. Why, just on Friday when we had lunch..." Suddenly disheartened, Mary let her words fade.

"What's wrong?" Greg asked.

All the combativeness went out of her. "I can't blame Sarah entirely—I played a role in this, too."

"What role?"

Once again, she was amazed by her husband's obliviousness. "This business with Thom. Now that I think about it, I'm convinced he wanted to talk over his engagement with me, only I was so rattled by the Value-X incident I didn't give him a chance. Oh, Greg, how could I have been so self-absorbed?"

"What makes you think he was going to tell you he was getting engaged? Why don't we call and ask him when we get home?" Greg suggested.

"And let him think we're interfering in his life? We can't do that!"

"Why not?"

"We'd ruin his surprise, if indeed there is one."

Greg merely sighed as they wheeled the cart to the checkout counter.

Ten minutes later, once everything was safely inside the trunk, Mary turned to him. "I just don't know what I'll do if *she's* the one he's interested in. I couldn't stand it if he married into *that* family."

"I don't think we need to worry about it," he told her as they started back to the house. "There's no evidence whatsoever."

"He *danced* with Noelle McDowell!"

"He danced with lots of girls."

The engine made a coughing sound as they approached the first intersection. "What's that?" Mary asked.

"It's time for an oil change," her husband said. "I'll have the car looked at after the holidays."

She nodded. She trusted the upkeep of their vehicles to her husband and immediately put the thought out of her mind. Car troubles were minor in the greater scheme of things.

By the end of the day, when clouds thickened the sky and the cold swept in, fierce and chilling, Thom finally had to admit that replacing the silver tea service wasn't going to be easy.

He'd tried everything he could think of, called friends and associates who might know where he could find an antiques dealer who specialized in silver—anyone who might lead him to his prize. Far more than a gift lay in the balance. It was possible that his and Noelle's entire future hinged on this.

At seven, after an exhaustive all-day search, he went

home. The first thing he did was check his answering machine, hoping to hear from Noelle. Sure enough, the message light was flashing. Without waiting to remove his coat, he pushed the button and grabbed paper and a pen.

A female voice, high and excited, spilled out. "It's Carley Sue. Remember me? I'm Noelle's sister. Anyway, Noelle asked me to call you. She'd call you herself, but I asked if I could do it, 'cause it was my bedroom window you knocked on. And my computer Noelle used."

Thom laughed out loud, almost missing the second half of the message.

"Anyway, Noelle wanted to know if you could meet her at the park tomorrow morning. She said you should be there early. She said six o'clock 'cause you have to drive all the way to Portland. She said you'd know why, but she wouldn't tell me. When you see Noelle, please tell her it's not nice to keep secrets from her sister, will you?" She giggled. "Never mind, I could get it out of her if I really wanted to. Bye."

Thom smiled, feeling a surge of energy. Obviously Noelle had had better luck than he did.

A second message followed the first.

"Thom, it's me. I wasn't sure Carley got the entire message to you. When we meet at the park, come with a full tank of gas. If this conflicts with your Christmas Eve plans, call me on my cell phone." There was a short pause. "I don't want you to get your hopes up. I found a tea service that's not *exactly* like your grandmother's, but I'm looking for a Christmas miracle. We'll need to compare it to the picture. The dealer's only keeping his store open until noon, which is why we need to leave here so early. I'm sorry I can't see you tonight. I wish I could, but I've got family obligations. I know you understand."

He did understand—all too well. A third message started; he was certainly popular today. It was his mother and she sounded worried.

"It's Mom… I ran into a friend from the newspaper this morning and she mentioned seeing you at Mendleson's Jewelers. Were you…buying an engagement ring? Thom, it isn't that McDowell girl, is it? Call me, will you? I need reassurance that you're not about to make a big mistake."

This was what happened when you lived in a small town. Everyone knew your business. So, his mother had heard, and even with the wrong facts, she'd put together the right answer. Yes, he'd been at Mendleson's. And yes, it *was* "that McDowell girl."

Thom decided he had to talk about all of this with someone who understood the situation and knew all the people involved. Someone discreet, who had his best interests at heart. Someone with no agenda, hidden or otherwise.

The one person he could trust was his older sister. Suzanne was three years his senior, married and living ten miles outside of town; she and her husband, Rob, owned a hazelnut orchard. Thom didn't see Suzanne often, but he was godfather to his five-year-old nephew, Cameron.

A brief phone call assured him that his sister was available and eager to see him. Off he went, grabbing a chunk of cheese and an apple to eat on the way. Maybe his sister would have some wisdom to share with him.… How quickly life can change, he mused, and never more so than at Christmas.

Suzanne had a mug of hot cider waiting when he arrived. Rob was out, dealing with some late deliveries. His family owned the orchard and leased it to him. Rob worked long hours making a success of their business, and so did Suzanne. Both his sister and brother-in-law were honest, hardworking people, and he trusted their advice.

"This is a surprise," Suzanne said, pulling out a chair at the large oak table in the center of her country kitchen.

"Cameron's in bed already?" Thom asked, disappointed to miss seeing his nephew.

"He thinks if he goes to bed early Santa will come sooner." She gave a shrug. "Never mind that this is only the twenty-third. I guess he's hoping he can make time speed up," she said with a smile. "By the way, he had a ridiculous tale about you and some woman at the movies the other day. Throwing popcorn was a big theme in this story."

"I don't know what he told you, but more than likely it's true. We bumped into Noelle McDowell and her little sister at the theater."

"Noelle. Oh, no." Suzanne was instantly sympathetic. "That must've been uncomfortable."

"Yes and no." He hesitated, wondering to what extent his sister's attitude was a reflection of their parents'. "It was difficult at first, because we didn't exactly part on the best of terms."

"At first?"

His sister had picked up on that fast enough. "We've talked since and resolved our difficulties."

"Resolved them, did you?" Suzanne raised her eyebrows.

"I love Noelle." There, he'd said it.

"Who's Noelle?" Rob asked as he walked in through the kitchen door, shedding hat, scarf and gloves.

"I'll explain later," Suzanne promised, ladling a cup of cider from the pot on the stove. "Here, honey."

"Our families don't get along," Thom explained.

"Do Mom and Dad know?" his sister asked.

"Not yet, but Mom got wind of me going to Mendleson's. She must have her suspicions, since she left a message on my machine practically begging me to tell her I'm not seeing Noelle."

"Did you buy a ring?"

"That's not the point."

"Okay," his sister said slowly. "What *do* you plan to tell Mom and Dad?"

"I don't know."

Suzanne sipped her cider, then put down the mug to focus on him. "You're going to wait until Christmas is over before you say anything, right?"

Thom didn't know if he could. His mother was already besieging him with questions and she'd keep at him until she got answers—preferably the answers she wanted. He needed an ally and he hoped he could count on Suzanne.

"Let me play devil's advocate here a moment," his sister suggested.

"Please."

"Put yourself in Mom's place. Noelle's family has hurt our family. And now you're asking Mom to welcome Noelle into our lives and our hearts."

"Noelle is already in my heart."

"I know," Suzanne told him, "but there's more than one person involved in this. How does her family feel about you, for instance?"

That was a question Thom didn't want to consider. This wouldn't be easy for Noelle, either. Kristen and

Carley were obviously supportive, but Sarah McDowell—well, she was another matter.

"We were ready to defy everyone as teenagers," he said, reminding his sister of the difficult stand he'd taken at eighteen.

"You were a kid."

"I was in love with her then, and I'm still in love with her."

"Yes," Suzanne said, "but you're more responsible now."

"I can't live my life to suit everyone else," he said, frustrated by her response.

"He's got a point," Rob said. "I don't understand the family dynamics here, but I have a fairly good idea what you're talking about. I say if Thom feels this strongly about Noelle after all these years, he should go for it. He should live his own life."

Thom felt a rush of gratitude for his brother-in-law's enouragement.

"That's what you wanted to hear, isn't it?" Suzanne said, smiling. "For what it's worth, I agree with my husband."

"Thanks," Thom said. "That means a lot, you guys." He shook his head. "Noelle and I are well aware of the problems we face as a couple. We'd hoped to come to our parents with a solution."

"What kind of solution?"

"I've been pounding the pavement all day, checking out antiques stores and jewelry stores for a replacement tea service. Noelle's been doing an internet search."

His sister frowned. "I don't want to discourage you, but you're not going to find one."

She certainly had a way of cutting to the chase.

"Thank you for that note of optimism. Anyway, how can you be so sure? Noelle thinks she might have a lead."

"Hey, that's good," Rob said. "It's worth trying to find…whatever this thing is that you're looking for."

"An antique silver tea service—I'll fill you in later, Rob." She turned to her brother. "I don't want to be pessimistic. It's just that Mom and Dad looked for years. They've given up now, but for a long time they left no stone unturned."

"If we find one, we'll consider it a Christmas miracle."

"Definitely," Suzanne agreed. "And I'd consider it a lucky omen, too."

"But you don't think we'll succeed."

"No," his sister told him. "I don't think so, but who knows?"

"If I ask Noelle to be part of my life, will you accept her?"

"Of course." Suzanne didn't hesitate. "But I'm not the one whose opinion matters. However, Rob's right, you've got to live your own life, and we'll support you in whatever choice you make."

He visited with his sister a while longer and assured her that no matter what he decided, he'd meet the family for the annual Christmas Eve dinner, followed by church services.

The next morning Noelle was waiting in the park at the appointed time and place when he got there. His heart reacted instantly to the sight of her. She looked like an angel in her long white wool coat and cashmere scarf. A Christmas angel. He smiled at the thought—even if he *was* getting sentimental in his old age.

"Merry Christmas," he said.

"Merry Christmas, Thom." Her eyes brightened as he approached.

Thom folded her in his arms and their kisses were deep and urgent. His mouth lingered on hers, gradually easing into gentler kisses. Finally he whispered, "Ready to go?"

"I hope this isn't a wild-goose chase," Noelle told him as she leaned her head against his shoulder.

"I do, too." But if it was, at least he'd be spending the day with her.

If they couldn't carry out their quest, they'd simply have to find some other way to persuade both mothers to accept the truth—that Thomas Sutton and Noelle Mc-Dowell were in love.

It was Christmas Eve, nine in the morning, and Sarah McDowell was eager to finish with the Christmas baskets. She'd skillfully wrapped each gift to transport to the Salvation Army.

"You're coming with me, aren't you?" she asked her husband.

Jake glanced up from the morning paper, frowning. "I can't."

"Why not?" Sarah didn't know if she could face Mary alone—not again. She'd assumed Jake would drive with her.

"I've got errands of my own. It's Christmas Eve."

"What about you, Carley?" she said, looking hopefully toward her daughter.

"Can't, Mom, sorry."

But not nearly sorry enough, Sarah thought. Her family was abandoning her in this hour of need. "Where's Noelle?" she asked. Surely she could count on Noelle.

"Out," Carley informed her.

"She's left already?"

Carley nodded.

Sarah thought she saw Jake wink at Carley. Apparently those two were involved in some sort of conspiracy against her.

At least Jake helped her load up the car, shifting his golf clubs to the backseat, but he disappeared soon afterward. Grumbling under her breath, Sarah drove out to the Women's Century Club.

Mary's car was already in the lot when she arrived. So, Mary Sutton was breaking a lifelong habit of tardiness in her eagerness to finish this charity project. For that, Sarah couldn't blame her. She, too, had reached her limit.

The cold air cut through her winter coat the instant she climbed out of the car. The radio station had mentioned the possibility of an ice storm later in the day. Sarah only hoped it wouldn't materialize.

"Merry Christmas," Melody called out as Sarah struggled through the front door, carrying the largest and most awkward of the boxes.

Sarah muttered a reply. Her Christmas Eve was *not* getting off to a good start.

"Mary's waiting for you," Melody told her. "I understand there was a mix-up with the lists. I'm so sorry. It was crazy that morning, wasn't it?"

Sarah wasn't fooled by the other woman's cheerful attitude. Melody Darrington had done her utmost to manipulate the two of them into working on this project together, and Sarah, for one, didn't take kindly to the interference. It was clear that Mary hadn't realized anything was amiss, but then Mary Sutton wasn't the most perceptive person in the world. Still, Sarah wasn't going to make a federal case of it, on the off chance that it *had* all been an innocent mistake as Melody was implying.

Sarah made her way into the meeting room, where Mary had the six baskets set up on a long table, as well as six large boxes, already filled with the makings for Christmas dinner.

"Is that everything you've got?" Mary asked, peering into Sarah's carton. Her tone insinuated that Sarah had contributed less than required.

"Of course not," she snapped. "I have two more boxes in the car."

Neither woman leaped up to help her carry them inside, although Melody did make a halfhearted offer when Sarah headed out the front door.

"No thanks—you've already done enough," she said pointedly.

"You're sure you don't need the help?" Melody asked.

Shaking her head, Sarah brought in the second of the boxes and set it on the table.

"I thought you'd bring one of the girls with you," Mary said in that stiff way of hers.

"They're busy." She started back for the last of the cartons.

"Noelle isn't with Thom, is she?"

The question caught her off guard. No one had said where Noelle had gone, but it couldn't be to meet Thom Sutton. Could it? No, she wouldn't do that. Not her daughter.

"Absolutely not," Sarah insisted. Noelle had already learned her lesson when it came to the Suttons.

"Good," Mary said.

"Noelle's with friends," Sarah returned and then, because she had to know, she asked a question of her own. "What makes you ask?"

"Oh—no reason."

Sarah didn't believe that for a moment. "You tell your son Noelle's under no illusions about him. She won't be so easily fooled a second time."

"Now just one minute—"

"We both know what he did."

"You're wrong, Sarah—but then you often are."

Melody stepped into the meeting room and stopped abruptly. With a shocked look, she regarded both women. "Come on, you two! It's Christmas."

"And your point is?" Sarah asked.

"My point is that the least you can do is work together on this. These baskets need to get to the Salvation Army right away. They're late already, and my husband just phoned and said there's definitely an ice storm coming, so you shouldn't delay."

"I'll get them there in time," Mary promised. "If we could get the baskets filled…"

"Fine," Sarah said. "I'll bring in the last box."

"We wouldn't be this late if you'd—"

Sarah ignored her and hurried out the door, only to hear Melody mutter something about an ice storm developing right in this room.

She knew that the minute she left, Melody and Mary would talk about her. However, she didn't care. Right after Kristen's wedding, she was letting her membership in the Women's Century Club lapse.

Once the third box was safely inside, Sarah placed the gifts in the correct baskets. Then both women sorted through the family names by checking the tag on each present. Sarah had spent a lot of time wrapping her gifts, wanting to please the recipients…and, to be honest, impress Mary and Melody with her talents. Given the opportunity, she could have decorated the clubhouse to match Mary's efforts. No, to exceed them.

"You did get that Firefighter Barbie doll, didn't you?" Mary asked.

"Of course I did," she answered scornfully.

They attached ribbons to each basket, then prepared everything—gifts and groceries—for transport.

"Would you like help loading up your car?" Sarah asked. Since Mary was driving and this was a joint project, she felt constrained to offer.

Mary seemed surprised, then shook her head. "I can manage. But…thanks."

Sarah had wanted to make a quick getaway, but Melody stopped her at the door, appointment book in hand.

"I have a few questions about Kristen's wedding."

"What do you need to know?"

Melody flipped open the book. "Will you require the use of our kitchen?"

"I'm not sure because we haven't picked the caterer yet, but we'll do that right after the first of the year."

"I have a list, if you'd like to look at it."

"I would." Sarah wanted to make her daughter's day as special as she could. But as she answered Melody's questions, her mind drifted to Noelle. Mary had brought up a frightening possibility. Noelle had been absent from the house quite a bit since the dance on Saturday night. She was at the mall on Sunday, and then on Monday— oh, yes, she'd worked on Carley's computer most of the day. Reassured now, Sarah relaxed. Mary's fears about her son and Noelle were unfounded.

She glanced around the lot; Mary's car was gone.

She'd apparently left for the Salvation Army already. She must have moved her vehicle to the side entrance in order to load up the baskets and boxes more easily and Sarah hadn't seen her drive off. That was just fine. Maybe this was the last she needed to see of Mary Sutton.

Now she could enjoy Christmas.

"Merry Christmas, Melody," she said. "I'm sorry for the way I snapped at you earlier."

Melody accepted her apology. "I realize this was hard on both of you but what's important are the Christmas baskets."

"I couldn't agree with you more."

Sarah's spirits lifted considerably as she walked to her car or rather, Jake's. He'd insisted she take his SUV, and she was glad of it. If possible, it seemed even colder out; she drew her coat more closely around her and bent her head as she trudged toward the car.

As she turned out of the parking lot, she saw that the roads were icing over. The warning of an ice storm had become a reality, and even earlier than expected. This weather made her nervous, and Sarah drove carefully, hoping she wouldn't run into any problem.

She hadn't gone a mile when she noticed a car pulled off to the side of the road. She slowed down and was surprised to see Mary Sutton in the driver's seat. Mary was on her cell phone; she looked out the passenger window as Sarah slowed down. Mary's eyes met hers, and then she waved her on, declining help before Sarah could even offer it.

A NOTE FROM NOELLE McDOWELL

Christmas Eve

Dear Carley Sue,
Good morning. I'll be gone by the time you read this.
I'm meeting Thom in the park and we're driving to an an-
tiques store outside Portland to check out a tea service.
Kristen knows I'm with Thom, but not why.
I'm asking you to keep my whereabouts a secret for
now. No, wait—you can mention it to Dad if you want.
Mom's the only one who really can't know. I don't think
she'll ask, because she's got a lot to do this morning de-
livering the Christmas baskets.
This whole mix-up with those baskets has really got
her in a tizzy. I find it all rather humorous and I suspect
Dad does, too.
I'm trusting you with this information, little sister. I
figured you (and your romantic heart) would want to
know.

Love,
Noelle

Eight

The car had made a grinding noise as soon as Mary started it—the same sound as the day before. Greg had said he'd look into it after the holidays, but she'd assumed it was safe to drive. Apparently not.

The car had slowed to a crawl, sputtered and then died. That was just great. The Salvation Army was waiting for these Christmas baskets, which, according to Melody, were already late. If Mary didn't hurry up and deliver them to the organization's office before closing time, six needy families would miss out on Christmas. She couldn't let that happen.

Reaching for her cell phone, she punched in her home number and hoped Greg was home. She needed rescuing, and soon. Greg would know what to do. The phone had just begun to ring when Sarah McDowell drove past.

Mary bit her lip hard. Pride demanded that she wave her on. She didn't need that woman's help. Still, she felt Sarah should've stopped; it was no less than any decent human being would do.

Well, she should know better than to expect compassion or concern from Sarah McDowell. Good Christian that she professed to be, Sarah had shown not the slightest interest in Mary's safety.

Mary clenched her teeth in fury. So, fine, Sarah didn't care whether *she* froze the death, but what about the Christmas baskets? What about the families, the children, whose Christmas depended on them? The truth was, Sarah simply didn't care what happened to Mary *or* the Christmas baskets.

The phone was still ringing—where on earth was Greg? Suddenly an operator's tinny voice came on with a recorded message. "I'm sorry, but we are unable to connect your call at this time."

"*You're* sorry?" Mary cried. She punched in Thom's number and then Suzanne's and got the same response. She tossed the phone back in her purse and waited. The Women's Century Club was on the outskirts of Rose. On Christmas Eve, with an ice storm bearing down, the prospect of a Good Samaritan was highly unlikely.

"Great," she muttered. She might be stuck here for God knows how long. Surely *someone* would realize she wasn't where she was supposed to be. Still, it might take hours before anyone came looking for her. And even more hours before she was found.

With the engine off, the heater wasn't working, and Mary was astonished by how quickly the cold seeped into the car's interior. She tried her cell phone again and got the same message. There was obviously trouble with the transmitters; maybe it would clear up soon. She struggled to remain optimistic, but another depressing thought overshadowed the first. How long could she last in this cold? She could imagine herself still sitting in the car days from now, frozen stiff, abandoned and forgotten on Christmas Eve.

Trying to ward off panic, she decided to stand on the side of the road to see if that would help her cell phone reception. That way, she'd also be ready to wave for assistance if someone drove by.

She retrieved her phone, climbed out of the car and immediately became aware of how much colder it was outside. Hands shaking, she tried the phone. Same recorded response. She tucked her hands inside her pockets and waited for what seemed like an eternity. Then she tried her cell phone again.

Nothing. Just that damned recording.

Resigned to waiting for a passerby, she huddled in her coat.

Five minutes passed. The icy wind made it feel more like five hours. The air was so frigid that after a few moments it hurt to breathe. Her teeth began to chatter, and her feet lost feeling, but that was what she got for wearing slip-on loafers instead of winter boots.

A car appeared in the distance and Mary was so happy she wanted to cry. Greg was definitely going to hear about this! Once she got safely home, of course.

Stepping into the middle of the road, she raised her hand and then groaned aloud. It wasn't some stranger coming to her rescue, but Sarah McDowell. Desperate though she was, Mary would rather have seen just about anyone else.

Sarah pulled up alongside her and rolled down the window. "What's wrong?"

"Wh-what does it l-look like? M-my car broke down." She wished she could control the chattering of her teeth.

"Is someone coming for you?"

"N-not yet… I c-can't get through on my cell phone."

"I'm here now. Would you like me to deliver the Christmas baskets?"

Mary hesitated. If the gifts were to get to the families in time, she didn't really have much choice. "M-maybe you should."

Sarah edged her vehicle closer to Mary's and with some difficulty they transferred the six heavy baskets and the boxes of groceries from one car to the next.

"Thanks," Mary said grudgingly.

Sarah nodded curtly. "Go ahead and call Greg again," she suggested.

"Okay." Mary punched out the number and waited, hoping against hope that the call would connect. Once again, she got the "I'm sorry" recording.

"Won't go through."

"Would you like to use my phone?" Sarah asked.

"I doubt your phone will work if mine doesn't." It was so irritating—Sarah always seemed to believe that whatever she had was better.

"It won't hurt to try."

"True," Mary admitted. She accepted Sarah's phone and tried again. It gave her no satisfaction to be right.

"Go ahead and deliver the baskets," Mary said, putting on a brave front.

"I'm not going to leave you here."

Mary hardened her resolve. "Someone will come by soon enough."

"Don't be ridiculous!" Sarah practically shouted.

"Oh, all right, you can drive me back to the club. And then deliver the baskets."

Sarah glared at her. "Aren't you being a little stubborn? I could just as easily drive you home."

Mary didn't answer. She intended to make it clear that

she preferred to wait for Greg to rescue her rather than ride to town with Sarah.

"Fine, if that's what you want," Sarah said coldly.

"I'm grateful you came back," Mary told her—and she was. "I don't know how long I could've stood out here."

This time Sarah didn't respond.

"What's most important is getting these baskets to the families."

"At least we can agree on that," Sarah told her.

Mary climbed into the passenger side of Sarah's SUV and nearly sighed aloud when Sarah started the engine. A blast of hot air hit her feet and she moaned in pleasure.

Sarah was right, she decided. She *was* being unnecessarily stubborn. "If you don't mind," she said tentatively, "I would appreciate a ride home."

Sarah glanced at her as she started down the winding country road. "That wasn't so hard, now was it?"

"What?" she asked, pretending not to understand.

Just then, Sarah hit a patch of ice and the vehicle slid scarily into the other lane. With almost no traction, Sarah did what she could to keep the car on the road. "Hold on!" she cried. She struggled to maintain control but the tires refused to grip the asphalt.

"Oh, no," Mary breathed. "We're going into the ditch!" At that instant the car slid sideways, then swerved and went front-first into the irrigation ditch.

Mary fell forward, bracing her hands against the console. The car sat there, nose down. A frozen turkey rolled out of its box and lodged in the space between the two bucket seats, tail pointed at the ceiling. Sarah's eyes were wide as she held the steering wheel in a death grip.

Neither spoke for several moments. Then in a slightly breathless voice, Sarah asked, "Are you hurt?"

"No, are you?"

"I'm okay, but I think I broke three nails clutching the steering wheel."

Mary couldn't keep from smiling. Sarah had always been vain about her fingernails.

"Do you think we should try to climb out of the car?" Sarah murmured.

"I don't know."

"One of us should."

"I will," Mary offered. After all, Sarah would've been home by now if she hadn't come back to help.

"No, I think I should," Sarah said. "You must be freezing."

"I've warmed up—some. Listen, I'll go get Melody."

"It's at least a mile to the club."

"I know how far it is," Mary snapped. Sarah argued about everything.

"Why can't you just accept my help?"

"I'm in your car, aren't I?" She resisted the urge to remind Sarah that she hadn't actually been much help. Now they were both stuck, a hundred feet from where she'd been stranded. The charity baskets were no closer to their destination, either.

"Maybe another car will come by."

"Don't count on it," Mary told her.

"Why not?"

"Think about it. We're in the middle of an ice storm. It's Christmas Eve. Anyone with half a brain is home in front of a warm fireplace."

"Oh. Yes."

"I'll walk to the club."

"No," Sarah insisted.

"Why not?"

Sarah didn't say anything for a moment. "I don't want to stay here alone," she finally admitted.

Mary pondered that confession and realized she wouldn't want to wait in the car by herself, either. "Okay," she said. "We'll both go."

"Tell me what you found out about the tea service," Thom said as they headed toward the freeway on-ramp.

"The internet was great. Your secretary's list was a big help, too. I scanned in the photograph you gave me and got an immediate hit with the man we're going to see this morning."

"Hey, you did well."

"I have a good feeling about this." Noelle's voice rose with excitement.

Thom didn't entirely share her enthusiasm. "I don't think we should put too much stock in this," he said cautiously.

"Why not?"

"Don't forget, my mom and dad searched for years. It's unrealistic to think we can locate a replacement after just one day."

"But your parents didn't have the internet."

She was right, but not all antiques stores were online. Under the circumstances, it would be far too easy to build up their expectations only to face disappointment. "You said yourself this could be a wild-goose chase."

"I know." Noelle sounded discouraged now.

Thom reached out and gently clasped her fingers. "Don't worry—we're going to keep trying for as long as it takes." The road was icy, so he returned his hand to the steering wheel. "Looks like we're in for a spell of bad weather."

"I heard there's an ice storm on the way."

Thom nodded. The roads were growing treacherous, and he wondered if they should have risked the drive. However, they were on their way and at this point, he wanted to see it through as much as Noelle did.

What was normally a two-and-a-half-hour trip into Portland took almost four. Fortunately, the roads seemed to improve as they neared the city.

"I'm beginning to wonder if we should've come," Noelle said, echoing his thoughts as they passed an abandoned car angled off to the side of the road.

"We'll be fine." They were in Lake Oswego on the outskirts of Portland already—almost there.

"It's just that this is so important."

"I know."

"Maybe we should discuss what we're going to do if we don't find the tea service," Noelle said as they sought out the Lake Oswego business address.

"We'll deal with that when we have to, all right?"

She nodded.

The antiques store was situated in a strip mall between a Thai restaurant and a beauty parlor. Thom parked the car. "You ready?" he asked, turning to her.

Noelle smiled encouragingly.

They held hands as they walked to the store. A bell above the door chimed merrily when they entered, and they found themselves in a long, narrow room crammed with glassware, china and polished wood furniture. Every conceivable space and surface had been put to use. A slightly moldy odor filled the air, competing with the piney scent of a small Christmas tree. Thom had to turn sideways to get past a quantity of comic books stacked on a chest of drawers next to the entrance. He led Noelle around the obstacles to the counter, where the cash register sat.

"Hello," Noelle called out. "Anyone here?"

"Be with you in a minute," a voice called back from a hidden location deep inside the store.

While Noelle examined the brooches, pins and old jewelry beneath the glass counter, Thom glanced around. A collection of women's hats filled a shelf to the right. He couldn't imagine his mother wearing anything with feathers, but if she'd lived in a different era…

He studied a pile of old games next, but they all seemed to be missing pieces. This looked less and less promising.

"Sorry to keep you waiting." A thin older man with a full crop of white hair ambled into the room. He was slightly stooped and brushed dust from his hands as he walked.

"Hello, my name is Noelle McDowell," she said. "We spoke yesterday."

"Ah, yes."

"Thom Sutton." Thom stepped forward and offered his hand.

"Peter Bright." His handshake was firm, belying his rather frail appearance. "I didn't know if you'd make it or not, with the storm and all."

"We're grateful you're open this close to Christmas," Noelle told him.

"I don't plan on staying open for long. But I wanted to escape the house for a few hours before Estelle found an excuse to put me to work in the kitchen." He chuckled. "Would you like to take a look at the tea service?"

"Please."

"I have it back here." He started slowly toward the rear of the store; Thom and Noelle followed him.

Noelle reached for Thom's hand again. Although he'd warned her against building up their expectations, he couldn't help feeling a wave of anticipation.

"Now, let me see…" Peter mumbled as he began shifting boxes around. "You know, a lot of people tell me they're coming in and then never show up." He smiled. "Like I said, I didn't really expect you to drive all the way from Rose in the middle of an ice storm." He removed an ancient Remington typewriter and set it aside, then lifted the lid of an army-green metal chest.

"I've had this tea service for maybe twenty years," Peter explained as he extracted a Navy sea bag.

"Do you remember how you came to get it?"

"Oh, sure. An English lady sold it to me. I displayed it for a while. People looked but no one bought."

"Why keep it in the chest now?" Noelle asked.

"I didn't like having to polish it," Peter said. "Folks have trouble seeing past the tarnish." He straightened and met Thom's gaze. "Same with people. Ever notice that?"

"I have," Thom said. Even on short acquaintance, he liked Peter Bright.

Nodding vigorously, Peter extracted a purple pouch from the duffel bag and peeled back the cloth to display a creamer. He set it on the green chest for their examination.

Noelle pulled the photograph from her purse and handed it to Thom, who studied the style. The picture wasn't particularly clear, so he found it impossible to tell if this was the same creamer, but there was definitely a similarity.

The sugar bowl was next. Peter set it out, waiting for

Thom and Noelle's reaction. The photograph showed a slightly better view of that.

"This isn't the one," Noelle said. "But it's close, I think."

"Since you drove all this way, it won't hurt to look at all the pieces."

Thom agreed, but he already knew it had been a futile trip. He tried to hide his disappointment. Against all the odds, he'd held high hopes for this. Like Noelle, he'd been waiting for a Christmas miracle but apparently it wasn't going to happen.

Bending low, Peter thrust his arm inside the canvas bag and extracted two more objects. He carefully unwrapped the silver teapot and then the coffeepot and offered them a moment to scrutinize his wares.

The elaborate tray was last. Carefully arranging each piece on top of it, Peter stepped back to give them a full view of the service. "It's a magnificent find, don't you think?"

"It's lovely," Noelle said.

"But it's not the one we're looking for."

He accepted their news with good grace. "That's a shame."

"You see, this service— " she held out the picture "—was stolen years ago, and Thom and I are hoping to replace it with one that's exactly the same. Or as much like it as possible."

Peter reached for the photograph and studied it a moment. "I guess I should've looked closer and saved you folks the drive."

"No problem," Thom said. "Thanks for getting back to us."

"Yes, thank you for your trouble," Noelle said as they left the store. "It's a beautiful service."

"I'll give you a good price on it if you change your mind," the old man said, following them to the front door. "I'll be here another hour or so if you want to come back."

"Thank you," Thom said, but he didn't think there was much chance they'd be back. It wasn't the tea service they needed.

"How about lunch before we head home," he suggested. The Thai restaurant appeared to be open.

"Sure," Noelle agreed.

Thom shared her discouragement, but he was determined to maintain her optimism—and his own. "Hey, we've only started to look. It's too early to give up."

"I know. You're right, it was foolish of me to think we'd find it so quickly. It's just that…oh, I don't know, I guess I thought it *would* be easy because everything else fell into place for us."

They were the only customers in the restaurant. A charming waitress greeted them and escorted them to a table near the window.

Thom waited until they were seated before he spoke. "I guess this means we go to Plan B."

"What about pad thai and—" Noelle glanced up at him over the menu. "What exactly is Plan B?"

Thom reached inside his coat pocket and set the jeweler's box in the middle of the table.

"Thom?" Noelle put her menu down.

This wasn't the way he'd intended to propose, but—as the cliché had it—there was no time like the present. "I love you, Noelle, and I'm not going to let this feud stand between us. Our parents will have to understand that we're entitled to our own happiness."

Tears glistened in her eyes. "Oh, Thom."

"I'm asking you to be my wife."

She stretched her arm across the table and they joined hands. "And I'm telling you it would be the greatest honor of my life to accept. I have a request, though."

"Anything."

"I want to buy that tea service. Not you. Me."

Thom frowned. "Why?"

"I want to give it to your mother. From me to her. I can't replace the original, but maybe I can build a bridge between our families with this one."

Thom's fingers tightened around hers. "It's worth a try."

"I think so, too," she whispered.

"I'm going to try my phone again," Sarah said. Technology had betrayed them, but surely it would come to their rescue. Eventually. Walking a mile in the bitter cold was something she'd rather avoid.

"Go ahead," Mary urged. She didn't seem any more eager than Sarah to make the long trek.

Sarah got her phone and speed dialed her home number. Hope sprang up when the call instantly connected, but was dashed just as quickly when she heard the recording once again.

"Any luck?" Mary asked, her eyes bright and teary in the cold.

She shook her head.

"Damn," Mary muttered. "I guess that means there's no option but to hoof it."

"Appears that way."

"I think we should have a little fortification first,

though," Sarah said. Her husband's golf bags were in the backseat, and she knew he often carried a flask.

"Fortification?"

"A little Scotch might save our lives."

Mary's look was skeptical. "I'm all for Scotch, but where are we going to find any out here?"

"Jake." She opened the back door and grabbed the golf bag. Sure enough, there was a flask.

"I don't remember you liking Scotch," Mary said.

"I don't, but at this point I can't be choosy."

"Right."

Sarah removed the top and tipped the flask, taking a sizable gulp. Wiping her mouth with the back of her hand, she swallowed, then shook her head briskly. "Oh my, that's strong." The liquor burned all the way down to her stomach, but as soon as it hit bottom, a welcoming warmth spread through her limbs.

"My turn," Mary said.

Sarah handed her the flask and watched as Mary rubbed the top, then tilted it back and took a deep swallow. She, too, closed her eyes and shook her head. Soon, however, she was smiling. "That wasn't so bad."

"It might ward off hypothermia."

"You're right. You'd better have another."

"You think?"

Mary nodded and after a moment, Sarah agreed. Luckily Jake had refilled the flask. The second swallow didn't taste nearly as nasty as the first. It didn't burn this time, either. Instead it enhanced the warm glow spreading through her system.

"How do you feel?"

"Better," Sarah said, giving Mary the flask.

Mary didn't need encouragement. She took her turn with the flask, then growled like a grizzly bear.

Sarah didn't know why she found that so amusing, but she did. She laughed uproariously. In fact, she laughed until she started to cough.

"What?" Mary asked, grinning broadly.

"Oh, dear." She coughed again. "I didn't know you did animal impressions."

"I do when I drink Scotch."

Then, as if they'd both become aware that they were having an actual conversation, they pulled back into themselves. Sarah noticed that Mary's expression suddenly grew dignified, as though she'd realized she was laughing and joking with her enemy.

"We should get moving, don't you think?" Mary said in a dispassionate voice.

"You're right." Sarah put the flask back in the golf bag and wrapped her scarf more tightly around her neck and face. Fortified in all respects, she was ready to face the storm. "It's a good thing we're walking together. Anything could happen on a day like this."

They'd gone about the length of a football field when Mary said, "I'm cold again."

"I am, too."

"You should've brought along the Scotch."

"We'll have to go back for it."

"I think we should," Mary agreed solemnly. "We could freeze to death before we reach the club."

"Yes. The Scotch might make the difference between survival and death."

Back at the car, they climbed in and shared the flask again. Soon, for no apparent reason, they were giggling.

"I think we're drunk," Mary said.

"Oh, hardly. I can hold my liquor better than this."

Mary burst into peals of laughter. "No, you can't. Don't you remember the night of our Halloween party?"

"That was—what?—twenty-two years ago!"

"I know, but I haven't forgotten how silly those margaritas made you."

"You were the one who kept filling my glass."

"You were the one who kept telling me how good they were."

Sarah nearly doubled over with hysterics. "Next thing I knew, I was standing on the coffee table singing 'Guantanamera' at the top of my lungs."

"You sounded fabulous, too. And then when you started to dance—"

"I *what*?" All Sarah recalled was the blinding headache she'd suffered the next morning. When she woke and could barely lift her head from the pillow without stabbing pain, she'd phoned her dearest, best friend in the world. Mary had dropped everything and rushed over. She'd mixed Sarah a tomato-juice concoction that had saved her life, or so she'd felt at the time.

Both women were silent. "I miss those days," Sarah whispered.

"I do, too," Mary said.

Sarah sniffled. It was the cold that made her eyes water. Digging through her purse, she couldn't find a single tissue. Mary gave her one.

"I've missed you," Sarah said and loudly blew her nose.

"I've missed you, too."

The cold must have intensified, because her eyes began to water even more. Using her coat sleeve, she wiped her nose.

"Here," she said to Mary, handing her the flask. "I want you to have this. Take the rest."

"The Scotch?"

Sarah nodded. "If we're not found until it's too late—I want you to have the liquor. It might keep you alive long enough for the rescue people to revive you."

Mary looked as though she was close to bursting into tears. "You'd die for—me?" She hiccuped on the last word.

Sarah nodded again.

"That's the most beautiful thing anyone's ever said to me."

"But before I die, I need to ask you something."

"Anything," Mary told her. "Anything at all."

Sarah sniffled and swallowed a sob. Leaning her forehead against the steering wheel, she whispered, "Forgive me."

Mary placed her hand on Sarah's shoulder. "I do forgive you, but first you have to forgive *me* for acting so badly. You were right—I *was* jealous of Cheryl. I thought you liked her better than me."

"Never. She's one of those people who move in and out of a person's life, but you—you're my...my soul sister. I've missed you so much."

"We're idiots." Mary returned the flask. "I can't accept this Scotch. If we freeze, we freeze together."

Sarah was feeling downright toasty at the moment. The world was spinning, but that was probably because she was drunker than a skunk. The thought made her giggle.

"What's so funny?" Mary wanted to know.

"We're drunk," she muttered. "Drunk as skunks. Drunk as skunks," she recited in a singsong voice.

"Isn't it wonderful?"

They laughed again.

"Jake always insists I eat something when I've had too much to drink."

"We have lots of food," Mary said, sitting up straight.

"Yes, but most of it's half-frozen by now."

Mary's eyes gleamed bright. "Not everything. I'm sure the families would want us to take what we need, don't you think?"

"I'm sure you're right," Sarah said as Mary climbed over the front seat and into the back, her coat flipping over her head.

Sarah laughed so hard she nearly peed her pants.

Women's Century Club
Rose, Oregon

December 24

Dear Mary and Sarah,
Just a note to let you know how much the Women's Century Club appreciates the effort that went into preparing these Christmas baskets. You two did a splendid job. I could see from the number of gifts filling the baskets that you went far beyond the items listed on the sheet I gave you. Both of you have been generous to a fault.

Sarah, I realize it was difficult to come into this project at the last minute, but you are to be commended for your cooperation.

Mary, you did a wonderful job making all the arrangements, and I'm confident the baskets will reach the Salvation Army in plenty of time to be distributed for the holidays.

If you're both willing to take up the task again next year, I'd be happy to recommend you for the job.

Sincerely,
Melody Darrington

Nine

Jake McDowell glanced at the kitchen clock and frowned. "What time did your mother say she'd be home?"

"I don't know." His youngest daughter was certainly a fount of information. Carley lay flat on her stomach in front of the Christmas tree, her arms outstretched as she examined a small package.

"She should be back by now, don't you think?" Jake asked, looking at the clock again.

"I suppose."

"When will Noelle be home?"

Unconcerned, Carley shrugged.

Jake decided he wasn't going to get any answers here and tried Sarah's cell for perhaps the fiftieth time. Whenever he punched in the number, he received the same irritating message. "I'm sorry. We are unable to connect your call...."

Not knowing what else to do, he phoned his golfing partner. Greg Sutton answered on the first ring.

"I thought you were Mary," he said, sounding as worried as Jake was.

"You haven't heard from Mary?"

"Not a word. Is Sarah back?"

"No," Jake said. "That's why I was calling you."

"What do you think happened?"

"No idea. I could understand if one of them was missing, but not both."

Greg didn't say anything for a moment. "Did you phone the Women's Century Club?"

"I did. Melody said they were there and left two hours ago. She told me the ice storm's pretty bad in her area. She's going to stay put until her husband can come and get her this afternoon."

"What did she say about Mary and Sarah?"

"Not much. Just that they got the baskets all sorted and loaded into Mary's vehicle. Melody did make some comment about Sarah and Mary being pretty hostile toward each other. According to her, they left at different times."

"That doesn't explain why they're both missing."

"What if one of them had an accident and the other stopped to help?" Greg suggested.

Jake hadn't considered that. "But wouldn't they have been back by now?"

"Unless they got stuck."

"Together?"

"I wouldn't know."

Jake laughed grimly. "If that's the case, God help us all."

"What do you think we should do?"

"We can't leave them out there."

"You're right," Greg said. "But I have to tell you the idea is somewhat appealing. If they *are* stuck with each other for a while, they just might settle this mess."

"They could murder each other, too." Jake knew his wife far too well. When it came to Mary Sutton, she could be downright unreasonable. "I say we go after them— together."

Jake had no objection to that. Greg owned a large four-wheel-drive truck that handled better on the ice than most vehicles. "You want to pick me up?"

"I'm on my way," Greg said.

Sarah reached for another Christmas cookie. "What did you call these again?" she asked, studying the package. Unfortunately, the letters wouldn't quite come into focus.

"Pfeffernusse."

"Try to say *that* three times when you're too drunk to stand up."

Mary giggled and helped herself to one of the glazed ginger cookies. "They're German. One family on the list had a German-sounding name and I thought they might be familiar with these cookies."

Sarah was touched. Tears filled her eyes. "You're so thoughtful."

"Not really," Mary said with a sob. "I... I was trying to outdo you." She was weeping in earnest now. "How could I have been so silly?"

"I did the same thing." Sarah wrapped her arm around Mary's shoulders. "I was the one who got us thrown out of Value-X."

Mary sniffled and dried her eyes. "I'm never going to let anything come between us again."

"I won't, either," Sarah vowed. "I think this has been the best Christmas of my life."

"Christmas!" Mary jerked upright. "Oh, Sarah, we've got to get these baskets to the Salvation Army!"

"But how? We can't carry all this stuff."

"True, but we can't just sit here, either." She looked into the distance, in the direction of the Women's Century Club. "We're going to have to walk, after all."

Her friend was right. They had to take matters into their own hands and work together. "We can do it."

"We can. We'll walk to the club and send someone to get the baskets. Then we'll call Triple A. See? We have a plan. A good plan. There isn't anything we can't do if we stick together."

Sarah felt the tears sting her eyes again. "Is there any Scotch left?"

"No," Mary said, sounding sad. "We're going to have to make it on our own."

Clambering out of the car, Sarah was astonished by how icy the road had become in the hour or so they'd dawdled over their comforting Scotch. Luckily, she was wearing her boots, whereas Mary wore loafers.

Her friend gave a small cry and then, arms flailing, struggled to regain her balance. "My goodness, it's slippery out here."

"How are we going to do this?" Sarah asked. "You can't walk on this ice."

"Sure I can," Mary assured her, straightening with resolve. But she soon lost her balance again and grabbed hold of the car door, just managing to save herself.

"It's like you said—we'll do it together," Sarah declared. "We have to, because I'm not leaving you behind."

With Mary's arm around Sarah's waist and Sarah's arm about Mary's shoulder, they started walking down the center of the road. The treacherous ice slowed them down, and their progress was halting, especially since both of them were drunk and weepy with emotion.

"I wonder how long it'll take Greg to realize I'm not

home," Mary said. Her husband was in trouble as it was, leaving her a defective vehicle to drive.

"Probably a lot longer than Jake. I told him I wouldn't be more than an hour."

"I'm sure there's some football game on TV that Greg's busy staring at. He won't notice I'm not there until Suzanne and Thom arrive for dinner." Mary went strangely quiet.

"Are you okay?" Sarah asked, tightening her hold on her friend.

"Yes, but... Thom. I was thinking about Thom. He's in love with Noelle, you know."

"Noelle's been in love with Thom since she was sixteen. It broke her heart when he dumped her."

"Thom didn't dump her. She dumped him."

Sarah bristled. "She did not!"

"You mean to say something else happened?"

"It must have, because I know for a fact that Noelle's always loved Thom."

"And Thom feels the same about her."

"We have to do something," Sarah said. "We've got to find a way to get them back together."

"I think they might've been secretly seeing each other," Mary confessed.

Sarah shook her head, which made her feel slightly dizzy. "Noelle would've told me. We're this close." She attempted to cross two fingers, but couldn't manage it. Must be because of her gloves, she decided. Yes, that was it.

"We're drunk," Mary said. "Really and truly drunk. The cookies didn't help one bit."

"I don't care. We're best friends again and this time it's for life."

"For life," Mary vowed.

"We're on a mission."

"A mission," Mary repeated. She paused "What's our mission again?"

Sarah had to stop and think about it. "First, we need to deliver the Christmas baskets."

Mary slapped her hand against her forehead. "Right! How could I forget?"

"Then…"

"There's more?" Mary looked confused.

"Yes, lots more. Then we need to convince Noelle and Thom that they were meant to be together."

"Poor Thom," Mary said. "Oh no." She covered her mouth with her hand.

"What?"

"I left a message on his answering machine. I may not remember much right now, but I remember that. I told him I didn't think he should marry Noelle…."

"Why would you do that?"

"Well, because—oh dear, Sarah, I might have ruined everything."

"We'll deal with it as soon as we're home," Sarah said firmly.

A car sounded from behind them. "Someone's coming," Mary cried, her voice rising with excitement.

"We've got to hitch a ride." Sarah whirled around and held out her thumb as prominently as she could.

"That's not going to work," Mary insisted, thrusting out her leg. "Don't you remember that old Clark Gable movie?"

"Clark Gable got a ride by showing off his ankle?"

"No… Claudette Colbert did."

The truck turned the corner; Sarah wasn't willing to

trust in either her thumb or Mary's leg, so she raised both hands above her head and waved frantically.

"It's Greg," Mary cried in relief.

"And Jake's with him." Thank God. Sarah had never been happier to see her husband.

To their shock and anger, the two men drove directly past them.

"Hey!" Mary shouted after her husband. "I am in no mood for games."

The truck stopped, and the driver and passenger doors opened at the same time. Greg climbed down and headed over to Mary, while Jake hurried toward Sarah.

"We're friends for life," Mary told her husband, throwing her arm around Sarah again.

"You're drunk," Greg said. "Just what have you been drinking?"

"I know exactly what I'm doing," she answered with offended dignity.

"Do *you?*" Jake asked Sarah.

"Of course I do."

"We're on a mission," Mary told the two men.

Jake frowned. "What happened to the car?"

"I'll tell you all about it later," Sarah promised, enunciating very carefully.

"What mission?" Jake asked.

Sarah exchanged an exasperated look with Mary. "Why do we have to explain everything?"

"Men," Mary said in a low voice. "Can't live with 'em, can't live without 'em."

Her friend was so wise.

The drive back to Rose took even longer than the trip into Portland. The roads seemed to get icier and more slippery with every mile. Keeping her eyes on the road, Noelle knew how tense Thom must be.

"Would you rather wait until after Christmas?" she asked as they neared her family's home. It might be better if they got through the holidays before making their announcement and throwing their families into chaos. Noelle hated the thought of dissension on Christmas Day.

"Wait? You mean to announce our engagement?" Thom clarified. "I don't think we should. You're going to marry me, and I want to tell the whole world. I refuse to keep this a secret simply because our mothers don't happen to get along. They'll just have to adjust."

"But—"

"I've waited all these years for you. I'm not waiting any longer. All right?"

"All right." Noelle was overwhelmed by contradictory emotions. Love for Thom—and love for her family. Excitement and nervousness. Happiness and guilt.

"Do you know what I like most about Christmas?" Thom asked, breaking into her thoughts.

"Tell me, and then I'll tell you what I like."

"Mom has a tradition she started when Suzanne entered high school. On Christmas Eve, she serves fresh Dungeness crab. We all love it. She has them cooked at the market because she can't bear to do it herself, then Dad brings them home. Mom's got the butter melted and the bibs ready and we sit around the table and start cracking."

"Oh, that sounds delicious."

"It is. Does your family have a Christmas Eve tradition?"

"Bingo."

"Bingo?"

"Christmas Bingo. We play after the Christmas Eve service at church. The prizes aren't worth more than five dollars, but Mom's so good at getting neat stuff. I haven't been home for Christmas in years, but Mom always makes up for it by mailing me three or four little Bingo gifts."

"My favorite carol is 'What Child Is This,'" he said next.

"Mine's 'Silent Night.'"

"What was your favorite gift as a kid?"

"Hmm, that's a toss-up," she said. "There was a Christmas Barbie I adored. Another year I got a set of classic Disney videos that I watched over and over."

Thom smiled. "As a little boy, I loved my Matchbox car garage. I got it for Christmas when I was ten. Mom's kept it all these years. She has Dad drag it out every year and tells me she's saving it to give to my son one day."

She sighed, at peace with herself and this man she loved. "I want to have your babies, Thom," she said in a soft voice.

His eyes left the street to meet hers. The sky had darkened and he looked quickly back at the road. "You make it hard to concentrate on driving."

"Tell me some of the other things you love about Christmas. It makes me feel good to hear them."

"It's your turn," he said.

"The orange in the bottom of my stocking. Every year there's one in the toe. It's supposed to commemorate the Christmases my great-grandparents had—an orange was a pretty special thing back then."

"I like Christmas cookies. Especially meringue star ones."

"Mexican tea cakes for me," she said. "I'll ask your

mother for the recipe for star cookies and bake you a batch every Christmas."

"That sounds like a very wifely thing to do."

"I want to be a good wife to my husband." Noelle suddenly realized that she was genuinely grateful they hadn't married so young. Yes, the years had brought pain, but they'd brought wisdom and perspective, too. The love she and Thom felt for each other would deepen with time. They were so much more capable now of valuing what they had together.

"What's it like to be born on Christmas Day?" Thom asked.

"It's not so bad," Noelle said. "First, I share a birthday with Jesus—that's the good part. The not-so-good is having the two biggest celebrations of the year fall on the same day. When I was a kid, Mom used to throw me a party in June to celebrate my half-year birthday."

"I remember that."

"Do you remember teasing me by saying it really wasn't my birthday so you didn't need to bring a gift?"

Thom chuckled. "What I remember is getting my ears boxed for saying it."

Twenty minutes later, they were almost at her family's house. They'd decided to confront her parents first. Their laughter, which had filled the car seconds earlier, immediately faded.

"You ready?" Thom asked as he stopped in front of the house.

Noelle nodded and swallowed hard. "No matter what happens, I want you to remember I love you."

His hand squeezed hers.

Glancing at her family's home, Noelle noticed a truck

parked outside. "Looks like we have company." She didn't know whether to feel relief or disappointment.

"Oh, no." Thom's voice was barely above a whisper.

"What is it?"

"That's my parents' truck."

Dread slipped over her. "They must've found out that we spent the day together. That's my fault—I left a note for Carley telling her I was with you." Noelle could imagine what was taking place inside. Her mother would be shouting at Thom's, and their fathers would be trying to keep the two women apart.

"Should we wait?" Noelle asked, just as she had earlier.

"For another time?" His jaw tensed. "No, we face them here and now, for better or worse. Agreed?"

Noelle nodded. "Okay…just promise me you won't let them change your mind."

He snorted inelegantly. "I'd like to see them try."

Thom parked behind the truck and turned off the engine. Together, holding hands, they approached the house. Never had Noelle been more nervous. If this encounter went wrong, she might alienate her mother, and that was something she didn't want to do. In high school, she'd self-righteously cast her family aside in the name of love. But if the years in Dallas had taught her independence, they'd also taught her the importance of home and family. Her self-imposed exile was over now, and she'd learned from it. Listening to Thom talk about his Christmas traditions, she'd realized that he'd find it equally hard to turn his back on his parents.

He was about to ring the doorbell when she stopped him. "Remember how I said I was looking for a Christmas miracle?"

Thom nodded. "You mean finding a tea service similar to my grandmother's?"

"Yes. But if I could be granted only one miracle this Christmas, it wouldn't be that. I'd want our families to rekindle the love and friendship they once had."

"That would be my wish, too." Thom gathered her in his arms and kissed her with a passion that readily found a matching fire in her. The kiss was a reminder of their love, and it sealed their bargain. No matter what happened once they entered the house, they would face it together.

"Actually, this is a blessing in disguise," Thom said. "We can confront both families at the same time and be done with it." He reached for the doorbell again, and again Noelle stopped him.

"This is my home. We don't need to ring the bell." Stepping forward, she opened the door.

Noelle wasn't sure what she expected, but certainly not the scene that greeted her. Her parents and two sisters, plus Thom's entire family, sat around the dining room table. Her mother and Mrs. Sutton, both wearing aprons, stood in the background, while her father and Thom's dished up whole Dungeness crabs, with Jonathan pouring wine.

"Thom!" his mother shouted joyfully. "It's about time you got here."

"What took you so long?" Sarah asked Noelle.

Stunned, Thom and Noelle looked at each other for an explanation.

"There's room here," Carley called out, motioning to the empty chairs beside her.

Noelle couldn't do anything other than stare.

"What…happened?" Thom asked.

"It's a long story. Sit down. We'll explain everything later."

"But…"

Thom put his arm around Noelle's shoulder. "Before we sit down, I want everyone to know that I've asked Noelle to be my wife and she's accepted."

"Nothing you say or do will make us change our minds," Noelle said quickly, before anyone else could react.

"Why would we want to change your minds?" her father asked. "We're absolutely delighted."

"You can fight and argue, threaten and yell, and it won't make any difference," Thom added. "We're getting married!"

"Glad to hear it," his father said.

A round of cheers followed his announcement.

Thom's mother and Noelle's mother embraced in joy.

"One thing this family refuses to tolerate anymore is fighting," his mother declared.

"Absolutely," her own mother agreed.

Both Thom and Noelle stared back at them, shocked into speechlessness.

"There's no reason to stand there like a couple of strangers," her mother said. "Sit down. You wouldn't believe the day we had."

Sarah and Mary put their arms around each other's shoulders. "At least the Christmas baskets got delivered on time," Mary said with a satisfied nod.

"And no one mentioned that the two of us smelled like Scotch when we got there," her mother pointed out.

They both giggled.

"What happened?" Noelle asked.

Her father waved aside her question. "You don't want to know," he groaned.

"I'll tell you later," her mother promised.

Thom leaned close to her and whispered, "Either we just walked into the middle of an *X-Files* episode or we got our Christmas miracle."

Noelle slipped an arm around his waist. "I think you must be right."

Sarah McDowell
9 Orchard Lane
Rose, Oregon

December 26

Dear Melody,
Mary and I found your note when we delivered the baskets on Christmas Eve. We did have a wonderful time, and Mary has agreed to head up the committee next year. I promised I'd be her cochair.

   Now, about using the club for Kristen's wedding reception… Well, it seems there's going to be another wedding in the family, and fairly soon. Mary and I will be in touch with you about that right after New Year's.

Sincerely,
Sarah McDowell

* * * * *

MERRY EX-MAS

Sheila Roberts

Dear Reader,

I'm delighted to be included in this book along with my wonderful friend and mentor Debbie Macomber. And the fact that we're celebrating this festive season together with you makes me hugely happy.

I've got to say, I love Christmas. Love everything about it—the decorations, the goodies, the presents, the Christmas Eve service, even the crazy busyness. I especially love getting a chance to gather with my family to celebrate. Believe me, my family knows how to celebrate. We are fun, fun, fun!

But I realize that for many of us the holidays can sometimes be more stressful than fun, especially when dealing with difficult family members. And when you start adding former spouses to the mix, it can make you want to say more than "Ho, ho, ho."

I'm hoping Cass Wilkes, her friends and their exes will give you a laugh and maybe even some hope. I sure enjoyed writing about them, especially Ella and her ex-husband, Jake.

I must confess, Jake stole my heart. He even wound up with his own country music video, "Merry Christmas, Mama," which I hope you'll all check out on YouTube (youtu.be/MssZlpob0os). He was kind enough to give me a role in it. Of course, he conveniently neglected to tell me the rude indignities I'd suffer. Oh, well, that's showbiz.

Meanwhile, I hope you'll enjoy the ride as Cass, Ella, Charley and their friends get ready for a crazy Christmas filled with everything from jingle bells to wedding bells.

You can find me on Facebook and Twitter, and please stop by my website, www.sheilasplace.com. Happy holidays and happy reading.

Sheila

For my pal Kathy

One

Once in a while, if a woman is really lucky, the perfect day she envisioned turns out to be just that. This was going to be one of those days, Cass Wilkes thought as she set the platter of carved turkey on her dining table.

She surveyed her handiwork with a smile. Everything was Martha Stewart–lovely from the china and crystal to the Thanksgiving centerpiece she'd bought at Lupine Floral, and her old Victorian home was filled with the aroma of herbs and spices. The dining room window framed a greeting-card-worthy winter scene—her front lawn with its trees and shrubs draped in frosty white and the snowcapped mountains looming beyond.

The snow had done what all good snow should do; it had stopped in plenty of time for road crews to clear the way for travelers. Unlike Thanksgiving last year, the town of Icicle Falls was humming with visitors looking for a holiday getaway. Great for business, especially when you owned a bakery. This weekend, gingerbread boys and girls would march out the door of Gingerbread Haus in droves and money would march right into Cass's bank account—a good thing since she suspected she was going to have a wedding to pay for in a year or so.

A whoop of male excitement came from the living room, followed by cheers. The football game on TV was nearing its end and obviously the favored team had scored a touchdown.

"Okay, that's everything from the kitchen," said Dot Morrison, Cass's mentor and former boss, as she placed a serving bowl heaped with stuffing, along with another full of mashed potatoes, on the table. Normally Dot would have been celebrating with her daughter, but Tilda was on patrol, keeping Icicle Falls safe from…who knew? Their town wasn't exactly a hotbed of crime.

Dot had dressed for the occasion, wearing jeans and a white sweatshirt decorated with a turkey holding a sign that said "Think Outside the Box. Serve Ham." Dot, who owned the town's most popular pancake place, Breakfast Haus, had encouraged Cass to think outside the box years ago, even lent her money to start her bakery. Cass owed her Thanksgiving dinners for life.

"Get those clowns in here," Dot said. "There's nothing worse than cold food."

Cass could suggest a few things—taxes, yeast infections, exes.

Oh, no, she wasn't going to ruin a perfectly good holiday with even a hint of a thought about her ex-husband. That man, that self-centered, undeserving rat who'd tried to lure the kids away this weekend with a trip to Vail, who…

No, no. No thoughts about Mason. It was Thanksgiving, after all, a time to count her blessings.

Three of those blessings were sitting out there in the living room—her kids Danielle, Willie and Amber. Dani's boyfriend, Mike, was there, too, tucked beside her in an overstuffed easy chair.

Twenty-year-old Dani was Cass's oldest and her right-hand woman at the bakery. She'd inherited Cass's passion for creating in the kitchen, and after a year of community college had opted to work full-time at the bakery. Cass had hoped she'd put in at least another year, but she'd had no interest. "I can learn more from you than I can from any college professor," she'd told Cass. When it came to baking, well, what could Cass say? Dani was right.

Amber, her youngest, sat curled up on one end of the couch, texting. A few months earlier she'd been adding to Cass's gray-hair collection, hanging out with the kind of kids no mother wants her child to be with or, worse, become. Thank God (and, possibly, Cass's pal Samantha Sterling) Amber had changed direction and found some new and improved friends.

Willie, Cass's high school jock, was sprawled on the floor, holding the favored stuffed toy of high school boys everywhere—a football. The only trouble she had with Willie was keeping him full. The boy was a two-legged locust.

Then there was her younger brother, Drew, who'd come over from Seattle. Recently divorced (was this tendency toward divorce something in their genes?), he'd been more than happy to spend the weekend hanging out with her family. He'd never had kids of his own, so she'd shared. He made a great uncle and a better father figure than her ex.

No, no, no. Not giving him so much as a thought today.

Cass stood in the archway like a lady butler and announced, "Dinner, guys."

Of course, no one was listening. Another touchdown happened in TV Land. "Yeah!" whooped Mike.

"My team sucks," Willie muttered, giving his football an irritable bounce.

"My dinner's going to suck if you don't get out here and eat it *now*," Cass warned.

"The game's pretty much over, anyway," Mike said, demonstrating good boyfriend etiquette. He stood, pulling Dani up with him. He was a big boy, a former football star and her son's new hero. Mike was currently employed at the local hardware store, which, as far as Cass was concerned, was ideal. Once he popped the question, he and Dani would get married and live in Icicle Falls, near family and friends, a win-win for everyone.

"You're right," Drew agreed. He shut off the TV and led the parade to the dining room table.

Cass only had to look at a cookie to gain five pounds. Her brother, lucky dog, was tall and reedy, and could eat anything. He was a better dresser, too, always had been. And better-looking. But he couldn't cook, and when he came to town he was her best customer. He was also her best friend, and she was glad he'd come here for the holiday.

The only ones missing as everyone settled around the table were Cass's mother and stepfather, who'd become snowbirds and were with his family in Florida. But Mom and Fred planned to come out for Christmas, and if Cass had to choose she'd rather have her mother with them for that holiday.

Drew reached for the turkey and Cass rapped his hand with a serving spoon. "Grace first, you heathen."

Willie snickered, which earned him the privilege of

offering thanks. He barely had "Amen" out of his mouth before he was into the dressing, piling it high on his plate.

Normally she'd remind him that other people might actually want some, too, but not today. Thanksgiving was for feasting and she'd made plenty. Besides, she was going to have an extra serving herself.

For a while conversation consisted of comments like "Pass the rolls" and "Where'd the olives end up?" As plates and then stomachs filled, new topics arose: whose fantasy football team was going to win, how well Cass and Dani's new gingerbread necklaces were selling, Dot's upcoming bunion surgery.

Then it was time for pie. In spite of how crazy-busy Cass had been with work, she'd managed to bake pumpkin, pecan and her brother's favorite, wild huckleberry. "This will be enough for me," he joked, grabbing the whole pie.

With dessert came another tradition, one Cass had started when the kids were small.

"Okay," she said once everyone had been served, "it's gratitude time. Who wants to go first?"

Gratitude. Sometimes the challenge to be grateful had been as big as the word. Often she'd been a world-class hypocrite, encouraging her children to look on the bright side while she indulged in resentment.

It seemed like she'd spent most of her married life in that particular mental state. She'd resented Mason's decision to join the navy when they were engaged. They'd barely set up housekeeping when he shipped out the first time. He'd missed his daughter's birth; Cass's childbirth partner had been her mother. Better her mother than his, she'd told herself. That was something to be grateful for. And she'd been grateful when he got out of the navy. Not so much when he went back to school and neglected his family for his studies. Not so much when he carved out a career that seemed to keep him gone more than it allowed him to be home. Mason had been determined to find the path to success but that path had little room for his family. She was the one who'd always been there to soothe every heartbreak, puzzle over every math problem, cheer at every ball game. And what had *he* done?

Gratitude, remember? Okay, she was grateful she wasn't with him anymore.

"I'm grateful for something," Dani said. She reached into her jeans pocket and pulled out a diamond ring and slid it on her finger.

"Oh, my gosh, you're engaged!" cried Amber.

Cass set down her fork and gaped. Of course she'd known this was coming, but she was a little upset that her daughter hadn't told her before everyone else. "When did this happen?" she asked.

Dani's brown eyes sparkled with excitement. She looked at Mike and they shared the smile reserved for a couple in possession of newly minted love. "Last night. We wanted to wait and surprise everyone."

Well, they had.

"Don't know how surprised anyone is," Dot said, "but I think you made your mother's day."

Of course she had. Why was Cass sitting there like a turkey in a pan? She jumped up and went to hug her daughter and future son-in-law. "This is wonderful. You two are going to be so happy."

How could they not be? Unlike her mother at that age, Danielle had been wise and thoughtful when selecting a mate. She hadn't rushed into a relationship with her hormones on fire and her brain dead from smoke inhalation.

She'd held out for the right man. They even *looked* perfect together, Mike with his dark hair and eyes and that big frame, Dani with her lighter coloring and sandy hair and willowy figure. In their wedding garb they'd look fit for the top of a wedding cake.

"This calls for more pie," Drew said with a grin, and helped himself to another piece.

"I'm going to be a bridesmaid, right?" Amber asked her sister.

"Of course," Dani said.

"You'd better dig out your Armani," Cass said to Drew. "Dani's going to need you to walk her down the aisle."

Dani's face lost some of its bride-to-be glow and she bit her lip.

"Hey, I'm cool sitting in the front row with your mom," Drew said quickly. "I don't have to be the one."

Oh, yes, he did. Who else was going to? Oh, no. Surely not...

"Actually, I was hoping Daddy would walk me down the aisle," Dani said.

The undeserving absent father? The man who'd been M.I.A. for most of Dani's life? Cass fell back against her chair and stared across the table at her daughter.

Dani's cheeks bloomed with a guilty flush and she studiously avoided her mother's gaze.

"Daddy?" Cass echoed. It came out frosted with scorn. *Way to be mature and poison your daughter's happy moment,* she scolded herself.

With her sunny disposition and eagerness to please, Danielle was generally easy to get along with, but now her chin jutted out at a pugnacious angle. "I know he'll want to."

Oh, he always *wanted* to be there, but he never had been.

Until lately. Now that their children were practically grown. He and his thirty-two-year-old trophy wife, Babette, seemed to think they could have the kids come over to Seattle anytime he swooped in from his business trips and buy their affection with shopping expeditions and Seahawks tickets.

Obviously it was working, and that made Cass want to break the wishbone she'd been saving into a thousand pieces. This wasn't right. How to get Dani to see that, though?

She cleared her throat. "You know he travels a lot."

"I know," Dani said, "but we want a Christmas wedding and he'll be here for Christmas."

"Christmas Day?" Willie made a face.

Dani frowned at him. "What, are you afraid Santa won't come?" To the others she said, "We thought the weekend before."

"That's not much time to plan a wedding," Dot pointed out. "What's the rush?"

Now Mike was beaming like a man with a big announcement.

"Because Mike got a job as assistant manager at a hardware store in Spokane," Dani announced for him, "and when he moves for his new job I want to go with him."

Everyone at the table got busy offering Mike congratulations.

Except Cass, who was in shock. They'd be moving away. Her daughter would be leaving practically the minute after she got married. The vision of Dani raising her family here in Icicle Falls, of someday taking over the bakery, went up in smoke. It was all Cass could do not to cry. She pushed away the plate with her half-finished pumpkin pie and hoped nobody asked her what she was thankful for.

"Anyway, we just want a small wedding," Mike said. "Nothing fancy."

Nothing fancy? Dani had always wanted a big church wedding. What happened to that?

"And I know Daddy can come that weekend," Dani added.

"You already talked to your father?" *Before you even shared the news with me?* Hurt welled up in Cass, giving her the worst case of heartburn she'd ever had.

"Just to see if he's going to be around," Dani said. "I thought maybe everyone could come up and stay for the week."

"Here?" Cass squeaked.

"Whoo boy," Drew said under his breath.

"There's no room," Cass said firmly. No room at the inn.

Dot shrugged. "You could probably put them up at Olivia's."

Thank you, Dot. Remind me never to invite you over for Thanksgiving dinner again.

"Dani, you know how crazy it gets this time of year," Cass said. "I'm sure the B and Bs are booked solid."

"Olivia still has a couple of rooms," Dani said.

"You talked to her?" She'd told Olivia, too?

"This morning. I just called to ask if she had any left."

"Well, then, I guess that settles it," Cass said stiffly.

"You'll help me plan it, won't you?" Dani asked her in a small voice.

Cass was hurt and she was mad, but she wasn't insane. "Of course I will. And I'll make the cake."

"Well, duh." Amber rolled her eyes.

Dani ignored her sister and smiled happily. "Thanks, Mom."

Cass sighed. She'd even suck it up and be nice at the wedding. It would be wrong to spoil her daughter's big day with petty jealousy.

It's not petty, whispered her evil twin. Cass told her to shut up.

"I know it's a busy time of year," Dani said.

"'Tis the season," Dot cracked.

The season to be jolly. That was going to be hard with her ex-husband strutting around town, pretending to be the world's best dad. It was going to be hard to greet his bimbo trophy wife with good cheer. And she didn't even want to *think* about dealing with her ex-mother-and sister-in-law. If Santa thought this was what Cass wanted for Christmas, he needed to retire.

"This is going to be a pain in the butt for you," Dot said to her later, after the dishes were done and the kids were playing on the Wii.

Cass leaned against the kitchen counter and stared at the contents of her coffee mug—black, just like her mood.

"But you'll get through it."

Of course she would. Exes were a part of life. She'd put on her big-girl panties and cope. After all, it was only a couple of days. Anyway, they'd all be staying at Olivia's place. She'd hardly have to see them.

Cass managed a reluctant smile and raised her mug. "Well, then, here's to getting through."

Dot clinked mugs with her. "Merry Ex-mas, kiddo."

Two

It was Black Friday, a big day for retail in Icicle Falls. For Ella O'Brien that made two black days in a row. How different this Thanksgiving had been from the year before.

Not that her mother hadn't tried to make it special. Mims had hauled Ella over the mountains to Seattle for an overnight in the city, and on turkey day they'd eaten their holiday dinner at a high-priced restaurant. Surrounded by strangers. Well, except for Gregory, Mother's longtime friend and fellow fashionista, who had a condo on the waterfront.

Ella hadn't invited the thought that came to her as they were eating, but it had come, anyway, making an unwelcome fourth at the table. *This is pathetically different from last Thanksgiving with your in-laws.* Correction: former in-laws.

That had been a typical O'Brien celebration, rowdy and exciting, especially for a woman who'd always wanted brothers and sisters. Mims, who had been included, kept a superior distance while grown-ups and children alike had worked up an appetite by running around in the woods playing capture the flag. After din-

ner her mother-in-law (ex-mother-in-law, darn it) had
helped her figure out a tricky knitting pattern.

And later, when it was time for dessert, Mims the
fishaterian learned that the slice of mincemeat pie she
was enjoying was a hunter's version with moose meat
added to the sweet filling and had to make a dash for
the bathroom.

There'd been no bathroom dash this year. And no Jake.
That was fine with Ella. Really. Mims was right; she
was better off without that skirt-chasing, irresponsible,
overgrown child. And her life would be perfect once she
didn't have to see him every day.

But she missed his mother and his sister and brothers.
It had been fun to have someone to call Mom.

She'd never called her own mother Mom. Instead,
she'd wound up mimicking Mims's fashion-model friends
and calling her Mims. Ella had never gotten the full story
on that nickname, beyond that fact that it had something
to do with her mother's fondness for mimosas. Oh, and a
tycoon and a yacht. Her mother had never wanted to be
Mom, anyway. That was simply too unglam. And Lily
Swan brought glamour to everything, including moth-
erhood. So that was how it was growing up and that was
normal, and that was what Ella told her friends whenever
they asked why she didn't call her mother Mom.

And when they asked why she didn't have a daddy, she
recited the Swan party line—a girl didn't really need a
daddy. She'd sure wanted one, though, and had watched
with longing when she saw other little girls riding on their
daddies' shoulders or getting taken out for ice cream.

When she'd married Jake and gotten a father-in-law
it was the world's best bonus.

Jake's dad always greeted her with a hug and a "How's

my girl?" He checked the air in her tires and whittled little wood raccoons for her to put on her mantelpiece in the living room. Mims had pronounced them tacky but Ella loved them because every time she looked at them she could see her father-in-law's big, smiling face.

"We're so sorry to lose you," Mom O'Brien had written in a sweet card after Ella and Jake broke the news. She'd been sorry to be lost. Too bad a girl couldn't shed the husband but keep the family, she thought as she turned the sign hanging on the door of Gilded Lily's to Closed.

She was tired—working with people all day could be exhausting—but it was a good kind of tired, she decided as she started to add up the day's receipts. From now until New Year's Eve the shop would be busy. Gilded Lily's was the closest thing Icicle Falls had to a Neiman Marcus or a Nordstrom. It was owned by her mother but Ella managed it. She loved pretty clothes and she loved helping her customers find a special dress for that special occasion, whether it was a party or a prom, as well as all the accessories to enhance it. There'd been a lot of enhancing taking place this Black Friday.

Now the business day was over and it was time to go home. Home is where the heart is. There's no place like home.

Bah, humbug.

She stepped out into the brisk mountain air and locked the door behind her. Winter darkness had settled in for the night and downtown Icicle Falls was a-twinkle. Christmas lights decked out the trees in the park and the potted fir trees nestled against the shops, and red ribbons adorned the old-fashioned lampposts that ran along Center Street.

Every weekend there would be a tree-lighting ceremony, and the skyscraper-size fir in town square would
come to life with hundreds of colored lights, making the
winter village scene complete. With its mountain setting
and Bavarian architecture, Icicle Falls was like an animated postcard, quaint and charming—a perfect setting
for a perfect life. Except Ella's life wasn't so perfect these
days; it was like a dress that no longer fit.

It didn't take her long to walk the half mile from the
shop to her two-bedroom Craftsman-style cottage on
Mountain View Road. Her dream home. In the summer
she'd put two wicker rockers with plump cushions on the
porch, and she and Jake had sat out there on warm weekday nights. She'd work on her knitting with their Saint
Bernard, Tiny, lazing at her feet, while Jake serenaded
her on his guitar. Last Christmas she'd taken great satisfaction in stringing colored lights and cedar boughs
along the porch, while Jake had strung lights along the
roofline—a team effort.

Ella sighed at the memory. She'd thought she'd have
that house for life, had envisioned raising a family there
or, once Jake became a famous country star, keeping it
as a vacation home.

Her mother hadn't shared the vision. "You shouldn't
buy a house so quickly," Mims had cautioned when they
first looked at it. "You're both young and you don't even
know if this marriage will last."

"Of course it'll last," Ella had insisted. "Why wouldn't
it?"

Her mother said nothing, just pursed her lips like a
woman with an ugly secret. How had Mims known things
wouldn't work out with Jake? What early warning signs
had she seen that Ella hadn't?

Whatever she'd seen, she'd kept it to herself, and to show her support (once the decision was made and the papers were signed), she'd given them a gift certificate to Hearth and Home to buy a new couch, saying, "Really, Ella, you can't decorate in Early American Garage Sale. What will people think?"

"Maybe they'll think we're happy," Ella had suggested.

Mims had ignored that remark. "Go look at the couches at Hearth and Home, baby. You'll find one you love, I promise."

Ella did find a couch she loved, and Mims heartily approved of the brown leather sofa with the carved mahogany accents that Ella picked out. "You have wonderful taste," she'd said, and then added, "In most things." Translation: your taste in men is questionable.

"Really, darling, you can do so much better," Mims advised when Ella and Jake started getting serious. "Sleep with him if you must, but for God's sake don't saddle yourself with him for life."

What kind of mother told her daughter stuff like that? Lily Swan, that was who. Mims hadn't felt the need for a husband, so Ella supposed she thought her daughter would see the wisdom of her choice and follow suit. "Men are fun, but not necessary," she'd once overheard her mother say.

How much fun had Mims had with Ella's father? And what had happened to keep them from becoming a family? That, like her mother's age, was classified information and Ella had finally given up asking.

She opened her front door in time to see her own Mr. Not Necessary, her ex-husband, coming down the hallway wearing nothing but his boxers and carrying a basket of laundry, Tiny trotting at his heels. She hated it when Jake did that—not the laundry, parading around in his boxers.

Jake O'Brien had a poster-worthy body and looking at it was, well, distracting. He'd had all day to do the laundry. Why was he waiting until now?

She frowned at him.

He frowned back. "What?"

Tiny rushed up to her, his huge tail wagging with joy, and she bent to give him a good rub behind his ears. "You couldn't have done the laundry earlier?" That sounded snippy, and she wasn't a snippy sort of person. At least she hadn't been before their divorce.

"I was busy," he said.

Probably with some woman. Not that she cared. It was no longer any of her concern what he did or who he did it with.

"Anyway, what does it matter to you when I do my laundry? We're not married anymore."

"That's my point," she said, straightening up. "We're not married and I don't think you should be running around the house in your underwear." Now she sounded both snippy and bossy. She was never bossy. Never!

He stopped next to her. That close proximity still did things to her.

Used to do things to her. Used to! She told the goose bumps on her arms to settle down.

He grinned at her, a wicked, taunting grin. "Does it… bother you?"

She could feel a guilty-as-charged heat on her cheeks. "It's not proper." Snippy, bossy and prissy—who was this new and unimproved Ella? "You don't see *me* running around the house in my underwear."

"I wouldn't mind."

She upgraded her frown to a scowl. "We may be sharing this house but it's strictly business."

"I am strictly business, and if my boxers bother you, move."

Like she could afford to move? She didn't have any more money in the bank than he did.

"Go stay with your mama."

He might as well have added, "Mama's girl."

She wasn't a mama's girl and she had as much right to be here until the house sold as he did. She was an adult. She didn't have to run home to her mother.

Anyway, Mims had downsized to a condo in the spiffy new Mountain Ridge condominiums outside town and they didn't allow dogs Tiny's size. If Jake thought she was leaving Tiny to him, he could think again. Tiny needed a mommy and a daddy. Even when they went their separate ways, they'd have joint custody of him. And besides, Ella needed to stay to make sure the house was kept in good condition to show. If she wasn't there, potential buyers would see nothing but dirty toilets, dishes in the sink and beer cans on the coffee table, and they'd never be able to sell the place.

Sell the place—the thought of doing that still hurt. But it was only one in a string of many hurts she'd endured in the past year. For one wild, crazy moment, she wanted to put a hand to Jake's face and ask, "What happened to us? Why are we doing this?" But she knew what had happened, and there was no going back now. The jet hadn't just taxied down the runway or left the airport. It had left the city. The state. The country. They needed to move on, both of them.

She sighed. "Look, we're stuck here until the place sells. Can't we try and get along?"

He regarded her with those beautiful, dark Irish eyes. Roving eyes! "I'm not the one who started all this, El," he said softly.

"Oh?" Who had "started" it by coming home with another woman's phone number in his pants pocket?

There was no point in bringing that up. He'd just stick with his stupid story about the keyboard player dying to be in his band. Yeah? That wasn't all the woman was dying for. The voice message Ella had gotten when she called the woman's number said it all. *I'm not home right now so leave a message. If this is Jake, I can meet you anytime, anyplace.*

For what? A private audition? It had all been downhill from there.

He'd already let his perfect-husband mask slip before that, though, flirting with every little groupie who sashayed up to the bandstand when his band Ricochet was playing. She'd even caught him taking some girl's black thong one night when the band was on break and he was supposed to be getting a Coke. He'd seen Ella coming and handed it back like it was a hot potato. A lacy hot potato.

"That came out of left field. I was so surprised I didn't know what to do," he'd said.

Just like he hadn't known what to do with a certain keyboard player's phone number? How dumb had he thought she was? And once she had proof…oh, he'd climbed on his high horse and acted all insulted that her mother'd had the nerve to hire a private detective to follow him. Who could blame her after hearing about the way he was sneaking around behind her daughter's back, collecting other women's panties?

But there was no denying what was plain in those pictures—her husband on another woman's doorstep, hugging that woman. After being in her house for an hour. An hour! He'd *claimed* that he'd simply stopped by to drop off some music lead sheets. The kind of sheets they'd been using had nothing to do with music. How many quickies could an unfaithful husband squeeze into an hour? She didn't want to do the math. Boy, whoever said one picture was worth a thousand words must have had a cheating husband.

Well, he'd gotten his keyboard player and Ella had gotten her divorce. They both got what they wanted. "You're better off without him," Mims had said. "He's never going to amount to anything and you'd have been poor all your life. Starving musicians are a losing proposition."

"I didn't marry Jake to get rich," Ella had protested.

"Congratulations, you succeeded," Mims had retorted. Men might not have been necessary, but as far as her mother was concerned, once a girl had one, he darn well needed to earn his keep.

Her mother was right. Jake was immature and irresponsible and, worst of all, a cheater. She was well rid of him. Even if he did look hot in his boxers.

He frowned at her again. "Never mind. There's no point talking anymore. I could talk till I'm blue in the face and you wouldn't hear a thing I said." With that parting remark, he marched up the stairs.

Ella turned her back on him. She was not—not!— going to look at his butt.

In fact, she wasn't even going to stay in this house. By

eight he'd be gone, on his way to the Red Barn, a honky-tonk a few miles outside of town. There he'd spend the night crooning country songs for people who were more interested in brawling and hooking up than listening to his band.

Ella had always loved listening to the band.

Oh, enough already, she scolded herself.

A moment later Jake was downstairs again and on his way down the hall to the kitchen. He'd covered the boxers with jeans but he was still bare-chested and that brought the goose bumps back for another visit. "The kitchen's mine for twenty more minutes," he called over his shoulder.

"Stay there as long as you want." *Messing everything up.* "I'm leaving," she called.

"Got a hot date?"

None of his business. She declined to answer. Instead, she grabbed her purse and started for the door. Tiny followed her hopefully.

She knelt in front of him and rubbed his side. "I promise I'll be back as soon as he's gone," she whispered. "Then I'll give you a good brushing."

Tiny let out a groan and drool dripped from his chin. (Tiny did his share of mess-making, but unlike the other male in this house, he couldn't help it.)

She kissed the top of his head, then slipped out the door, guilt riding on her shoulder. Poor Tiny. He felt the unhappy vibes in the house. In his doggy heart did he wonder what he'd done to deserve getting adopted into a broken home? If she'd known this was going to happen she'd never have visited that rescue site.

There was nothing she could do about that now. She'd make it up to him, somehow. How, exactly, she didn't know. She hoped she could find someplace to rent that allowed big dogs that drooled and had a tendency to shed. *Oh, dear.*

Her Black Friday was getting blacker by the minute. She left the house, punching in Cecily Sterling's phone number on her cell as she walked.

Ella and Cecily had been friends since high school. In fact, it was Cecily who had gotten Ella and Jake together. They'd lost touch when Cecily moved to L.A. but had reconnected when she returned to Icicle Falls earlier in the year. Cecily had been shocked to hear about the divorce but she'd been sympathetic and supportive. She had men interested in her, two to be exact, but she was done with men (or so she claimed), which made her the ideal dinner companion.

"Have you eaten yet?" Ella asked.

"Nope," Cecily answered. "I just got in the door."

"I don't suppose you'd like to go back out the door, would you?"

"Maybe. What did you have in mind?"

"I need a place to hang out for a couple of hours. Dinner at Zelda's?" Even though it was Friday night and the town was packed with tourists gearing up for Saturday shopping, Charlene Albach could always find a table for her friends.

"Jake's still home?" Cecily guessed.

"Yeah," Ella admitted. This was silly. She couldn't keep running over to Charley's restaurant every time Jake was home.

"I could go for a huckleberry martini," Cecily said.

Oh, yes, a huckleberry martini sounded good. Or two. Whatever it took to wash away the image of Jake in his boxers.

* * *

Jake slammed a pot on the stove and pulled a can of chili from his side of the cupboard. Canned chili. He might as well have been a bachelor again.

Oh, yeah. He was.

He frowned at the can as he secured it to the electric can opener. This sucked. His life sucked. From perfect to puke in less than a year.

Was there a song in there somewhere? Probably not. He emptied the chili into the pot, along with a can of stewed tomatoes and a can of corn, his own secret recipe.

Tiny was in the kitchen now and looking expectantly up at him. "Yeah, I know. You like chili, too," he said to the dog. He opened another can and added that to the pot. "You know this will make you fart."

Tiny wagged his tail.

"Yeah, you're right. Who cares? We're guys, it's what we do." And they also walked around the house in their boxers.

Except not anymore, now that he and Ella weren't together. Walking around in his boxers was no longer allowed. So maybe he should talk to her about leaving her bras hanging out in plain sight when she did the laundry. Did she have any idea how crazy that made him? All it took was one glance at those lacy little cups and he could picture Ella with him in that sleigh bed they'd found at an estate sale, going at it like rabbits.

He heaved a sigh. How had he gone from happily married to miserably divorced so fast?

He and Ella were meant to be together. They should've gone to counseling, worked things out.

Aw, heck, they wouldn't even have needed counseling if he'd explained when she first started singing her version of "Your Cheatin' Heart," accusing him of being unfaithful. He'd tried to, but she'd cut him off. Then she'd thrown those pictures down in front of him and he'd been so shocked that his mother-in-law would do something that outrageous, and so offended and just plain pissed... he'd lost it. Wounded pride and anger had escorted him to the edge of the matrimonial cliff and then pushed him off.

It had been a fast fall and he learned firsthand that once the *D* word's been said, there's nothing else left to say.

So here he was, broken and miserable. The woman who'd once thought he hung the moon now wanted nothing more to do with him.

And his chili was burning. He swore and pulled it off the burner. "You're getting the crusty part," he informed Tiny. "You don't care."

You don't care. Ella had thrown those words at him, insisting he sign the divorce papers.

"I'm not the one who filed for this," he'd shot back.

"Just sign it, Jake. Please."

When he'd seen those tears in her eyes, he should have pulled her to him and kissed her breathless. Then he should've torn up the papers, borrowed some money from Pops and moved them to Nashville. *There* was someplace he was sure her mother would never have followed. And that was probably what they needed. It could've been the two of them rather than the three of them.

He put his culinary creation in a bowl, gave Tiny the rest and then went back to his room. His room. That sucked, too. This was the guest room. Someday it was supposed to have been the nursery. Now it was his room.

He sat on the single bed that was six inches too short for him (a garage sale find), and sighed. Here he was, a squatter in his own home. Maybe Lily Swan was right. Maybe he was a loser. Maybe he had no talent. If he'd just admitted it, quit the band and taken a job in the warehouse at Sweet Dreams Chocolates, maybe he and Ella would still be together. There'd have been no groupies, no Jen, no reason to be jealous. Instead, he'd had to dream of a songwriting career and stardom. He'd tried to support his habit (and them) by working in the music shop on Fourth, but then the music shop had gone out of business. He still had a few guitar students but he wasn't exactly getting rich. In short, these days he was a loser, unable to hang on to his woman and barely able to hang on to his dreams.

He looked at the dresser and the diamond in Ella's engagement ring winked at him mockingly. He'd made payments on that for a whole year. Then he'd bummed the rest of the money he needed from Pops, paid it off and asked her to marry him that same night. She'd given him back both the engagement and wedding rings the day she'd shoved the divorce papers in front of him. "I can't keep them," she'd said. Just like she couldn't keep him.

"No. I gave them to you. Keep them," he'd insisted.

Ella loved jewelry and she'd especially loved that engagement ring, but she'd shaken her head and backed away.

Jake couldn't bring himself to get rid of either ring. They still meant something to him, even if they didn't to Ella.

Damn, he was a walking country song.

With a growl, he set aside his chili and finished getting dressed. No sense hanging around here any longer.

He'd go to the Red Barn. Maybe he'd find some cute chick there who appreciated him and his music.

Even if he did, he'd look at her and see Ella.

And that sucked the most of all.

Three

Charlene Albach, Charley to her friends, surveyed her domain with satisfaction. *Six o'clock and all is well.*

Zelda's restaurant was filled with diners, many of them out-of-towners who'd come up to enjoy a Thanksgiving weekend getaway. Charley had been happy to oblige. She'd hated to miss going to her sister's in Portland to be with family, but the restaurant was entirely hers now and she simply couldn't leave. So she'd focused instead on giving other families a spectacular holiday, serving turkey dinner with all the trimmings, including stuffing made from her great-grandmother's recipe. Well, with a few new twists. That was part of the fun of owning a restaurant. You got to create new recipes, dream up taste sensations that would keep customers coming back for more.

They were sure coming tonight. People had obviously worked up their appetites sledding and spending money in the shops. Tomorrow there'd be more sledding and shopping and more diners crowding into Zelda's. And that meant more money in the cash register, which was bound to make for a very merry Christmas. This year

Charley planned to be extravagant when shopping for her friends. They'd been there for her at every painful bump on the road to unexpectedly single, and she intended to show her thanks in a way that would make Santa proud.

She had just seated a fortysomething couple with a texting teen in tow when Ella O'Brien and Cecily Sterling came in. "And I thought my shop was crazy," Ella observed, looking around.

The scene was a feast for the eyes. People of all ages and sizes, dressed in winter garb, consumed house specials such as salmon baked in golden puff pastry, squash seasoned with curry, baked winter vegetables and wild huckleberry cheesecake. There was plenty to occupy the other senses, too. The tantalizing scent of sage drifted out from the kitchen, encouraging diners to try the special turkey lasagna Charley's head chef, Harvey, had created, and the clink of silver and hum of voices reminded her that life was good.

No, better than good. Great. Who needed a man, anyway? Getting free of her louse of a husband had freed up her creativity. The restaurant was better off without him. And so was Charley. Anyway, sex was overrated.

And if she kept telling herself that, she might begin to believe it.

"Can you find us a spot?" Cecily asked.

"I can always find room for a former employee. Are you sure you don't want to come back to work for me?" Charley added as she led them to her last remaining twotop. "Like now?"

"Samantha's keeping me busy enough at Sweet Dreams," Cecily said with a smile. "I think my restaurant days are over."

Just like her matchmaking days, or so Cecily claimed.

Sometimes Charley entertained the idea of seeing if Cecily would put on her matchmaker hat one last time and find her a perfect man. But then she remembered there was no such thing, which was probably why Cecily was out of the matchmaking business and helping run her family's chocolate company instead.

And there's a reason you're single, Charley told herself. Men were a liability, and they had no staying power. Richard, her ex, had proved that.

Never mind him. You're having a really successful Black Friday. No need to turn it blue.

"So, business was good today?" she asked Ella as she handed her friends their menus.

"We moved a lot of inventory," Ella said, sounding pleased.

Hardly surprising. Ella had a gift for creating irresistible displays in her shop. Charley had certainly succumbed to temptation often enough. How could a girl not when a hot top paired with a sweater that begged to be touched called her over, whispering, "Just try us on. Oh, and don't you love this amazing scarf that's hanging out with us?"

Ella herself was a walking ad. Tonight she was dolled up in jeans tucked into brown suede winter boots trimmed with a faux fur, along with a cream-colored cashmere sweater. She'd finished the look with a jaunty red jacket and a beret. It took style to pull off a beret. Ella had style in spades. Hardly surprising, considering who her mother was.

"That'll make your mom happy," Cecily predicted.

Did anything make Lily Swan happy? Charley could count on one finger the number of times she'd seen the woman smile. Well, really smile. How had such a snobby sour lemon produced such a nice daughter?

It was one of life's mysteries, right up there with the mystery of how Charley could have been so dumb as to miss the fact that her husband was conducting an affair right under her nose…with the woman who worked as their hostess, for crying out loud. Somehow, Ariel hadn't gotten the memo that her hostess duties applied only to paying customers. They did not extend to making your boss's husband at home in your bed.

That was past history. Charley returned to the present. "So, you here celebrating?" she asked Ella.

"More like avoiding," Cecily suggested, making Ella frown. "Jake's still home," she added for Charley's benefit.

"I can see this house-sharing thing is working out great," Charley cracked.

Ella shrugged. "It won't be for long. Anyway, he can't afford a place on his own and I can't afford my half of the house payment plus rent somewhere else."

"Your mom would probably help you."

"I know, but I wouldn't feel right asking her."

"I'd have kicked his butt to the curb," Charley said in no uncertain terms. "Let him stay with one of his band buddies."

"Their wives and girlfriends would have been all over that," Cecily pointed out with a grin.

"Beggars can't be choosers," Charley said. "Neither can cheaters." Oooh, how she hated men who cheated on their wives!

"I know he looked as innocent as a man going to the bank in a ski mask, but I still have a hard time picturing

Jake cheating on you," Cecily said to Ella. "It doesn't seem like him."

Good old Cecily, always trying to see the best in people, even when there was no best to see. Although Charley had to admit, Jake had seemed like a nice guy. He and Ella had been Cecily's first successful match, back when she and Ella were in high school. Going their separate ways for college hadn't quenched Ella and Jake's passion, and after graduation had come the big church wedding. Her mother hadn't approved of Jake, but she gave Ella a wedding fit for a princess. They'd not only been a lovely bride and groom, they'd also seemed like the ideal couple, united for life.

Well, she and Richard had seemed like the ideal couple, too. Things weren't always what they appeared.

"I don't want to talk about it," Ella said stiffly.

"Good idea," Charley approved. "Keep this table a heartbreak-free zone." She caught sight of another couple coming in the door and excused herself to greet them.

They were somewhere in their thirties. The man was going bald and his woman was no beauty, but the way they looked at each other proved that love was blind. She hung on to his arm like she'd never let him go.

Charley could remember when she'd held on to Richard like that. Somewhere along the way she'd released her hold....

She yanked herself back into the present and smiled at the newcomers. "Hi, how are you doing?" As if she had to ask. They were still happily in love.

"Great," said the man.

"Do you have a reservation?" Charley asked.

He shook his head. "Someone told us this is a good place to eat. How long is the wait?"

"About twenty minutes, but we're worth it." Charley smiled. "If you like, you can wait in the bar and we'll call you when there's a table. Try the chocolate kiss," she told the woman.

"That sounds good," the woman said, and squeezed her man's arm.

"We'll wait," he said, and gave Charley his name.

Watching them go, she wondered if they'd be happy together for the rest of their lives. Yes, she decided, they would be. And on their twenty-fifth wedding anniversary they'd come back to Zelda's to celebrate. On that pleasant thought she went to help a frazzled-looking Maria clear the corner table.

As Ella and Cecily enjoyed huckleberry martinis while waiting for their food to arrive Cecily took another stab at convincing her friend that she might have made a mistake.

It wasn't the first time she'd tried, but Ella had been determined to divorce Jake even though Cecily was sure she was still in love with him. Yes, he wasn't perfect, but he was perfect for Ella—a good guy with a nice family. Easygoing, fun-loving, just what Ella needed to balance the life of perfection her mother expected from her.

"I know it seems too late now that the divorce is final," Cecily said, "but I can't help thinking you should reconsider this. It doesn't feel right."

Ella stared into her martini glass. She looked like she was going to drop a few tears into it. "I know you're famous for those hunches of yours, but this time you're wrong, Cec. We just aren't a match. He's irresponsible. And untrustworthy."

"But all you really had were suspicions."

"I had more, believe me," Ella said, and took a giant sip of her martini.

Jake was such a stand-up guy, Cecily found that hard to believe. What the heck had happened to these two? They'd been madly in love when she moved to L.A., yet by the time she'd moved back home they were done.

"Well, he's not really irresponsible," she defended Jake. "I mean, I know he doesn't have a normal nine-to-five job, but he has a dream."

"You can't live on dreams."

That sounded more like Lily Swan than Ella O'Brien. Ella's mother had never liked Jake, probably thought he was too much of a redneck for her elegant daughter. Ella had beautiful taste in clothes and decorating, but when it came right down to it, she was a simple, small-town girl, not a New York jet-setter. That was Lily Swan, though. She'd settled in a small town to raise her daughter but she'd always fancied herself a sophisticated woman. Having a son-in-law who was a country musician and who eked out a living teaching guitar and playing in a band didn't line up with her idea of a successful life.

Had Lily herself been all that successful? Surely if she'd been a top model she'd have wound up living in London or New York or L.A.—some place other than Icicle Falls. If you asked Cecily, Lily Swan had started believing her own press.

Not that anyone was asking Cecily, and not that she would've said what she thought even if she *was* asked. And she wouldn't be saying anything now, except that Ella was miserable and she hated seeing her friend miserable.

"I don't know," she said. "It seems to me if you don't have dreams you're not really living." She'd dreamed of coming home and carving out a new life for herself, and so far that was working out pretty well.

Her new life didn't include love, though. She'd had enough misery in that department. She had to remind herself of this on a regular basis, every time she saw Luke Goodman, Sweet Dreams' production manager. She also had to remind herself that sexual attraction did not equal love every time she ran into Todd Black, who owned the Man Cave, the seedy bar at the edge of town.

Ella finished off her drink. "It just wasn't meant to be. Mims was right."

Mother knows best? Lily Swan had done a fabulous job of brainwashing her daughter. Of course, she'd brainwashed herself, as well, convincing both of them that Ella could do better than Jake. Maybe she could if she was looking for wealth and status. But that wasn't Ella. Hopefully, she'd realize it before it was too late and some other girl came along, picked up Jake's broken heart and put it in her pocket.

The evening went by in a busy blur for Charley. By nine-thirty her feet hurt. That was nothing new. Her feet always hurt by nine-thirty. A few diners remained, savoring coffee and dessert or an after-dinner drink, but most of the crowd had moved on or relocated to the bar at the back of the restaurant. The dining area was now a burble of soft voices and an occasional clink of silverware on plates.

Sore feet aside, this was Charley's favorite time of the night. The dinner rush over, she could bask in the satisfaction of having delivered a memorable dining experience to people celebrating and connecting over food.

Food. It was the centerpiece of life. From dinners of

state to family gatherings, sharing food was an essential part of human connection. And it was the spice of love. How could you *not* fall in love when you were gazing across the table at someone? And when your sense of taste came alive over a Chocolate Decadence dessert or a crab soufflé the other senses joined the party. There was a reason lovers went out to dinner.

Some might say she simply owned a restaurant. Charley knew better. She owned a slice of people's lives.

Tonight she'd had a great slice. She smiled, remembering how the texting teen had actually stopped on the way out to tell her she loved the wild blackberry pie. Her smile grew with the memory of the couple in love strolling out the door hand in hand. Oh, yes, a very successful night, she concluded as she loaded dirty dishes onto a tray.

She had just lifted it up to haul off to the kitchen when a cold gust of wind blew in the door. She looked up to see who the latecomer was and received a shock that made her heart jump and the tray slip from her hands, sending dishes and glasses to shatter on the floor. Oh, no. It couldn't be.

But it was. The Ghost of Christmas Past. Her ex.

Four

Charley stood gaping at her former husband. Random thoughts circled her brain like so many spinning plates. *What's he doing here? Am I hallucinating? Let's test that theory by throwing a broken plate at him.*

Maria hurried over to help her clean up, saw Richard and managed a shocked "Oh."

Okay, now Charley knew she wasn't hallucinating

He stepped into the dining area. "Hello, Charley. You look good."

So did he. Richard wasn't a tall man, coming in at around five foot eight, but what there was of him was yummy. Yes, he'd added some gray strands to his dark hair—she hoped the new girlfriend had given him every one—but other than that he was sailing pleasantly into his forties with only a hint of lines around those gray eyes. He still had that full mouth and the misleadingly strong jaw. Anyone would mistake him for a movie hero. Movies, yes. Hero? Definitely not.

He stood there in his jeans and winter jacket, looking at her—how? Hopefully? No, that couldn't be it. She had nothing he wanted. He'd made that abundantly clear when he chose another woman.

"What are you doing here?" she asked, her voice flat.

"I wanted to see you."

"Well, I don't want to see you. Ever again." Charley bent next to Maria and began to pick up some of the bigger pieces of dishware.

Richard joined them, loading a chunk of broken glass onto the tray.

"I don't need your help," Charley growled. "Anyway, you might cut yourself and sue me." She was already giving him enough money. Talk about adding insult to injury. As part of the divorce settlement she'd had to buy out his share of the restaurant. *Her* restaurant!

Oh, yes, he'd worked it with her, but it had been hers— her vision, her creation. She'd sunk her entire inheritance from her grandmother into the place when it was a dying dump, and with imagination and hard work she'd built it into a popular community gathering spot. Richard had only come along for the ride.

And then taken her for a ride.

He laid a hand on hers. "I really need to talk to you."

Maria gave a disgusted snort before hauling the tray full of breakage off to the kitchen.

Charley's sentiments exactly. She sat back on her heels and regarded her ex. "You can't want more money. God knows you've taken enough from me."

He looked at her as if she'd stabbed him with a steak knife. "Charley…listen, we can't talk here."

"I don't want to talk at all."

"I know I don't deserve so much as the time of day from you, but please, can we go back to the house?"

"*My* house," she reminded him. She was buying out his share of that, too.

"Please?"

Maybe she was curious, or maybe the desperation in his voice gave her an appetite for more of the same. She could feel herself weakening.

Still she hedged. "I'm not done here."

"I'm staying at Gerhardt's. Call me on my cell when you're finished."

The same cell phone he'd used to text messages to Ariel, setting up stolen quickies in the bar before the employees arrived. Before Charley arrived.

"Charley, please. I know I don't deserve it but please."

"I'll think about it," she said. "And that's the most I can promise."

He managed an awkward nod. "I'll be waiting," he said, and then walked out the door.

Charley stood slowly. She was only thirty-nine but she suddenly felt ninety and weary right down to her soul.

Maria was back with a whisk broom and dustpan, frowning. "What did that *bastardo* want?"

"I'm not sure." And she wasn't sure she wanted to find out. "But he wants to see me later."

"Don't do it," Maria cautioned. "He already hurt you once."

"Don't worry, I won't let him do it again," Charley assured her.

But when she finally got home she found herself calling him. He probably wouldn't leave until she gave in, so the sooner she saw him, the sooner he'd go.

He was at her door ten minutes later.

"Make this fast," she said as he stepped in. "I'm tired

and I want to go to bed." *Alone, like I've been doing ever since you left.*

He motioned to the living room. "Can we sit down?"

The last thing she wanted was Richard back in her living room. Bad enough that almost everything in it held a memory of their life together, from the brown microfiber sofa where they'd cuddled watching football or the Food Network to the Tiffany-style lamp he'd bought for her birthday three years ago. She should have gotten rid of that lamp. Heck, she should've gotten rid of everything. "I don't understand why you're here," she said bitterly, leading the way to the couch. She sat down, crossed her arms over her chest and scowled at him.

He sat close to her—too close—and looked at her earnestly. "I'm here to ask you to take me back."

This was the biggest shock she'd had since, well, since she'd discovered him cheating on her. "What?"

"I don't know what I was thinking."

"I don't either, but I know what you were thinking with," she retorted.

His face flushed, but he held her gaze. "If I had it to do over…"

"You wouldn't have done her?" Charley finished for him. "What's the matter, Richard, did she dump you for a younger man?"

The flush deepened. Bingo! "I was a fool."

"Yes, you were," Charley agreed, "and for all I know you still are. Why should I take you back?"

"Because I love you."

That produced a bitter laugh. "Oh, please. Don't make me sick."

"I do," he insisted. "I always have. Ariel was a mistake."

"A mistake you were happy enough to make," Charley said. "You had a chance to give her up and you didn't."

"I wasn't thinking clearly."

"Well, I am." She stood, signaling that this ridiculous conversation was over.

He stood, too. He was barely taller than she was. Why had she picked such a small man?

"All I'm asking is that you give me a chance to prove I've changed. Twelve years together, Charley—that has to count for something."

"It should have counted for something when you were looking around for a side dish."

He sighed. "You're right."

"You know where the door is."

His eyes filled with regret. "What would it take to convince you I've changed?"

She studied him. "You know…"

He regarded her hopefully.

"I can't think of a thing." She walked to the door and opened it. "Good night, Richard."

He took the hint and walked out the door, but as he passed her he said, "I'm not giving up. You're worth fighting for."

He hadn't thought that a year ago. She slammed the door after him and locked it.

The Gingerbread Haus opened at ten but Cass was always in by six, baking cookies and, at this time of year, assembling gingerbread houses, many of which would be shipped all over the country.

She got plenty of appreciation in her hometown, too, and Olivia Wallace arrived at eleven to pick up the creation Cass had made for the lobby of the Icicle Creek

Lodge. A perfect replica of Olivia's B and B styled after a Bavarian hunting lodge, it even sported a blue-frosting creek running past it.

"It's lovely as usual," Olivia said. "I don't know how I'll be able to resist nibbling at it."

Olivia's well-rounded figure testified to her lack of willpower. But Olivia was a widow and, as far as Cass was concerned that gave her unlimited nibbling rights. Anyway, Cass was in no position to say anything. She was a nibbler, too.

"Here's a little something extra for when you get the urge," she said, and handed Olivia a box containing a baker's dozen frosted gingerbread cookies cut in the shape of Christmas trees.

"Oh, thank you," Olivia said. "How much do I owe you for these?"

"Nothing. They're on the house. The gingerbread house," Cass added with a wink.

Dani came in from sending off the day's shipment of gingerbread creations. "Here's our bride-to-be," Olivia greeted her.

Dani's cheeks flushed with pleasure and she smiled at Olivia.

She's going to be a beautiful bride, Cass thought. If only they had more time to plan this wedding.

"I just gave your grandmother and aunt our last room," Olivia said to Dani. "It's a good thing you called when you did, or that one would've been gone," she added. "I've had three calls since."

"One of them was probably my stepmother," Dani said, and now the pink in her cheeks wasn't from pleasure.

Babette. Cass could feel her mouth slipping down at

the corners. *Bimbette* was more like it. Cass hadn't met her, but she'd seen pictures. The woman was nothing more than arm candy. Cass had it on good authority (her son's) that she couldn't cook.

Not that Mason had married Babette for her culinary skills. She'd been a professional cheerleader for the Seattle Seahawks, a Sea Gal, and she had the body to prove it. Of course, once she snagged Mason at the ripe old age of thirty, she gave that up. Now she was all of what, thirty-one? And stepmother to a twenty-year-old. What a joke.

Olivia looked distinctly uncomfortable. "I wish I'd known earlier. I'd have reserved a block of rooms for you."

"If any of us had known earlier we would've been more organized," Cass said. She'd meant that as an explanation, not an accusation of her daughter. Judging from the deep rose shade blooming on Dani's cheeks, she'd taken the remark to heart. "But Mike got a job in Spokane and he starts in January and they want to be together."

"Of course you do," Olivia said to Dani. "I sure hope the rest of your guests find someplace. I know Annemarie is full up and so is Gerhardt."

No room at the inn. What a shame. Mason and Bimbette might have to miss the wedding. Not a very gracious thought, Cass scolded herself.

"Oh," Dani said, a world of worry in her voice.

"Mountain Springs over by Cashmere might have something," Olivia suggested. "That wouldn't be too far away."

Dani nodded and whipped her cell phone out of her jeans.

As she stepped away to make the call, Olivia lowered her voice. "I imagine this is all a little awkward."

There was an understatement. "A little," Cass said.

"I almost felt like a traitor saving a room but Dani asked."

"It's okay. In fact, I really appreciate it. Otherwise, they might have had to stay with me."

The very thought of that was enough to make Cass shudder. Her judgmental ex-mother-in-law and her gossipy ex-sister-in-law staying with *her?* Ugh.

Two middle-aged women had come in and were waiting patiently in front of the glass display case. Olivia, like everyone else in Icicle Falls, knew the value of a tourist dollar. "Well, I'd better be going," she said. "I've got to get to the grocery store or my guests won't have breakfast tomorrow." To the newcomers she said, "The gingerbread boys are delicious, but make sure you get a couple of those cream puff swans, too. They're to die for."

The women took her advice, purchasing gingerbread boys and girls and a couple of cream puffs. One of them bought a gingerbread house, as well.

Meanwhile, more customers had come into the bakery. Normally Dani would be helping Cass, but right now she and her cell phone were in the kitchen looking for lodging for Mason and Bimbette.

Let them find their own place to stay. Cass moved to the kitchen area. "I could use some help out here."

Dani turned her back and held up a hand, which meant—what? Trying to hear? Be there in a minute?

"Now," Cass added in her stern mama-bear voice.

"Okay, thanks," Dani said, and ended the call.

"Honey, you're going to have to do that later," Cass said. "We've got customers."

"We've always got customers," Dani muttered grumpily.

Which was how they paid the bills. This had never bothered her daughter before.

But then she'd never been engaged.

Twenty minutes rushed past before they had a lull. Cass knew it was temporary. Once the lunch hour was finished, the customers would return.

She turned the sign on the door to Closed. "We'll Be Back by One," said the clock below. That gave them time for lunch, and in Dani's case, time to go back to calling every motel and B and B within a twenty-mile radius.

Cass sat down at a corner table with her cup of coffee and watched as Dani became increasingly desperate with every conversation. That desperation began to make Cass's coffee churn in her stomach. If her daughter didn't succeed in her mission it boded ill—not for Dani, and not for Mason and Bimbette, but for Cass.

Sure enough. At a quarter to one Dani plopped onto the chair next to her and tossed her smartphone on the table.

Tell me we're out of eggs, tell me someone's order never arrived, tell me anything but what you're about to tell me.

"There's no vacancy anywhere," Dani announced miserably.

Cass spoke before her daughter could say the dreaded words. "It'll be okay. Seattle's not that far. Your dad can drive over the day of the wedding."

Dani looked at her, eyes wide in horror. "But what about the rehearsal dinner the night before? And what if something happens? What if they close the pass?"

Then we can get on our knees and thank God.

Okay, that was truly rotten. This was her daughter's

big day and she wanted her father there. "I'm sure he'll figure it out," Cass said, trying to sound as if she cared.

"Mom, how can he when there's no place anywhere?"

Surely that was a rhetorical question. She kept her mouth shut.

"Can they stay with us for a couple of days?"

There it was, what she'd known was coming all along. Just what she wanted for Christmas, her ex and his bimbo bride staying with her. "We have no place to put them," she argued.

"They can have my room. I can sleep with Amber."

"I was going to give your room to Grandma Nordby." Cass would jump into boiling oil before she'd turn her mother out in favor of Mason and Bimbette.

"Then give them Willie's room and put him on the sleeper sofa. Or put them on the sleeper sofa."

That was what Cass wanted, to come out and find her ex and his second wife curled up together in her living room.

"We could find a place for them for just one night, couldn't we?" Dani begged. "Two at the most."

There had to be some other way they could work this out. Cass stalled for time. "Let me think about it, okay?"

Dani made a face like she'd just eaten baking soda. "I know what that means."

So did Cass, and she felt like the world's meanest mother.

A woman with two little girls had come to the door, and the girls were peering inside.

"Go unlock the door," Cass said wearily.

"Sure. Fine," Dani said in a tone of voice that showed how un-fine everything was.

"It would be nice if you could greet our customers with a smile instead of a frown," Cass called after her.

"I'm smiling," Dani called back. Smiling on the outside, seething on the inside.

They'll find someplace to stay, Cass told herself. Now, if she could only believe that.

Five

It was Sunday evening, time for Cass's weekly chick flick night. The friends had decided to watch Christmas movies during the month of December and Cass's pal Samantha Sterling had picked the one for tonight—*The Family Man*.

"I love that movie," she'd said. "Love how the hero changed from a Scrooge to a great husband and dad."

"I never knew you were so sentimental," Cass had teased.

"I'm not," Samantha had retorted, "but I know what's important."

Cass would give her that. Samantha Sterling had fought hard to save her family's chocolate company. In the process she'd resuscitated the town of Icicle Falls, which had been in an economic slump, by sponsoring a chocolate festival. Spurred on by that success, the town leaders had caught festival fever. October had seen Oktoberfest, December's tree-lighting event had been expanded from one weekend to every weekend and there was talk of a wine festival in the early summer.

Samantha and her sister Cecily were the first to ar-

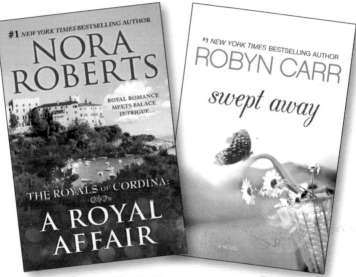

Dear Debbie Macomber Fan,

Since you are a lover of our books, your opinions are important to us... and so is your time.

That's why we made sure your **"FAST FIVE" READER SURVEY** can be completed in just a few minutes. Your answers to the five questions will help us remain at the forefront of women's fiction.

And, as a thank-you for participating, we'd like to send you **4 FREE THANK-YOU GIFTS!**

Enjoy your gifts with our appreciation,

Pam Powers

To get your
4 FREE THANK-YOU GIFTS:

✱ Quickly complete the "Fast Five" Reader Survey
and return the insert.

"FAST FIVE" READER SURVEY

1 Do you sometimes read a book a second or third time? — ○ Yes ○ No

2 Do you often choose reading over other forms of entertainment such as television? — ○ Yes ○ No

3 When you were a child, did someone regularly read aloud to you? — ○ Yes ○ No

4 Do you sometimes take a book with you when you travel outside the home? — ○ Yes ○ No

5 In addition to books, do you regularly read newspapers and magazines? — ○ Yes ○ No

YES! I have completed the above Reader Survey. Please send me my 4 FREE GIFTS (gifts worth over $20 retail). I understand that I am under no obligation to buy anything, as explained on the back of this card.

194/394 MDL GLDT

FIRST NAME	LAST NAME

ADDRESS

APT.#	CITY

STATE/PROV.	ZIP/POSTAL CODE

READER SERVICE—Here's how it works:

◄ If offer card is missing write to: Reader Service, P.O. Box 1867, Buffalo, NY 14240-1867 or visit www.ReaderService.com ►

BUSINESS REPLY MAIL
FIRST-CLASS MAIL   PERMIT NO. 717   BUFFALO, NY

POSTAGE WILL BE PAID BY ADDRESSEE

READER SERVICE
PO BOX 1867
BUFFALO NY 14240-9952

NO POSTAGE
NECESSARY
IF MAILED
IN THE
UNITED STATES

rive, rosy-cheeked and smiling, stomping snow off their boots. Blue-eyed, blond-haired Cecily was the beauty of the family, but with her red hair and freckles, Samantha wasn't exactly a troll. She'd married Blake Preston, the bank's manager, in August and still sported a newlywed glow. That would wear off eventually.

Listen to you, Cass scolded herself. *Queen of the cynics.*

"We brought vitamin C," Samantha said, handing over a holiday box of Sweet Dreams Chocolates.

Chocolate, the other Vitamin C, and a girl's best friend. "This takes care of me. I don't know what the rest of you are having," Cass joked. "Did you bring the movie?"

Cecily held up the DVD with Nicolas Cage on the cover. "We're set."

Ella was the next to arrive. She wasn't as beautiful as her glamorous mother, Lily Swan, but she was cute and she knew how to dress. Tonight she looked ready for a magazine shoot in skinny jeans paired with a crisp white shirt, a black leather vest and a long, metallic red scarf, and bearing a bowl of parmesan popcorn, her specialty. Ella even did popcorn with flair.

Cass decided that flair was something you either soaked up in the gene pool or you didn't. She could create works of art in her bakery, but when it came to personal style she couldn't seem to get beyond unimpressionist. Oh, well. What did she care? She didn't have anyone she needed to impress.

Not even your ex-in-laws?

No, she told herself firmly. Living well was the best revenge and she was living quite well, thank you. She didn't need to look like a cover model to prove it.

She pushed aside the thought of Babette, who would, of course, show up for the wedding with her hair perfectly highlighted and her skinny little bod draped in something flattering. Maybe Cass would pass on the chocolate and popcorn tonight.

Charley was the last to arrive. She came bearing wine and looked frazzled enough to consume the entire bottle single-handed.

"Okay, what's wrong?" Cass asked once the women were settled in the living room with their drinks and goodies.

"Richard's back." Charley took one of Cass's gingerbread boys and bit off his head.

Cass nearly dropped her wineglass. "What?"

Charley nodded. More of the gingerbread boy disappeared.

"Why is he back?" Cass asked. "What does he want?"

"Me," Charley said.

"You? He left you for another woman! Tell him to take a hike off the mountain," Samantha advised.

Cass couldn't have said it better herself. "I'll second that."

"So he's left Ariel?" Cecily asked.

"He says it was all a mistake."

Men always said that when they got caught with their pants down. Cass frowned. "Not as big a mistake as taking him back would be."

"You're not going to, are you?" asked Samantha.

"Absolutely not," Charley shook her head vigorously.

"Good for you," Cass said. Charley had the kind of never-ending legs that made men drool and gorgeous long hair and plenty of personality. She didn't have to settle for letting a loser back in her life.

"Did you tell him that?" Samantha asked.

"Of course I did."

"Then why is he still here?" Samantha persisted.

Charley was on her second gingerbread boy now. "He says he's not giving up."

"Oh, brother," Ella said, rolling her eyes.

"Why is it men only want you when you don't want them?" Charley grumbled.

"Because they're bums," Cass said.

"Not all of them," Samantha murmured.

"Blake is the exception to the rule," Cass told her.

"There are other exceptions out there," Cecily added.

"Like Luke Goodman?" her sister teased.

"Like Luke," Cecily agreed, her voice neutral.

Ella sighed. "So why do we always like the bad boys?"

Charley sighed, too. "Because we're masochists?"

"There's something about bad boys," Cecily said, then seeing her sister's frown, got busy inspecting a lock of hair for split ends.

"Yeah, something bad," her sister said firmly. "Men like Richard and Todd Black are nothing but heartbreak on two legs."

"I wasn't talking about Todd," Cecily said, her cheeks pink.

"I was," Samantha said.

Cecily grabbed a handful of popcorn. "I don't know about the rest of you, but I'm ready to watch the movie."

With Samantha in bossy older sister mode that was understandable. Cass started the movie.

As the plot unfolded, chronicling the life of the fictional Jack Campbell, she couldn't help thinking of her own choices, of Mason. What if they'd been given a glimpse of a better future, one where they stayed united and lived as best friends instead of combatants? What would her life look like now?

What did it matter? She and Mason had made their choices and no hip angel was going to drop into their lives to give them a second chance. The best glimpse she could get was one of her daughter's wedding going smoothly, of herself managing to be civil. If she could pull that off, it would be a miracle.

What a wonderful movie. And what a wonderful way to start the holidays. Ella was teary-eyed by the end of it. She always cried at movies. She cried over movies with sad endings because she felt so bad for the poor people. A movie with a happy ending, especially a romantic movie, brought her to tears because, well, it was all so overwhelmingly hopeful. Somewhere out there in the real world a man could be coming to his senses, realizing that he didn't need to go off in search of El Dorado, that there was gold right in his own backyard. Maybe like the Jack Campbell character, Charley's husband had figured that out.

Jake had insisted he had, that Ella was all he needed.

What big fat lies! Thank God her mother had opened her eyes to the truth. Otherwise, she'd have wasted the best years of her life, keeping the home fires burning on a shoestring budget while he carried on with other women.

"Well." Cass raised her glass. "Here's to the Jack Campbells of the world, wherever they're hiding."

"I'll drink to that. I found mine," Samantha said.

"And here's to Christmas," Cecily toasted.

"And Christmas weddings," Samantha added. "Do these guys know Dani's engaged?"

"That's wonderful! Why didn't you tell us?" Ella asked Cass.

"You've been anticipating this for months. I'm surprised you haven't been crowing from the rooftops," Charley said.

"I was going to tell you all." Cass shrugged. "I got distracted."

When Ella and Jake had gotten engaged, she'd told everyone. How did a woman get distracted from sharing such big news? "That's so exciting. Tell us now."

"She's getting married the weekend before Christmas at Olivia's."

"Oh, that'll be gorgeous," Cecily said. "Olivia always has the place decorated like something out of a magazine."

Especially at Christmas. The outside of the lodge would be awash with white twinkle lights, and inside cedar swags and red bows would adorn the banisters. But the best decoration of all was the vintage sleigh, decked out with swags and ribbons, surrounded by decorative gift boxes. Ella could envision Dani and Mike in that sleigh, posing for pictures in their wedding day finery.

"But wow, it doesn't give you much time," she said. It had taken her nine months to plan her wedding.

"And I thought we had a challenge putting together our chocolate festival in six weeks," Cecily joked.

"Why so quick?" asked Ella, and then blushed as one obvious possibility occurred.

"No, they don't have a baby on the way," Cass said. "Just a move to Spokane in January."

"Are you going to be able to pull it off?" Ella asked after Cass had explained about Mike's new job.

"Are you stressed about getting everything done?" put in Cecily. "We can help, you know."

"Absolutely," said Charley, and Ella nodded her agreement.

"That's not the bug in the soup, is it?" Samantha looked at Cass.

"Then what?" Ella asked. "Are you worried that she's too young?"

"She is young," Cass admitted. "And I was figuring she and Mike would wait a year before getting married. But she's had her life mapped out since she was twelve—baking, husband and babies."

Ella could identify with that. Well, except for the baking part. She'd always wanted a family, complete with husband. "Then what's the bug in the soup?"

Cass frowned. "Dani wants her father to walk her down the aisle."

They all knew how Cass felt about her ex. "Oh," Ella said, at a loss for anything else to say.

"Yeah, *oh*. And it gets better. Guess where my daughter wants him and stepmommy to stay?"

Charley's eyes got so big Ella thought they'd pop out of her head. "Seriously?"

"Pathetically seriously," Cass said.

Cecily picked up the box of chocolates. "You need one of these."

Several chocolates and much commiseration later, the party broke up.

"How are we going to help her get through this?" Cecily asked as the women made their way down Cass's front walk.

"We could beat up Bimbette," Charley cracked. "Or

poison the ex." She shook her head. "Cass is nuts if she goes along with this."

"She'll cave," Samantha predicted. "She likes to pretend she's tough, but when it comes to her kids she's softer than a marshmallow. I think we're going to have to be available 24/7 so she's got someone to vent to."

"For sure," Charley agreed. "I can't imagine being stuck in the same house with your ex." She seemed to realize what she'd said and her face turned as red as a poinsettia. "Sorry, Ella."

"It's okay," Ella said. "And I can tell you from experience, it's going to be hard."

"Hopefully your place will sell soon and you can move on," Samantha told her.

Move on. Move. Ella's holiday spirit suddenly moved on without her. "Hopefully," she echoed.

She said goodbye to the others and returned to her empty dream house.

Jake was at an open mike at the Red Barn so the only one home was Tiny. He greeted her with a woof and a wagging tail.

"I know," she said, rubbing the top of his massive head. "You're ready for some exercise, huh, boy?"

Tiny woofed again and danced back and forth. She opened the front door and he darted out into the night.

Ella followed at a more sedate pace, wondering what it was like to be a dog. Did dogs ever worry? Did they ever question whether they'd made the right choice, done the right thing?

Silly thought, of course. All a dog had to do was enjoy being a dog. Someone else made the tough decisions.

If she and Jake had been Saint Bernards…

She shook her head at her own foolishness and whistled for Tiny to heel. Too bad she couldn't have whistled for Jake to heel before he went bounding off.

Jake wasn't the kind of man to heel. Instead of saying how sorry he was and asking her to forgive him after his fling with that keyboard player, he'd gotten combative. "I'm tired of this shit, Ella. If you can't trust me, then we can't be together."

It had been all downhill from there.

"You don't need a man to be happy," Mims had told her.

Except Ella no longer had a man and she wasn't happy.

She stewed over that for twenty minutes while Tiny sniffed and marked his territory. Then it started to snow and she turned them toward the house. By the time they got back she was in need of some bedtime hot chocolate.

She shed her coat and went to the kitchen to get her last packet of instant cocoa. She was pleasantly surprised to see that Jake had actually cleared his dishes from her vintage red Formica table. And then not surprised to find them in the sink. From the sink to the dishwasher was only one more step. How hard was that? He'd probably left them there, figuring she'd do it for him.

She opened the cupboard beneath the sink to get out the dish soap.

What was this? Water. A little pool of water. How had he managed that?

She mopped it up, then loaded the dishes. Now all that was left was a pot crusted with bits of burned chili. It didn't take long to deduce that the chili was welded to the pan, so after a futile attempt to dislodge it, she added more soap and filled it to the brim with water to soak overnight. Then she rinsed out the sponge and the sink and opened the cupboard to put away the dish soap.

Oh, no. Here was a fresh puddle. Just what they needed right now, a leaky sink. She'd have to call a plumber first thing in the morning. Another bill to split down the middle.

She picked up the phone and called Jake's cell. He was probably up on the bandstand singing about love with that man-stealing keyboard player or sitting at a table nursing a Coke and flirting with some cowgirl poured into tight jeans. That was his life—fun, glamorous and irresponsible. And while he flirted and played his guitar she dealt with leaky faucets.

She was well rid of this relationship. Next time she'd be smart when it came to choosing a man. Maybe she'd even find herself a plumber.

She'd expected her call to roll over to Jake's voice mail but he answered on the second ring. "Everything okay?"

Why did he immediately think something was wrong? Oh, yeah. She was calling him. "The pipe under the kitchen sink is leaking. I just wanted to let you know so you wouldn't use it when you got ho—back." *Home,* that would've been the wrong word to use. This house wasn't a home anymore. "I'll call the plumber tomorrow." Maybe he could squeeze her in that same day. It would make life simpler, since the shop was closed on Mondays.

"Don't do that," Jake said.

"We can't leave it." No one would want to buy a house that was falling apart.

"I know. I'll fix it."

Jake wasn't the world's best handyman. Last summer he'd gone through a pile of two-by-fours trying to fix one broken front-porch step. "I don't think that's a good idea."

"Hey, any guy can fix a leaky pipe," he said. "I'm not paying a plumber."

She sure wasn't going to foot the entire bill. "Okay," she said. "But you'll fix it first thing tomorrow, right?" Their Realtor, Axel Fuchs, had cautioned her to always have the house in tip-top shape. You never knew when a potential buyer would want to look at it.

"I'll do it tomorrow," Jake said. "Don't worry."

Don't worry? That would be possible only if she were a Saint Bernard.

Six

Richard was history. He needed to stay history, and that was exactly what Charley was going to tell him next time he popped up like the Ghost of Christmas Past. It wasn't right to come back into a girl's life after she'd worked through her anger (well, most of it) and gotten on with things. And she'd tell him that, she decided as she put on her makeup.

It was Monday and the restaurant was closed. She never bothered with makeup on Mondays.

She glared at her reflection. *Why are you doing this?*

Pride. She wanted Richard to see her at her best when she told him to set his boxers on fire and get lost.

"You liar," she scolded herself. "You just want him to see you looking your best, period."

Charley tossed her mascara in her makeup basket and left the bathroom.

She always stayed home on Monday mornings. She did her laundry in the morning and fooled around on Facebook. After lunch she'd read or watch the Food Network and then she'd take a run to Bruisers for a quick workout on the treadmill. Or go to the bakery for a little something—always more fun than the treadmill.

No hanging around the house this morning, she told herself. If Richard tried a surprise attack he'd find the fort deserted. She could finish her Christmas shopping. She'd hang out in Gilded Lily's, Hearth and Home and Mountain Treasures. Oooh, and for lunch she'd indulge in a bratwurst at Big Brats. Then maybe she'd stop in at Sweet Dreams and say hi to Samantha. Or wander over to Gingerbread Haus and treat herself to a gingerbread boy.

She donned the knitted hat Ella had made for her and grabbed her winter coat.

And opened the door just in time to see Richard coming up the front steps, bundled up for winter in a parka and ski cap and carrying a thermos. She didn't know which irritated her more, the fact that he'd ignored her command to bug off or that at the sight of him her heart lost its groove and gave a nervous skip. "What are you doing here?"

"Kidnapping you."

"That's against the law. Anyway, you're not big enough to overpower me," she added, and hoped that hurt. She shut the door after herself and started past him.

"Kidnapping you to go on a sleigh ride," he said, ignoring her barb.

She stopped in her tracks. A sleigh ride. Other than chocolate, there was nothing more tempting. Sleigh rides were becoming a popular tourist activity in Icicle Falls. Ever since she and Richard had moved to town, Charley had wanted to take one, but somehow she'd never found time. There was something so romantic about a sleigh ride.

There would be nothing romantic about taking one

with her ex. "Currier's doesn't offer sleigh rides on week-days."

"They do this week. I made special arrangements with Kirk Jones."

Special arrangements. What strings had Richard pulled to get the owner of the Christmas tree farm to harness up his horses on a Monday?

Richard held up the thermos. "Hot chocolate with pep-permint schnapps."

"I don't care if it's champagne."

"That's for brunch. At the Firs."

The Firs was an exclusive resort compound that ex-tended for acres and included everything from hiking trails to outdoor hot tubs and pools surrounded by moun-tain rock. Cabins were outfitted with luxury furnishings and the dining hall provided feasts prepared by the kind of top chefs Charley only dreamed of hiring.

Now she was doubly tempted.

Don't do it.

"All I'm asking for is a chance. Just give me today."

One day, that was all he was asking.

She sighed. "Why did you have to come back?"

"Because I need you."

"You didn't need me a year ago when you were boink-ing Ariel in the bar."

Richard grimaced. "Charley, I've changed. Let me prove it."

Eating at the Firs was the equivalent of eating at Canlis in Seattle. She had no intention of getting back together with Richard, but that didn't mean she couldn't use him. Just deserts, she concluded. She'd use him like he'd once used her. Then he could see how it felt.

"Okay, I'll go," she said. "It's not going to do you any good, but I'll go."

He grinned like she'd just offered to sleep with him. "It's a beginning."

Currier's Tree Farm was rustic and picturesque. The snow-frosted split rail fence along the property was draped with cedar swags and red bows. The big tree in the yard was adorned with lights and huge colored balls and a shawl of snow. Behind the house, the tree farm stretched out with every imaginable kind of holiday tree. Off to the left she saw a stand where visitors could enjoy complimentary hot cider and to the right sat a big, red barn. There, in front of it, stood an old-fashioned sleigh decked out in cedar swags and ribbon. The chestnut draft horses looked equally festive, with jingle bells in their harnesses, their manes and tails braided with red ribbons. One of them stamped a foot. Another let out a soft nicker.

A lean, gray-haired man in winter garb came out of the barn and waved at them. "You're right on time," he called to Richard, and motioned for them to join him. "Got a perfect day for a sleigh ride," he greeted Charley.

"It was nice of you to open for us," Charley said.

He grinned, a big, broad smile that filled his face. "Anything for lovers."

Lovers! Was that what Richard had told him? "Not exactly," Charley said, frowning. "We're exes."

That made Kirk Jones's bushy gray eyebrows shoot up and Richard's mouth turn down.

"Oh, well," Kirk said, and then cleared his throat. "It's a great day for a sleigh ride."

"No matter who it's with," Charley said, ignoring Richard's helping hand and climbing into the sleigh.

Kirk had provided a plaid wool blanket and Richard spread it across her legs.

"Thanks. Lover," she said with some asperity.

"You can't blame me because people jump to conclusions," he said.

"Did you give him a little push?"

"No. I told him the truth."

Charley cocked an eyebrow. "Oh? And what was that?"

"That this is for a special lady. No lie." He uncorked the thermos and pulled two disposable cups from his coat pocket.

As he poured she remembered how good he'd always been at romantic gestures—creating a dish and naming it after her, taking her over the mountains to Seattle one year to look at Christmas lights and then spending the night in a downtown hotel, hiding a bit of anniversary bling under her pillow.

What romantic things had he done for Ariel?

He handed over her hot chocolate. Then he poured himself a cup and capped the thermos. "To new beginnings," he said, and raised his cup to her.

She said nothing in return, just took a sip and looked away.

"Or the hope of new beginnings," Richard amended.

In your dreams, Charley thought, and downed some more.

Kirk was up in the sleigh now. He clicked his tongue and gave the horses' rumps a gentle slap with the reins and they lurched forward.

Good thing her cocoa was half-gone, or she'd have been wearing it. And that would have been a shame because it was delicious. This was no instant stuff, she could tell. It had been made with cream and fine Dutch chocolate. Chocolate, the way to a girl's heart.

But not this girl's. Richard would never find his way back to hers, not even with a GPS made of solid Sweet Dreams dark.

Still, she decided, she might as well enjoy the ride.

There was plenty to enjoy. The sleigh ride was everything it should be. They wooshed past fir and pine trees clad in frosty white and open fields that beckoned them to come play in the snow, and all the while the sleigh bells on the horses' harnesses jingled. The air was crisp and Charley could see her breath but the cocoa and the blanket kept her warm. Meanwhile, Richard was looking at her like he was a starving man and she a six-course meal. The best salve in the world for wounded pride.

Except it had been Richard who'd wounded her pride in the first place. Starvation was too good for him.

"This is perfect, isn't it?" he said, and placed an arm around her shoulders.

She slid out from under it. "Almost."

He was smart enough not to ask what kept it from being perfect.

They turned onto a path that led down a small incline and took them under a canopy of snowy tree boughs. This was magical. Charley sighed and leaned back against the seat cushions.

Up front Kirk was crooning a song about lovely weather for a sleigh ride.

"With you," Richard whispered. "Aw, Charley, there's no one like you."

"You're right," she agreed.

"I'm just sorry I had to learn that the hard way."

"Yes, you are a sorry man," she said, making him frown. And that made her snicker.

After a brunch that involved several glasses of champagne she'd switched from snickering to giggling.

"I drank too much," she realized as he drove her home.

"Maybe a little," he said.

"Why did you let me drink so much champagne?" She groaned. "I'm going to have the mother of all headaches later."

"Well, we can fix that," he said. "You just need some water, and lucky for you I've got Perrier."

She eyed him. "You thought of everything, didn't you?"

"And then some," he replied with a smile.

She shivered, but not because of what his smile did to her. She'd gotten chilled on the sleigh ride, that was the problem.

"How about I build you a fire?" he offered as they pulled up in front of the house that used to be theirs.

All she needed was him in her house building a fire. "I don't think so. I have things to do." Except after their gargantuan meal and those glasses of champagne, all she wanted to do was take a nap. She got out of the car before he could come around and let her out. "Thanks, Richard," she said, and shut the door.

He got out, too, and held up the green bottle. "Water. Remember?"

"I think I can manage to turn on the faucet."

"This tastes better," he said, and followed her up the walk. Like a bad smell.

She opened the door and before she could tell him goodbye and close it in his face he'd slipped in.

* * *

Ella returned home from running errands to find a village of dishes in the sink and the water still turned off. Jake's voice and the sound of his guitar strumming drifted down to her. Great. He'd forgotten to fix the sink.

She marched up the stairs and into his room. There he sat on the bed, wearing jeans and T-shirt, his feet bare—a gorgeous country balladeer with tousled dark hair, looking good enough for a CD cover and completely oblivious to the rest of the world. Once upon a time Ella had thought that was so cute. Now she just thought it was irresponsible.

Tiny, who'd been lying at his feet, enthralled, bounded up at the sight of her and came over, tail wagging. Jake's singing stopped and his hands froze on the guitar strings. He turned his head, his expression both guilty and surprised. "You're home already?"

"It's 5:20," she informed him. "You said you were going to fix the sink today."

"I was. I am."

"Well, it's not fixed. I'm going to call a plumber."

He set the guitar on the bed. "I'll get the stuff right now and have it fixed in an hour."

"The hardware store closes in ten minutes."

"I can make it."

She frowned but said nothing. She knew she shouldn't have trusted him to take care of this. Thank God no one was coming to see the house tonight.

By the time he returned from the hardware store she'd changed into her jeans and a sweater and was heating up leftover chicken soup.

"That smells good," he said.

He'd always loved her chicken soup. These days, though, they didn't share food.

"Fix the sink and I'll give you some."

He grinned and spread his tools on the floor—a wrench, a flashlight, some sort of hose and a bowl he'd gotten from the cupboard.

"That's all you need?" she asked.

"It's a simple job. All I gotta do is replace the flex hose for the cold-water line. I'll need you to hold the flashlight, though."

Assuming she'd be there (like he'd always assumed), he opened the doors below the sink, got on his knees and crawled in, taking the bowl with him. She turned off the soup and picked up the flashlight.

"What's the bowl for?" she asked, trying to ignore the sight of his finely crafted behind.

"To catch whatever water is left in the line. Hey, where are you?"

"I'm here." She got down on her knees, too, and aimed the flashlight at the pipe.

"I need you to come in here farther. Shine the light on the hose. Right there."

She came in farther. And now there they were, side by side under the sink, closer than they'd been in a year. His spicy aftershave reached out to her, bringing back memories of his kisses. She could see the play of his muscles as he worked the wrench. She'd never realized how quickly it got hot under a kitchen sink.

Now the old hose was off. "Hand me the other hose," he said.

Feeling a little like a nurse in an operating room, she handed it over. "Scalpel, doctor," she cracked.

"That's me. Dr. Fix-it."

Too bad he couldn't have fixed what was wrong with them.

It didn't take long to connect the new flex hose, but that was long enough for her to entertain all kinds of ridiculous thoughts that a divorced woman shouldn't invite into her mind, at least not about her ex.

He gave the wrench one final twist. "There, just like new." Now he turned to her and his easy smile gave way to something else, a look she knew well, one that always led straight to the bedroom. "Anyone ever tell you that you look good under a sink?"

The gift of blarney. Jake O'Brien had it in spades.

"Anyone ever tell you you're full of it?" she replied, and backed out.

Tiny, who had been sitting there watching the proceedings, gave a woof. Then they heard the front door opening and the sound of voices drifted into the kitchen. With another woof, Tiny was off down the hall.

"Anyone here?" called Axel Fuchs, their Realtor. "Tiny, down!"

Ella stared at Jake in wide-eyed panic. "Axel!" She scrambled to her feet and hurried down the hall.

Sure enough, there he was, suave as usual in his business clothes and camel-hair overcoat. Axel was a tall, slim man with blond hair and strong Germanic features. He always dressed to the nines and could have posed for the cover of *Gentleman's Quarterly.* Ella was very aware of her grubby jeans and messy hair. Even more so looking at the well-dressed couple he had in tow. They appeared to be in their late forties and practically smelled of money. A potential sale.

And there was Jake in the messy kitchen with tools on

the floor and a dead kitchen hose. She'd get him to ditch all that while the couple was looking around upstairs. She thought of the rumpled, unmade bed Jake had been sitting on. Ugh. Still, it was better than letting them see the kitchen mess.

Tiny was doing his best to welcome the newcomers. Ella grabbed him by the collar. "No, Tiny. Down. Don't worry, he won't bite," she assured the woman, who had ducked behind her husband.

"But does he chew?" the man asked, looking around suspiciously, as if checking for damage.

"No, he's a well-behaved dog," Ella said.

The woman was relaxing now. "Something smells good."

"Oh, I was just heating up some soup," Ella said, smoothing her hair. *And repairing our leaky faucet.*

It was so embarrassing getting caught like this. Normally she wouldn't have even been here. Neither of them would. Axel preferred the owners to be gone when he showed a house. Why hadn't he let them know he was coming?

"I love to cook," the woman volunteered. "Let's see the kitchen first." And before Ella could stop her, she was off down the hall.

Once they were in the kitchen, Ms. Potential Buyer came to a halt at the sight of Jake gathering up his tools and the dead flex hose. "Oh."

Oh...no. "Just a little leak," Ella said, willing Jake to take his hose and scram.

The man, who'd said nothing so far, grunted. Ella didn't know much about real estate but she did know that grunts were not good.

"Let's go see the rest of the house," Axel said smoothly. "It really is in excellent condition."

"Yeah, I can tell," the man said, and that was worse than the grunt.

They went down the hall and Ella shot an angry look at Jake.

"What?"

"You had all day to fix that sink," she hissed.

"I was working on a song."

"Well, I hope it was a good one because it might have cost us a sale."

"There'll be other buyers," he said.

"When? Darn it, Jake! That was the only thing I asked you to do. Why couldn't you have done it?"

"I did. Just now."

There was no point in talking to him. He was hopeless. She hurried after Axel and the couple. They were in the living room now, looking around. "We recently painted in here," she said.

"Mmm," the woman murmured.

"We've taken excellent care of the house," Ella continued.

The husband responded with another grunt and Axel quickly said, "Let me show you the bedrooms." His clients started up the stairs and Ella got ready to follow them. "Why don't you wait down here," he suggested.

"Oh." Feeling frustrated and foolish, Ella sat on the couch with an issue of *Martha Stewart Living* and hoped against hope that the couple would forget what they'd seen in the kitchen. They probably wouldn't, though, thanks to Jake. At this rate they were going to be here forever, stuck in limbo.

Axel and the buyers came back downstairs and took

another trip out to the kitchen. The woman was smiling politely, but her husband looked like he'd had a close encounter with the Grinch. Another five minutes and they were out the door.

"I'll be right with you," Axel called after them.

Ella was at his side in a minute. "Did they like it?"

"Most of it. I'm afraid the leaky sink didn't make a good impression. Neither did Jake's bedroom. Ella, everyone wants to buy something that looks like a picture from a magazine. You two have to keep on top of things."

That stung. She was *trying* to keep on top of things. It was that ball and chain she was no longer married to who was messing up her perfect house. "I have been," she protested. "I had no way of knowing the sink was going to break. And I didn't know you were coming."

"I told Jake I was, this afternoon," Axel said.

"You did?" Jake had known all afternoon and he hadn't gotten the sink fixed? She was going to strangle him with a string of Christmas lights.

"He didn't tell you?"

Ella shook her head.

Axel frowned. "That guy is a disaster."

Ella sighed. "He is."

"What did you ever see in him?" Axel wondered, and then before she could say anything, added, "I'll see what I can do with Mr. and Mrs. Winters and get back to you."

She thanked him and shut the door with a weary sigh.

Now Jake was coming down the hallway. "Well, did they like it?"

"They might have, if they hadn't seen the leaky sink," Ella said frostily.

"Hey, sinks leak."

"Yes, they do. And Realtors call."

His cheeks took on a ruddy tinge.

Ella pointed a finger at him. "You knew we had people coming to look at the house. Axel called you this afternoon."

"It was late afternoon."

"That is beside the point," Ella said, throwing up her hands in frustration.

"No, it's not. It must've been four when he called. I was right in the middle of working on a song. I didn't want to lose it."

She was about to lose it. "So you just played on. What did you think, Jake, that the fairies were going to come and fix the sink and wash the pots and pans?"

"I was going to get to it," he said sullenly.

"But you didn't, and that probably cost us a sale." Ella marched back to the kitchen and Jake followed, with Tiny bringing up the rear, whining.

Ella pulled her pan of soup off the stove. "Here, you can eat all of this. I'm not hungry anymore."

Now Jake was beside her, "El, I'm sorry. I should have fixed the sink right away."

He should have done a lot of things. Ella kept her back to him.

"I really did lose track of time."

"Oh, and that makes it okay? If you'd just fixed the sink this morning it would've been done. Were you writing this morning, too?"

"No."

Ha!

"I was working on arrangements for the band."

"The band," she growled. Of course, the band and his home-wrecking keyboard player came first. It was all Ella could do not to dump the pan of chicken soup over his head.

Her cell phone called to her from the table in the entryway where she'd dumped her purse and she hurried to dig it out. "I'll bet that's Axel. Maybe he's talked that couple into making an offer." She picked up just before the call could go to voice mail and said a breathless hello.

"Sorry, Ella, it's a no-go."

She was going to cry. She went back to the living room and fell onto the couch. "I thought they liked it. At least the woman did."

"They did, but not enough to make a offer. Don't worry, we'll find you a buyer."

At the rate they were going, that could be years from now. She scowled at the copy of Jake's favorite book sitting on the coffee table. *Do What You Love and the Money Will Follow.* How about do what you promised and a sale will follow?

If she stayed here with Jake much longer she was going to kill him. They had to get the house sold and move on with their lives. "What can I do to make this place sell?"

"Keep it looking good."

"I will," she promised. "Anything else?"

"Have dinner with me tomorrow and we'll brainstorm," Axel suggested. "You need to get out, get away from that loser."

Now Jake was in the living room. He was a loser. It would make her life so much easier if he looked like one.

"Dinner sounds good," she said.

"Dinner?" Jake echoed. "With who?"

"I'll make reservations at Schwangau for Wednesday," Axel said.

"Schwangau sounds great."

Jake frowned. "You're not going out with that fat-headed wuss, are you?"

"Fine. I'll pick you up at seven."

"Perfect," Ella said.

"That guy is as far from perfect as a man can get," Jake muttered.

"See you tomorrow," Ella said, and Jake made a disgusting noise as she hung up. "Oh, very mature," she said.

"Yeah, as mature as you going out with that twit just because you're mad about the sink."

"Yes, I am mad about the sink but that has nothing to do with why I'm going out with Axel."

"Then why are you going out with him?" Jake demanded.

"None of your business," she told him. "We're not married anymore and I can do what I want. And at least I waited until we were divorced to do what I want."

"So did I! But I'm still not getting to do what I want, 'cause what I want is— Oh, never mind," he ended grumpily, and stomped off upstairs.

What had he been about to say? *What* did he want?

What did it matter? Ella picked up her magazine and stared unseeingly at it.

Tiny came over, sat on the floor and laid his big head in her lap. "I know," she said as she petted him. "It makes you sad when we fight."

Tiny belched and licked his chops. The belch smelled suspiciously like chili.

"Has Daddy been feeding you chili again?" Ella asked.

Tiny whined and thumped his tail.

She frowned. Tiny had been gaining weight. There could be only one person responsible for that and it wasn't her. "He's not supposed to give you people food. I'll bet he's been sneaking you cookies, too."

Tiny wisely kept his doggy mouth shut. Instead, he just looked at her with his big brown eyes.

"Don't worry, you're not in trouble," she told him. "I know whose fault it is."

The same man whose fault it was that their potential buyers had decided to take their money elsewhere. Jake O'Brien was a thorn in her side.

A sudden memory of the two of them picnicking up at Lost Bride Falls the day he proposed made tears sting her eyes. She'd thought she'd seen the ghost of the lost bride, who was a local legend. It was an experience everyone in Icicle Falls knew portended engagement. And Jake had been ready with her ring in his pocket.

"Marry me, El. Make my day, make my life. Say yes."

She'd said, "Yes, yes, yes!" and they'd sealed the deal with a kiss. That had been the happiest day of her life.

Now it seemed like a million years ago. Jake O'Brien wasn't a thorn in her side. He was a thorn in her heart, and the sooner she pulled him out, the better.

Jake kicked his pile of dirty clothes across the floor. He'd meant to get that sink fixed before Ella got home and before Axel the twit came over, but he really had been absorbed in a new song. Ella knew how he got when he was busy songwriting. Why hadn't she believed him? Hell, why didn't she *ever* believe him?

The answer to that could be summed up in two words. Her mother. Lily Swan had never liked him from the start. His family were simple people who hunted and fished and cleaned their own houses, and that didn't make them cool enough for old Ms. America's Top-Model-Who-Never-

Was. She'd obviously wanted her daughter to marry some jet-setter and not a country boy from Eastern Washington, so she'd immediately set out to break them up.

And that was a downright sin because he and Ella had been happy together. They were meant to be together. He would've made it as a country singer in time and Ella could have lived that fancy life. He'd have been able to buy her anything she wanted.

She'd believed that once. She obviously didn't anymore. Now, in her eyes, he was nothing but a skirt-chasing, lazy loser. Thanks, mother-in-law, for poisoning the waters. Thanks for ruining our lives. Thanks for putting that stuck-up nose of yours where it didn't belong.

Too bad he hadn't hit the big time yet. He'd have sent good old Mom on a nice long trip—to the edge of the world. And then pushed her off.

The thought made him smile. Then it made him think. Then it made him chuckle as he picked up his guitar. "Mama, I'm about to write you a song for Christmas."

Seven

Dani still hadn't found lodging for Mason and his child bride, and Cass was feeling the pressure. Every sigh, every accusing you-could-fix-this look from her daughter sent guilt and anger racing through her veins. She finally did what any sensible woman would do. She called her mother.

"And now Dani wants me to find room for them at our place," she finished miserably.

"Well," her mother said, "I think you have two choices. You can refuse, which will make you feel better…for about two minutes, or you can squeeze us all in and make your daughter happy."

Cass sighed. "This is not what I envisioned when I thought of Dani getting married."

"He would have been at the wedding, Cassie," her mother said reasonably

"I never dreamed she'd want him to walk her down the aisle!"

"Not want her father to walk her down the aisle?"

"Her mostly absent father."

"Her father all the same."

"Sad but true. So, okay, somewhere in the back of my mind I might have known that was a possibility, but I never figured I'd have Father of the Year and Bimbette staying in my house."

"Life rarely goes according to plan," said Mom.

Maybe that was why Cass had become a baker. Baking was easy. You followed the recipe and everything came out just as it should. Perfect.

There was no recipe for a perfect family, though. Unlike flour, sugar, butter and eggs, people were unpredictable and often uncooperative. Rather like she was being right now.

"It's only for a couple of days," her mother said. "If I were you I'd play nice."

Play nice. Ugh. Cass ended the call and went back inside the bakery, where Dani was in the kitchen, putting the finishing touches on a special-order gingerbread house. They'd been working together in strained silence since 7:00 a.m. Heck, they'd been working together in strained silence since Saturday. It was almost ten now, and in another few minutes, they'd open and be busy with customers for the rest of the day. Now was the time to settle this.

Cass's heart began to race. She didn't want to do this. She *so* didn't want to do this.

She took a deep breath and plunged in. "Okay, I give. Call your father and tell him Hotel Wilkes has a vacancy."

Dani's expression went from glum to thrilled in a millisecond. "Really?"

Cass frowned. "Really. God knows where we'll put them, but we'll find a place somewhere." Maybe at the bakery, in the walk-in fridge.

Dani dropped her icing bag and rushed across the

kitchen to hug Cass. "Thank you! You're the best mother in the whole world."

Or the stupidest.

Dani grabbed her smartphone and made a call. It didn't take a genius to guess who she was calling. Sure enough. "Daddy? I've got great news!"

For someone, but not for Cass. Oh, well. Onward and upward. "Now we can start planning," she said after Dani ended her conversation with her father.

"That'll be fun," Dani said.

Yes, it would, and the fun of planning this big event with her daughter would make up for the irritation of having to host her former husband. "To start, we'll need to get invitations out as of yesterday. I'm thinking we should close a little early and run over to Wenatchee."

"Oh, we're not going to do invitations," Dani said breezily.

"No invitations?" How did you have a wedding with no invitations?

"We're doing evites."

"Email invitations?" Was that tacky or was Cass just getting old? No, forty-two was not old. So that left tacky.

"It's quicker," Dani said. "Anyway, most everyone already knows."

"Well, one less thing to do. Good idea," Cass said, going with the flow. "There's still the flowers, though, and the cake and of course—"

Before she could even mention the gown Dani said, "I was thinking cupcakes."

"Cupcakes," Cass repeated. Her daughter wanted cupcakes for a wedding in three and a half weeks. At their busiest time of the year. A cake Cass could do in her sleep, but cupcakes, the little devils, were much more labor-intensive. At least they would be for her, because she'd want to make each one special. And where one slice of cake was sufficient for the average wedding guest, cupcakes went down fast and easy and few people would eat just one, which meant she'd need to bake and decorate a lot of them. "Dani girl, you know what things are like around here right now."

Dani bit her lip. "I really wanted cupcakes."

She hated to disappoint her daughter, but... "I'm just not sure," Cass began.

"Okay, fine," Dani snapped, and marched off to unlock the door for their customers. "It's my wedding, but do what you want."

If Cass was doing what she wanted, Mason and his child bride would be off the guest list. Cass frowned, grabbed the icing bag and went to work finishing the trim on the gingerbread house.

Where had that outburst come from, anyway? She'd bent over backward for her daughter, practically turning herself into a human pretzel, but that hadn't been enough.

Cass knew about the bridezilla phenomenon, but she'd never expected to experience it. Dani was a sweet-tempered (well, usually) cooperative, responsible girl. Correction: Dani used to be a sweet-tempered, cooperative, responsible girl. It looked like that was about to change. And they hadn't even started talking about food, flowers or the bridal gown. Or the budget, which—due to the unexpected early advent of this wedding—wasn't exactly going to be huge. What fireworks lay in store if they clashed over the budget?

The gingerbread house was now complete, temptingly decorated with icing and a lavish variety of candy. The stained-glass sugar windows gave the illusion of a cozy fire within. For a moment, Cass imagined herself safely huddled inside it, nibbling at its walls in peace and quiet.

Then the door of her gingerbread sanctuary opened and in came a gingerbread man who looked suspiciously like Mason, with a lady in tow. And here came a girl, stamping her little gingerbread foot and demanding her mother bake enough cupcakes to feed all of Icicle Falls.

Cass shook her head to dislodge the horrible vision. Ugh. Where were those sugarplums when you wanted them?

Wednesday morning Ella was just finishing her remer-chandizing, putting back the blouses her last customer had left in the dressing room, when Charley came into Gilded Lily's to browse.

"Are you shopping for any special occasion?" Ella asked.

Ella loved helping women look their best, and Charley, with her long legs and size-eight figure made that fun, rather like playing dolls on a large scale. Ella couldn't say the same for all her customers. Some of them were a real fashion challenge. Still, she tried hard to help everyone find colors and styles that would flatter them, and women who entered Gilded Lily's left feeling good about themselves.

"Not really," Charley said. "I'm just looking. Maybe a sweater. Or a new blouse to wear with my black pencil skirt when I'm at the restaurant."

Only a couple of weeks ago Charley was saying she didn't need any new clothes. "Who's there around here to impress?" she'd joked.

Who, indeed? "Um, you haven't seen Richard, have you?" Ella ventured. Okay, that was none of her business.

But…she and Charley had become good friends since Ella joined Cass's chick-flick nights. Didn't friends watch out for one another?

Charley suddenly became busy inspecting a white silk blouse. "He took me to the Firs."

"Oh."

"He claims he's sorry. He wants to try again."

If Jake asked to try again, Ella wondered, would she give him a second chance?

"Of course I'm not going to."

"That's probably a good idea," Ella said. "If he cheated once he'd cheat again."

Charley took the blouse off the rack. "Do you think people can change?"

If they could, wouldn't Jake have dismantled his flirt mechanism? Wouldn't he have been able to stay true to her? And wouldn't he have proved he was serious about settling down by getting a real job somewhere when the music store closed instead of teaching a handful of students in the afternoons and playing in his band? Teaching teenage boys with dreams of getting on *American Idol* was barely letting him make a living, and in ten years he'd probably be doing the same thing—playing his guitar and helping his father in the family orchard during apple harvest season. By sixty he'd be playing on street corners in Seattle.

Or Nashville. He was still determined to write a hit song and get to Music City. Once upon a time they'd both dreamed of going there. He would make it big. They'd buy an old house somewhere in town that she'd decorate to the hilt, and when he went on tour she'd come along.

But then she'd grown up.

"Some people change," she said. They put away their little-girl dreams and got practical.

Charley nodded thoughtfully. "I think I'll try this on."

It would look lovely on her, especially if she put up her hair and showed off her long Audrey Hepburn neck. Ella handed her a necklace of freshwater gray pearls. "This would accessorize nicely. Add that black skirt and some heels and you'll be good to go."

Charley took the necklace. "Why not?"

A couple of minutes later, she stepped out of the changing room to model for Ella. "Oh, yes," Ella approved.

"That's what I thought," Charley said with a smile. "Sold. I'll wear this to work tonight."

Where Richard was sure to put in an appearance. *Oh, Charley, be careful.* Should she say that? Maybe not. But she wanted to. She bit her lip as she rang up the sale.

"I know what you're thinking," Charley said.

"That I don't want to see you get hurt?"

"Don't worry. I have no intention of getting hurt."

Ella nodded. Charley was a strong woman, and once she made up her mind it stayed made up. But the best of intentions could easily get lost in a romantic fog. She hoped Charley's didn't.

She left with her fashion finds and the store fell quiet. Ella treated herself to a ten-minute break and pulled a Vanessa Valentine romance novel out from under the counter.

She should've been able to jump right into the story because when she'd stopped reading she'd left Ophelia and the duke caught in a compromising situation. But the words on the page refused to register. Instead, Charley's question kept repeating itself over and over in her mind. *Do you think people can change?*

She finally gave up on the book and decided she needed to make a new window display.

She'd just finished when her mother stopped by. Mims ran the shop on Sundays, so Ella could have the day off, but she also came in a couple of times during the week. Today she was all in black, except for the brown cashmere coat she wore over her V-neck sweater and wool pants. She'd accented the outfit with an Hermès scarf and gold jewelry. Between the outfit and her perfectly highlighted blond hair, she looked like a modern-day Grace Kelly.

"Nice display." She nodded at Ella's handiwork. "When did you do that?"

"Just now. It's been quiet."

"The calm before the weekend tourist storm," Mims said. "I see someone bought the pearl necklace." Mims saw everything. "You might want to put out another one so we don't have a bare space."

Of course, she should've done that right away. Good as she was, she always managed to forget something. She hurried to the back room to get another necklace out of their stock. This time she chose a multibead red one that was ideal for the holidays and bound to sell in a hurry.

Mims followed her. "I thought you might like to go to Schwangau tonight. I hear they have a new vegetarian menu."

"I can't tonight," Ella said.

Her mother frowned. "Why not? You certainly don't want to stay in the house with…that person."

Her mother had had trouble remembering Jake's name for the first six months they were together. He was James,

Jack and sometimes even George. Now Mims seemed to take delight in not having to say his name at all. Ella wasn't sure why, but it bugged her.

"I'm not going to be in the house with Jake," she said, emphasizing his name. "But I do have plans for dinner."

"Oh?" Now Mims's eyes had an inquisitive glint. "Who?"

"Axel Fuchs."

"Axel." Mims gave this information great consideration. "He's not bad-looking." The way Mims said this made it sound as if, for once, her daughter had managed to show good taste. "I hear he might run for mayor next year." That, along with Axel's more metrosexual style, would be a winning combination as far as Mims was concerned.

Was it a winning combination for Ella? She wasn't sure. But he was nice-looking, and going out beat staying home and feeling frustrated with her current state of affairs.

"He drives a Lexus," Mims continued.

Well, that settled it. Axel was the catch of the year. Ella couldn't hide her disgust as she hung up the necklace.

"There's nothing wrong with dating a man who's going somewhere," Mims said.

"I don't know if this is a date. We're going out to talk about ways I can make the house more appealing so it'll sell."

"What a flimsy excuse," Mims scoffed. "Of course it's a date. What are you wearing? Not that outfit, I hope. You look like a shopgirl."

She *was* a shopgirl. Ella shrugged but didn't bother to comment.

"Where's he taking you?"

"Schwangau."

Mims nodded approvingly. "You can try the wild mushroom lasagna and tell me how it is. And wear the ABS trapeze necklace dress I got you for Christmas."

"I was thinking of something more casual," Ella said.

"Not too casual. It only inspires men to pinch pennies."

"I don't need a man to spend a fortune on me," Ella protested.

Her mother gave her a long-suffering look. "And that is exactly what got you into the mess you're in now. Be a little wiser this time around, baby."

And marry a millionaire. Or a prince from some small European country.

Ella sighed inwardly. Her mother still had hopes that some of her glamour would rub off on Ella, but it was too late. If Mims had wanted to turn her into a jet-setter, she should never have settled in a small town.

When Mims had inherited the house in Icicle Falls, she'd expected to use it as a mere way station in life while she recovered from what she'd referred to as a slight career setback (translation: aging), but she'd stayed too long and Ella had become too attached to the town. She'd tried to rectify her mistake (and find her footing in the world of glam once more) by hauling Ella to New York for fashion week on a regular basis, but New York had been too big and too crowded for Ella. Mims finally realized her daughter wasn't enjoying those trips and abandoned the effort, taking her buying trips alone or with her fashionista sidekick, Gregory.

"Ella, where are you?"

Ella dragged herself back to the present with a blink. "I'm here."

"That boy will be a millionaire by the time he's fifty," Mims predicted. "You could still land on your feet."

"I don't even know if I like him...that way."

"At least give it a chance. This isn't New York, baby. Your options are limited."

Rather like Mims's had become since settling here. Why on earth didn't her mother move to New York or Paris or...someplace?

Ella knew the answer to that. It was because of her. Mims had her faults, but she took her mothering seriously, and living far from her daughter had never been a consideration. If Ella wanted to live in a small town, then Lily Swan would live in a small town. And make regular trips to Seattle, the East Coast and Europe. The only downside to all of that was, every time she returned, she became less enchanted with Icicle Falls. She had a condo in Seattle. She could live there. Ella had once pointed this out.

"Not until I see you well established," Mims had said. "What kind of mother would I be if I just ran off and lived for myself?"

The answer to that was easy—a happy one.

"I know you'll have a fabulous time tonight," Mims said. "And I can hardly wait to hear about it." She kissed her daughter on the cheek and left, the fragrance of her perfume lingering like a nosy ghost.

"I *will* have a fabulous time," Ella decided. And she wouldn't think about Jake even once.

Could a person change?

Eight

Jake saw the silver Lexus pull up in front of the house and frowned. Axel Fuchs was a predator in a silk tie, and it wasn't hard to guess who his prey was. So he drove a Lexus, so what? He had to be at least ten years older than Ella and he looked like a Viking reject—blond and blue-eyed, but too skinny and wimpy to be allowed to go pillaging with the big boys. What would any woman see in him? Oh, yeah, the silk tie and Lexus.

Naturally, he was taking her to Schwangau. It wasn't as hip or fun as Zelda's but it was the most expensive restaurant in town. Overpriced, if you asked Jake, especially the beer. Who cared if it was imported?

He had taken Ella there for their anniversary once and she'd raved over it like it was Disneyland. White linen tablecloths on the tables, soft lighting provided by little candles that made it hard to read the menu.

"You're paying for the atmosphere," Ella had said, taking in the dark wood paneling and the paintings on the walls.

Atmosphere. Why was that a big deal to women? Jake had never understood. He was more a burger-and-fries kind of guy. Or a picnic kind of guy. On sunny Sunday afternoons they used to pack sandwiches and chips and a couple of apples and find a spot on Icicle Creek. They'd spend the day on the bank, dangling their feet in the water and talking. Sometimes he'd throw his guitar over his shoulder and take it along and sing to her. She'd loved that. Or so she'd said.

Axel was coming up the walk now. How much had he paid for that suit? Ella would be able to guess right down to the penny. She loved nice clothes and knew how to dress, but she never got that it wasn't the clothes that caught a man's eye. It was the woman wearing them.

Clothes make the man—whoever said that was wrong.

The doorbell rang and Jake considered letting Axel stand out there in the cold and keep ringing. Maybe his finger would freeze off. Maybe he'd give up and go away. Not likely, though.

Jake was halfway to the door when Ella came running down the stairs, Tiny racing behind her. "I'll get it."

Scowling, Jake went back into the living room and picked up his guitar.

He started strumming. Loudly.

He could still hear Axel say, "Ella, you look incredible."

Like that was unusual? Ella never looked anything *but* incredible. Tonight she'd taken extra care—had her hair down (all that gorgeous long hair he loved to play with) and wore what women called a little black dress along with black heels. How women could run or even walk in those was a mystery. But man, a chick in heels—what a turn-on.

And she was wearing them for Axel. Jake strummed

harder. But he still heard Ella say, "Thanks, Axel. It's always nice when a man notices how you dress."

Jake always noticed how she dressed. And then he thought about undressing her. He'd lay odds that Fuchs was thinking the same thing, the bastard.

The door shut and they were gone. Tiny lumbered into the room and sat down at Jake's feet. Actually, sat on one of them. That foot would be numb in a matter of minutes. If only Jake could numb his heart as quickly.

He strummed a C 2 chord. "Wish my heart was ice." Followed by an A minor seventh. "Then I couldn't feel." The chords flowed and the words poured out. "How long will this hurt go on? How long before I heal?" Dumb question. He would never heal.

He shoved his guitar back in its case with enough force to make the strings twang in protest.

Ella studied the menu. Everything here at Schwangau was expensive, even the schnitzel. Of all the restaurants in town, this was Mims's favorite. Ella's, too, although on the rare occasion she went out to eat she usually went to Zelda's—partly because she enjoyed the food but mostly because Charley was a friend and she liked to support her friends. So, this was a rare treat.

Axel was making a great show of selecting their wine. "Since we're in a German restaurant we should start with a Rhine wine, don't you think?" he asked her.

"That sounds fine," she agreed, although it would probably be wasted on her.

She was no connoisseur. Other than an occasional huckleberry martini at Zelda's or some rum-spiked eggnog at Christmas, she drank soda pop or juice. She supposed it would come across as unsophisticated if she confessed that to Axel. And if he wanted to spend money on an expensive bottle of wine, she'd let him. In fact, if he was going to spend that much on wine, then she certainly wasn't going to look for the cheapest meal on the menu.

Once the wine was ordered, he leaned back in his chair with a satisfied smile. "I think you'll love this. It's unpretentious but tasty, and a good way to begin the evening."

"I'm sure I will," she lied.

"It's a favorite of mine. There's nothing better after a long day than relaxing to some jazz with a glass of wine."

Jazz. Ick. Ella was more of a country music girl.

"Jazz is the true American music," Axel said.

"So is country," she added, trying to keep up her end of the conversation.

"Not very sophisticated," he said with a shake of his head. "Twang, beat-up trucks and beer. Oh, that's right. Jake plays in a country band, doesn't he?"

Jake had a beat-up truck, but he sang hip country and he drank organic fruit juice. Even at the clubs he played he stuck to soft drinks. "Booze and music don't go together well," he said. "Makes you sloppy. Anyway, if a guy can't get high on the music, he shouldn't be in the business."

Why was she remembering things Jake said? Who cared what he had to say about anything? She was here with Axel, who was rich and sophisticated—everything Jake wasn't.

"Let's not talk about Jake."

"Excellent idea," Axel said. "So, what kind of music do you like?"

"Oh, just about everything." It was always good to keep an open mind, expand your horizons.

"What do you listen to when you get home from work?"

Jake, playing his guitar. She'd miss that once the house was sold and they'd divided the money and split. The final split. "Well, right now it's hard to listen to anything. Jake is either giving guitar lessons or working on a song."

Axel frowned. "A bad situation. You need to get out of there." He sounded like her mother.

"There must be something I can do to make the house more appealing," she said.

"It's already a nice house. The Craftsman style works well here."

"I'd so hoped that couple was going to buy it," she said with a sigh. "Would it help if we had some Christmas decorations, a tree maybe? Make it feel more homey?"

"Possibly. If you don't go overboard. These days it's all about staging."

"I was thinking it looks a little, I don't know, bare."

"A tree might be a nice touch."

So she'd put up a Christmas tree. And maybe string some cedar boughs along the mantel and put out a few candles. Cinnamon. People were drawn to a house with good smells; she'd known that even before Axel told her. Anyway, she liked decorating her home for the holidays. She pushed aside the thought that this would be her last Christmas there with a new thought—next year she'd have a new place to fix up. A new place and a new beginning.

Their wine arrived and the waiter poured the obligatory sip for Axel to sample. He sniffed, swirled and swilled, then nodded his approval and the waiter poured. They placed their food orders—sauerbraten for her, rolladen for him and an appetizer for both that promised plenty of lobster—and then Axel raised his glass to her. "Here's to a sale and freedom."

"To freedom," she said. The house was a millstone around her neck. She couldn't move on until it was sold and Jake was out of her life completely. She raised her glass and drank deeply, then caught sight of Axel's raised eyebrows. "It's been a long day."

"I can imagine," he said.

They talked about the house some more and how hard Axel was working to get her out of there. After that, the conversation moved on to a new topic, which was really more of a move back to a topic they'd already touched on—Axel. He liked to travel. He had a condo in Seattle that he'd acquired in a short sale. He loved going into the city to see plays at ACT or musicals at the Fifth Avenue. TV, other than the offerings on PBS, was for morons, and why would anyone bother with those dumb reality shows and sitcoms when he (or she) could be enjoying a James Joyce novel?

Maybe this wasn't the moment to confess that her TV viewing consisted of shows like *The Bachelor* and her favorite read was always a good romance novel.

"What do you like to read?" Axel asked.

"Vanessa Valentine," she blurted.

"Who?"

"She writes about…relationships."

Axel nodded slowly, unimpressed and trying to hide it.

"I like to read all kinds of authors."

He smiled approvingly and took another sip of his wine. "Your mother was right. You and I have a lot in common."

Her mother! "You were talking to my mother?"

"A while back," he said with a shrug. "You know it's not that easy to find a woman with class in a small town."

Maybe he needed to move to New York. There was a reality show about Realtors in New York. He could be on it, drinking Rhine wine.

"Of course, I knew *you* had class the minute I saw you," Axel continued.

"Did you?" It was hard not to be flattered. It was hard not to be impressed. Axel had it all—success, money, nice looks. And he liked jazz. Well, no man was perfect.

Now he began to wax eloquent. "I've got to tell you, a man can have all the success in the world, but without the right woman to share it, it doesn't mean much. I mean, where's the fun in taking a gondola ride down a Venice canal by yourself or strolling the banks of the Seine alone?" He smiled at Ella. "A beautiful woman completes the experience."

He thought she was beautiful. With her snub nose and round face she'd never thought of herself that way. Who could when comparing herself to the incomparable Lily Swan? Even Jake had never told her she was beautiful. Cute, yes. Hot. But beautiful?

She could learn to like jazz.

Jake was in a foul mood when he got to band practice.

"What's eating you?" asked Tim the drummer.

"Nothing," Jake lied. Even though these guys were all his pals, he wasn't ready to tell them that his ex was on a date.

Jen offered him mock comfort, playing the chorus of Elton John's "Sorry Seems to Be the Hardest Word" on her keyboard. "You need some comfort, Jake," she said silkily.

"Got some Southern Comfort in the cupboard," offered Larry, who played lead guitar. Larry had agreed to the no-drinking-on-the-job rule, but during practice everyone was allowed a beer or a shot of booze. Jake was the only one who never indulged.

"Nah, he needs to start jamming," said Guy, his bass player. "Did you bring the new song you told us about?"

Oh, yeah, and Jake was in just the mood to play it.

By the end of the first chorus everyone was guffawing, proof that, as Jake suspected, this was a kick-ass country song. His ex-mother-in-law had her uses, after all. The others joined in with the instruments on the second verse and chorus and, great players that they were, had the song sounding good within only a few measures.

Once they'd finished the last chorus Larry said, "That rocks, man. We should do it this weekend, kick off the holidays."

"Hell, it could kick off more than the holidays. This could be a hit," Guy said. "There hasn't been a mother-in-law song on the charts since the sixties. Has there?"

"I dunno," Larry said, "but there should be. Every guy on the planet could relate."

Guy shook his head. "Not me," he said. "My mother-in-law rocks. She bakes my favorite cookies at Christmas and makes a steak dinner for my birthday every year."

"That ain't normal," Larry said.

"Well," Jake said, "I know guys who like their mamas-in-law." Too bad a man couldn't mix and match. *I'll take this woman and her best friend's mother.*

Larry made a face. "They're probably lying. Chrissie's mom drives me bonkers."

"She don't count as a mother-in-law," Guy told him. "You and Chrissie ain't married."

"And we're not gonna be until she gets a new mother," Larry said.

Guy turned to Jake. "All I can say is that if your ex's mom inspired this, it was worth all the pain."

"Not really," Jake muttered.

He forced himself to set aside all further thoughts of his ex-wife and concentrate solely on arranging the song. They worked on that, then ran over a couple more Christmas songs and the new Brad Paisley hit. After an hour and a half, he began wondering if Ella was still out with Axel. Maybe he'd taken her home by now. Had he dropped her off and left, or had she invited him in? If she'd invited him in, was he still there? What were they doing?

"Let's pack it in for the night," he said.

"This early?" Jen protested, looking disappointed. "Come on, Jake, I'm ready to make a night of it." Jen was always ready to make a night of it.

Guy looked at him like he was nuts. "We never quit this early. Are you sick?"

He had to be sick in the head to be obsessing over the woman he was no longer married to. "Yeah, I feel like shit." He'd felt like shit for a long time but that was beside the point.

"Okay, fine with me," Larry said. "We'll kick back and have a beer in your honor. Just make sure you're well by Friday."

"I've never missed a gig," Jake assured him, and loaded his guitar in its case.

He pulled up in front of the house fifteen minutes later, just as Ella and the slime in a suit were arriving. Jake got out of his truck and eyed the Lexus with disfavor. What a wussy car.

They didn't seem to be in any hurry to get out so he took his time going up the walk. They kept sitting in the wussmobile. Jake ditched his guitar and let Tiny out for some air. Tiny was happy to see him and equally happy to trot around the front yard, sniffing the bushes. Jake stood on the porch and watched... Ella and Axel.

Finally Fuchs got the hint and vacated the car, going around and opening the door for her. She slid out and flashed a well-curved leg from under her winter coat. Ella had great legs. Heck, Ella had great everything.

Here they came up the walk together, both frowning. *Three's a crowd, huh? Too bad.* He stood in the open doorway, leaning on the door frame. "Hey, kids, how was the dance?"

Ella glared at him, but Axel refused to rise to the bait, merely smiling pleasantly. Always the good businessman.

Now they were on the porch. "Were you going in?" Ella asked pointedly.

"Tiny's not done."

"I can watch him," Ella said.

"I don't mind."

Axel gave up. "Well, I guess I'll be going."

"I had a great time," Ella told him.

Great? Really? It was just dinner. Oh, but dinner with fancy tablecloths. That made all the difference.

"We'll do it again," Axel said.

Not if Jake had anything to say about it. Oh, yeah. He didn't.

Axel went back down the walkway and Ella marched past Jake into the house. He called Tiny and followed her in, wearing a smirk.

But once inside she wiped the smirk off his face. "That was mature," she said as she slipped off her heels.

He played dumb. "What?"

"You know what. You're such a hypocrite."

"What!"

"You can have other women but I can't have other men? Is that it?"

"I never—" he began.

She cut him off. "You always. I'm going to see Axel again and I'm going to have a life. And I'm going to get a Christmas tree and get this place sold!"

He wasn't sure what a Christmas tree had to do with anything, but he got the general gist of that tirade. He was out of the picture. And once they sold the house, he'd be out of her life for good. Now would be the time to say, "Baby, we've been so wrong. Let's sit down and talk, really talk. Let's lose the suspicion and the anger. Let me make love to you." Instead, he just stood there in the hallway, glaring as she went upstairs.

His life was like a bad country song. All he needed now was for his truck to break down and his dog to die.

As if reading his thoughts, Tiny whimpered.

"I didn't mean it, boy," he said. "Come on. We'll go out to the kitchen and get us some chili."

Ella threw her shoes in the closet and fell on her bed. She could hardly wait to sell this house and get away from Jake O'Brien. Him and his immature behavior and his tacky country songs. He was probably downstairs right now, messing up the kitchen, just like he was trying to mess up her life.

Well, she wasn't going to let him. And she was going to learn to appreciate jazz if it killed her.

Nine

Ella was getting ready to go to the shop on Friday when Axel called. "I just wanted to give you a heads-up that I've got a couple arriving in town who are looking for a second home. I think they might like your place."

"That's great," Ella said. If these people were looking for a second home they obviously had money. They might even be willing to pay the asking price.

"We'll be over this afternoon, so if there's anything you need to do…"

Like have Jake pick up his underwear and clean the sink? Very diplomatic. "I'll make sure the place looks good," Ella promised.

As soon as she ended the call, she went searching for Jake. It wasn't hard to find him. She just had to follow her nose to the kitchen, where he was frying an egg, spattering grease all over the stove. Everywhere he went he was a mess in progress.

"Axel's bringing over some people to see the house this afternoon," she said.

His only response was a grunt.

He'd been downright hostile since her dinner out with

Axel, which meant it was difficult to make any kind of reasonable request. She made hers, anyway. "So, you will clean up the kitchen, right?"

"Yeah," he said, obviously insulted.

"Thanks," she said and left the kitchen. She didn't have time to stand around and exchange rude looks. She had to get to work. But first, she'd run up to the attic and get a few decorations, Christmas the house up a little. Staging was important.

So was getting to the shop on time. Mims was a stickler for that. Ella picked up her pace, opening the door to the attic and hurrying up the narrow stairs.

The closed door kept it nippy. She rubbed her arms and did a quick scan of the odds and ends lying around, pieces of their life together. There was the picnic basket Cecily had given them for a wedding present. Off in the corner lay Jake's old catcher's mitt. She'd gone to all his softball games back when they were a happy couple. There sat the old trunk they'd gotten at a garage sale. And over in the corner, carefully preserved and bagged, hung her wedding gown. She quickly averted her gaze.

Jake had put the decorations away last Christmas and the boxes were shoved in a corner every which way. Fortunately, she recognized the one with her candles and the Fitz and Floyd snow globe. Those would be perfect on the mantelpiece. Just the right touch until she could get a tree.

Maybe she wouldn't even need a tree. Maybe the couple Axel was bringing by would fall in love with the house and make an offer today.

Conscious of the ticking clock, Ella took the box and hurried down from the attic.

After arranging her decorations, she ditched the box

in the coat closet and left for the shop. Hopefully, before the day was over, the house would be sold. History. Like her and Jake.

Jake had just finished some song charts and was recharging with a cup of coffee when he saw the silver Lexus pull up in front of the house. The wuss was here. And he wouldn't be happy to see Jake. Well, Jake wasn't going to be happy to see him, either, so that made them even. Anyway, this was still half his house and he had every right to stay.

He stood by the window, watching as Axel and his clients got out of the car and started up the front walk. The couple was older, maybe in their fifties. He looked like a model for The North Face. She was wearing a coat trimmed with some kind of fake fur over slacks and heels. Her hair was as phony as the trim on her coat, a youthful blond chin-length and carefully coiffed. Everything about her said, "My man has money." Yuck. *This* was going to buy his house?

Axel spotted him at the front window and his smile stiffened.

Yeah, I know. You were hoping I'd be gone. You've been hoping that ever since you started drooling over Ella. Jake saluted him with his coffee mug and chuckled to see the smile slip into a frown. But then Axel put his salesman's game face back on and began talking to the two fish he had on the line as he ushered them up the steps and onto the porch.

Suddenly, Jake heard a noise that didn't bode well for Axel and the fish. It was a great thundering woosh that sounded like Santa and a million reindeer were using the metal roof as a slip 'n' slide. Uh-oh. Ella had been in the attic getting Christmas decorations before she left for work. She must've left the door open—not a good thing because that meant a lot of heat had been rising up to the attic for a long time, enough to melt the snow accumulation and send it sledding down onto—

He heard the scream, saw the avalanche and then watched in horror as one of the icicles he'd forgotten to knock down hurled itself like a sword at the feet of three snow people, making them all jump back. The woman's shriek was enough to break off all the other icicles that hadn't already been dislodged.

Jake ran to the door and pulled it open. "You guys okay?"

"What do you think?" Axel said through gritted teeth.

The couple was in shock. They both looked like the abominable snowman's cousins. The woman blinked out at Jake from behind a snowy mask. She whimpered as she brushed at her face and then raked the cap of snow from her hair, leaving it plastered to her head. "Oooh, my hair." That wasn't her only problem. Her eye makeup had run and she looked like Barnabas Collins in drag. Her husband, who was sweeping the snow from his shoulders, appeared ready to murder someone.

So did Axel. Jake was sorry his clients got dumped on, but Axel—that was another story. It was somehow satisfying to see the guy drenched in snow from the top of his smarmy head to the tip of his expensive shoes. Jake almost laughed, but the realization that Ella was not going to be happy about this kept him sober.

"What was that?" the man demanded.

"This happens sometimes with metal roofs," Axel said smoothly. "Nothing to be concerned about."

"Nothing to be concerned about?" the man echoed,

his voice rising. "One step closer and that icicle would have gone through Annabel's skull."

There probably wasn't much in there, anyway, Jake thought. "Come on in and get dry," he offered.

The woman took a step back. "I don't think so."

Now Tiny was at the door and let out a bark of greeting. "Eeep!" cried Annabel.

Another icicle stabbed the front porch. "Eeee!" Annabel turned and fled down the steps.

"Show us a condo," her husband said, and hurried down the walk after her.

"You blew that sale," Axel told Jake, glaring at him.

"Hey, I'm not responsible for snow sliding off my roof," Jake snapped. "That was an act of God."

Axel looked as if he'd like to say more, but instead, he brushed the last of the snow from his expensive overcoat and stalked off down the walk after his clients.

"Good riddance," Jake said, and slammed the door after him.

Ella wasn't going to think that.

Sure enough. An hour later Jake's cell phone rang. Figuring the best defense was a good offense, he didn't give her a chance to say anything. "El, that was not my fault."

"You didn't knock down the icicles and I asked you to. How is that not your fault?"

"Okay, that part is," he admitted. "But not the snow thing. I went up and checked. You left the door to the attic open. All that warm air drifting up there all day warmed the roof and loosened the snow."

That shut her up. But a moment later he could hear sniffling. "Oh, come on, El, don't cry. Someone will buy the house."

"Not if we try to kill them with snow and icicles."

"Look, the icicles are all gone and I shoveled the snow off the porch. So next time…"

"I don't even know if there'll be a next time. Axel was really mad."

"Well, Axel can go—" Jake bit off the rest of the sentence, realizing it would hardly be productive.

"Oh, why am I talking to you, anyway?" she said miserably.

Then she hung up before he could say, "Because I'm the one you come to when you're upset, because you still love me." He looked down at Tiny, who was watching him, head cocked to one side. "Let me tell you, being a guy is a lot easier for you than it is for me." Love shouldn't be this hard.

Now, there was a good title for a song. Too bad it was also the story of his life.

Cass closed the bakery an hour early on Friday so she and Dani could pop over to Lupine Floral and pick out flowers for the wedding. It was December 1, and the town was buzzing with shoppers.

About this time the following day the town square would be packed with visitors, watching the tree-lighting ceremony. This included a carol sing, an appearance by Santa and an invocation from one of the local pastors. Then there'd be a countdown and the hundreds of lights on the giant fir in town square would burst into glorious colored bloom and the handbell choir would play "Joy to the World." The week before Christmas there'd be something going on every night, including performances by choirs and the local folk-dancing club. In addition to all that, bonfires would blaze by the skating rink every evening so families could enjoy roasting hot dogs and

toasting marshmallows. Icicle Falls knew how to celebrate the holidays.

And bring on the visitors. They'd had a rough winter
the year before with little snow for the skiers and winter sports enthusiasts, but they'd learned from that. The
town was now holiday party central. Besides Christmas,
they'd found a festival to celebrate something every season. And more were in the works. Their little town was
quickly becoming a destination.

Even Lupine Floral had come up with a way to lure in
holiday visitors, offering special Christmas corsages featuring red carnations and small candy canes that women
could pin on their winter coats and hats. Cass counted
half a dozen as she and Dani hurried through the Friday
afternoon crowd toward the florist's.

The shop window was a winter work of art, a study
in white and silver, with a river of silver ribbon running among arrangements of white roses and carnations
in silver mercury-glass vases. A small forest of baby's
breath stood tall in milk-glass vases linked by faux-pearl
swags. A table-size flocked tree sported silver balls and
shiny blue ribbons.

"I could go for that," Dani said as they walked in.

"Which part of it?" Cass asked.

"All of it."

Cass could see the money flying away. She nodded
gamely and followed her daughter inside, wishing she'd
saved more.

Even if Dani had given her a year, she wouldn't have
been able to sock away the kind of money she suspected
they'd end up spending on this "small" wedding. She
should have started saving long ago. *Cheer up. By the
time you've paid for this Amber will be engaged and*

you can start all over. Thank God one of her children was a boy.

Kevin Carlyle, looking spiffy in designer jeans and a gray cashmere sweater, was just saying goodbye to a customer when they walked in. "Here's the bride-to-be!" he greeted them. "Congratulations, Dani. We're so happy for you."

"Thank you," Dani said.

"There's nothing more beautiful than a Christmas wedding," Kevin went on.

Or more expensive, Cass thought. If Dani and Mike had been getting married in the summer they could have culled flowers from all their friends' gardens and saved a bundle. But that would have been tacky, she scolded herself. It was important to support local businesses, and heaven knew Heinrich and Kevin had bought enough goodies from her bakery.

Heinrich emerged from the back of the shop where he'd probably been working on a floral arrangement. Kevin was barely into his forties, but Heinrich was pushing fifty. His brown hair had begun to thin and he was edging toward fashion's dark side—a Donald Trump comb-over. He, too, wore expensive jeans topped with a black mock-turtleneck sweater.

"Ladies," he greeted them, "this is going to be so much fun. I haven't done a December wedding in ages."

"I hope you can do one on a budget," Cass said, earning her a dirty look from her daughter.

Heinrich laughed. "We'll make it work. Come sit down and let's talk." He took a slim laptop from under the counter and led the way to a white ironwork table and chairs in the corner. Like everything else in the shop, this little meeting spot was a delight for the eyes, the table covered with a white cloth and, on top of that, a square glass vase bearing a holiday floral arrangement.

Kevin brought them bottles of Perrier, and Heinrich opened the laptop. "What's your color scheme, darling?"

"Gosh, I thought I wanted red and white," Dani said. "My gown's white with white faux-fur trim."

"Your gown?" Dani had already picked out a gown?

"I was going to show it to you," Dani said to Cass. "I saw it last month when I was visiting Daddy in Seattle."

"You went to a bridal shop with your father?" The green-eyed monster landed on Cass's shoulder, and began breathing down her neck, souring the moment.

"No," Dani said. "I just…went."

"All by yourself?" Where was the fun in that?

"Babette and I were out shopping."

Babette! The child bride, Mason's trophy wife? Her daughter had been looking at wedding gowns with Babette?

"We happened to walk by the shop and I saw it," Dani said. "I didn't buy it or anything, Mom. I was waiting for you to come with me."

But she'd already tried it on. Babette had seen it. *So what,* she told herself. *So what, so what, so what!*

It didn't help. She could feel tears pricking her eyes.

Heinrich cleared his throat. "Well, red and white are perfect for Christmas."

Cass jerked her petty self out of that Seattle bridal shop and back to the present. "I think Dani might be leaning toward something else now."

She must have succeeded in straining the hurt from her voice because the pink in Dani's cheeks faded and her shoulders relaxed. "I really like the white and silver combination you have in the window."

"That would go with almost anything," Heinrich said. "What color are your bridesmaids' dresses?"

"We haven't decided yet," Dani said, "but Ella has some great dresses at Gilded Lily's. There was a really pretty gray one that my bridesmaids liked."

"That would go well with silver and white. And we could accent with red, maybe in your bouquet." Heinrich smiled at Cass. "And your mother could design an amazing cake using silver and white, maybe a little red."

Good old Heinrich, trying to use flattery as a salve for wounded motherly pride.

"I like that," said Dani.

"And where are we holding the wedding and reception?" he asked.

"All at Olivia's," Dani said. "The wedding will be in that big conference room and the reception in the dining hall."

"Ah, perfect. And the view from the dining hall." Heinrich kissed his fingers. "We can bring the outdoors inside."

With that they were off.

"It's all gorgeous," Cass said finally. "What are we looking at costwise?"

"What's your budget?" Heinrich asked.

Not much probably wasn't a helpful answer. Cass had been doing some rough calculations in her head, which had given her a headache. She threw out a figure she hoped wouldn't make her sound like the cheapskate of Icicle Falls.

Her daughter looked at her like she *was* the cheapskate of Icicle Falls.

Heinrich had been taking notes as they talked. Now

he said, "Let me run some figures," and disappeared into the back room, taking Kevin with him.

"Jeez, Mom. That won't buy much more than my bridal bouquet and boutonnieres."

"We still have to pay for food and your gown and a DJ, and we have to pay Olivia."

"I have some money saved up," Dani said. "I can pay for the flowers."

"No, I'll do it. You need to keep your money for the move," Cass said quickly. Dani had asked for little enough growing up. She deserved the wedding she wanted. And the flowers she wanted. Cass would just have to load up her credit card, that was all. How much was that wedding gown going to cost?

Don't think about it.

Now Heinrich was back, with a smiling Kevin right behind him. "Okay, we're good to go."

"So you can do the flowers for that amount?" Cass asked. Surely not.

"Not quite," Heinrich said.

"Well, then," Cass began, ready to drain her account.

"But we're picking up the difference," Kevin added before she could finish. "As a wedding present."

"Oh, thank you," breathed Dani.

Cass felt those pesky tears burning her eyes again. "Thanks, you two. Anything you want from the bakery, anytime."

Kevin grinned. "I'll remember that when we throw our New Year's Eve party."

So there it was, the first wedding hurdle safely jumped. Now all she had to worry about was…everything else.

Mason could pay for half of this, she told herself. But the idea of asking him galled her. He'd been little more than a child-support check when the kids were growing up, and obviously he didn't want to be involved now or he would have offered. No, she'd find a way to get whatever her daughter needed all on her own. Like she always had.

Dani slipped her arms through Cass's. "Thanks, Mom. It's going to be beautiful."

Yes, it was. No matter what it cost.

Richard strolled into Zelda's toward the end of the evening. Charley was visiting with Ed York and Pat Wilder as they enjoyed their pie and coffee. The sight of him whipped up more than one emotion in her. When he'd first reentered her life she'd felt anger and resentment. But tonight's mix bore something new—yearning. *What if?*

What was she thinking? This was not a good ingredient to add to the stew.

She tried to keep her easy smile but it must have faltered because now Pat was looking at the door. "Oh, my," she murmured.

There was an understatement. Charley found herself wishing she'd hired a hostess for weekday evenings. Yes, she was the general manager, but she didn't need to live here 24/7 as if she had no life. If she hadn't been on duty tonight she could have hidden in her house, kept the door locked. Pretended she had a life.

Why wouldn't he give up? She made her way up to the front, stopping to check with a diner here and there en route. *Let him wait.*

He seemed to have no problem waiting and greeted her with a smile when she finally got to him. "Looks nice in here," he observed, taking in the red bows she'd put up at the windows and the small tree in the lobby done in red and gold.

"Glad you approve." *Now, scram.*

"You look nice, too. In fact, you look good enough to eat," he said, taking in the black pencil skirt and the new blouse and necklace she'd gotten at Gilded Lily's. What, did he think she'd worn it for him?

If not him, then who did *you wear it for?*

She pleaded the fifth.

"Is it too late to get a table?"

"You know it's not," she said, and led him to a corner table by the kitchen. Not the best seat in the house by any means, but he didn't deserve the best seat. He didn't deserve any seat.

"Perfect," he said. "Now I can observe the new chef in action. Is he as good as me?"

"There are lots of men who are as good as you. Better even." She handed him his menu, then walked away.

"Take your time getting to him," she told Ginny, his waitress.

Ginny looked at her wide-eyed, and no wonder, since she had only one other occupied table in her station, but she nodded.

Richard didn't seem to mind. Every time Charley glanced at him, he was sitting there smiling contentedly, observing everything. As if he still had a stake in this place. The old anger fired up. How dared he! She avoided him for the rest of the night, even when he was the last person sitting at a table.

Finally, at ten, she told him, "The restaurant is closing. You need to go."

"I'm not done." He held up the glass of wine he'd been nursing for the past half hour. It had one sip left in it.

She took the glass and downed the wine. "Now you are."

He leaned back in his chair. "I didn't see your car outside. How about I walk you home?"

"How about you don't."

"It's only a walk home, Charley."

It would be too long a walk. She shook her head. "No, thanks."

"Please."

He looked so contrite. And so handsome. Oh, jeez. What was wrong with her?

"Charley, I want to make up for how I hurt you."

The very mention of what he'd done strengthened her resolve. "You can't," she said, her face stony.

"I can try, if you let me."

After several more minutes of contrition wrapped in flattery she gave in. *Fool. What are you thinking?* She had a suspicion, and it left her feeling uneasy.

Charley exchanged her shoes for the boots she'd worn to work and they walked home in a wintry wonderland, the houses along her street looking like frosted gingerbread. Many had their Christmas lights up already and they glowed like giant gumdrops. Charley huddled inside her long coat, trying to fight off the shivers. She should've worn pants.

"You're cold," Richard said, and put an arm around her.

"Not that cold," she lied, and removed it, then hunched inside her coat collar like a giant turtle.

"Won't even let me fight off the cold, huh?"

"I can do my own fighting."

He acknowledged that with a nod.

They walked the rest of the way in silence, and when

they got to the front porch, she turned and said, "See? I didn't need you to walk me home."

"You've never needed me."

Was that some sort of accusation? "Is that why you found Ariel so attractive? She needed you?"

He shrugged.

"How convenient to have an excuse." Charley turned her back on him and unlocked the front door.

She tried to shut it in his face but he blocked the move and slipped inside, just like last time. Well, he was going to get nowhere now, just like last time.

"One nightcap, then I'll go. I promise."

She should tell him to go now. *So, tell him.* "One nightcap," she said. She hung up her coat and then went to the dining room sideboard where she kept the liquor. She didn't need to ask what he wanted. She knew. Jack Daniel's, straight up.

She handed him the glass.

"You're not having anything?"

"No."

"No peppermint schnapps?" he coaxed.

"No." Charley liked a glass of wine now and then, and this time of year she enjoyed cocoa laced with peppermint schnapps. But she preferred companionable drinking. There was no companionship here. There was something else, though, and that was giving her shivers worse than she'd had on the walk over.

"Well," he said, raising the glass to her, "here's looking at you, kid."

Casablanca, their favorite movie. "Did you make the same toast to Ariel?"

He gave a snort. "Like she would even have known where it came from?"

"Everyone knows where that comes from." Yet it had sounded so special when Richard said it to her.

She should have left her coat on. The house was cold. She didn't usually bother to heat it though, not when she came straight home from work every night and went to bed. Alone. The shivers returned full force.

"Let me build a fire," Richard offered, and moved to the fireplace.

"No!" Her voice was sharper than necessary, certainly sharper than she'd intended. "I'm not planning on staying up that long." She sat on the couch and pulled an afghan around her shoulders.

"Or having me here that long?"

"What would be the point?"

"To talk, and remember why we got together in the first place."

"Temporary insanity?"

"We had something good. Until I blew it," he added quickly, probably before she could. "And I'm not sure you can call twelve years temporary."

"I thought it was going to be for a lifetime." Charley found an inconvenient sob rising to choke her.

"It should have been." Now he was next to her on the couch, his drink forgotten on the coffee table. "Oh, baby. I'm sorry. I blew it."

She pulled away. "Yeah, you did. And now I'm supposed to simply forget that and welcome you back with open arms?"

"No. I wouldn't expect you to do that. All I'm asking is that you think about starting again. Remember how good we had it?"

She remembered. Maybe that was why his betrayal

hurt so much. She stood. "It's late, Richard, and I'm tired."

He nodded and stood, too. "Walk me to the door."

She remained where she was. "You know where it is."

He nodded, took her hand and led her toward the entryway.

In only a few nervous heartbeats they were standing in the archway that separated the entryhall from the living room, right where Charley had always hung a satin ball decorated with mistletoe.

He pointed to the spot. "The mistletoe isn't there this year."

"No, it's not," she agreed. "I haven't exactly been in a kissing mood." Now she wished she'd hung it there, found some great-looking guy to kiss her under it. She could have taken a picture, posted it on her Facebook page, sent a copy to Richard with a note that said, "See what you're missing?"

"Let's pretend it is," he murmured, and then, before she could stop him, he kissed her. Oooh, how long had it been since she'd been kissed? Richard had always known how to turn her to mush. He hadn't lost his touch.

He'd had plenty of practice. With another woman. She pulled away and yanked the front door open. "Good night, Richard."

He grabbed his coat from the coat tree where he'd tossed it. "I like that."

She couldn't resist asking, "What?"

"You said good-night. You could have said goodbye." He turned and ran down the steps.

"Goodbye!" she called after him. But it was belated and halfhearted and they both knew it.

Ten

Charley was enjoying a leisurely Saturday morning with her December issue of *Bon Appétit* when Richard showed up on her doorstep bearing eggnog lattes from Bavarian Brews.

She scowled at him. "Would you like me to tell you what you can do with those?"

He held up a cup, letting the aroma of coffee and nutmeg drift her way. "It would be a shame to waste this."

She snatched the cup from him. "Lattes for life couldn't atone for what you did."

"Charley, I'm trying. Please, let me come in."

She hated him for the pleading expression on his face, hated how it almost made her feel sorry for him. She opened the door wider and he stepped inside.

Great. You've let the snake slither back in your house in exchange for an eggnog latte. Smart, Charley. She turned her back on him and took a sip. The latte was better than her judgment. "What do you want, Richard?"

"I want you to go out to breakfast with me."

"I don't think so."

"You have time. It's only ten."

"Just because I have time doesn't mean I have the inclination." Her phone rang. Saved by the ringtone. Whoever it was, whatever that person wanted, it would make the perfect excuse to ditch her ex.

"Uh, Charley, it's Bruno."

Why was her grill chef calling her at ten in the morning? Why was he calling her at all? If there was a problem she should've been hearing from Harvey, her head chef.

Dread dropped in to wish her happy holidays. "Where's Harvey?"

"I don't know. That's why I'm calling you."

"What?" She fell onto the nearest chair. Her chef should have been in at seven. By now he should have had all the orders put away, the goose portioned and the kitchen crew prepping the night's set menu. Instead, there was... Bruno. Good old Bruno, who never operated on all four burners. And who'd waited three hours to call her.

"He's not here," Bruno said. "And there's nothing in the walk-in. The meat guy hasn't shown up and Sysco hasn't brought the produce order. I don't know what I'm supposed to be prepping for the set menu."

The mayor's holiday dinner—thirty movers and shakers, politicians, even the representative for their district would be present. "I know you'll come up with a wonderful meal for us, Charley," Mayor Stone had said.

"Oh, yes," she'd assured him.

"Oh, yes," her head chef had assured her. "We can give him goose, roasted winter vegetables, a traditional figgy pudding for dessert."

Now Bruno was telling her they had nothing, and *her* goose was cooked. "I'll be right there," she said. She ended the call and raced for the door, both her latte and her ex forgotten.

Richard hurried after her. "Charley, what's going on?"

Hell's kitchen, that was what. "My head chef didn't show up." Richard said something but she didn't listen. She was too busy panicking. This was a disaster. Her life was flambéed, all thanks to Harvey's disappearing act. She raced to her car, putting in a call to Harvey as she went. His phone rang. And rang. And rang some more. Finally his voice mail kicked in. "Harvey, where are you?"

As if she had to ask. She knew. Harvey had broken his promise to go to AA. Harvey was out with his best friend, José Cuervo. Harvey, the worm in the bottle. They'd had this conversation only two weeks ago when she'd caught him helping himself from the bar. For his sauce, he'd claimed. But she'd smelled his breath. His kitchen creations weren't the only things getting sauced. She'd given him another chance; now she wanted to give him a black eye. Oh, she was going to murder the little weasel! How good it would feel to be able to break a plate over his head.

Except who had been the fool who gave him a second chance? No, she was the one who deserved to have a plate broken over her head.

The kitchen at Zelda's was normally a beehive of busyness on a Saturday morning, with staff cutting tomatoes and tearing lettuce leaves into big bins, pulling desserts out of the oven, cutting and weighing steak. Instead, Charley found Bruno, leaning against the counter, a block of cement with a head, wearing a white chef's jacket and a befuddled expression. Next to him stood Andy, her salad and dessert man, a short, skinny guy, also in a white jacket. "There's no produce," he informed her.

She marched to the walk-in cooler and threw open the door. All she saw was bare metal shelving, giant

Sysco containers of mayonnaise, mustards, garlic, shallots, pan racks with vacant metal trays, plastic inserts filled with sauces and dressings, but no produce or meat to be dressed. Bruno had told her but she hadn't wanted to believe him.

She stood for a moment, staring at shelves full of empty, then she left the cooler. There, in the middle of the kitchen, stood Tweedledum and Tweedledumber, looking at her, waiting for their orders.

She went back into the walk-in, shut the door after her and, woman of action that she was, grabbed two fists full of hair and screamed. Then she marched to the door. She was going to bang her head on it until her brains fell out. Brains for dinner, hahahaha.

She was just about to whang her head on the door when it opened.

There stood Richard.

"Excuse me, but I have to go stick my head in the oven," she said, and started past him.

He caught her arm and pulled her back inside the walk-in, shutting the door. Not exactly the warmest place for a cozy conversation but Charley had worked up enough of a sweat having her meltdown that she was barely aware of the cold.

"You have to get a grip," he said.

"I intend to get a grip—around Harvey's neck."

"Harvey's history. Right now we have to make a list of what you need."

What she needed? She needed all her deliveries. And a head chef, pulling together the set menu for the evening. "I need—" she threw up her hands "—everything! I need a miracle. I need to murder Harvey, and serve his head on a platter. The mayor's dinner party is tonight and there's *nothing!*"

Richard grasped both her arms. "Charley, calm down. This isn't like you."

"This *is* like me," she growled. "This is like the new me."

"Well, get in touch with the old you and calm down," he said firmly. "Let's come up with a game plan."

She ran a hand through her hair. "Right. You're right."

"Okay. You calm now?"

She nodded. "I'm cool. Call me cucumber." How was she going to fix this mess?

"Good. Now, first of all, what's the set menu for the mayor's dinner?"

She told him, trying not to sound as hysterical as she felt.

When she'd finished, he said, "Okay, we'll have to alter the menu."

"Wait a minute," she said. "You don't have to help. This isn't your problem."

"I know. I want to."

"Then I'll pay you." The last thing she wanted was to be indebted to her ex.

"Don't be ridiculous." He picked up a clipboard and disappeared into the walk-in to do inventory. Of course, there was little enough to inventory and he was back out in a couple of minutes. Oooh, she was going to get hauled away in a straitjacket before this day was over.

Richard was unfazed, however. While Charley fantasized about hunting down Harvey and flogging him with a frozen salmon, Richard went on a wild-goose hunt, putting in a couple of calls to fellow chefs at other restaurants. Once more he was the head chef at Zelda's, throwing together a special menu on the fly, compiling a shopping list, calling their suppliers and barking out orders to Bruno and Andy, sending them scurrying to the grocery store for food to tide them over.

Charley was scurrying, too, getting the new menu printed, then helping Richard and the rest of the crew prep the food. Lunch was crazy, with a ton of tourists, hungry from a morning of shopping and exploring town, but they made it through. Then they had to gear up for the dinner service. By the time that was done, she had less than an hour to run home, freshen up and change into an evening outfit suitable for greeting diners. She made it back just in time to open, and when the mayor's party arrived everything at Zelda's was running as it should—smoothly.

"We're looking forward to this dinner, Charley," Mayor Stone said to her when he entered the restaurant, a pudgy blonde on one arm and his sister, Darla, on the other.

"I know you'll love it," Charley said.

And they would. Richard had managed to find a goose—not enough to serve thirty, but enough to make a goose soufflé. In addition to that, he'd produced a prime rib, the roasted winter vegetables Harvey had promised, a crab-artichoke salad and bread pudding (faster to make than figgy pudding), complete with rum sauce.

Like the Lone Ranger, Richard had ridden in and saved the day. Who knew? Ex-husbands were good for something, after all.

Jake was coming out of the kitchen with a hot dog when Ella came downstairs. He glanced disapprovingly at her short skirt and clingy black sweater. She'd accessorized with suede boots, gold earrings and bracelet and a nice Hermès knockoff scarf.

"You look like a hooker," he informed her. "Are you going out with that wuss again?"

Oh, he had his nerve! "Just because Axel doesn't wear cowboy boots and run around shooting helpless deer—"

"For food," Jake cut in.

"Whatever. It doesn't make him a wuss. And I don't look like a hooker."

"Could've fooled me. What do you think is gonna go through that man's mind when he sees you like that?"

"Maybe every other man doesn't have the same kind of dirty mind you have," Ella retorted.

"Trust me. They do."

"Axel is a gentleman, and unlike some people he actually has self-control."

"I have self-control!"

Yes, she could tell by the way his voice was now bordering on a roar. "Anyway, I can dress how I want and see who I want. And at least I waited until I was divorced," she couldn't help adding.

"I never did anything with anyone!"

Oh, please. "Well, you're free to do whatever you want now, and so am I," she said. Saying those words should have made her happy but it didn't.

"Fine." He threw up his hands. "Go out with that turkey, but he's only after one thing."

She refused to dignify his remark with a response. And she refused to stay in the living room with Jake while she waited for Axel, so she marched out to the kitchen. She'd probably find it a mess.

She looked around in surprise. There was no mustard

jar on the table, which had been wiped down. She walked to the sink. No dishes. He'd even cleaned it.

"I'm not a total slob, you know."

She turned to see Jake leaning in the doorway, Tiny by his side. Tiny seemed to like him best these days. Of course, why wouldn't he? Jake was home all the time, feeding him treats, making him fat.

Jake had always been the messy one. You'd never know it now to look at the kitchen. He obviously wanted to sell the house and get out of there as much as she did. That should've made her happy, too, but it didn't. Maybe she was never going to feel happy again.

You're happy now, she told herself, and decided to believe it.

The doorbell rang and she brushed past Jake and hurried down the hall. She shrugged into her coat and met Axel at the door, not even giving him a chance to come in. The last thing she needed was Jake standing there in the background, an unwanted third party.

"A woman who's ready on time? Now, that's impressive," Axel said. He took in her outfit. "You're impressive in so many ways, Ella."

She could read in his eyes what he was thinking. Jake was right.

Well, so what if he was? It was nice to be desired.

Once in the car she felt the need to apologize for the last disastrous showing—or, rather, nonshowing—of the house.

"Don't worry," Axel said. "I'll find the right buyers, I promise. Tonight I want you just to relax and have fun."

Fun was a local artists' show at D'Vine Wines. Modern art. She almost lost her appetite for the brie cheese she was nibbling.

What was she supposed to make of that picture of a path lined with crazy-colored trees that could've been painted by a third-grader? At the end of the path stood a naked woman with a tulip for a head. And here was a painting of a red couch spread out over four panels. It was hard to see the couch for the random black-and-white squiggles all over it. To Ella it looked as if someone had vandalized the painting.

"Striking, isn't it?" Axel said by her side.

"Striking," she repeated. It struck her as stupid.

The artist was approaching now, a fortysomething man with carefully cut shaggy hair, wearing an old gray sweater thrown on over jeans. She supposed he thought his outfit made him look like an artist. She thought it made him look dowdy.

"Dorian," Axel greeted him. "Great show."

"I'm pleased with it," the man said. Easy to tell from the self-satisfied expression on his face.

Ella couldn't help comparing him to Jake. When Jake had written a song, he was all excitement. And humility. "Do you really think it's good?" She'd be willing to bet this man never asked anyone that. Just as well. It spared people from having to choose between lying and answering honestly.

"This is Ella," Axel said.

Dorian looked her up and down. "Now, here's a work of art."

"Thanks," Ella murmured.

"You should model for me sometime," he suggested.

So she could end up naked with a tulip for a head? Anyway, she wasn't her mother. "I'm not into modeling."

He shrugged. "Shame." Then he turned his attention

to Axel. "I have the perfect painting for you. Have you seen *New Day?*"

"No, show us," Axel said. He looked so eager, like a man about to be shown buried treasure.

Wineglasses in hand, they followed Dorian to a corner of the room to... Oh, that one? Seriously? Ella gaped at the primitive painting of a bloodred sun rising from a river of chartreuse toxic waste.

"That makes a statement," Axel said.

It made a statement, all right: *take Pepto-Bismol before looking at me.*

Axel was nodding at it. "Yes, I think I might have to get that."

Oh, he had to be joking. Ella glanced at the price. Rather an expensive joke.

"Do I know your taste or what?" Dorian asked.

"Tell Bridget to save it for me. I'll be by for it tomorrow," Axel promised.

Dorian sauntered off in search of a new victim and Ella turned to Axel. "You really like that?"

"Absolutely. Don't you?"

She could learn to like jazz. She could get into reading the classics, but this? She shook her head.

"Modern art grows on you once you understand the symbolism," Axel told her. Was that true or was he simply repeating something he'd heard from some other sucker who'd purchased an overpriced painting?"

"Trust me, this man's work is going to be hanging in MOMA someday."

"Who?"

"The Museum of Modern Art, in New York."

Oh, that museum. All right, maybe she *was* ignorant. Maybe she could learn to like modern art.

"I've got some great pieces at my place. Why don't we go over there? I'll show them to you, give you an art lesson."

Ella was sure he had more in mind than an art lesson.

"Okay," she said. Why not? She wasn't married anymore. She was ready for art lessons.

Axel's house was a huge, modern number with glass windows everywhere. The great room had hardwood floors covered with expensive Persian rugs and sleek, modern furniture that suggested you admire it rather than get comfy in it. And there over the equally uncomfy fireplace hung a huge painting of...nothing. Only white space.

"Um, is it waiting for inspiration?" she asked.

He chuckled. "It's called *Vacuum*," he said, and launched into a detailed explanation.

She sighed. "To me, it just looks like a canvas waiting for someone to do something with it." She wondered if Axel thought of her that way. Was he trying to make her more polished?

"Well," he said, "art is subjective." He sat on the uninviting couch and patted the space next to him. "If you sit and study it, you'll be surprised by what you see."

She sat, she studied, she saw nothing. And she wasn't at all surprised when Axel decided to kiss her.

The kiss was as good as any a certain ex-husband could manage and it stirred up interest in all the right places. But it stirred up something else, too, something that protested, *What are you doing?*

She pulled away. "Axel, I'm sorry. I can't."

"Oh, of course. You're still angry over your divorce, but you need to know that not every man is a bum like your ex-husband. You can trust me."

That was what Jake used to say. Maybe a woman couldn't trust any man. "I think I need more time," she said. That was the problem.

"Understandable," Axel agreed, but he kept his arm around her shoulders.

They sat a moment and contemplated the painting of nothing hanging over his sterile fireplace.

"It grows on you, doesn't it?" he finally said.

She hoped so.

Charley's day had rushed past in a blur, and by the time the last diner left Zelda's she was a zombie. She and Richard had run on adrenaline for the past sixteen hours. She fetched a bottle of wine from the bar, along with two glasses, and invited him to join her at the little table in the back of the kitchen where the staff took their breaks.

She kicked off her shoes and he did the same, watching as she filled the glasses. She handed him one, saying, "You saved the day."

"No, *we* saved the day," he corrected, and raised his glass in salute. He took a drink, then leaned back in his chair and regarded her. "What are you going to do tomorrow?"

She shrugged. "See if I can haul Harvey out of whatever bottle he crawled into."

"So he can do this to you again?"

"Oh, believe me, I'll be looking for his replacement." Harvey should be thanking his lucky stars that she wasn't looking for a hit man. "I should never have believed him when he promised he'd go to AA."

Richard shook his head. "You're too softhearted, Charley. Don't keep him another day. Eighty-six his ass."

"And be both general manager *and* head chef?"

"I'll help you."

"You have your own restaurant," she reminded him.

"I know. But I can stay here a little longer."

Long enough to help her find a decent chef? That was easier said than done. "You don't want to be away from your place, though."

"Let me worry about that. Okay? Right now there's only one place I want to be and that's here," he added with a smile.

She felt his stockinged foot creep up her leg. A day ago she would have not only moved her leg out of range, she'd have tossed her wine in his face. Tonight, well, she was just too tired. And too grateful.

"Let's do the new song," Jake's bass player said.

Good idea. Jake had left the house ready to punch something and his mood hadn't improved as the night went on. He had to keep reminding himself to smile. Then he'd think about Ella out with that prissy Axel Fuchs and want to smash his guitar, preferably over Axel's head.

Of course he would never do that. It would be a waste of a fine instrument.

A cute little number with hair like honey, wearing skintight jeans, came up to the bandstand. "Can you play a Christmas song?"

"Sure," Jake said. "We've got just the song." To the dancers on the floor, he said, "We've got a song for all you married men out there. It's called 'Merry Christmas, Mama.'" He turned to Tim, the drummer. "Count us in."

And with that they were off. The cute little number frowned as her man shuffled them along the floor in a slow two-step but he was grinning. So were a lot of men in the room. The brotherhood of the sons-in-law. Once the song ended, there was much hooting and clapping.

"Looks like we got ourselves a hit," Larry said.

The cute little number was back at the bandstand now. "Can't you play something a little nicer?"

"How about 'Grandma Got Run Over by a Reindeer'?" Jake asked. Take out mother-in-law and Grandma in one fell swoop.

"I love my grandma," she informed him, and stomped off.

"Yeah? Well, I love my grandma, too," he called after her.

"Dude," Guy said, "what the hell's eating you?"

"Nothing," Jake growled. "Let's do 'Santa's Flying a 747 Tonight.'"

It was an old country song, but a great dance number and people loved it.

Not nearly as much as they loved Jake's song, though. Lots of guys gave him a thumbs-up or slapped him on the back as he made his way to the band's table when they went on break.

Yeah, he'd nailed it. If all the mothers-in-law in the U.S. could be rounded up and sent out to sea, the divorce rate would plummet, Jake was sure of it. Well, okay, not Guy's, whose mama-in-law baked him cookies and served steak dinners in honor of his birthday. She could stay.

"You guys were great," said Larry's girlfriend, Chrissie. She held up her smartphone. "I recorded it."

"Sweet," Larry said. "Let's put it up on YouTube and see what happens."

Jake shrugged. "Why not?" *Payback's a bitch...kinda like my ex-mother-in-law.* He grinned and downed his Coke.

By the time he got home Ella was in bed, her door firmly shut against him. As he passed her bedroom, a tiny germ of a thought two-stepped across the back of his mind. Maybe putting that song up wasn't such a good idea. Maybe writing it hadn't been such a good idea. Maybe he should tell Larry to hold off.

But then he asked himself, why? What did it matter now? Ella was moving on. He should, too. Like a gambler in Vegas, he said to himself, "Let it ride."

Eleven

Sunday afternoon found Ella at Santa's tree lot, along with half the residents of Icicle Falls, who were all bundled up in winter coats and hats. She spotted Cass and her kids and went over to say hi. "Looks like you're getting a tree early, too."

"Busy as we are with the wedding, we decided we'd better do it now," Cass said.

"How are the plans coming?" Ella asked.

"We picked out the flowers yesterday," Dani said.

And that launched a discussion about colors and bridesmaids' dresses. "I can stay open a little later on Tuesday if you want to bring Mikaila and Vanessa in after they're done with work," Ella offered.

"That'll be great since Mom and I are going over to Seattle tomorrow to check out bridal gowns."

"Oh, fun!" Ella could still remember standing in front of the mirror at the bridal shop, looking at herself in that elegant white gown and envisioning her perfect life with Jake. Parts of it *had* been perfect. "Sure. Anytime that works for them. Just let me know."

Willie was busy inspecting trees one row over. "Hey, Mom, how about this one?"

"Guess I should get back to business. See you tonight," Cass said, and went to join her son. Ella could hear her. "That's a good one, but it's out of our price range."

"Come on, Mom," Willie wheedled. "It's Christmas. Don't be a Grinch."

Ella couldn't help smiling. Cass would cave. When it came to her children, she was a softy.

Ella had thought that by now she'd be looking at trees with a little one in tow, maybe a girl dressed in pink Baby Gap. Life never turned out the way you planned. Why was that?

She wandered down the rows, inspecting trees, searching for one that would say Home, Sweet Home to potential buyers. Finally she found it. This tree would look lovely in the window. Anyone entering the house would think a happy family lived there. Well, until they saw the his-and-hers bedrooms.

"You've picked out a beaut," approved Al, Mr. Santa himself. He looked around, making his Santa hat wag like a tail. "Where's Jake?"

Last year Jake had been with her. They'd bought a small tree, taken it home and decorated it with strung popcorn. Jake had eaten more popcorn than he'd strung and she'd given him a hard time about not doing his fair share. It had all been in fun, but come February, when Mims was sitting her down for a serious talk, she'd realized how true those words had been.

"We're not together anymore," Ella said, and the merry smile disappeared from Al's face. She hated having to tell people, hated seeing the embarrassment and pity on their faces. *Poor kid. She couldn't make her marriage work.*

"Oh. Well, that's too bad," Al said. "So, uh, let me get this tree over to your car. Got some rope to tie it on?"

"I've got some in the trunk."

With the help of his son, Al hoisted the giant tree onto the roof of her car. It promptly swallowed the vehicle.

"Good thing you don't have far to drive," Al said. "That's a traffic ticket waiting to happen."

"Better hope Tilda's not on the road," his son added. "She'll give you one for sure."

Ella thanked them, then got in her car and drove home, peering through the fir fringe. She parked in front of the house in time to see Jake and Tiny strolling up the street. At the sight of her Tiny raced over to the car and greeted her as she got out.

"Hey, boy," she said. "Did you have a good walk?"

Now Jake was at the car. "You didn't tell me you were getting a tree."

Why should she have? It wasn't like they were going to spend a cozy afternoon together trimming it. "I didn't think you'd be interested."

He scowled at it. "I don't see the point."

"Maybe that's why I didn't tell you."

"How much did it cost?"

She'd spent more than she should have, but she didn't need him pitching in. She could handle it on her own. She was going to be handling things on her own from now on, and that included Christmas trees. "Never mind," she said, and began fumbling with the rope.

"Here, let me," he said, stepping in and taking over. "I don't know why the hell you bought a tree."

"To make the house look nice."

"Oh, yeah. That figures."

"What?" she demanded.

"Nothing," he said irritably.

Mims had always hired decorators, so for Ella trimming the tree was still a novelty and a delight. But it was an activity that should be done with smiles. There would be no smiles today. What a dumb idea. What had she been thinking? As if a tree alone would sell her house. It probably wasn't the lack of holiday decor or faulty plumbing that was keeping this house on the market. It was the lack of love inside it. People picked up on things like that.

Jake lifted her purchase down from the car and hauled it up the front walk, rather like a cave man bringing home a dead animal. "Be careful," Ella said as he went up the steps, the tree dragging along behind him.

"Don't worry about it."

She sighed and followed him in. Definitely a dumb idea.

He propped the tree by the front door. "Do we need the tree stand?"

"I need the tree stand," she said. "I'll get it."

He held up a hand. "I can do it. I'll get the ornaments out of the attic, too."

Half an hour later, the tree was planted in its stand by the front window, waiting to get dressed for the holidays. She assumed Jake would leave now, his part in the process over, but instead he opened the storage container with the lights and pulled out a string. "Tell me how you want 'em," he said, and started stringing them around the tree.

That was how they'd done it in the past. He'd string the lights and she'd look on with an artist's eye and direct operations. She swallowed a sudden lump in her throat.

"How's this?" he asked.

"Nice," she managed.

Once the lights were on, he vanished into the kitchen. His job was done.

She opened the container of ornaments they'd collected and felt sadness fly out at her. All the memories in here were good ones. It was so wrong that they didn't mean anything anymore.

Many of the ornaments were simple colored balls, but they had a few special ones, and she felt tears springing to her eyes when she took out one shaped like a miniature Christmas present. Jake had gotten it for her their first Christmas. "Wish I could buy you a box full of designer jewelry," he'd written on the card, "but for now will you settle for all my love?"

She sniffed and hung it up.

"I remember that," he said, and she turned to see him coming back into the room holding two mugs. He handed her one. "Eggnog. We always drink eggnog when we decorate the tree."

She accepted the mug with a murmured thanks and took a sip. "You spiked it."

"I always spike it."

And she always got tipsy and crazy. They weren't married anymore. There was no point getting tipsy and crazy. She set it on the coffee table and went back to the ornaments. Jake joined her. "You don't have to help," she told him.

"I know, I want to." He took out a porcelain angel in a lacy gown. "Remember this?"

She nodded. He got it for her three years ago at the Kris Kringl Mart on Thanksgiving weekend. They'd shopped at the merchants and artist booths and drank hot chocolate, and then walked home in the snow. Later that evening, they'd built a fire in the fireplace and made love on the couch. She averted her eyes as he hung it up.

"El, I didn't mean to sound like a bastard earlier. I just thought we weren't going to do a tree. And…"

"And what?" she prompted.

He shrugged. "It sucks that we're doing a tree to get rid of this place."

"You wanted to move to Nashville," she reminded him.

He clenched his jaw, a sure sign that he was keeping back something he'd thought the better of saying.

This had been such a stupid idea. Ella took a big gulp of eggnog.

Jake pulled out the little jukebox topped with a black cowboy hat and she downed the last of her eggnog in one long guzzle.

He looked at the ornament. "Remember when you got this for me?"

She'd found that ornament at a kiosk in a mall when they went to Seattle to celebrate their first anniversary. The company personalized the ornaments and the banner across this one read "I Do and I Will." It was the title of the song he'd written and sung to her at their wedding.

"I need more eggnog," she muttered, going to the kitchen, Tiny trotting after her hopefully. "This wouldn't be good for you," she said as she poured the eggnog. Heck, all those calories wouldn't be good for her, either. She'd be sorry when she stepped on the scale tomorrow but tonight she needed comfort food.

She heard footsteps and a moment later Jake was at her side. "I could use a refill, too," he said, taking the carton from her. He filled his mug, then picked up the bottle of rum he'd left on the counter and added a generous splash. Before she could protest he'd added some to hers, as well. "'Tis the season."

Not to be jolly. She went back to the tree. Enough with the special ornaments, she decided, and dug out a box of plain gold balls. Even those made her want to cry.

Jake gave the jukebox a flick with his finger. "I still think that song could be a hit." He began to sing, painting a musical picture of their wedding.

She grabbed her eggnog and downed more. "Stop."

He frowned. "What happened to us, El? Why didn't we try harder to work things out?"

"What was the point? You're never going to change."

"You liked me just the way I was when we were first together," he said softly.

She didn't say anything to that and they worked in silence for a while, decorating and, every time a new memory came out of the ornament box, drinking. Her mug emptied, he filled it back up. And then it emptied again. How fast the eggnog disappeared when you were trying to wash away memories!

At last the tree was done. "Looks good," Jake said. "There's something missing, though."

She glanced at the stack of boxes. "I don't think so."

He grabbed some old newspaper and started crumpling it. "We always have a fire in the fireplace when we put up the tree."

Had. They always *had.* Ella didn't say anything. Instead, she cleared away the empty boxes while Jake piled on the kindling. By the time she returned, the kindling had caught and he was adding a couple of logs. The fragrance of burning pine began to fill the room. A decorated tree, a husband building a roaring

fire—this was a scene fit for a magazine ad selling...
what? Happiness.

No, this wasn't *true* happiness, just an alcohol-induced
buzz.

Buzzing was good, though.

Jake fetched more rum and joined her on the couch.
"Remember the first time we lit a fire in that fireplace?"
he asked as he freshened her mug.

She took another sip. How could she forget? He'd
thought he was opening the damper and instead had
closed it. She smiled. "You've gotten pretty good at building fires since then." He'd gotten good at a lot of things,
especially making love to her. He knew every inch of
her, exactly what turned her on.

She felt his fingers caressing the back of her neck,
right below her hairline. That was one of the things.

"This is our last Christmas," he whispered, then began
singing again, the chorus of that first song he'd written
for her.

Tell him to stop, she commanded herself, but she
couldn't. She'd always loved it when he sang to her. It
had made her feel special. She wanted to feel special
one last time.

He took her mug and set it on the coffee table. Then
he took her face in his hands and looked at her with longing in those gorgeous dark eyes of his.

He still loves you.

It was the rum talking. She wouldn't listen.

Be honest. You still love him, said the rum. *And you
want him.*

The rum was right. She let Jake kiss her. And kiss her
again. And then she let him slide his hand up her midriff.

Every nerve ending along the way did the Wave. *Woooh!* Oh, this wasn't leading anywhere good.

No, said the rum. *It's leading somewhere great.*

Cecily looked at the clock in Cass's living room. "I wonder what's going on with Ella. It's not like her to be this late."

Cass had the DVD of *Miracle on Thirty-Fourth Street* in the player, waiting for their last movie buff to arrive. Ella loved these movie nights. Where was she?

"I say give her ten more minutes and then we start without her," Samantha said, popping a chocolate mint truffle in her mouth.

"I saw her at Santa's tree lot today." Cass helped herself to another Christmas cookie from the platter on her coffee table. "Maybe she got busy decorating and forgot."

"Kind of early to put up a tree, isn't it?" Samantha asked. "We used to wait until mid-December to put ours up so it wouldn't dry out."

"Al claims his trees are so fresh you don't need to wait," Cass said. "Although, come to think of it, the one we got from him last year was practically a fire hazard by Christmas Eve."

"So when are you putting up your tree?" Charley asked her.

"Good question," Cass said. "Somewhere in between the wedding dress and the DJ."

Samantha shook her head. "Pulling this wedding together so fast is—well, I don't know how you're doing it."

"Piece of cake," Cass said.

"Spoken like a true baker." Samantha grinned. "Have you picked a caterer yet?"

"It's on the to-do list. I need to find someone Dani will like and I can afford."

"Well," Samantha said slowly, "Bailey's planning on coming up for the holidays. She's the queen of caterers and I bet she could be persuaded to come up early. She'd give you a deal."

"Now, there's a good idea," Cass said. "I wouldn't have to worry with Bailey in charge."

"Well, other than worrying about her tripping and falling into the wedding cake," Samantha joked.

Cecily couldn't help smiling. Bailey wasn't the most graceful girl on the planet. But of the three of them, she was the bubbliest. A girl could get away with a lot of klutziness when she was adorable.

Cass poured herself a glass of wine. "Well, I say we start the movie. I have to get up with the birds."

The life of a baker. Ugh. But Cass was right. They couldn't wait indefinitely. "Let me just call her," Cecily said. She picked up her cell phone and called Ella's house.

Jake answered on the third ring.

Now that they were divorced, Cecily never knew quite what to say to him. It was so awkward when friends broke up. Heck, it was more than that. It was heartbreaking. "Oh, Jake. Hi. Sorry to bother you, but we're getting ready to watch our movie and we're wondering where Ella is. Do you know if she left?"

"She's not gonna make it tonight," Jake said. "She had too much eggnog and she can't drive."

It was a fifteen-minute walk from their place to Cass's. "Too much eggnog?"

"We were decorating the tree," Jake said, as if that explained it.

Before Cecily could say anything more, he added, "I'll tell her you called, Cec." And then he hung up. Cecily stared at her phone, trying to figure out what was odd about that conversation.

"So, is she coming?" Samantha asked.

"No," Cecily said. "She had too much eggnog."

"Too much eggnog," her sister repeated.

"Eggnog and tree-trimming. Something is going on over there," Cecily said.

"You think they're getting back together?" Charley asked.

"Bad plan if you ask me," Samantha said, choosing another chocolate.

"Not necessarily," Cecily argued. "Maybe they've come to some sort of compromise." She hoped so.

Cass shook her head. "I don't know. Getting back together with her ex? It doesn't sound smart to me."

"People can change," Charley said.

Cecily hadn't been a matchmaker for nothing. She could read between the lines, and Charley's statement read like a potential horror story. "Not all people," she cautioned.

Charley pretended not to see her friend's warning look. Instead, she loaded a bowl with popcorn and said, "So, let's start the movie."

Okay, *there* was a heart destined for the heartbreak trail. Charley was going to do what she was going to do, and there'd be no stopping her. Just like there'd been no stopping Ella when she let her mother convince her that she needed to dump Jake. Cecily was the resident love expert here. Why didn't her friends ever listen to her?

Maybe because you've gone through two fiancés? Well, there was that. She filled another bowl with popcorn and sat back to watch the movie. What was going on over at Ella's?

Twelve

Ella stumbled out of a deep sleep Monday morning to find she had three arms. One was under her pillow and another was stretched out in front of her. Over that arm lay the third, a muscular one with dark hair. She blinked herself the rest of the way into consciousness to see that the third arm was attached to a second body tucked up against hers, a body that didn't belong in her bed. Jake.

With a yelp she hurled herself out of bed. This sudden movement didn't do wonders for her head, which was throbbing.

He was awake now and looking confused. "El?"

"What are you doing in my bed?" *Someone's been sleeping in my bed. And doing other things, too.*

"I was sleeping," he said, sitting up.

"Before that?" Why was she asking? She knew.

He grinned.

"But we're divorced." She ran a hand through her hair. How had this happened? Of course, that was a stupid question. She'd gotten sloppy sentimental and tipsy.

"We can fix that," he said easily. He slid from under the covers and started toward her.

"Where are your clothes?" For that matter, where were *her* clothes? Naked. She was naked. She grabbed the bedspread and held it in front of her like a shield.

"Scattered all over the living room, along with yours. And it's a little late for that, isn't it?" he teased, pointing at her makeshift covering. He tried to hug her but she jerked away, tripping over the bedspread in the process. "This was wrong. You seduced me!"

"Oh, yeah? Well, you seemed pretty anxious to be seduced. Come on, Ella, quit pretending you didn't want that as much as I did."

"I…" She had. "This doesn't mean anything."

"It means a lot. It means we belong together."

"No, we don't." Jake had been a mistake. Last night had been a mistake. She was done making mistakes. "I'm not doing that again. Ever." At least not with him.

A new thought occurred to her. What if she'd gotten pregnant? It only took once and she wasn't on the Pill anymore. "Did you use protection?"

"Uh, no."

One time, it was just one time. What were the chances? "Ooooh. I feel sick," she moaned. Morning sickness? Already?

"I'll make us some coffee," he said.

Exactly what she wanted, a cozy cup of coffee with her ex-husband. *You didn't have any objections to sharing a cozy mug of eggnog with him last night.* Actually, several.

She hurried to the shower, determined to wash away the fuzzy memory of his touch and any latent traces of longing.

By the time he came out of the kitchen with her coffee, she was on her way out the door.

"Where are you going? It's only eight."

"I need to get to the shop."

"It's not open on Mondays. Don't run away, El."

"I'm not running away," she said haughtily. "I'm just… not staying. I have extra work to do." She'd come up with something.

He frowned. "What a little chicken you are."

"I'm not a chicken."

"Yeah, you are. By the way…"

"What?"

He nodded at her chest. "Your sweater's on backward."

She looked down. He was right. She was so upset she couldn't even dress herself properly. "Thank you," she said, trying for some dignity. Then she shut the door and ran down the walk.

It wasn't until she got to the shop that she realized she'd also put on one black pump and one brown one and she had a black sock on one foot and a navy blue one on the other. Great. Now she looked as messed up on the outside as she was on the inside. Gilded Lily's didn't carry shoes so she was stuck. Unless, of course, she wanted to run back home and change. And see Jake. Which, she insisted sternly, she didn't want to do. It was a good thing they weren't open on Mondays. No one would see her messed-up feet and ask what the heck she'd been thinking when she got dressed this morning.

She spent the next hour updating the store's website and Facebook page, trying to ignore her mismatched shoes and her mixed-up feelings, then got busy ordering merchandise. There was always plenty to do in a small shop. Sadly, nothing she did was enough to take her mind off Jake. She could still remember the touch of his lips on hers, the feel of his arms around her.... *Oh, stop,* she scolded herself, *you sound like one of your romance novels.*

And what was wrong with that?

Plenty, when you were romancing the wrong man.

Sigh.

Jake had finished cleaning up the kitchen. Not so much as a speck of dirt anywhere. That would make Ella happy. He'd done the laundry, too. He could never fold clothes right, but he hoped she'd be pleased that he'd tried. And now the house stuff was finished, or at least all that he could see. He had several hours until Curt Whalen came for his after-school guitar lesson. Jake wished he could pop on over to the shop and take Ella out to lunch. He used to do that when he was working at the music store. They'd go to Big Brats and grab something. Sometimes they'd eaten sandwiches at the shop while she was between customers. Those had been good times, living simply and loving it while they waited for him to catch a break, sell a song.

Last night it was like it had been when they were first married—no worries, no disagreements, no mother-in-law telling lies about him. Why couldn't they go back in time?

Back in time. Was there an idea in there? He went in search of his guitar. Two hours later he'd poured his heart into a kick-ass song, perfect for Lady Antebellum. He went to the spare room downstairs, where he'd set up a small recording studio with secondhand equipment, and got to work on a song demo. Any day now a publisher would pick up one of his songs. He was getting closer all the time. Little Big Town Publishing had been encouraging. A song picked up by a Nashville publisher—maybe that would be enough to win Ella back. A guy could dream.

Cecily called Ella's cell shortly before lunch. "Want to get a salad at Zelda's?"

No way was Ella going out in public dressed like this. 'Um, I'm working at the shop."

"On a Monday?"

"I had a lot to do." *And a lot to run away from.*

"Oh. Well, how about I pick up something and come by?" Before Ella could think up some excuse to keep her away, Cecily said a breezy, "See you in a bit," and ended the call.

Ella looked at her mismatched shoes and frowned. She should've told Cecily she didn't have time for lunch. The last thing she needed was her friend the matchmaker coming by. Cecily could be unnervingly astute, and Ella was already unnerved enough.

Half an hour later Cecily was tapping on the shop door. Ella opened it and she walked in bearing a big take-out bag, the aroma of chicken dancing in with her. "I got a couple of hot chicken salads," she said just in case Ella's nose wasn't working.

"That sounds good." Ella hurried back to the other side of the counter to hide her feet.

Cecily allowed her a moment to savor her first bite, then said, "We missed you last night."

Ella could feel her face catching fire. "We got busy putting up a tree. I thought it might help sell the house."

"Uh-huh," Cecily said diplomatically. She took a bite of salad, then picked up the multibead red necklace Ella had put on the counter earlier. "This would be cute for the holidays." She checked the price tag. "I think I'll get it for Mom. Even though you're not open, you wouldn't mind ringing it up, would you?"

Ella could feel her friend's assessing gaze on her. Oh, this was awkward. She gnawed her bottom lip as she rang up the sale.

"Everything okay?" Cecily asked.

Ella slipped the necklace in a gift bag. "I think I made a mistake."

"Which time? When you got divorced or when you slept with Jake last night?"

Ella stared at her friend in wide-eyed shock. "Are you psychic?"

"When we called and Jake said you'd been drinking eggnog and couldn't drive, it wasn't too hard to figure out something was up."

Ella groaned. "I was stupid. I don't know what I was thinking."

"I guess you weren't thinking of Axel."

Axel. She'd forgotten all about him. "Oh, if he found out…"

"Don't worry," Cecily said. "Nobody's going to tell him."

Except maybe Jake. "I should never have slept with him," Ella said. "And I'm sure not going to do it again."

"Never say never." Cecily leaned over the counter and looked at Ella's feet. "By the way, am I hallucinating or are you wearing two different shoes?"

"You're hallucinating."

"Uh-huh," Cecily said, and left it at that.

The bakery was closed on Mondays, so after Willie was out the door for school, Cass and Dani and Amber (who'd been allowed to miss school so she could be part of the all-important mission) had made the trek to Special Day Bridal in Seattle. Now Cass and Amber waited in the seating area for Dani to model the dress of her dreams.

The shop was a feast for the eyes, with celebrity-worthy bridesmaids' dresses and white gowns fit for a princess hanging everywhere. Lace, organza, satin—money, money, money. The velveteen chair Cass was sitting on probably cost more than all her living room furniture put together. She wouldn't be surprised if this dress cost more than all the furniture in her house. *And* the appliances.

Amber hadn't stopped prowling the place since they arrived. "Look at this one, Mom." She pulled out a tiered organza number.

"It's beautiful," Cass acknowledged. Everything here was.

Dani came out of the dressing area, followed by the shop owner, who'd had been hustling in and out with goodies.

"Oh, my," Cass breathed. A montage of scenes flashed through her mind: Dani as a smiling baby, jumping up and down in her crib with excitement, waiting for Cass to lift her out; five-year-old Dani blowing out the candles on the doll-shaped birthday cake Cass had made her; Dani at seventeen, wearing her first prom dress. Her daughter had grown up overnight. Now, here she stood, a beautiful woman in her bridal gown, every mother's dream come true. She wore an off-the-shoulder long-sleeved white silk taffeta dress with a formfitting bodice and sweeping, full skirt. The cuff, neckline and hem were trimmed with white angora to match the white angora hat. Scalloped layers of tulle trimmed with lace and silver sequins added bling. Cass could see why her daughter had fallen in love with the dress.

Dani looked at her hopefully. "Well, what do you think?"

"Wow," Amber said.

"It's stunning," Cass said.

Dani beamed. "I love it so much."

Cass swallowed and asked, "How much is it?"

Dani brushed a hand along the soft trim. "Twelve hundred and sixty dollars for the dress."

"It's on sale, thirty percent off," the store's owner threw in. "And we won't have to do any alteration, which is unusual."

"And the hat?" Cass asked weakly.

"Two hundred dollars."

So, fourteen hundred and sixty dollars. Plus tax. She'd pay it, though. It was worth every penny to see that radiant smile on her daughter's face.

"Don't worry, Mom," Dani said. "Daddy's going to pay for it."

He was? "Oh."

"I talked to him yesterday."

Without telling her. *Be glad he's picking up the tab,* Cass advised herself. *Be glad he wants to be involved.*

"That's…great," she said, injecting goodwill into her voice.

"He said to call him and he'll give you his Visa number," Dani told the woman.

"That was really cool of Daddy," Amber said.

"Yes, it was." In spite of the pep talk she'd just given herself, Cass found it difficult to get the words past the jealous bone caught in her throat. She'd worked so hard, done everything for her kids, and now she felt like she was being displaced. Bought out and squeezed out.

"I know it's not rational," she said to Dot later that day when she was back in Icicle Falls. "But, damn, it bugs me that he gets to ride in on his white horse after being such an absent father. And it's so…passive-aggressive. He doesn't talk to me at all, discuss what he will and won't pay for. He just cherry-picks and coughs up the money for the big, high-drama items."

Dot's bunion surgery had been a success and now she sat enthroned on her couch, her foot propped up on a pillow. The coffee table in front of her hosted a get-well box of Sweet Dreams chocolates from Dot's friend Muriel Sterling, a glass of water, a crossword puzzle book and the TV remote. And now a bowl of the chicken stew Cass had brought.

"Come on, kiddo," Dot said. "Everything's a high-drama item when you're planning a wedding. You know that. And if your ex is like most men, he's clueless. He wouldn't think to offer—he just waits around with his checkbook. Your daughter's got his number, in more ways than one. She calls and says, 'Daddy, I need money,' and he forks it over. The silver lining is that you don't have to pay."

And Dani had the gown of her dreams. Still… "I feel like I'm paying in other ways."

"Everything has a cost. I know it's hard to share when you've pulled most of the load and had the kids all to yourself for so long, but it looks like that's changing and there's nothing you can do about it. It's all part of the for-better-or-worse thing."

"Well, it shouldn't be, since we're not married anymore," Cass said grumpily.

"Divorce doesn't cancel out for better or worse, not when you've got kids."

Dot was right, Cass told herself as she drove home. She had to come to grips with the fact that Mason was in her children's lives (and hers) to stay. Why was that so hard to do?

Because it wasn't fair, that was why.

How many times had the kids said that to her over the years? And how many times had she replied, "Who said life is fair?" Of course, it wasn't, and now she'd have to follow her own advice: make the best of it.

She remembered how happy Dani had looked standing in that bridal shop in her wedding gown. Her daughter was getting married and she got to be a part of it. If she couldn't make the best of *that,* she had something seriously wrong with her.

"I'm not going to keep encouraging Richard," Charley told her reflection. The woman looking back at her was all dressed to party in charcoal slacks, a black sweater and a diamond pendant necklace—the very necklace Richard had given her for Valentine's Day three years ago.

Not going to encourage him, huh? That was why she'd let him play footsie with her on Saturday night. That was why she'd bought mistletoe and hung it up. That was why she was wearing a Victoria's Secret black bra under her sweater. *Planning on removing your sweater later tonight?*

She frowned at her reflection. "You are pathetic." She had to stop being pathetic. Didn't she?

No, she answered herself. Everyone deserved a second chance. Richard really was sorry and he was doing everything he could to prove it. And she was sticking with Victoria.

The doorbell rang, sending butterflies swirling in her stomach. Silly. She felt like a teenager getting ready to go to the prom instead of a woman about to go out to dinner. She opened the door and he stepped in, smelling like Armani cologne.

"You're gorgeous," he said.

"It's just pants and a sweater," she said, feeling ridiculously pleased.

"I wasn't talking about the clothes." He held out a small box.

"What's this?"

"Just a little something I thought you might like."

She opened the box to find a pair of etched silver open teardrop earrings. "They're lovely."

"I thought they'd look good on you."

Pricy earrings, sleigh rides, expensive brunches, pitching in to help during a crisis—no man went to all that trouble unless he was truly sorry for his wicked ways.

And now they were off to the Orchard House Bed and Breakfast several miles outside of town for a five-course dinner sponsored by one of the local wineries. Another pricy bit of penance, and a penance she was happy to let him pay.

Zelda's was closed on Sunday and Monday evenings, and after the crazy weekend they'd had, a spectacular dinner that she didn't have to plan and prepare was exactly what the doctor ordered—although a heart specialist might have suggested she attend with someone else.

The Orchard House's restaurant was a feast for the senses, with a fire burning in the river rock fireplace, sparkling silver and crystal on linen tablecloths and holiday floral arrangements that must have cost an arm and a leg. In addition to a treat for the eyes, diners were given a treat for their ears with a harpist in one corner of the room, playing Christmas carols. Charley took it all in, making mental notes on how she could improve her own place.

The food was incredible, from the first course, which offered caramelized apple with brie and red wine cherry glaze, to the dessert—white chocolate strawberry shortcake paired with a cabernet sauvignon.

"That was fabulous," she said as they drove back.

"Like the woman I'm with." He smiled at her in a way that turned her poor insides to mush.

She was a goner. Tonight she was going to cave. She knew it, Richard knew it. A woman could only hold out for so long. Anyway, it didn't feel right to hold out any longer. Driving home together, sharing this intimate space while Aerosmith serenaded them with "I Don't Want to Miss a Thing" felt like the good old days when they were happy together. They could be happy again, couldn't they? Heck, they were happy right now.

Still, she was going to make him fight for this last bit of ground. When they pulled up in front of the house she didn't invite him inside. She knew she didn't need to, anyway. Just as he'd been doing since he hit town, he'd invite himself in.

Sure enough. "Can I talk you into a nightcap?" he asked softly.

"I'm stuffed."

"How about some conversation, then?"

"Talking is good."

Talking was, indeed, good. They took a stroll down memory lane and then his hand took a stroll along her arm. A minute later he was kissing her. "You are an amazing woman. You know that?" he murmured.

"You're just now realizing?"

"I knew it all along. Take me back."

She pretended to consider. "I might. Depends on whether you're still any good in bed."

He grinned and proceeded to show her.

They'd gotten as far as playing show and tell with her Victoria's Secret bra when she heard sirens. "Do you hear that?"

"Hmm?" he said as he kissed his way down her neck.

"Sirens," she said, stating the obvious.

"Someone probably left a candle burning."

One of her friends or neighbors. She pushed Richard away and sat up, straining to hear. A fire right before Christmas would be a nightmare. She made a mental note to give whoever was dealing with it a gift certificate to Zelda's.

"They're nowhere near us." Richard ran a hand up her back.

She ignored the flutter it caused in her chest. "It sounds like they're somewhere downtown. If that's the case, it's someone's business."

She'd barely finished speaking when her phone rang. Suddenly, she knew who the fire victim was.

Thirteen

Charley stood across the street in shock, watching as her baby went up in flames. She'd poured everything into this restaurant—her money, her time, her heart and soul—and now it was dying before her eyes. So was a part of her.

The flames lit the night and the faces of bystanders as firefighters scrambled to put out the blaze. The heat blew in her face, taunting her. It took the chill from the night but Charley couldn't stop shivering. How could this be happening? She stood rooted to the street, hardly noticing Richard's arm around her, watching the place that had hosted so many people, so many events, turn black.

As the fire hoses did their work, the flames evolved into giant plumes of smoke. That was even worse than the flames, a real-life illustration of what was happening to her dreams.

It was difficult to see past the tears, but she became aware of her friends, coming to stand by her. Cass positioned herself on Charley's other side, opposite Richard, and Samantha and Cecily fell in line next to Cass. Finally, Ella slipped behind her and draped a big blanket over her shoulders. They stood around her like palace guards, deflecting inquisitive townspeople and curious tourists alike, wrapping her in love.

Fire Chief Berg came up to her. "I'm sorry, Charley."

"What caused it?" she asked, barely able to speak.

"We won't be able to tell for a while. Once the fire is completely out, we'll do salvage and investigate the area of origination. I'll call you as soon as we know something, I promise."

She nodded and managed to thank him.

"You can't do any good here and tomorrow will be busy," Richard said, attempting to lead her away.

She resisted. "No. I'm going to stay until the fire is out."

"Charley."

"I'm staying," she said through gritted teeth.

He gave up. "Okay."

People began to drift away, but her friends remained until Zelda's restaurant was nothing but a charred shell.

"Now we need to go home," Richard said.

This time she didn't resist. There was nothing more to see.

She didn't cry until she got home. Then she curled up in her bed and sobbed. Richard climbed in behind her. Pulling the blankets over them both, he wrapped her in his arms and let her have at it. She cried until her head throbbed and she was hoarse. Finally, exhausted, she fell into a fitful sleep. But with dawn she was awake and staring at the ceiling while the tears slid down her cheeks.

"I'll make coffee," Richard said.

He brought her coffee in bed, along with a croissant, which she had no interest in eating.

"Try," he urged. "It's going to be a tough day."

That was an understatement. The worst part of her

morning was when she got the news about the cause of the fire. It appeared that one of her kitchen workers—probably Bruno—had left a burner on after the Monday lunch shift. A pot on top of the stove, which should have been put away, had eventually ignited and the fire had spread from there. The sprinkler system had failed to activate, and if not for the fire alarm system, the place would have burned to the ground. Charley couldn't help thinking it might as well have for all that remained of it. Renovation would take months. With a heavy heart, she put in a call to the insurance company.

Midafternoon Cecily came into her sister's office at Sweet Dreams Chocolate Company. "We need to take some vitamin C over to Charley." Chocolate was so much better than the other vitamin C when a friend was under stress.

"I'm sure she's buried in paperwork. The last thing she wants right now is visitors," Samantha said.

"We're talking about the woman who threw herself a party when her divorce was final," Cecily argued.

"That was different. She was celebrating then. I don't think she's celebrating today."

"Chocolate is good for celebration *and* commiseration," Cecily said.

Samantha considered this for a moment. "You're right."

Fifteen minutes later they were on their way to Charley's house with a ten-pound box of salted caramels, her favorite.

"You can still smell the smoke from the fire," Cecily said, wrinkling her nose.

"As if it isn't bad enough that she has to see her ruined restaurant," Samantha said, shaking her head, "she has to smell it, too. I can't imagine what I'd do if Sweet Dreams burned down."

"You'd rebuild, of course, just like Charley will. But don't even say things like that. It creeps me out."

"Don't worry, we've already had our share of misery."

"Poor Charley, I hope this is the last misery she has to go through," Cecily said as they walked up her front porch steps.

Samantha rang the doorbell but they didn't hear any sounds of life from inside the house. "I told you this was a bad idea," she said, and turned to go.

Cecily stayed put and rang the bell again. "Give them a minute. She needs this candy, and she needs her friends."

This time they heard approaching footsteps. A moment later Richard opened the door.

"We brought something for Charley," Samantha said, holding out the box.

He took it and nodded solemnly. "That was nice. She could use it."

Cecily expected him to invite them in. After all, they were two of Charley's closest friends. Instead, he said, "Thanks. I'll see that she gets it," and shut the door.

"I don't like that guy," Samantha muttered as they walked down the porch steps.

Cecily frowned and pulled up her coat collar. "I've got a bad feeling about him."

"You should tell Charley."

"I doubt she puts much stock in my hunches."

"She should. They're rarely wrong."

Cecily shrugged. "Even if she did, she wouldn't want to hear this one. Once a woman's made up her mind about a man, it isn't easy to steer her in another direction. When it comes to love, sometimes we have to learn the hard way." Boy, did she know that. Experience was a thorough teacher.

"Someone should invent a spray," Samantha said. "Like bug spray, only for losers."

Cecily chuckled. "Bad-boy spray?"

"Something like that. I'd buy you a bottle."

"Me?" Cecily protested.

"Yeah. Then you could shoot it at Todd Black every time he drops by the gift shop to buy chocolate for his mom. Since when is *he* such a good son?"

Since he'd run into Cecily at the drugstore when she'd returned to Icicle Falls to stay. She'd also encountered him at the gym. Several times. That was a bad place to run into a man you were determined not to be attracted to—T-shirts and muscles and...did sweating release pheromones? Todd Black was a bad boy, a heartbreak waiting to happen. Cecily strongly suspected he was the type of man who'd sleep with her, steal her heart and then steal away, move on to the next conquest. Everything he said was a double entendre, meant to tickle her hormones, and every encounter with him hit her zing-o-meter. It was stupid to let herself be attracted to a man who was so wrong for her. But if he suggested she stop by his seedy tavern to try out his pinball machine one more time, she was afraid she might just give in. If she could go a couple of months without seeing him, it would help, but that was next to impossible in a small town.

But if it wasn't Todd, it would be someone else. Bad boys were her Achilles' heel. And, darn it all, bad boys were everywhere. *It doesn't mean you need to get involved with one,* she reminded herself.

That last thought led her back to Charley and Richard. Hopefully, her intuition was off for once and Charley's bad boy had reformed.

Ella had just sent Pat Wilder out the door with a floating-petals coral top and a new bracelet when Axel Fuchs called.

"I'm bringing some people by to see the house around five-thirty," he said, "so make sure Jake cleans."

"I will," she promised. She could close a little early, run home and pitch in.

"And maybe you'd like to go out with one of your friends for a while after work," Axel added.

He probably didn't trust her to stay out from underfoot. "Okay."

"And get Jake to take Tiny for a walk."

No woman, no man, no dog—make the house look like anything but a home, she thought. Why did that bug her? It already wasn't a home even with them in it.

"These people have driven by and love the place from the outside. And they like the price," Axel continued. "So fingers crossed that we'll have a sale for you this time."

"I hope so," she said fervently. Then she could get Jake gone and move on with her life.

She called his cell. Naturally, he didn't answer. Why did the man have a cell phone when he never bothered to use it? "We might have a sale tonight," she told his voice mail. "Can you see that the kitchen is clean and your bedroom picked up?" She ended the call and frowned. She felt like his mother instead of his wife. Ex-wife, she quickly corrected herself.

An hour later her cell rang. "Got your message," Jake said. "Everything's clean."

Hmm. Jake-clean or really clean?

"I'm running the dishes right now."

"Can you sweep the kitchen floor?"

"Already done."

"Check to be sure the bathrooms—"

"Did it."

This was, indeed, surprising. "Oh. Well."

"Anything else?" he asked shortly.

"Um, Axel wants us both gone when he shows the house."

"When is he bringing them?"

"Around five-thirty."

"Well, I'm not done with my last student until then," Jake said, and his tone of voice added, *And I'm not leaving one minute before.*

"Fine."

Her tone of voice must have added, *Be that way,* because he said, "But Tiny and I will get out of here right after."

"Good."

"Yeah, good," he muttered.

Now she felt bad, like she'd somehow turned him out in the cold. Well, she was out in the cold, too. And anyway, this was for his benefit as well as hers.

She stayed late at the shop, then stopped by Charley's house to see how she was doing. Her friend looked like a zombie, her eyes bloodshot with purple shadows beneath them. She was wearing sweats and her hair was tied up in a sloppy bun.

"Come on in," she said. "Richard's out in the kitchen making dinner. Want to stay?"

"You guys probably don't want company," Ella hedged. She'd really meant to stop by for only a few minutes.

Charley swung the door wide. "I always want company. Anyway, how can you say no to stuffed pork loin?"

It turned out she couldn't. Ella watched as Richard waited on her friend, refilled her wineglass. And the one time Charley grew despondent, he said, "It's okay. We'll go on to do something even better."

How sweet.

"You're right," Charley said. "The kitchen really needed a remodel, anyway, and I'd like to make the bar bigger." She stared at her plate. "I just hope people don't switch loyalties while we're rebuilding."

"Of course they won't," Ella assured her. "Everyone loves Zelda's and everyone loves you."

That made Charley tear up. Richard patted her hand.

"You should rest, babe," he said after they'd finished eating.

Ella got the hint and left, feeling hopeful that things would work out for her friend. And only the slightest bit jealous.

She came home to the smell of Jake's chili. If she'd known he was going to heat that up again, she'd have hurried over and sprayed the house, or lit a scented candle. Except that leaving a candle unattended was never a good idea. Fire hazard.

She thought again of poor Charley's restaurant. Life had a way of taking turns you never expected. It sure had for her. Who would've guessed she'd be divorced and sharing her dream house with her ex-husband?

She heard Jake's voice and realized he was back home. That meant their potential buyers had come and gone. She slipped off her shoes and padded out to the kitchen, where she caught him feeding Tiny crackers.

"That's why he's getting fat," she accused.

"Hey, it's comfort food. He needs comfort."

Comfort and joy. There was none of that this holiday season. Ella sighed. "Has Axel called? Did the people like the house?"

Jake nodded. "Yeah. He's coming over at seven with their offer."

"Our asking price?"

"Within five thousand."

That was close enough as far as Ella was concerned. "Great. Let's take it."

"May as well," Jake said. He turned his back on her and got busy removing his bowl of chili from the microwave.

She walked out of the kitchen and went to the living room to fidget. There wasn't anything to do here, and she'd read her latest *Martha Stewart Living* from cover to cover. She went upstairs and brushed her teeth. Then she freshened her makeup. Then she was out of things to do once more. She went back downstairs, feeling like a prisoner awaiting sentencing.

What was *that* about? She should be doing a jig. They had an offer on the house. By the new year she'd be done with this ridiculous living arrangement. She'd be a free woman. *You should be celebrating,* she told herself.

Jake came into the living room and sprawled on the couch, staring into the cold fireplace. The sight of him made her feel even less like celebrating.

The doorbell rang and he gave her a stony stare. "You gonna let him in?"

Yes, she was. A moment later Axel was in the living room, brimming with satisfaction. "They want to know if you'll include some of the furniture," he said.

"May as well," Jake said, still stone-faced.

"What furniture?" Ella asked.

"Your bedroom set."

The sleigh bed. They'd shared more than heated en-counters in that bed. They'd shared laughter and dreams.

Ella looked over at Jake. He was scowling at the winter darkness outside the window. "Are we cool with that?" she asked.

He shrugged. "We're not gonna use it."

"I guess so, then," Ella said to Axel. Like Jake said, they weren't going to use it.

Within a matter of minutes, the papers were signed and she was seeing Axel to the door.

"I think you got a good deal," he said.

"Yes, we did. Thank you so much."

"Now you can get on with your life."

Exactly what she kept telling herself. "Yes, at last."

"Let's go out Friday night and celebrate. The Icicle Falls chorale is doing their winter concert at Festival Hall. Handel's *Messiah*. We can have dinner before."

Classical music wasn't her favorite, but she certainly liked it better than jazz, and the *Hallelujah Chorus* seemed appropriate, considering that she'd just unloaded her house and her unwanted roommate. "Sure." She had nothing better to do with anyone else. Her thoughts veered to Jake, scowling in the living room.

"Good. The concert's at eight. I'll make dinner reservations at Schwangau for six-thirty."

Just like that, without asking her where she wanted to go. Granted, Zelda's wasn't an option at the moment, but what about Italian Alps or Der Spaniard?

No, not Mexican. That was where she and Jake always went.

Oh, who cared where she and Jake always went. "How about Der Spaniard?"

Axel looked momentarily surprised that some of the planning was being taken out of his hands but he recovered quickly enough. "All right, if that's where you want to go."

"It is." She could eat at that restaurant with anyone and have a good time. Anyone!

With Axel out the door, she turned back toward the living room to find Jake still on the couch where she'd left him, Tiny lying at his feet.

"So, I guess you're going out to celebrate," he greeted her.

"Why not?" she retorted. She sat down on the opposite end of the couch, wishing she could feel more excited by this turn of events. "I mean, this is a relief. We're rid of a house we can't afford." *And a sleigh bed.*

Jake studied her from his end of the couch, those dark eyes of his filled with sadness. "Do you ever ask yourself how we got here, El?"

Suddenly she wanted to cry. She bit her lip and shook her head.

He looked around the living room, taking in everything. "I'm gonna miss this place. We had some great times here."

"Stop." The words came out sharper than she intended.

"You already took away our future, El. Don't take away my past, too."

"Me! Oh, no. Don't make me the bad guy here."

"I wasn't the one who wanted a divorce."

"No, you had a good thing going, didn't you?"

He made no reply to that. Instead, he left the couch and disappeared down the hall. Probably off to the kitchen for more chili. She could hear him out there, opening cupboard doors.

But a moment later he returned with something very different. She saw the Christmas mugs and knew instantly what was in them. "Oh, no. No more eggnog."

He held out a mug. "We were happy once. Let's drink to that. Let's part friends. Can we do that much?"

All right. They could do that much.

She took the mug and he sat down next to her on the couch and clinked his against it. "To new beginnings."

"To new beginnings," she repeated.

Now he was looking around the room again. "I hope the new owners enjoy this house as much as we did. Do you think they'll put their tree in the same place?"

This resigned kindness was unnerving. Ella took a sip of her eggnog. Spiked, of course. "I don't know."

"I hope they don't repaint."

She and Jake had spent an entire weekend painting the living room. She still loved her red accent wall. "Isn't that the color of passion?" Jake had joked, and then proceeded to demonstrate the passion it inspired in him.

She had to stop thinking about all of that. It was in the past. They were done. Through. Finished. That was how she wanted it. She started to cry.

"Aw, babe," he said, his voice anguished.

The next thing she knew he was kissing her. And then she was kissing him. And then they were taking one final ride in the sleigh bed.

Fourteen

Jake awoke to discover that he was alone in bed. Dang. He'd been hoping for another round with Ella. He rolled over to check the clock on the bedside table and there sat Tiny looking at him. "Where's, Mom, boy?"

Tiny woofed, doggy encouragement for Jake to get up and find out for himself.

It was only eight-thirty. Ella wouldn't have left for work yet. Maybe she was in the kitchen, making breakfast for them. Now there was a pleasant thought. Except if she was in the kitchen, Tiny wouldn't be up here. He'd have been down there with her, looking hopeful.

Jake threw off the covers and went downstairs to investigate. In his boxers. There'd probably be no more complaining about that now that they were back together. They *were* back together, weren't they?

The kitchen was empty, and clean, with not so much as a dish in the sink. Or a love note on the table. Maybe she'd been in a hurry. Maybe she had to do inventory at the shop. No, inventory didn't happen until January. Maybe someone had an appointment for a private style consult. Ella often did that, and when she did, she always went to the shop early to prepare.

He picked up his cell phone from the coffee table and called her.

She said a wary hello.

Okay, the clues were adding up, making it hard to stay in denial. "Hey, babe. You left before I could kiss you awake."

"Jake, last night was a mistake. We should never have slept together."

Oh, not this again. "Come on, El. You can't believe that. The only mistake we've made was getting divorced."

"I'm sorry, but—"

He cut her off before she could finish. "Let's talk this out. I'll come by the shop and take you to Der Spaniard for dinner." He'd cancel band practice. Or better yet, he'd take Ella with him and she could meet Jen, check out the competition she'd been so jealous of. Ha.

"I can't. I'm going out with Mims."

Her tone of voice guaranteed she wouldn't break that date. And once she'd spent an evening with her mother, it would be all over. *Mims strikes again.* He had to convince Elle to listen to reason before the wicked witch of the Pacific Northwest brainwashed her any more. "Look," he began.

"I'm sorry, Jake, I've got to go," she said and ended the call.

Jake tossed his cell phone on the couch and sat staring at the dead fireplace. Then he swore. Then he drop-kicked a pillow across the room while Tiny cheered him on with a hearty woof. He drop-kicked another pillow but the second kick didn't help, either, so he marched back upstairs. He threw on sweats and went out the door to Bruisers to work off his anger.

An hour later, most of it was still riding his back. He left the gym, returned home and took Tiny for a long walk. After that he ate a big bowl of sugary cereal, then showered and dressed in his favorite jeans and Washington Huskies sweatshirt. As he stepped out of his pathetic single-guy bedroom, he couldn't help looking into the master where he'd slept last night. The sleigh bed mocked him. *No more rides for you, pal.*

He heaved a sigh. Why was Ella being so stubborn? She had to know deep down that this was all wrong. She couldn't make love like she had the night before and not want to be together. They'd come about as close to heaven as two people could get. Close to heaven. Now there was a good hook. Already humming, he went downstairs in search of his guitar.

Cass was exhausted. Not from work, but from hammering out the food details for the reception with Dani. Dani had sneered at the more affordable suggestions Bailey Sterling had emailed.

"For a wedding? Jeez, Mom."

"There's nothing wrong with Alfredo," Cass had objected, "especially with shrimp in it, and this has shrimp and smoked salmon."

"Probably a teaspoon of each," Dani had said sarcastically.

"Not if Bailey's doing it, and if we add appetizers…"

That had produced an eye roll. "What? More shrimp?"

"In endive, with avocado. And we can add chicken. Everyone loves chicken wings."

"No one loves chicken wings. They're stupid!"

"So is paying a fortune for salmon filets, especially if you want a band."

At that Dani had thrown up her hands. "Fine. Why don't we just make it a potluck?"

Now there was an idea. Before Cass could say anything cheeky, her daughter was crying and threatening to call Mason. Again.

"Go ahead," Cass had snapped. "Let your father pick up the bill for everything. It can make up for all those years he did nothing." Oh, that had been wrong.

"Maybe if you hadn't moved us all the way over here, he would've been able to do more."

"And maybe if I hadn't, you'd never have met Mike."

Their voices got loud enough to break the sound barrier in the kitchen, where Cass had staked out a corner for the family computer. Willie poked his head in the door. "What's going on?"

"Nothing," Cass had growled.

"Yeah, right," he'd scoffed, but neither Cass nor Dani bothered to say anything to that. They had enough to say to each other.

Finally, Cass did something she never did. She cried. Who said brides should have all the fun?

That had ended the fight. Dani knelt in front of her, all remorse and crying, too. "I'm sorry, Mama. I didn't mean all those things I said. It's just…"

"I know. It's your big day. Of course you want it to be special, and so do I." But she couldn't afford to give her daughter a Kardashian-style wedding. Why, oh, why wasn't she rich?

They'd compromised, bagging the salmon and settling for three-cheese-stuffed chicken, fettuccini (minus the shrimp and salmon) and Caesar salad. And no appetizers.

"But we have to have champagne," Dani had insisted. "For the toast."

"How about champagne for the toast and champagne punch for the rest of the meal?"

That, along with a nonalcoholic punch, had been another good compromise.

Now Dani was off with Mike, Willie and Amber were watching a Netflix movie and Cass was going to take a long soak with some peppermint bubble bath from Bubbles, the bath shop that had opened last summer. She did her best to avoid the bathroom mirror as she undressed, but it was hard to ignore the fat woman lurking there.

She was sure she'd put on another five pounds since Dani got engaged. Potato chips and Sweet Dreams chocolates would do that to a woman, particularly when she was stressed.

She didn't care what Dot said. It would've been nice if Mason had called her when Dani got engaged and suggested picking up half the tab for the wedding instead of playing this passive-aggressive game of offering nothing but coming through like a superhero every time Dani called him. Cass would have had twice the money and half the misery.

You could have called him.

She pushed the thought firmly away. She'd hated taking child support money from him when they were divorced, even though they were his kids, too, and it was money she was due. Those monthly checks had felt more like a sop to his conscience than support. It would've felt the same now, too.

In all fairness to Mason, he'd never been a deadbeat dad. He'd occasionally been late with his child support check, but that had been because of his crazy work schedule and forgetfulness rather than deliberate irresponsibility. And he wasn't hurting for money now. So why hadn't he offered up front to fork some over?

The answer was simple. He wasn't merely clueless. He was still the same self-absorbed man he'd always been.

Let him keep his money. She didn't need it. She didn't need him. Hadn't for years. In fact, she didn't need any man. She was fine on her own. Fine.

Were there any potato chips left?

"I'm so glad the house has sold," Mims said as Ella forked into a slice of hazelnut torte.

Once more Ella was eating at Schwangau, the most expensive restaurant in town, and the maître d' was becoming her new best friend. But when they'd walked in and she saw how packed the place was, even on a weeknight, she couldn't help thinking about poor Charley. Would her former customers return once she'd rebuilt her business or would they get in the habit of frequenting other places? Ella sure hoped they'd return. She'd be back.

"The sooner you're out of the house, the better," Mims said as their waiter filled her coffee cup.

"I still have to find a place that will allow Tiny," Ella said.

"Let your former husband have him," Mims said with a dismissive flick of her hand. And that took care of Tiny.

Mims had dismissed Jake just as easily when Ella decided on a divorce. "Really, baby, you're better off without him. The boy was subpar."

But Tiny wasn't subpar, and Ella had no intention of letting Jake keep him and feed him until he exploded. "He belongs to both of us."

Mims rolled her eyes and took a sip of her coffee. "It

was ridiculous to get such a big dog. Really, Ella, I don't know what you were thinking."

She was thinking they'd stay in that house for years, have a child to go along with the dog once they had a little more money. Child. Baby. What were the chances that one of Jake's sperm had succeeded in its egg hunt? She pushed aside the rest of her torte.

"You're not finishing? I'm surprised."

"I'm not hungry." Now she sounded sullen. Well, she felt sullen.

"You shouldn't eat that fattening garbage, anyway."

Mims had raised Ella to believe that sugar was the devil's tool. If a woman had to consume calories they should come floating in a glass of white wine. Well, once in a while, Ella liked to flirt with the devil, especially at Christmas. She'd even tried her hand at baking Christmas cookies the year before last. They weren't as good as Cass's but Jake had liked them.

Him again. She had to stop thinking about Jake. And his sperm. *You made your choice*, she told herself sternly. *Now you have to live with it*. And if that included a baby, fine. She'd wanted a baby.

She'd never wanted to raise a baby by herself, though. If Jake moved to Nashville that was exactly what she'd be doing.

Well, her mother had managed fine on her own and she would, too. She could see it now, Mommy and baby having a little talk. *Sorry your daddy isn't around, but daddies are overrated. Just ask your grandma.*

Mims reached a hand across the table. "Why the glum face? Everything is finally smoothing out in your life."

Smoothing out. Was that what you called it? She'd lost her marriage, her dreams and now her home. Smooth.

* * *

"Not again," Larry said.

Jake scowled at him. "What?"

"You've got that same bee up your butt that you had last week. What is bugging you now?"

"Nothing," Jake said, sounding completely bugged.

"I can take away the sting," Jen said. "Did any of you guys check out our song on YouTube?"

The song. With everything else that had been going on, Jake had forgotten about it.

"Oh, yeah," Larry said. "This should make you smile, bro. You wanna guess how many views we're up to already?"

Jake shrugged. "Fifty."

"Try eight hundred," Larry said.

"Eight hundred?" Guy echoed. "I've only got twenty people to my name, including family and friends. Who all is looking at this?"

"People are forwarding the link, dope," Larry told him. "Hell, everyone at the packing plant has sent it to their friends. I knew you were on to something," he said to Jake.

"Yeah, he was," Tim agreed. "Talk about inspired. And what a great way to get back at the mother-in-law from hell for screwing up your life."

"Poetic justice," said Jen.

"Huh?"

"It means she's getting what she deserves," Jen said, and smiled at Jake.

And with all the poisonous crap she was probably still pouring in her daughter's ears, she deserved a lot. Jake found himself smiling for the first time all night. *Yeah, Merry Christmas, Mama.*

By Friday he concluded that his former mother-in-law was deserving of much more than a tacky song. Maybe a nice winter cruise—down Icicle Falls, in an inner tube, buck naked, in the middle of the night. Or a visit to some-place special in one of her favorite cities—a back alley, with hopefully a mugger or two. If not for her, he and Ella would be together again, he was sure of it.

But instead, they were back at square one, sharing the house with an invisible force field between them. Jaw clenched, he watched Ella drive off with Axel Fuchs yet again. God only knew where they were going tonight. Ella hadn't told him. Ella had hardly spoken to him.

The house was sold and she was getting on with her life. He should, too.

He took Tiny for a good, long lope in the snow and then turned back toward home. Not home, he corrected himself. The house. Just a house. Then he got ready to go play his gig at the Red Barn.

"Sorry you're on your own tonight," he told the dog.

Tiny whined and wagged his tail. He'd seen the guitar sitting by the front door and he knew that meant doggy solitary.

Jake gave the dog a goodbye scratch behind the ears. "Maybe she won't stay out too late."

Unless she decided to stay over at Axel's.

Would she do that? Jake frowned. He'd been Ella's one and only. The thought of that slimy wuss having her was enough to make him clench his fists.

She'd do it. Eventually, she'd do it just because she could.

So why was he being a choirboy?

He asked himself again later that night when a cute

little groupie named Allison stopped by the band's table to flirt.

"She's hot for you," Larry said.

"Who isn't?" Jen said, and winked at him.

It was obvious Jake could move on with his life, starting tonight if he wanted to.

Well, maybe he did. Maybe he was sick of chasing after Ella like a dumb puppy. He downed the last of his Coke. Maybe he could get laid before the night was over. Why not? Ella always thought he was a player. It was time to live up to the legend.

Fifteen

The snoring was loud enough to wake the dead. Jake rolled over and gave his bedmate a shove.

Tiny startled awake and lifted his big head as if to say, "Where's the emergency?"

"You're snoring again," Jake informed him. He glanced at the clock—10:00 a.m. Ella would be long gone.

At least she'd come home the night before. He'd looked in the bedroom when he rolled in around one and found it gratifying to see her slender form under the covers in the sleigh bed—until it occurred to him that she might have had sex with Axel and then come home.

Sex. He'd planned on making a night of it. Until his conscience reminded him that revenge sex wasn't good for anyone, especially the other person. He couldn't do that to someone. He didn't want to be a player. He only wanted to be with Ella.

He sat on the edge of the bed and dragged his hands through his hair, giving it a good pull in the process, hoping to wake up his brain cells. What the hell was he going to do?

Finish that song he'd started for her, that was what.

* * *

Cecily was going to meet Luke Goodman, Sweet Dreams' production manager, and his daughter, Serena, at the little downtown skating rink dropping in at Johnson's Drugs first. She'd added mascara to her basket of goodies when Todd Black came strolling down the aisle.

"Hey, there," he greeted her.

Zing went her insides. Why, oh, why did they do that every time he came around? *Cut it out,* she told them, then said a casual hi to Todd.

He stopped next to her and peered into her basket.

She frowned and shifted it away from him.

"You don't need that."

What, the Midol or the mascara?

"Why do women wear makeup, anyway?"

Okay, not the Midol.

"To look nice," she said.

"Guys don't care, you know," he said. "They're not that interested in your eyelashes."

"So you say, but if a woman walked around without makeup you wouldn't even look at her."

"Sure I would," he said. "I'd just be looking somewhere else." He demonstrated, letting his gaze drift down to her chest.

"You're pathetic," she said in disgust.

"No, I'm not. I'm honest."

"Well, thanks for the honesty."

"Just trying to tell it like it is." He threw her a cynical smile. "But you were a matchmaker. You already know how it is. Or did a lot of your clients ask for women with big…eyelashes?"

"No, and maybe that has something to do with why

I'm not in that business anymore. And not dating." She started to move down the aisle.

Instead of getting the message to buzz off, he fell in step with her. "Funny how you can be so smart and still not see what's right in front of your face."

She stopped. "Okay, I'll bite. What's right in front of my face?"

He moved to stand in front of her, very *closely* in front of her. "Me."

Zing! All that heat… Her lips were suddenly dry. *Don't lick your lips.*

She couldn't help it, they were dry.

Now the cynical smile had turned much more intimate. He reached up and ran his thumb along her lower lip. "You should get some lip balm, gorgeous. It would be a shame to see those pretty lips get all cracked."

Zing, zing, zing! Her zing-o-meter was going through the roof. She took a step back. "Thanks. I'll do that." She slipped around him and started walking again.

And there he was, still keeping her company. "You know what else is good for fighting off the cold?"

"What?"

"Hot chocolate. I'll buy you some."

She cocked an eyebrow at him. "Have some candy, little girl?"

He chuckled. "Get into my car. Take a ride."

"Sorry, I don't take rides with strange men."

"Come on, Cecily. Quit being such a wimp. You know you want to be with me."

Yes, she did.

And she didn't. The smart part of her didn't.

"One cup of cocoa. What's it going to hurt?"

Probably her heart. "Sorry," she said. "I've got plans."

Not a date. Luke wanted them to be more, but they were just friends, and she was determined to keep it that way. Letting things get serious wouldn't be fair to him. She'd sworn off men, the good, the bad and the…drop-dead gorgeous.

Todd shrugged off her rejection. "One of these days, you're not going to be able to take it anymore. One of these days you'll be knocking on my door, ready for a dance lesson."

She remembered their conversation a few months ago when she'd fainted and wound up in the back room of his tavern. The idea of seeing Todd in action was as tempting now as it had been then. Oh, yes, Todd Black had the moves, and he'd given her a sample of them since she'd come home.

But she wasn't in the market. She wasn't in the market for any man. "I hope you're not holding your breath."

"You'd be surprised how long I can hold my breath. You'd be surprised how long I can do a lot of things."

She rolled her eyes and shook her head and left it at that.

Enough of him. She had better ways to spend her time than sparring with the pirate of Icicle Falls. She made her purchases, then headed for the park.

The ice rink, dotted with skaters clad in colorful winter clothes, would have inspired Norman Rockwell. Around the edges, people sat on park benches and enjoyed hot chocolate or roasted nuts, or stood at fire pits, warming up for the next round. Farther up the hill that led to the highway, a group of boys were having a snowball fight. The scent of cinnamon and vanilla from a nut vendor's booth made Cecily's mouth water.

Luke was already at the edge of the rink, lacing up

his daughter's ice skates. Serena, now five, looked adorable in pink leggings and her pink parka, a knitted hat pulled over her curls. The child always appeared ready for a magazine cover, thanks to her grandmother, who'd stepped into the mother role when Luke's wife was killed in a car accident.

Serena saw Cecily approaching and began waving, not a sedate wave, but one that had her bouncing on the bench. Luke turned and waved, too. No bouncing, but the big grin on his face said it all.

She had to stop seeing this man. It wasn't fair.

"Cecily, I have new skates!" Serena called.

"Those are very nice," she said, coming to stand in front of them.

"My feet grew," Serena told her. "Daddy says I'm going to be tall like him and be a lady basketball player."

"Would you like that?" Cecily asked.

Serena wrinkled her forehead. "No. I just want to make cookies with Grandma."

"Maybe you'll grow up to be a baker like Mrs. Wilkes," Cecily suggested.

"And make gingerbread boys!" cried Serena.

"You make 'em and we'll eat 'em," Luke said.

Serena hopped off the bench and began teetering toward the ice. "Let's skate!"

"Wait a minute, kiddo," Luke said, reaching out and grasping her with a big hand. "No going on the ice by yourself. Remember?"

Serena frowned. "Hurry up, Daddy. Get your skates on."

Luke sat on the bench and indicated the spot next to him, and Cecily set to work putting on her own skates.

Serena stood watching the other skaters and Cecily

took a moment to watch, too. It seemed half the residents of Icicle Falls were enjoying the fresh air this particular Saturday, with teenagers zipping past more sedate older people. Small children wobbled around, safely tucked between their parents, and one or two advanced skaters practiced jumps at the center of the rink. A little boy in hot pursuit of a squealing girl fell down, blinked in shock at the impact and then scrambled back up and returned to the chase.

Next to Cecily, Luke chuckled. "Maybe by the time they're grown-ups he'll actually catch her." He finished tying his lace, then stood and held out a hand to Cecily. "Ready?"

Ready to be caught? Of course that wasn't what he'd meant. And she wasn't.

But she gave her laces a final tug and let him take her hand. He held out his other hand to his daughter, and the three of them went onto the ice.

Sometimes people forgot what a risky business skating was. A person could fall and break an arm. Or worse. Yet look how many people were out here. There was a thrill in racing over the ice, the wind in your face. And that, of course, was why people took the risk. Wasn't it the same with love?

After this she really had to stop hanging out with Luke. Really.

Ella found herself squirming in church on Sunday as Pastor Jim talked about the importance of self-control. Hers had been sadly lacking of late. Was it wrong to sleep with someone you weren't married to if you'd *been* married to him? Maybe she could get off on a technicality.

Right or wrong, it was stupid, and she wasn't going to be stupid again, no matter how much Jake kissed her.

No, no kissing! She let out her breath in a hiss.

"Are you okay?" whispered Cecily, who was sitting next to her.

No, she wasn't. She was...confused. She nodded, though. Heaven forbid a woman should admit that she had problems when she was in church, surrounded by people who cared and would gladly help her.

After the service, she went to lunch with Cecily, Samantha and Samantha's husband, Blake Preston. Anything to avoid being at the house with Jake. They were through. Finished. Done.

He probably wasn't there, anyway. Since the divorce he'd taken to spending Sundays at his parents'.

Sunday dinner with the O'Briens—how she missed that! Pot roast with all the trimmings, homemade biscuits, a rowdy game of cards, maybe even a knitting lesson— those afternoons had felt to Ella as if she'd been dropped right in the middle of some vintage TV family show like *The Brady Bunch*. Now she was in...what? *Desperate Housewives*? *Lost*? She *felt* lost, and she hadn't touched her yarn and needles in months.

Once you're out of the house everything will be fine, she told herself. Once she didn't have to look at Jake every day. Once she was out of touching range. That was the problem, of course. He was using sentiment like a swizzle stick to stir up her hormones and make her think they— She stopped the thought before it could turn into a sentence and light up inside her mind like a neon sign. But it was still there, anyway. *Make her think they could get back together and be happy.*

Jake was a skirt-chasing loafer. She'd always have to

be the one earning the family income and she'd never know if she could trust him. If she got together with someone like Axel she could have it all. The family. The comfortable lifestyle. Venice. Paris.

Nashville.

No, not Nashville!

"Something's off," Cecily said as they all left Herman's Hamburgers.

Ella realized she hadn't been paying attention. Had Cecily been talking? "What?"

"You've been a zombie all morning. Are you sure everything's okay?"

Ella nodded. It was. Well, it would be. Someday.

She was still telling herself that when she showed up at Cass's for their weekly movie night. Cass had her tree up now, and it was decorated with a mishmash of ornaments, many obviously made by small hands, a colorful testament to a happy family. Unlike her tree, which was a sad reminder of family failure. *Oh, yes, you're doing fine.*

The selection for this night was the classic version of *A Christmas Carol,* with Alastair Sim. The happy ending was very satisfying.

And more than a little thought-provoking. "Do you guys think people can change?" Ella asked. She suddenly realized she was echoing the question Charley had asked her the last time she was in the shop.

"I don't think so," Cass said.

"I didn't used to." Charley helped herself to one of the appetizers she'd brought. "But I think I was wrong, especially after the way Richard jumped in when Harvey went on his bender and left me in the lurch. And he's been so supportive since the fire."

Ella saw Samantha and Cecily exchange looks. "It pays to be cautious," Samantha said.

Charley narrowed her eyes suspiciously. "What do you mean by that?"

"I mean it pays to be cautious."

"Are you talking about Richard?"

Samantha took a deep breath, a clear indication that she was getting ready to dish out something unpleasant. "I don't want to see you rush into anything."

"I'm not rushing," Charley insisted. "Anyway, why are you so suspicious?"

"Because he screwed you over once and he could do it again," Samantha said bluntly.

"She doesn't want to see you hurt," Cecily added. "None of us do."

Now Charley looked ready to smack Samantha. "Just because he made a mistake in the past—"

"Doesn't mean he can't make another," Samantha finished for her.

"That wasn't what I was going to say!"

"I know. Listen," Samantha continued. "It's easy not to notice the red flags when all you're seeing is hearts and flowers. I'm just suggesting you be a little cautious."

"*What* red flags?"

"How about the fact that he can hang around here indefinitely? What businessperson can do that? What restaurant owner can do that?"

"One who has a good general manager," Charley retorted. "You want to come right out and tell me what you're implying?"

"I'm implying that maybe he hasn't been so successful on his own. Maybe he's come back to be with the goose who lays the golden eggs."

"In case you didn't notice, my golden egg got fried," Charley said, her voice icy.

Samantha wasn't deterred. "It's insured. You have insurance money and a valuable piece of property."

A big, ugly silence fell on the room. Ella felt as if each woman was holding her breath.

All except Samantha, who continued on boldly. "He hasn't taken you to Seattle to see his restaurant. Why is that?"

"Because he's been busy helping me," Charley said. "I couldn't just up and leave my place, you know." She glared at them. "Jeez, you guys."

"Wouldn't he want to show you how successful he is?" Samantha persisted.

Even Jake loved playing his songs for her, Ella thought. Men liked to show off to their women, to prove themselves worthy.

That saddened her. Had she failed to give Jake enough appreciation and driven him to look for it from other women?

Meanwhile, Charley and Samantha were still going at it. "Richard doesn't need to prove anything to me," Charley snapped. "Not anymore."

Samantha cocked an eyebrow. "Oh, really?"

Charley was blinking furiously now, obviously fighting back tears. "Yeah, really, and thanks for your support."

"This *is* support." Cass spoke in a quiet, even voice. "Like Cecily said, we don't want to see you hurt again. We want you to be cautious."

"Have you looked up the restaurant on the internet?" Samantha asked.

"I've been busy," Charley said defensively.

"At least check out the website," Samantha urged. "If his place looks like the next best thing to Wolfgang Puck, then you can forget I said anything."

The tears had spilled over now. Cecily handed Charley a tissue and gave her a hug. "He hurt you badly once. Nobody wants to see him do it twice. That's all. We really do care what happens to you, you know."

Charley dabbed at her eyes and nodded. "I know. I'm sorry I'm so bitchy."

"Your restaurant just burned down. You're allowed," Samantha said. "But you can rebuild it and make it even better. It's a lot harder to rebuild a broken heart."

How true.

A few more tears, some hugs, and then Charley was on her way, claiming she still had paperwork to fill out.

"And some research to do," Samantha murmured as their friend hurried out the door. "I hope she does it."

"Do you know something we don't?" her sister asked.

It was plain from Samantha's face that she did.

"Okay, spill," Cass commanded.

"Well, cynic that I am, I looked up this restaurant of his."

"Does he even have a restaurant?" Cass asked, her voice tinged with worry.

"Oh, he has one, all right. But it's not open."

Sixteen

Samantha's suspicions burrowed their way into the back of Charley's mind like so many termites and began crunching away.

Richard had moved from Gerhardt's Gasthaus into her bed, and she returned home to find him sprawled on the living room couch, watching the Food Network's *Hidden Surprises,* a show featuring small-town restaurants. After seeing how well getting featured on Mimi LeGrand's *All Things Chocolate* had worked for Samantha, Charley had been toying with contacting this show's producer and inviting him to Icicle Falls. Thanks to her unpleasant surprise, that would be a ways down the road.

She frowned. "You want to turn that off?"

He fired the remote at the TV and the cozy restaurant scene vanished from the screen. "I was just killing time until you got back home. How was the party?"

Fine until the movie ended. "It was okay."

"Just okay, huh?"

"It's hard to get excited about anything right now." Including Richard. Sometimes a woman shouldn't listen to her friends. Now Charley wished she'd covered her ears and chanted, "La, la, la, la, la, la."

"Anything?" He patted the cushion next to him on the couch, and she came over and sat down. "There's a new year right around the corner, babe." He put an arm around her and kissed her. "Meanwhile, I bet I can get you excited."

Sort of. Even as Richard was making love to her, the termites kept crunching. *He hasn't taken you to Seattle to see his restaurant. Why is that?*

Any number of reasons. Like maybe he simply wanted to concentrate on winning her back. Maybe he'd figured that bringing up the subject of the restaurant he'd started after he left her would be like pouring salt in a wound. It would.

So there was the reason. And now, with that resolved she could—

Check out Richard's restaurant on the internet the next morning. Masochist that she was, she'd done it when they first split. Try as she had, she'd never been able to forget the name: Piatto Dolce, Sweet Plate. The thought of him serving up sweet plates of anything with his little hostess with the mostest had set her teeth on edge. She'd glared at the webpage, hoped they gave whatever food critic visited them food poisoning and then closed the page, never to look again. She hadn't looked when he returned, either. She *had* been busy. Really. Maybe she also hadn't wanted to see how successful he'd been without her.

But now she had to get rid of those termites, so she left Richard snoring in bed and slipped downstairs to settle on the couch with her laptop.

Up came the website with the food-magazine-worthy picture of the restaurant's interior on the home page—a sophisticated slice of Italy complete with sexy lighting and linen tablecloths, a tribute to Richard's favorite cuisine. There was something else on the home page, too. A notice saying, "Piatto Dolce is currently closed for renovations. Please check back later. *Grazie.*"

Closed for renovations. Richard hadn't said anything about that. But so what? They'd had other, more important things to talk about. Like them. And this explained why he could afford to stay in Icicle Falls....

But wouldn't he want to be on hand to supervise those renovations? She planned to be on site at Zelda's every day, making sure things were getting done. She'd been over to the charred ruins any number of times, picking through things, meeting with the company in charge of cleanup, getting bids from contractors.

Maybe the work on his place hadn't started yet.

That was it. He was here winning her back while he had the time. Once the renovations were done they'd own two restaurants. It would mean double the work, of course, but double the success as long as they could manage both and be together. They'd find a way to work everything out, and he was up here to do just that. He was here for her. Samantha had been wrong. Well-meaning, but wrong.

"Hey, you awake already?"

Charley gave a guilty start and hid the evidence of her snooping with a click before Richard could see what she was up to. "I couldn't sleep anymore."

There he stood, his hair tousled, bare-chested, wearing his favorite black sweats. Dessert with legs. He came over to the couch and looked over her shoulder. "What are you working on?"

She suddenly felt like some kind of traitor. "Just doing some research," she said, and shut the laptop.

"It's going to be another long day. How about some coffee?"

"Please. I think I'll go shower."

"Want company?"

She shook her head. With all the stress of rebuilding her life, it seemed her sex drive had put itself in Park. That was it. The stress. Stress would do that to any girl.

"Like you said, it's going to be another long day," she said. "I'd better get started."

That day didn't turn out to be half as long as the next one. After the last conversation with her insurance agent, Charley finally had an idea of how much money she could expect for rebuilding Zelda's and just how far it would stretch.

"Everything's gone up in price," she lamented as she and Richard worked together on dinner. "There's so much to do. And that darned Dan Masters is going to drive me nuts."

"He's the best contractor in town," Richard said, slicing apples for their salad.

"And the most infuriating." Charley picked up her wineglass and took a healthy slug of pinot grigio, then moved to help him with the salad, shelling pistachios to go in the bowl with the tossed greens and apples. "He doesn't seem to understand that the longer I stay closed, the more customers I lose."

Richard set down his knife and leaned against the counter. "So run away."

She gave a snort. "Sometimes I'd like to." Lately she'd fantasized about running away from her problems. If it hadn't been for her friends and Richard, she didn't know what she would've done. Samantha could say whatever she wanted, but he really had been there for her, especially since the fire.

"No, I'm serious," he said. "There's nothing tying you here. You don't have to spend the rest of your life in Icicle Falls."

But she wanted to. She loved this town with its friendly people and its gorgeous mountain views. Still, she could keep an open mind. "What were you thinking?"

"Come to Seattle with me."

Maybe they could have two homes, one here and one in Seattle. Still… "It would be hard to run Zelda's from Seattle." How were they going to manage that?

"How about running a restaurant in Seattle instead?" He shrugged. "Don't waste your money rebuilding in this nowhere place."

Wait a minute. The termites began crunching again. "What should I do with it?" *Don't say what I think you're going to.*

"We could put it into my place in Seattle. That's where the action is. Anyway, you're not a small-town girl, Charley."

She wasn't a fool, either. She stopped shelling nuts. "What's going on with your Piatto Dolce, Richard? Do you need a cash infusion?"

The sudden flush on his cheeks answered before his lips even started moving. "A restaurant is a money pit, you know that. But that's beside the point," he added quickly.

"No. It *is* the point. I went to your website. It said you were closed for renovations."

"I'm making some improvements," he said defensively. And putting them on hold until he had her eating out of his hand and could convince her to take him back. Then he would've returned to live off her or done exactly what he was trying to do now—talk her into sinking *her* money into *his* place.

"And you need money to do that," she said. "My money."

He opened his mouth to speak but the look on his face had already said it all.

"You. Bastard." All the rage she'd felt the first time he left returned with double the force. She whacked the salad bowl and sent it crashing, spilling romaine and spinach leaves and apples across the kitchen floor.

He held up a hand. "Charley, babe, let me explain."

"No, let *me* explain. I can see it all so clearly now. Your restaurant is going toes-up and so you decided to come back to mine. Job security. And then when the place burned, there was all that lovely money to grab for. All I am to you is a cash cow."

"That's not true! I missed you. I told you, I made a mistake."

What a load of crap. He reached out for her and she slapped his hand away. "Well, I didn't miss you," she snarled. "And I must have been insane to even consider taking you back."

"Charley, you're overreacting," he said.

"You come back here to use me and I'm overreacting?" She grabbed the wine bottle with the vague notion of beaning him over the head with it

"I did not come back here to use you," he protested, taking a step back.

"That's not what it sounded like just now."

"Just now I was being practical."

"Well, now *I'm* being practical. Get out."

"You don't mean that."

"Oh, yeah? You want to stick around and find out how much I do mean it?"

His pleading expression hardened into something uglier. "God, Charley, you're such a selfish bitch."

Her jaw dropped. He'd come back to use her, the ultimate betrayal, and yet she was a selfish bitch?

"You always were," he added.

This from the man who'd left her for another woman and then returned to ride on her gravy train? *Rage* was too small a word for what she felt now. "You—" She hurled the bottle at him and he barely dodged it. It shattered against the wall, leaving white wine running down the wall like tears.

"You're psycho, too," he said as he turned and started for the door.

"Yeah, well you made me that way," she shouted after him.

He kept walking and flipped her off, and she slid down the cupboard amid the violently tossed salad, laid her head on her knees and sobbed.

Samantha and Blake had just sat down to enjoy a pizza from Italian Alps when the phone rang.

Blake groaned. "Do your friends have some kind of radar? Why is it they always call when we're about to eat?"

"How do you know it's for me?" she retorted, getting up to grab it.

"Because I've already talked to everyone I need to talk to."

She looked at the caller ID and frowned. "Go ahead

and start." She had a sinking feeling that this call might take some time.

"You were right." The voice on the other end sounded like a zombie version of Charley.

How she wished she hadn't been! "Oh, Charley, I'm so sorry."

"What's wrong?" Blake asked.

She shook her head to signal she'd update him later. "What happened?"

Charley heaved a shaky sigh. "Well, I scattered salad all over the kitchen floor and christened my wall with white wine."

"And Richard?"

"Not to worry. No skunks were harmed in the filming of this farce," Charley said bitterly. "My God, how could I have been so blind?"

"Easily," Samantha said. "You wanted to believe the best." And Richard had, once more, managed to give her the worst.

"His restaurant is closed for renovations," Charley said, scorn dripping from her voice. "More like closed for lack of cash flow. You know what he wanted me to do with my insurance money?"

"I can guess," Samantha said. How different from her man, who'd actually gone into debt to help her save her company. Well, there were men and there were male snakes. And she knew which category Richard fell into. She'd known all along. She didn't say so, though. Instead, she said, "I'm really sorry. He deserves to be roasted over a giant spit."

"That's too good for him," Charley said, and her voice broke on a sob. "And you know what else? He told me I'm a selfish bitch."

"You?"

Now Charley began to cry in earnest.

"You know that's not true," Samantha said.

"Do I?"

"Of course you do," Samantha said. "Your ex is not only bad at business, he's bad at being a human being."

"He broke my heart all over again." The words ended on a sob.

Poor Charley. First her restaurant and now this. The year was not ending well for her. "Come on over and hang with us," Samantha offered. "I'll give you chocolate."

"No. I need to clean up this mess."

"You need your friends," Samantha said sternly.

"I'll be okay," Charley said. "And thanks for opening my eyes. If you hadn't, I might've just drifted along with whatever Richard wanted, never knowing I was being taken."

"You'd have figured it out," Samantha assured her.

"Thanks for being such a good listener."

"That's what friends are for."

They were for a heck of a lot more than that, too. "Charley's in trouble," Samantha told Blake after ending the call.

"I kind of guessed that," he said. "I won't wait up. I have a feeling this is going to be a long night."

Forty minutes later Charley's seafood lasagna was out of the oven and the kitchen was clean. The house was empty, too. Richard had packed up his bags and left without another word. Which was fine with Charley. He'd said enough.

Selfish bitch. Was she really? Had it been selfish to sink her inheritance into that restaurant? She hadn't thought so at the time. Yes, she'd had to do some talking to persuade Richard they wanted to settle here. But she'd felt so sure he'd grown to love the town, the same way she had. She'd believed he was happy. Anyway, this had been all she could afford. It would've cost twice as much to start a restaurant in the city. She'd wanted to be practical. And she'd liked being a big fish in a small pond.

But somehow, she'd become a bigger fish than her husband. Looking back now, she realized that hadn't gone over well. He used to jokingly refer to himself as her kitchen slave or Mr. Charley. But he'd been the chef.

Still, she'd been the front person, the one people saw when they came in. And people had liked her. Richard not so much. She thought back to the party she'd thrown herself when she got divorced, how so many of her friends had said they'd never really liked him. Yes, Cass, was right. Love was blind. And dumb.

The doorbell rang. Richard. He was back to say he was sorry, he'd never meant those mean words. He'd stay and help her rebuild Zelda's.

You can't take him back, she told herself. *You've been a fool twice. Don't go for a third time.*

She remembered the ugly expression on his face when she'd proved herself immune to the old Richard charm. Was she that insecure, that desperate for love? The answer was no. Hell, no.

She marched to the door and yanked it open.

And there stood the Sterling sisters, Cass and Ella, bearing gift bags, chocolates, cookies and wine. "We're here for another party," Samantha said.

Girlfriends. What would she have done without them? She could feel tears pricking her eyes. "You're just in time for seafood lasagna."

"All right," Cecily said, handing over a bottle of wine. "Let's party."

And party they did. They ate every bit of Charley's lasagna and consumed enough goodies to put themselves in a sugar coma (the gingerbread boys with their heads cut off were a huge hit). They played games—Stick the Knife in the Ex-husband (crafted by Cass), Hangman (every word was an unendearing term for Richard) and a movie trivia game Samantha had thrown together that involved bad men getting what they deserved. Then Charley opened presents—bubble bath, chocolate, more cookies and the hit of the night, Man Away Spray, which was really an old can of bug spray wrapped in a funny label Cecily had made.

"I hope you've got an extra can of that for yourself," Samantha told her sister.

Cecily stuck her tongue out at her sister, then returned her attention to Charley. "Next time Richard comes near you, aim this at him."

"I doubt he'll ever come near me again," Charley said, and felt a moment of melancholy. "Especially after I threw that bottle of wine at him." Just remembering the shock on his face was enough to make her feel better and she actually giggled.

"I'd love to have been a fly on the wall for that," Cecily said.

"Heck, I can top that," Cass told them. "I once threw a flour canister at Mason."

Samantha shook her head. "We're a violent bunch."

"Men drive us to it," Cass said.

The final present, this one from Ella, was the hit of the evening. Charley read the words engraved on the silver pendant, *True to Myself,* and teared up.

"First to thine own self be true," Samantha murmured.

"And if you find yourself having trouble doing that, call one of us. We'll get you through," said Samantha. "That's what friends are for," she said again.

"Absolutely." Cass nodded. "Men may come and go but girlfriends are forever."

"To girlfriends," Cecily said, raising her glass.

"To girlfriends," everyone chorused.

Yes, that was all she needed, Charley told herself.

But later that night when she finally went to bed, she remembered there were a few things men were still good for. Yes, she had her friends and they were fabulous, but when it came to sharing dreams and building a life (and a sex life), marriage was still the gold standard. At least it was for her. No matter how many parties she threw herself, no matter how many friends she had, in the end she still went to bed alone.

Maybe she'd always be alone. She hugged a pillow and let the tears fall.

Seventeen

Ella was closing out the till on Thursday when someone tapped at the door of Gilded Lily's. Good customers would sometimes have a wardrobe emergency and need help after hours, and she always opened up for them, but today she was in no mood. She was pooped and didn't want to open up for anyone.

It had been a long day. Dani's bridesmaids had come by to pick up their dresses, and that had been the only bright spot. Hildy Johnson had come in looking for something to wear to a Christmas party and kept insisting she was one size smaller than she really was. Of course, nothing fit and she finally left in a huff. Darla, the mayor's sister, had returned a bracelet with a faulty clasp. She didn't have a receipt—hardly surprising since Ella had sold her that bracelet two years ago. Two bargain-hunters had spent an hour wandering around, asking questions and getting free fashion advice and then left with their wallets still securely in their purses. Of course, this often happened in retail, but it was discouraging when you spent so much time and tried so hard to help people and got nothing in return. Finally, Charley had come in for some retail therapy and had spent a small fortune, then left wearing a smile that never quite reached her eyes.

That had been depressing, partly because Ella felt bad for her friend but also because watching Charley was a little like hanging out with the Ghost of Christmas Yet to Come. Was this her future, loneliness and disappointment? Retail therapy?

With a sigh she looked up from her work and saw that her visitor wasn't a woman but a man with dark hair and gorgeous dark eyes. Oh, no. What did he want? A snatch of the Christmas carol "Jingle Bells" came jingling into her mind. *Oh, what fun it is to ride in a one-horse open sleigh.* No. No more rides in the sleigh bed.

She opened the door and stood there, her brain and her mouth not quite connecting.

It turned out she didn't need to say anything. He spoke first. "I thought you might be going somewhere after work and I wanted to ask you to come back to the house. I have something waiting there."

"What?"

"Just come home and you'll see."

Home, there was an interesting choice of word, considering that house wasn't their home anymore.

"Will you do that, El?"

He looked so earnest.

So what? He always looked earnest.

Except she was tired of avoiding the house and she hardly ever got to see Tiny. "Okay."

He grinned like a little boy who'd just impressed his mom with his school art project for Mother's Day. "Good. I'll wait for you in the truck."

She shut the door after him and realized she was smiling. *What are you smiling about? Nothing's changed. No one has changed. People don't change.*

Scrooge did. Of course, Scrooge wasn't a real person.

With a sigh, Ella fetched her purse. Then she locked up the shop and got into the truck with Jake. He had the radio tuned to her favorite station, one that played solid Christmas songs this time of year, and Rascal Flatts was singing "I'll Be Home for Christmas." She wasn't going home now. She was going to a house. *I'll be at a house for Christmas.* Boy, that sure didn't have the same ring.

You'll have a home someday, she told herself, snapping off the radio. This had been a starter marriage. Someday she'd have the real thing. Or maybe she'd end up like her mother, keeping men at a distance, keeping them as friends. Being a single mom, bossing her daughter around.

Whoa, where had that come from? She immediately shied away from the disloyal thought. Her mother never bossed her around. She simply gave advice. Good advice.

She could imagine what kind of advice her mother would give her if she were here right now. *Don't go back to the house with him. What are you thinking?*

Oh, what fun it is to ride... No, no. That was a bad thought.

The truck cab was heavy with silence. Boy, had that been rare back when they were happy.

Ella sighed and looked out the window at the houses on their street. Every one of them was all dressed up for Christmas. The Bennetts had their living room light on, and through the window she could see Cheron and Harold decorating their tree. Judging by the cars parked on the street, Sam Moyle, her former math teacher, and his wife, Selma, were hosting a party of some sort, and his brother Ben, who happened to live next door, was walking across the lawn with his wife, Marliss, who carried a huge platter of Christmas cookies. Everyone was in the holiday spirit. She wished she could join them.

Farther up the road, the houses were fewer and the trees denser. At the end of it sat their house. She wished they'd gone ahead and put up…lights! Jake had strung multicolored lights all along the roof. She turned to him, tears in her eyes, and stated the obvious. "You put up lights."

He smiled at her, his look tender. "I thought you'd like it."

She did. "Thank you," she murmured. Her gratitude felt out of place and awkward. Why was she thanking him? And why was he doing this? They weren't married. The house was sold. This was crazy.

Inside the smell of onions greeted her. She looked questioningly at him.

"I made dinner," he said.

"Meat loaf." It was the only thing he knew how to cook. That and, "Baked potatoes?"

He nodded.

She loved meat loaf. It was something Mims had considered beneath her and she'd never made it, but for Ella meat loaf spelled family.

"I thought we should have one last dinner together," Jake said, helping her out of her coat.

Their last supper.

He led her out to the kitchen, where she found the table set and decorated with a small vase of red and white roses. He'd even put on the tablecloth they'd bought at a garage sale three years ago.

"Sit down," he said.

She sat and watched, Tiny glued to her side, while Jake dished up meat loaf and baked potatoes with all the trimmings. And salad from the grocery store deli. Salads, easy as they were to prepare, were beyond him. Then he pulled a bottle of champagne from the fridge.

"Champagne?" she asked. There was nothing to celebrate.

"Why not?" He filled their glasses. Then he sat down across from her and raised his.

"What are we toasting?"

He shrugged. "To happier times, past and future."

She could do that. "To happier times," she said, and they clinked glasses.

The meat loaf was delicious, full of chopped peppers and onions and coated with barbecue sauce. She was going to miss Jake's meat loaf. She was going to miss a lot of things, but she was better off without him. Still, it was hard to remember that just now, and every bite she took came seasoned with guilt. Which was ridiculous. She had nothing to feel guilty about. She'd carried her weight in this relationship, working eight to five, five days a week. And she hadn't chased after other men.

"Why are you doing this?" she asked.

"I figured it might be our last chance to talk."

"There's nothing to talk about. It's too late."

He set down his fork and leaned back in his chair. "It's never too late. I've always loved you and I still do. You know that."

"Do I?"

He frowned. "You believed in me once. Why did you stop?"

Now she set down her fork. "You really need to ask? You know why. You couldn't be trusted."

"I was never unfaithful to you. I tried to tell you that."

Right. She rolled her eyes.

"But you listened to your mom instead of me."

"My mother was right," she said hotly.

"Why, just because she's your mother?"

"No, because she had proof."

"Those pictures looked like proof because you wanted them to. You chose to believe her over me. How do you think that makes me feel as a man? I know you love your mama, but you promised to build a life with me. And you didn't. You always kept bringing your mother into our relationship. And maybe that would've been okay if she'd liked me, but she never did."

"I…" Ella stopped, unsure how to finish that sentence.

"Do you remember how happy we were?"

She remembered, more often than was comfortable.

"We could still build a good life."

Somewhere deep down, past the hurt and anger, something glimmered, like a small candle determined to hold back the dark.

"And I want to. I think you do, too, El, but you've got some tough choices to make."

"What kind of choices?" she asked suspiciously.

"You're gonna have to choose whose side you're on, your mom's or mine."

"I was never on anyone's side," she protested.

"Oh, yes, you were. When it came time to choose sides, you always took hers."

"That's not true!"

"It is, El, and you know it. You stood in church before God and all our friends, and you promised to stick with me no matter what—sickness, health, for richer or poorer—but in the end you listened to your mom. You chose her over me, and all because of something you imagined. A phone number and a message and some pictures that didn't tell the whole story."

Ella shoved her plate away, no longer hungry. In fact, she felt slightly ill. Tears were sneaking into her eyes now, turning Jake's face to a blur. "They told enough."

"Jen was never interested in me. Those pictures are bogus."

Ella looked at him in disgust. Was he still insisting on that same tired story?

She got up to leave but he caught her arm. "Come and hear the band play the song I wrote for you tomorrow night. Meet this other woman you were so sure I was hot for."

She chewed on her lip, torn.

"At least give me that, El. Let me prove I never cheated on you."

She frowned. "Why now?" What was the point?

"Because I want you to know the truth. Hell, I should've done this back when everything first hit the fan, but I was mad. And proud, too proud to beg. But I've come to realize that my pride isn't worth a damn. I'd rather have you. So will you come? Will you do that much for me?"

All right. She could do that much. She nodded.

He smiled. "Good." Then he nudged her plate back toward her. "Tiny will love this, but I made it for you."

They finished their dinner in silence. She half expected him to bring out the eggnog, try to kiss her, something, but instead he simply said, "Why don't you go watch some TV? I'll clean up in here."

"I think I'll take Tiny for a walk," she said. Tiny needed the exercise and she had a lot to process.

She had even more to process Friday night at the Red Barn. She felt awkward joining the other women at the band's usual table. These women had stuck with their men. She'd been the defector.

"Hi, Ella," Larry's girlfriend, Chrissie, greeted her. "Glad you're back."

She wasn't back exactly. She was just…here. Sort of. Not much had changed since the good old days when she'd come and hung out on the weekends. Pretty much the same crowd of cowboys and farmers inhabited the place. The old hardwood floor was still scuffed and scarred, the table lamps were still cheap and the bar was still hoppin'.

There was one small change at the band table, though. A new member had joined Chrissie's and Guy's wives, Taylor. This woman had to be Tim's new lady, but Ella had a hard time imagining him with this tough-looking customer. Her hair was cut short and she wore jeans and a black T-shirt and she was the only woman at the table who hadn't bothered with makeup. She wasn't fat by any means but she wasn't the petite girlie-girl type Tim normally went for.

"This is Tanya," Chrissie said. "Jen's partner."

Partner. Partner? Partner! "You mean… I mean…" Ella could feel her face flaming.

"You mean what?" Tanya asked, her eyes narrowing.

"I mean, I thought…" Ella put her hand to her mouth. She was going to cry, she was going to laugh, she was going to…remember her manners. "Oh, my gosh, it is so great to meet you."

Tanya looked at her like she was nuts.

Jake's voice drifted over to her from the bandstand.

"And now I want to play a song I wrote for someone very special. It's called 'To Find Heaven.'"

Ella fell onto the chair next to Chrissie and let the song wash over her.

"'Sometimes this world is a hell of a place. And heaven feels so far away. But every time I've held you and you've made me come undone. That's the closest I have come.'" As he sang Jake looked at her with eyes so full of love she had to wonder what madness had possessed her to think they didn't belong together. And give their love—*almost* give their love—away to the green-eyed monster.

"'I'm close to heaven with you, closer than I've ever come. There's no hell I won't walk through to find heaven, girl, with you,'" Jake finished.

They had gone through hell, thanks to her. The band was just coming off break, and a moment later Jake was at her side, hugging her. "Hey, El. I see you've met Tanya."

Tanya didn't seem all that happy about it. Once more Ella's face sizzled. She managed to nod.

Now his keyboard player Jen had come up beside him. "And this is Jen."

"Hi," Jen said. She sat down, placed an arm around Tanya's shoulders and smirked at Ella. "I'm your competition. Nice to meet you."

"Still think I was cheating on you?" Jake asked softly.

What a fool she'd been. What a stupid, insecure, untrusting fool. "Oh, Jake!" She threw her arms around him and kissed him.

"Get a room," Larry cracked.

"You are such a jerk," his girlfriend said, swatting his arm.

Not half as much a jerk as Ella had been.

"But what about those pictures the detective took?" she asked later as they drove home.

"The detective your mom hired?"

The residual bitterness in his voice made her feel bad that she'd allowed Mims to overstep her boundaries. Still, "You've got to admit it looked bad."

"To someone with a suspicious mind," Jake said, not willing to cut either her or Mims any slack. "You remember in one of those pictures I was carrying some papers. Lyric sheets."

So he'd said. *I was just dropping off some lead sheets.*

She remembered what she'd said in response. "And it takes an hour to drop off lead sheets?"

That was when Jake had blown up. That was when everything had blown up.

"Yes," she said now.

"Well, I was. Just like I told you. Jen asked me if I had a minute to go over a couple of songs, which we did. Then she started crying, told me she was having problems with Tanya. They'd had a big fight about twenty minutes before I showed up. All I did was listen and then tell her everything would be okay. When I left she hugged me and said thanks. So, like I told you, it didn't mean a thing."

The damning picture had been a thank-you hug. One picture was, indeed, worth a thousand words. And this time those words all needed to be "I'm sorry."

"I should have told you back then that Jen wasn't into guys but, like I said, I was mad. And you know what? Even if I *had* told you, you wouldn't have believed me."

Much as she hated to admit it, he was probably right. By the time the Jen incident had happened, her insecurities had hardened into a wall of mistrust.

"El, there will always be women throwing themselves

at me. That goes with the territory if a guy makes it in this business. But there's only one woman I want, only one woman I'll ever want, and that's you." He reached over and took her hand and she gave his a squeeze. "Hmm," he said thoughtfully, "I wonder if there's a song in that."

Saturday morning Axel called Ella. "I thought you'd like to go to the tree-lighting ceremony tonight. I'll come by the shop and pick you up."

"Sorry, I can't," she said.

"Oh." He sounded shocked. "Why not?"

She grinned at Jake, who was standing next to her in the kitchen, flipping pancakes for their breakfast. "I'm back with Jake."

There was a moment of shocked silence on the phone. Then, "You can't be serious."

She smiled at her ex-husband, who was grinning from ear to ear. "I'm afraid I am. But thanks for the offer."

"Ella, I don't know where your head is," Axel said.

She didn't, either, actually, but she knew where her heart was.

"Sorry," she said. "It wouldn't have worked out between us." She still hated jazz.

The family had just come home from church when Cass's cell phone rang. It was her stepfather, Ralph. Probably calling from the airport. They were due to fly out today and had a layover in Detroit.

"How's it going?" she asked. Neither Ralph nor her mother was particularly fond of flying, but Mom had said nothing was going to keep her from coming up for her granddaughter's wedding.

"Not so good," Ralph said.

Cass could feel a dark cloud creeping up on her sunny Sunday. "What's wrong?" she asked, dreading the answer.

"Your mother had a fall."

The cloud shot out thunder and lightning. Cass fell onto the nearest chair. "Oh, no."

"What's wrong?" Dani asked, sitting opposite her.

"Grandma fell," Cass said, then asked Ralph, "Is she hurt?" Dumb question. Of course she was hurt or Ralph wouldn't have been calling.

"She broke her wrist. She has to have surgery on Friday."

The day before the wedding. *Poor Mom. Poor me,* Cass added as a new, more selfish thought occurred. There went her support system. She'd been counting on her mother to help her hold it together while dealing with Mason and his family. Now she was on her own.

She chided herself for being so egocentric and asked if she could speak to her mother.

"I'm afraid she's with the doctor right now," Ralph said. "We'll keep you posted, though."

"Thanks," Cass said. "Tell her I love her. We're going to miss you guys."

"Not as much as we're going to miss you," Ralph assured her.

"So what happened?" Dani asked as Cass set aside her cell.

"Grandma broke her wrist. She has to have surgery on Friday."

Dani looked horrified. "She's not coming to the wedding?"

"She can't travel the day after surgery," Cass said.

"It won't be the same without her."

Now Willie was back from the kitchen (always his first destination after church) with a bag of chips. "When are we eating?"

"It's not all about you," Dani told him. Then to her mother, she said, "Maybe Grandma will be well enough to fly by Saturday."

No, it wasn't all about Willie, but it certainly was all about the bride-to-be. Cass leveled a look at her daughter, who had the grace to blush. "Even if she was up for it, they wouldn't get here in time."

Dani fell back against the couch cushions. "This blows."

There was an understatement. Cass patted her leg. "Don't worry. We'll have plenty of family for your big day." Half of them unwanted.

"I know. I just feel bad Grandma won't be here."

Not half as bad as I feel. "I know, and I know she's disappointed. But Uncle Drew will be recording it, so at least she'll get to see you walking down the aisle later on."

Dani's scowl lessened to a frown. "Poor Grandma. Gosh, I really wanted her there."

Cass gave Dani a hug. "But the most important people will be there—you and Mike."

That coaxed a smile out of her daughter.

"Now, come on, let's make dinner," Cass suggested. "Amber, Willie, that means you, too."

"Aw, Mom," Willie protested. "I hate cooking."

"But you like eating, and if you want to eat well when you're out in the big bad world, you'd better know how to cook. Anyway, it's tacos, and that's easy."

"Tacos! All right!"

"It's your turn to grate the cheese," Amber informed him. "I had to last time."

Willie groaned. "I suck at grating cheese. I always scrape my fingers."

"Be a good sport," Cass told him, and then told herself the same thing. Having her mother missing from Dani's wedding party had hardly been part of her plan, but—as she'd told her kids—not all recipes turned out as you planned them.

She said as much when her brother called to console her.

"Wow, sis, you're sure taking this well," he said.

She was sure pretending to take it well, anyway.

By the time her friends arrived for their Sunday chick-flick night, she was tired of pretending.

"Not having your mom here for such an important event, that's awful," Ella lamented.

"Dani's really disappointed," Cass said. "And I've got to tell you, even though I put on a good face for her, I'm not doing so well, either. I was counting on Mom being here to help me get through this."

"We'll get you through," Samantha promised.

"Absolutely," Charley seconded.

"Speaking of getting through things, how are you doing?" Cecily asked her.

Charley's eyes turned steely. "I'm doing just fine. I've decided to become a man-hater. Too bad I've got to work with one rebuilding the restaurant."

"Who'd you end up hiring?" Samantha asked.

"Masters Construction."

"Dan Masters?" Samantha cocked an eyebrow.

"He's new in town, isn't he?" Cecily asked.

Samantha nodded. "And newly single from what I hear. I met him at Bavarian Brews the other day."

"Quite a hunk of beefcake from what I hear," Cass said, looking speculatively at Charley.

"Hey, you go for him if you want," she said, holding up a hand. "Me, I'm so done with men it isn't even funny."

"Never say never," Cecily said.

"Yeah, you never know what might happen," put in Ella, who was beaming.

Cass looked at her speculatively. "Okay, you've been acting like a woman who owns a diamond mine ever since you got here. What gives?"

"Well." After a dramatic pause, she announced, "Jake and I are getting back together."

This produced squeals of delight and hugs all around.

"You two belong together," Cecily said.

"That's what we decided." Ella dropped her gaze, suddenly self-conscious. "You know, I was wrong about Jake. I mean, yes, he's a flirt, but he never cheated on me."

"I smell a story in there somewhere," Samantha said.

Ella's face turned pink. "I met the keyboard player Friday. She has someone. I guess this is where you all say I told you so."

"We wouldn't dream of it," Cass said.

"But we did tell you," Cecily added with a wicked grin.

"I'm glad Cupid is being good to you," Charley said. "Jake really is a nice guy."

Ella nodded. "Now, if we can just figure out a way for him to make a little more money."

"You've been able to live okay on what you guys earn," Cecily pointed out.

"But you're right to be thinking about how you can earn more," her sister said. "Especially if you want kids…."

"It would be hard to raise a family on what we're making," Ella admitted, and the pink in her face deepened.

"A family?" Cecily looked at her speculatively.

"I mean, we'll probably end up having kids," Ella stammered.

"You'll figure it out," Charley said. "One thing's for sure, you'll have lots of aunties to help out."

Poor Charley, Cass thought. It seemed she was auntie to half the babies in town, and the rare times she wasn't at the restaurant, she was always watching someone's kid. At the rate she was going, was she ever going to have children of her own? Cass hoped she would, hoped her friend wouldn't give up on love.

She was in no position to encourage Charley to stay hopeful. She herself had given up years ago. Love was overrated.

It did produce children, though, and she'd gotten three good ones out of the bad deal she'd made with Cupid. And now she was about to add a son-in-law and, down the road, grandchildren. Everything was coming together for the wedding and it was going to be beautiful.

But as she watched Cecily's movie pick of the week, *National Lampoon's Christmas Vacation,* she couldn't shake the feeling that she was going to wind up living the sequel.

Eighteen

Monday morning Ella met Mims at Bavarian Brews to make her big announcement. So far she was finding it difficult to work up the nerve.

"Ella, baby, what's wrong?" Mims asked.

"Wrong? Nothing."

Mims raised a perfectly sculpted eyebrow. "You could have fooled me. You're fidgeting. And you ordered decaf."

Ella took a deep breath. "I have news." And it was good news, so she shouldn't be so nervous about telling her mother.

Mims smiled encouragingly. "Well, my darling, let's hear it."

"Jake and I are back together."

A disapproving frown devoured her mother's smile. "Ella, you can't be serious."

She'd never realized before how often she saw that frown. Ella lifted her chin. "I am."

"After the way he's behaved? Have you gone insane? My God, we need to find you a shrink." She took her cell phone from her purse. "I'm calling Gregory and getting the name of his."

"I'm not seeing a shrink and I'm not leaving Jake," Ella said firmly. "You were wrong about him, Mims."

Mims gave Ella her snootiest look, the one she reserved for incompetent store clerks. "Oh?"

"He wasn't seeing that keyboard player."

Now Mims looked heavenward as if praying for strength to deal with her obstinate daughter. "Ella. Baby. I don't know what he said to you."

"Everything those pictures didn't. I was wrong not to give Jake a chance to tell the whole story."

She'd wanted to believe her mother was right. She was already jealous of the attention Jake got from other women, already prone to suspicion when she found Jen's note and phone number in his pocket. She'd had springs on her feet, ready to jump to conclusions. And once she had those incriminating pictures, she'd closed her mind and her heart to anything Jake had to say.

"Those pictures—"

Ella cut her off. "He wasn't having an affair with that keyboard player. She has someone else."

"Now, maybe," Mims conceded, "but not then."

"Not then, either. Jen's not into guys. She's got a girl-friend."

"A…girlfriend?"

"I should never have divorced him."

"Oh, yes, you should have," Mims insisted "If not her, it would've been someone else. And he's never going to have any money. He's never going to amount to any-thing."

"There's more to life than money," Ella said.

There went the motherly eyebrow again. "When was

the last time you tried living without it?" Before Ella could say anything, she added, "I won't always be here as a safety net for you, Ella. I want you to be secure."

"I am secure. I'm secure with Jake."

"You think you can be secure with a selfish man who always puts himself first?"

Brandon Wallace, one of Jake's softball team buddies, and Todd Black, who were sitting at a table behind them, suddenly began to laugh like some kind of all-knowing Greek chorus.

Mims shook her head. "Men like him, they use other people. They say all the right things, but their actions never line up."

"Are you talking about Jake or my father?" Ella retorted.

"Both."

Ella heard another guffaw from the table behind them. And something else, some kind of country song.

"Ella, baby—"

Ella held up her hand for silence. That voice, it sounded like Jake's. She got up and moved to stand by the table, trying to subtly peer over Brandon's shoulder. Sure enough, there on YouTube was Jake and his band. When had he done this? And what was it? Now Mims was standing next to her.

Brandon glanced over his shoulder at them and his eyes got bigger than those of any deer looking into a truck's headlights. "Ella, hi," he said, and quickly closed the page.

"Brandon, that was Jake," Ella said.

His deer-in-the-headlight eyes shot to his buddy.

Okay, what was the problem? Jake was on YouTube. That should be good news.

"Uh, no, it was some—somebody else," Brandon stuttered.

"Bring that back up," Mims commanded.

Brandon and his pal exchanged uh-oh looks as he obliged.

Sure enough, it was Jake. "Oh, my gosh, he's going to be famous," Ella cried. Another thing her mother had been wrong about.

Then she heard the lyrics. What kind of sick song was this? Next to her, Ella could feel her mother stiffening. She listened in horror as the song proceeded on its nasty route, Jake mocking her mother, offering Santa beer for life if he'd just haul Mims away. That was supposed to be funny?

Mims didn't stay to hear the second verse.

"I didn't see you guys sitting there. Sorry, Ella," Brandon said sheepishly.

He wasn't half as sorry as her husband was going to be. Make that ex-husband. Again.

When Ella didn't come home Jake figured she and her mother were shopping. But the hours dragged by and no Ella. His afternoon guitar students came and went, and still it was only him and Tiny in the house. Finally, it was almost dinnertime and he was hungry—for more than food.

He called her cell and received a very stiff hello.

What the hell was going on? "Hey, where are you?"

"I'm with Mims."

"Did you guys go to Seattle or something?"

"No. I'm at her place."

"Oh." Disappointment and confusion made it difficult for his brain to come up with any other words. Finally some surfaced. "Uh, when are you coming home?"

"Not tonight." The words came out so cold he nearly got frostbite on his ear.

"Okay, what's up?"

"What's up? You really need to ask?"

"Yeah." How else was he going to find out what could have gone wrong between last night and today?

"Well, why don't you look on YouTube? That might give you a clue," she said. Then all he heard was dial tone.

He didn't need to hear any more. Now he knew what the problem was. Somehow, someway, she'd seen him singing THE SONG. She'd been with her mother today and that meant mama-in-law had heard THE SONG, too. *Shit.*

He sat on the couch with his laptop and brought up "Merry Christmas, Mama." He almost dropped it when he saw how many views they had. That was great—in a parallel universe. Here in Jake's world it was a disaster. There he was, big, dumb, guitar-playing dope, dissing his former mother-in-law for all the world to see. He shut the laptop and fell back against the couch cushions. What was he going to do now?

The invasion had begun. Louise, Cass's former mother-in-law, and Maddy, her former sister-in-law, stopped by the bakery midmorning to announce that they had arrived. Days early. "We don't want to miss the bridal shower," Louise had said. Next thing Cass knew, they were stealing Dani away for shopping and lunch. Cass was not invited, which she told herself was fine, since someone had to wait on the customers. The snub stung, though, and she could only imagine how many more she was going to endure before their visit was over.

The next torture began when Mason showed up at the house with his trophy wife, who also wanted to attend the shower—oh, joy. He looked as fit as he was on the day they got married and had only a scant salting of gray in his brown hair. Father Time was treating him much more kindly than Cass. Men. They always stuck together.

Babette, standing next to him, was arm candy with her petite figure and her perfectly highlighted, shoulder-length hair. Looking at her, Cass felt every extra pound on her body. And here was another treat. They'd brought their dog, Cupcake.

Some dog, Cass thought. The yippy apricot Pomeranian resembled an overgrown powder puff. Cass was not a fan of little dogs. She much preferred real dogs like Ella's Saint Bernard, Tiny, dogs who had a purpose in life beyond trying a person's patience.

"Oh, you brought Cupcake," Amber said as Babette walked in holding the stupid thing like a baby. Amber reached out a hand to pet it and the dog growled and barked at her. She yanked back her hand.

"No, Cupcake, this is family. Remember?" Babette cooed to the minibeast. "She doesn't know where she is."

She's in Icicle Falls, invading my house. And for longer than she'd originally agreed to, no less. She must have been insane to go along with this.

"She just needs time to warm up. She's really very sweet," Babette explained to Cass.

Compared to what?

"Thanks for putting us up," Mason said.

He was managing to be civil. She could, too. "No problem," she lied. Dani had given up her room and was

sleeping in Amber's, a sacrifice she was more than willing to make to have her father here. They were a full
house, but not as full as they would've been if Mom
hadn't broken her wrist. If Mom and Ralph had made it,
Mason and Bimbette would probably have been on the
sleeper sofa.

At least she'd been spared having to see *that* every
morning when she got up. "Dani will show you to your
room. Dinner's just about ready." After that, the women
would be off to Dani's bridal shower, which Cass was
determined to enjoy even if it killed her.

Dinner was lasagna with garlic bread and Caesar
salad. Size-six Babette passed on the lasagna, had a few
bites of salad and fed most of her garlic bread to the dog,
who came to the table and sat in her lap.

"I take it you don't like lasagna," Cass said, trying
(not very hard) not to be offended.

Babette wrinkled her pert little nose. "It's so fattening."

And that was why Babette was a size six and Cass
was...not. She should have gone on a diet when she first
heard this highlighted Barbie doll was coming.

Oh, what did she care? She didn't have to look good
for anyone.

This last thought didn't prove comforting. She dished
herself up a second helping of lasagna.

After dinner Mason and Willie got busy looking for a
guy movie to watch while the women cleaned up in the
kitchen. Babette cleared the table, all the while talking
about the "amazing" Murano glass she'd bought when
Mason took her to Italy. Cupcake helped by trying to get
into the garbage. And Cass reminded herself that they
were only here for a few days.

Then it was off with Dani and Amber and Ms. Size Six to pick up her ex-mother-and sister-in-law at Olivia's B and B and take them to Samantha's place for Dani's big night.

They were already standing outside the door when Cass pulled up under the port cochere. Maddy had gone lighter with her hair and it looked like she'd gained weight. She'd gotten divorced shortly before Cass and Mason. Like Cass, she'd obviously shed a husband and gained a couple of dress sizes. Louise, on the other hand, had gotten thinner. She looked like a stick with a wool coat. Even her lips were thin. That probably had something to do with the fact that they were pressed together in a semifrown.

"It's almost seven," she said as she got in the backseat. "We're going to be late."

Ah, yes, how Cass remembered that charming critical spirit. "Don't worry. Samantha lives five minutes from here. We'll be right on time," she assured Louise.

She was wasting her breath. Her former mother-in-law wasn't listening. She was already gushing a greeting to Dani. "And here's our bride. I'm looking forward to meeting all your friends, darling."

And they were looking forward to meeting her. Not.

"Thanks for picking us up," Maddy said. She checked out the interior. "Is this the same car you had way back when you were with Mason?"

Wouldn't that have been a fun bit of information to spread when she got back home and saw her friends? "Not quite. How've you been, Maddy?"

"Wonderful. I've just gotten engaged."

"Well, congratulations," Cass said, determined to be magnanimous.

"How about you? Did you ever find anyone?"

Maddy had a way with words. "I haven't been look-ing. I've been too involved with my business."

"Still single, then? Well, maybe you'll catch the bou-quet. Dani, you'll have to throw it in your mother's di-rection."

Oh, that was cute. "I think we'll save that opportunity for the younger girls," Cass said. "Speaking of bouquets, tell them about your flowers, Dani."

Her suggestion shone the spotlight where it needed to be. Talk turned to the wedding and they made it to Sa-mantha's without Cass having to stop the car and bitch-slap her ex-sister-in-law.

"What a pretty house," Babette said as Cass pulled up to the curb.

The Prestons' house was decked out for the holidays with white lights strung along the roof and a holiday wreath on the door. Inside it was just as lovely. Saman-tha was an amateur photographer, and a winter shot she'd taken of Icicle Falls frozen in action hung over the fire-place. To the side of it, several candles were arranged on the mantelpiece, and the scent of bayberry filled the house. The living room was packed with women, all dressed in their holiday finery and Samantha's coffee table was piled high with beautifully wrapped presents and gift bags.

Samantha herself looked chic in black jeans, ballet slippers and a green sweater that showed off her red hair.

"Thank you so much for including us," Babette said once Cass had introduced them. "It's so exciting to see our Dani getting married."

Our Dani. Cass managed to smile and grind her teeth simultaneously.

"You're welcome." Then before Babette could get too chummy, Samantha got down to business, offering to take everyone's coats.

Dani's bridesmaids, Mikaila and Vanessa, came running up to her, all squeals and excitement and adorableness. Looking at them, Cass wondered if she'd ever been that cute. Hard to remember ancient history, but she was pretty sure she'd once been equally happy and carefree. She was still happy, she reminded herself. And seeing all her friends and neighbors here to show their love and support for her daughter had proud-mama tears welling up.

Samantha had gone all out and her dining room table practically groaned under the weight of appetizers and cookies.

"When did you have time to do all this?" Cass asked as she handed over her coat.

"Me? Are you kidding?" She nodded to where her younger sister stood, chatting with Lauren Belgado. "Bailey's back. Wait till you taste the chocolate dessert she made."

"Can't wait," said Cass. Too late to start dieting now, she reasoned.

But first she needed to make the rounds and thank everyone for coming. Oh, yeah, and introduce the in-laws.

"It's lovely to meet you," the mother of the groom said to Louise.

Yeah, well, wait until you get to know her, thought Cass.

"We're delighted to be here," Louise said.

She'd certainly been delighted to tell Samantha how lovely her house was. So much roomier than Cass's, but then those old houses weren't really designed for modern living.

Who said? It had taken all Cass's restraint not to kick the gray-haired biddy in her skinny butt.

Now Louise was busy telling Mike's mother how lucky her son was to be getting such a sweet girl.

"Oh, we know it," said Delia, giving Cass an encouraging smile—one suffering daughter-in-law to another. Delia and Cass had become good friends over the past few months and had come to agree on several important things. Yes, their children were young to be getting married, but they were both mature, well-grounded kids and they'd be fine. And they were each getting a great mother-in-law, which was more than either Cass or Delia could say. And, no matter how strongly tempted, they would neither take sides nor interfere in their children's lives.

Once all the guests had arrived, Samantha's younger sister Bailey, who'd come home early to cater the wedding, took charge, making them all play a game, some sort of word scramble involving necessities for a successful wedding. Cass couldn't help smiling at one of them—*reacter,* which, unscrambled, spelled *caterer.* Good advertising.

Then it was time to open presents. Amber was happy to be put to work making a practice bouquet using ribbons from the package and a paper plate, while Dani's friend Vanessa kept track of who gave her what. Dani was over the moon with Cass's, which was a box filled with essential baking tools. Like her mother, she loved to bake both at work and at home, and Cass knew Dani would use every item. Delia gave her a cookbook and the Sterling women gave her a gift card to Hearth and Home. Ella had made a wedding towel cake. Louise, big spender that she was, had given Dani a 9" x 12" glass pan and Maddy had gone one better by getting her a set of ramekins. Her bridesmaids got her fun gifts—personalized bride flipflops and a sexy cookbook loaded with aphrodisiac recipes. But the hit of the shower was Babette's present—a huge Victoria's Secret gift bag packed with lingerie. Even perfume.

"Oh, thank you! I love this fragrance," Dani said happily.

"I know you do," Babette told her, smiling.

It was like they were best friends. Cass popped an entire snowball cookie in her mouth.

"That's quite the gift," said Dot, who was sitting next to Cass with her foot propped on a footstool.

It was hard to swallow…the cookie. "Yes, it is," Cass agreed, and went back to the refreshment table. *This is not a competition,* she reminded herself. *Try to remember you're a grown-up and be grateful your daughter has so many people in her life who care.*

That attitude adjustment made it much easier to enjoy the shower. And it hardly fazed Cass when her former mother-in-law eyed her second plate with disgust. They were small plates.

Bailey had created a special drink for the bride that she'd dubbed Wedding Night Bliss, a frothy white concoction consisting primarily of coconut juice and white chocolate liqueur, for which she was now taking orders. "I can do alcoholic or virgin," she said.

"I'd better make mine a virgin," Babette said.

"And I know why," Maddy murmured, with a conspiratorial grin. She leaned across Dani and said to Cass in a stage whisper, "She's pregnant."

Cass lost her grip on her plate and two cookies bounced onto the floor. "P-pregnant?" she stammered.

"Wow, I didn't know that," Dani said.

"They're thrilled about it," Maddy confided.

And Maddy would know, of course, Cass thought cynically, since she specialized in minding other people's business.

The rest of the evening became mechanical. Cass smiled and said all that was right while inside she battled with her less noble half once more. This time it was a losing battle. It was hard to shake the sense of injustice she felt. After doing such a lousy job with his first set of kids, Mason the absent father was getting a second chance with his hot young wife. Everything was going great for him the second time around.

You could have remarried.

As if she'd wanted to. She liked being on her own. No one to foul up her plans, no one to disappoint her, no one…well, no one.

That wasn't altogether true. She had her family and her friends and her business. She didn't need anyone else. Heck, she didn't have time for anyone else.

But her nest was starting to empty. In another ten years she'd have time. How was she going to fill it? She'd never given that any thought. She'd been so busy, and middle age had been a lifetime away. Now here it was. She found herself feeling relieved when the party ended.

She helped carry Dani's loot out to the car and load it in the trunk, then looked on with a motherly smile while her daughter hugged Louise and Maddy goodbye at the lodge. She kept her smile as she, her daughters and Babette drove back to the house and Dani said to Babette, "I didn't know you were pregnant."

"Well, I'm only three months," Babette said, and glanced nervously in Cass's direction.

"Congratulations," Cass said, and tried to mean it.

After all, there was no sense resenting Babette. She deserved a chance at happiness just like anyone else.

"Thanks," Babette said. "We're excited."

Mason had been far from excited when she got pregnant with Dani. "How did that happen?" he'd protested. As if it'd been all her fault. Of course, he'd backpedaled and said they'd make it work. And they had. They'd made it work by her doing everything. Well, maybe this time around he'd be more involved.

Mike had joined Mason and Willie, and they were on their second action flick when the women walked in the door, but they stopped it to help unload the trunk and then showed the proper interest in all of Dani's presents. Mike was especially interested in Dani's Victoria's Secret goodies.

"That's quite the haul," Mason said when she'd finished.

"We have so many great friends," Dani said happily, falling onto the couch next to Mike.

"You can say that again," he said.

"Man, you sure get a lot of stuff when you get married," Willie observed.

"You *need* a lot of stuff when you get married," Mason informed him.

"But it's all girl things," Willie said.

"Oh, not all of it," Mike said, picking up the Victoria's Secret bag.

That made Willie, big man on campus, actually blush. He leaned over his chair, reaching down to the plate sitting on the floor, only to discover Cupcake devouring the one remaining sugar cookie on it. "Hey!" he yelled.

Cookie in mouth, Cupcake made a dash for the kitchen.

"She ate my cookie!"

"Oh, Willie, I'm sorry," said Babette, who had squeezed in next to Mason on the other end of the couch.

"You know better than to leave food on the floor," Mason told him.

Cass bridled. This was her house. Willie could leave food on the floor if he wanted. "He's not used to having to worry about anything coming along and stealing his food," she said.

Mason shrugged off her comment, much as he'd shrugged off almost everything she'd had to say when they were married. She glared at him. That, too, bounced off him.

No glaring on the night of your daughter's bridal shower, she scolded herself. *And no more of these negative feelings.* At this rate she'd never get to sleep. And, unlike everyone else in the house, she had to be up before dawn.

She excused herself to go get ready for bed. Cupcake, now lurking by the stairs, yapped at her. *Good night, bitch.*

It was going to be a long week.

The next day wasn't any better for Cass. Her workday was an endless stretch of baking and waiting on customers, and the customer service turned out to be a one-woman operation once Dani disappeared to run errands in the afternoon and never returned. When Cass finally called her on her cell to find out where the heck she was, she learned Dani was out with Grandma and Aunt Maddy.

"Sorry, Mom. I've got so much to do."

"You've also got a job," Cass said. "I need help here."

"Okay, I'll get there as soon as I can," Dani promised.

Cass ended the call feeling guilty. It was unfair to expect Dani to work the week before her wedding. She'd been wrong and she'd apologize to her daughter—if she ever saw her.

In addition to realizing she was being unfair, she came to another conclusion. With her right-hand woman leaving, she was going to have to hire help.

This left her feeling a little low. Dani had been her baking sidekick, working alongside her for the past six years, first coming in after school and washing down tables and cleaning up in the kitchen, then taking on more responsibility as she got older. Cass had delighted in watching her daughter's skills develop and her creativity bloom, and she'd come to depend on her. Their shared passion for baking had kept them close. Now Dani was leaving, making plans to go back to school and get a catering degree. She'd be setting up both a business and a new life a hundred and seventy miles away.

Not the edge of the earth, Cass reminded herself. Why was it so hard to let go of that vision of Dani and her family here in Icicle Falls, of living close to her grandchildren? Family was important. Grandkids were important.

Maybe they'd been important to Louise, too.

Oh, no! Where had that come from? No place Cass wanted to visit.

She reined her thoughts away from the past and turned them toward the future. What was she going to do with Dani gone? Maybe she could teach Amber how to work the cash register and get her to come in after school on weekdays, even convince her she could sacrifice some of her social life to work on Saturday mornings. But Amber was more into clothes than cookies. Even if Cass could persuade her to put in some hours, that wasn't going to be enough; not with the way her business had been growing.

It was time to put an ad in the classifieds. Her daughter would be a tough act to follow, though. Maybe impossible.

That's life, she reminded herself. Children grow up and move on. She'd been perfectly happy with the growing-up part, and the moving on. It was just this moving *away* thing that upset her.

The future was out of her control. All she had was the present, and here in the present she had customers to wait on.

She'd just sent Darla on her way with a gingerbread house when Willie called to report that Cupcake had eaten his shorts.

"She *what?*"

"She ate my shorts!"

There was a gross visual. "How on earth did she manage that?"

"I don't know," Willie said grumpily. "I came home and found 'em all shredded. I hate that dog."

That made two of them. Still… "Did you leave your dirty clothes on the floor like I'm always asking you not to?"

"Yeah," he said grudgingly.

"And I'm guessing you didn't bother to close your bedroom door when you went to school."

"I shouldn't have to."

"No, you shouldn't. But if you don't want the dog going after your socks next, it might be a good idea to keep the door closed."

"Gee, thanks, Mom," Willie grumbled, and hung up.

Life was tough all over. Dani never made it back to the bakery, leaving Cass to soldier on alone.

Her daughter was apologetic when they met with the ex-in-laws for dinner at Der Spaniard later. Cass apologized, too, for being such a slave driver, and even managed a friendly greeting for Louise, along with a compliment on her Christmas sweater.

Louise accepted the compliment with as much grace as the cactus on the reception desk, which was also decked out for the holidays with colored lights and looked a lot cuter.

Once everyone was seated and the orders had been placed, talk turned to the happy couple's upcoming move.

"Spokane has some great wineries," Babette said. "We'll have to come check them out. After the baby's born," she added, and put a hand on her tummy.

Cass kept smiling.

By the end of the evening, the smile was wearing thin and she was glad to leave the restaurant. Mason picked up the tab. Mr. Generous.

Let him, she decided. She was tired of competing with him, tired of keeping score.

To prove it she offered to make coffee for everyone and serve up the cream puff swans she'd brought home from the bakery. Louise declined the invitation, claiming exhaustion. Yes, shopping all day could be wearing. Maddy said she'd come, though, promising to be there as soon as she'd dropped off Louise.

Won't that be fun? More smiling all the way home. Mouth muscles aching, Cass opened the front door and led everyone into the house.

And got an early Christmas present. Lovely. This was the icing on the cake.

Nineteen

It wasn't hard to figure out what she'd stepped in. Soft, squishy, stinky—a welcome-home present from Cupcake. With a growl, Cass lifted her foot to remove her shoe, while behind her Amber said, "Eew, gross."

"What?" asked Willie, lumbering in behind her.

"Watch where you step," Cass cautioned. "Amber, get some paper towels."

"What's wrong?" Babette asked. She halted just inside the door. "Oh."

"Yes, *oh*," Cass agreed. "That dog," she said through gritted teeth.

Now Mason was inside. "What's this?"

"If you can't guess, I'll be happy to let you take a sniff of my shoe," Cass snapped.

Her son, probably fearing that he'd get drafted to help with cleanup, made himself scarce, leaving the three adults to deal with the smelly problem.

"I knew we should've taken her for a walk before we left," Babette lamented.

"And lost her," Cass muttered.

"Cute, Cass," Mason said in disgust.

Amber returned with the paper towels, and Mason snatched them and got to work. Amber beat a hasty retreat, but Babette bent to help, all the while saying how sorry she was.

Cass ignored her. "Cute?" she retorted. "Kind of like you bringing that animal here without even asking if it would be okay?"

"Mason said it was all right," Babette protested. "I had no idea."

Cass glared at him. "Seriously?"

"I'd forgotten how uncooperative you could be."

"Oh, that's rich coming from you of all people," Cass snarled as she wiped off the bottom of her shoe.

"I'm so sorry," Babette said again.

Now the verbal battle began in earnest. "*You* don't need to be sorry," Cass told her. "It's the inconsiderate jerk you're married to who should be sorry."

"Hey, you're the one who invited us to stay," Mason said, his voice rising.

"Because I was suffering from temporary insanity."

"Temporary?"

"Oh, that is funny."

The door opened to reveal Dani and Mike.

For a moment all was silent as Dani stood gaping at her squabbling parents. Then she burst into tears. "Why do you guys have to do this?" she wailed. "Are you going to fight on my wedding day, too?"

Without waiting for an answer, she turned and fled, Mike following her.

"Now look what you've done!" Cass snapped at Mason. *"Me?"*

Babette was crying, too. And here came Cupcake,

trotting out to see what all the fuss was about. "You bad dog," Babette scolded.

Bad? How about demon-possessed? Cass tossed her smelly shoe out on the front porch and then stomped off to the kitchen.

"Don't make coffee," Mason yelled at her. "We're going out."

"Fine," she shouted. *Go out and don't come back.*

She didn't bother with the coffee but she did help herself to two cream puff swans. No sense letting them go to waste. Then she set the rest out on a plate. Willie and Amber would finish them off.

And now, after eating too much and saying too much, it was time for bed.

A knock on the front door reminded her that not everyone had gotten the message that the party was off. She opened it and there stood Maddy.

"Mason's car is gone," she told Cass.

"Sorry. I should've called you. We had a change of plans."

"A change of plans." Maddy repeated the words as if she were learning a foreign language.

"Yes, a change of plans," Cass said, trying to hold on to her patience.

Maddy pointed a finger at her. "You and Mason had a fight, didn't you?"

"Good night, Maddy," Cass said, and shut the door. Not in Maddy's face, not really. All right, she'd shut it in Maddy's face. Guilt prompted her to open the door again. Maddy was already marching down the porch steps. "We'll do it another time," Cass promised.

Maddy graciously accepted the offer with a one-fingered salute and kept walking.

Cass shut the door again and started upstairs. She met Amber coming down, holding the cause of all the commotion. Cupcake growled at Cass and let out an ear-piercing bark. *Bad Mom*.

"Are you and Daddy still fighting?" Amber asked in a small voice.

Nothing like a final dose of guilt to help a woman sleep well. Cass sighed. "We do that sometimes."

"Sometimes?"

"Okay, we do that a lot. But everything will be fine." She gave her daughter a pat on the arm. "There are cream puffs in the kitchen just dying to be eaten."

Amber nodded and continued on down to the empty living room, while Cass went upstairs and shut herself in her bedroom. What a lovely evening this had been.

And whose fault was that?

She tried to ignore the sobering thought as she got ready for bed, but it refused to be ignored. It followed her into the shower. Then it followed her to bed, where it camped on her pillow and nagged her for hours. She lay there, trying to not face it, as muted voices drifted up from downstairs. Dani was probably back, talking with Mason about her terrible mother. Eventually she heard footsteps on the stairs, and then in the hallway as, one by one, everyone made their way to bed. Had Willie done his homework? Amber had asked for help with her math earlier. Cass had completely forgotten. Great. Mother of the year.

Now the nasty thought was bouncing up and down on the bed. *Whose fault? Whose fault?*

She rolled over on her side and squeezed her eyes shut, told both the thought and herself to go to sleep.

It didn't. Neither did she.

At 1:00 a.m. she decided to see if warm milk really did help a person sleep and padded downstairs to the kitchen. To her surprise, she found Mason already there, seated at the kitchen table with a mug of cocoa and a book. He looked up at her entrance and frowned.

"I couldn't sleep," she said. "Hard to do when you've got a guilty conscience."

He grunted. Then he raised his mug. "Want some?"

"I'll have some hot milk," she said, and sat down at the table.

"That's for sissies."

"Sissies who have to be up early in the morning. The chocolate will keep me awake." Just like that nasty thought. Okay, it was now or never. She took a deep breath. "Mason, I'm sorry. I've been a rotten host."

He shrugged and put a mug of milk in the microwave.

"My attitude stinks," she admitted.

He turned and faced her. "I hate to say it, Cass, but it's stunk for a long time."

Her first instinct was to fire back an angry retort, but she didn't. Instead, she did something she hadn't done in years. She stopped and considered what he'd said.

The microwave dinged and he removed her cup and brought it to the table. Then he sat down and looked at her. "You know what I like about Babette?"

"The fact that she's young and gorgeous?"

He shook his head. "The fact that she's there for me."

Okay, now she was done holding back. "What, and I wasn't?"

"Not really." He took a sip of his cocoa and regarded her over the rim of his mug. "Come on, Cass, let's be honest."

"Okay," she agreed. "Let's. If you want honesty, try

this on for size. I hate it that you've been Mr. Absent Father for years and now all of a sudden you come waltzing in like you're Super Dad. You write a few checks, throw around a few bribes and everyone loves you. It makes me feel like everything I've done for the kids all these years doesn't matter."

He set down his mug with a heavy sigh. "I'm sorry you feel threatened, Cass. You've been a great mom. Nobody would say any different, certainly not me. I'm just trying to be a better dad. I'm tired of feeling left out. And if you want to know the truth, I always felt left out."

"Left out?" What was he talking about?

"It was always you and the kids, with me on the outside looking in, trying to figure out how I fit into the family. Sometimes all I felt like was a paycheck."

"That's all you were," Cass said bluntly. "You were so busy becoming important you didn't have time for us."

"I did it all for you," he protested.

"So you always said. But what good did that do when we never saw you?"

His jaw was set, which meant he was dealing with strong emotions. "I didn't want to be a loser like my dad. I wanted to be successful. And I wanted you there for me, Cass. You never were. Everything I ever did you resented."

"That was because it took you away." How often had she told him that? Had he never listened? Well, duh. Of course he hadn't. That had been part of the problem.

"Well, you got your revenge. You moved far enough out of reach that you made it damned hard for me to be anything *but* away. If I hadn't finally gotten a job in Seattle we'd still have been squabbling about when I could see the kids."

"I didn't want revenge. I only wanted a new start."

"Are you sure that's all you wanted?" he pressed.

She sat back against her seat. That *was* all she'd wanted, wasn't it? She'd been so angry, so bitter.

So out to get him? "I don't know now," she said. "I honestly don't know."

He shrugged. "It's all water under the bridge."

Troubled water.

"We probably didn't belong together in the first place."

He was right, but the statement stung, anyway.

"Still, you were so damned hot I couldn't resist you," he added with a hint of a smile.

She took the hint and managed to give him one in return. Then sighed. "If I hadn't gotten pregnant…"

"I'd have married you, anyway. You have to know that."

She nodded, accepting the truth of his statement. They'd been hot for each other, sure that what they had would last forever.

"But the instant-family thing had me panicked. I had to do something to provide for you."

Hence rushing into the navy. And that hadn't pleased her. Neither had anything else he'd done to try and better himself. "I'm sorry I wasn't more understanding," she said, and meant it.

"Past history." He shoved away his mug. "But it feels good to hear you say it. And I'm sorry I let you down."

"Well," she said thoughtfully, "you didn't let me down completely."

"Yeah?"

"You gave me three great kids."

"We gave each other three great kids," he corrected.

"I guess they were the one thing we did right." What

she and Mason once had together was definitely past history, but their children were the present and the future. And that was worth keeping in mind.

"Think we can work on being a team instead of adversaries?" he proposed. "For the kids' sake?"

She should have been the one proposing that, and she should have done it a long time ago. "I'm willing to try." After all, they'd be sharing these kids and probably grandkids for a lifetime.

"Me, too." He got up and took his mug to the sink.

"Mason?"

He turned, a questioning look on his face.

"You chose a nice wife."

He nodded. "I think so."

"I still hate her dog."

He smiled. "Me, too," he said, and left the kitchen.

Cass glanced at the kitchen clock and decided she'd better get back to bed. She didn't bother to finish the milk. She didn't need it anymore.

Jake tossed his cell phone aside and slumped against the couch cushions.

Tiny laid his head on Jake's leg and looked up at him in doggy concern.

"My life's in the toilet," he told the dog.

Ironic considering that his song was now up to 7400 views.

"You've got to take that thing down," he'd said to Larry.

"Are you nuts? Do you know how many views we're up to?"

"Yeah, and I don't care if we're up to a million."

"What the hell is the matter with you?"

"I'm trying to get back with Ella."

"So?"

"So my mother-in-law saw it."

"Ex-mother-in-law, dude," Larry had reminded him.

"She won't be an ex-mother-in-law once Ella and I are back together. And we were—until that song."

"I feel your pain," Larry had said. "Women. But, hey, what are you gonna do?"

"Take the song down, for starters."

"No can do, buddy."

"I can't get her back as long as that song is up there!" Jake had shouted.

"If her mom already saw it, it's too late, anyway. I'm not taking it down."

"You have to!"

"Hey, man, you may be our lead singer but I'm still the leader of this band. Now, I let you have your no-drinking onstage rule and your one-drink-during-practice rule, but I'll be damned if I'll let you screw things up for all of us just 'cause you're hot to get in your ex's pants."

It was a good thing they'd only been talking over the phone. Otherwise, Jake would have punched Larry's lights out. "You need to take that song down," he shouted.

"No, you need to get your shit together," Larry had said, and hung up.

And now, after that happy conversation, here came a call from Billy Joe Brown, a Nashville talent manager who had seen him on YouTube, wanting to know if he was under management. Did he have a CD in the works? Where had his band played? What were his plans for the future?

To win back his wife—that was his plan. But Jake had

been properly professional, and he and Billy Joe left it that he'd talk to his band, then call him back.

"The sooner, the better, son," Billy Joe advised. "When the snowball starts rolling you want to take advantage of it."

Well, the snowball had started rolling, and it had rolled right over Jake's love life.

Next to him, Tiny let out a groan.

"Yeah, I know. It's not all about me, is it? Tell you what, let's go for a walk and then get some firewood."

Tiny barked his approval of the plan.

Some people (Jake's ex-mother-in-law) thought that dogs couldn't understand human vocabulary, but Jake didn't agree. Tiny understood a lot. For sure he understood what *walk* meant. That translated into bounding across snow-covered lawns, sniffing and peeing on every shrub that crossed his path.

He also understood what *firewood* was. It was an exciting chore. Jake had a sled reserved for hauling in the wood that he harnessed to Tiny, so he could pull it from the shed to the house. It was more work harnessing Tiny and loading and unloading the wood than it was simply bringing in a couple of armloads, but Saint Bernards needed a purpose.

So did humans. A man needed to do what he was put on earth to do.

He probably hadn't been put here to diss Ella's mom.

Once he'd brought in the wood it didn't take him long to get a roaring fire going. He grabbed his guitar, plunked down on the couch and stared into the flames. How many times had he sat here like this on a winter's day, dreaming of a future filled with success? His dreams were finally starting to come true, but they wouldn't mean anything without Ella by his side. He was living in ashes.

He strummed his guitar. "I'm living in ashes. The fire is gone."

The song began to flow, and soon he was so caught up in what he was creating that he lost all track of time. He never heard the door open, never heard Ella walk into the room. He'd just finished singing his last chorus when he opened his eyes and there she stood by the fireplace. Was he hallucinating?

The hallucination spoke. "That's a beautiful song," she said softly. "Why couldn't you have put that up on YouTube?"

If he had they'd be solid now. He shook his head. "I don't know." That was a lie. He knew exactly why he'd put up his snarky holiday greeting to his ex-mother-in-law. He'd been angry.

And immature.

"That was a mean thing to do."

Yes, it had been.

She opened her mouth to say something else, then seemed to think better of it and started to leave the room.

"Wait," he begged. "What were you going to say?"

"What does it matter?"

"It matters a lot."

She pursed her lips and studied him. At last she spoke. "I know I married you, Jake, and I owed you my loyalty. I did a lot of stupid things. I was jealous for no reason, and toward the end I know I wasn't very supportive."

You could say that again. Jake wisely kept his mouth shut.

"But maybe if the shoe had been on the other foot,

you'd have gotten jealous. And maybe you'd have jumped to the same conclusions."

She had a point there. "Maybe," he conceded.

"And you can't blame Mims, either. She was only trying to help."

Was that what you called it?

Ella bit her lip. Sure enough. "You always want to make me choose—you or Mims. Do you know how impossible that is? What would you have done if I'd asked you to choose between your mother and me?"

Jake gave a snort. "That would never have happened because my mom likes you." *And my mom's cool and yours is a bitch.* "Anyway, your mom never wanted to share. She's hated me ever since I asked you to the senior prom."

"No, only since you picked me up for prom in that beat-up old truck," Ella corrected him. The memory brought a reluctant smile to her lips.

He grinned. "We took some rides I'll never forget in that old truck."

Ella sobered. "Oh, Jake."

Just then the doorbell rang. Jake swore. "Don't answer."

"I have to. It's Mims."

"Don't tell me, let me guess—you two are going out to dinner." The wicked witch of the Pacific Northwest, sweeping in again, just when she was most not wanted.

"We're going to dinner at   "

Jake cut her off. "Schwangau."

Ella nodded.

Big surprise there. Mims didn't like Mexican, and a pizza joint was beneath her. She sure as heck wouldn't be interested in Big Brats or Herman's Hamburgers.

Now that Zelda's was closed for repairs, the hoity-toity Schwangau was the only place this side of Seattle where Lily Swan would deign to eat. Why the hell couldn't she find someone her own age to go to dinner with?

Ella hurried down the hall. Jake could hear her opening the door, could hear Lily saying, "You ready, baby? I don't want to keep Axel waiting."

Axel! Who'd painted him back in the picture?

"Let me get my coat," said Ella.

There it sat on a nearby chair, along with her purse. For a moment Jake considered hiding them.

Now she was back, her expression unhappy, and he wasn't sure if she was unhappy about the conversation they'd been having or about the fact that her mother was taking her away. "I have to go," she said, not looking him in the eye.

"El," he pleaded. They could work this out if they could just have some uninterrupted time to talk.

She shook her head and rushed off, putting on her coat as she went.

In less than a minute he heard the door shut.

"*Now* what am I supposed to do?" he asked Tiny.

Tiny whimpered in sympathy.

Jake fell back against the couch cushions. "They're a matched set, aren't they?" he mused. "Hard to find a woman who doesn't come attached to her mama."

What was that about, anyway? Men left home and their moms accepted it. Why was it so hard for them to let go of their daughters? Or their daughters to let go of them? Was it some kind of female thing?

"You take one, you get the other," he informed Tiny. "No extra charge." He thought he'd been marrying one woman, but he'd gotten a twofer. Well, sort of. He would have if Lily Swan had ever approved of him.

She sure didn't approve of him now, thanks to that song. Who'd think one song could do so much damage?

"You should have known," he told himself. "Songs are powerful."

Hmm. Yes, they were. A song had gotten him into this latest mess. Could a song get him out?

Twenty

"Axel, I'm glad you could join us on the spur of the moment like this," Mims said after the waiter had taken their orders.

"My pleasure." He looked inquiringly at Ella. "I thought you'd have plans with Jake."

Lily spoke for her. "She doesn't. She and Jake are through for good."

"Really?" Axel sounded dubious.

"I don't want to talk about it," Ella said.

He nodded. "Well, this is some snowfall we're getting, isn't it?"

Ella gazed out the window at the scene of snowcapped shops lit by old-fashioned streetlights. When it snowed like this, she and Jake liked to be tucked in their house in front of a roaring fire.

He'd built a fire for her.

Who cared? What he'd done to her mother was unforgivable.

But was it understandable? She could still remember his angry words when they had their final fight, right before he accused her of not trusting him, and told her to go ahead and get that divorce. "I blame this on your mom. She's wanted me gone from the minute we got together."

"That's not true!" Ella had protested, but of course it was true. Weren't mothers supposed to be happy when their daughters found someone to love?

"Ella?"

Her mother's voice brought her back to the present.

"I'm sorry. What?"

Mims shook her head. "Where were you just now?"

With Jake. "It doesn't matter." Except it did. "You know, sometimes I don't understand why you never gave Jake a chance."

Both her mother's eyebrows shot up. "You must be joking."

"No, I'm not."

"Maybe I should go," Axel said.

"No, stay. We're not going to talk about this anymore," Mims said firmly.

Ella fell silent. Fine. She wouldn't talk at all. The waiter arrived with their salads, and she concentrated on the baby greens on her plate.

Axel tried to step into the breach with talk of plans to tour the California wine country.

Who cared? Ella broke her vow of silence. "I made a mistake."

"It's a little late to change your order now, baby," Mims said.

"No, I mean about Jake."

Axel stood. "You know, I'm going to leave you ladies to sort this out."

"Oh, Axel," Mims began.

"Good idea," Ella agreed. "Don't worry about dinner. My mother will pick up the check."

Axel nodded and left, and Mims let out an offended huff. "Really, Ella. That was high-handed."

"No more high-handed than you inviting him in the first place," Ella said in a tone of voice she rarely used with her mother.

"Well, you weren't seeing that—"

"Jake. His name is Jake. And what's Axel got that he hasn't?"

"Money, for one thing. Sophistication."

"Oh, Mims, he's a fathead. And he's controlling. Every time he asked me out it was to something he'd already decided on. I don't want to be controlled." Heaven knew she'd been controlled enough growing up. "By anyone," she added.

"Are you implying that I control you?"

She was on a roll now. *May as well keep rolling.* "You do. Actually, you always have. When I was growing up I never got to pick out my own school clothes."

"Of course you did, once you developed some fashion sense."

"Any friends you didn't like you weeded out of my life."

"For your own good," Mims insisted.

"There was nothing wrong with any of my friends, except that their moms worked at the Sweet Dreams factory or as cashiers in the grocery store." Mims had nothing to say to that and Ella moved on. "You're the one who decided I should work for you at the shop."

"And why shouldn't you? You have a flair for clothes."

"I have a flair for decorating, too. That's what I wanted to do." So she should have spoken up and said so instead of just going along. Well, she was done going along now. It was time to be her own woman.

"That was ridiculous," Mims said. "Go work for someone else when we had a family business? Ella, I don't know what's gotten into you."

"I want to be me. I don't want to be an imitation you. I want to be happy."

"You are happy," Mims said. "We're happy. We've always been happy, just the two of us."

Your mom never wanted to share.

Jake's words washed over Ella, a shower of icy reality. He was right. Surely, on some level, she must have known this. Maybe she'd never wanted to see it. Her eyesight was twenty-twenty now. The big question was, what was she going to do with her new, improved vision? Something every grown woman had to do at some point—claim her own life, for better or for worse.

She took a deep breath. "Mims, you know I love you."

"And I love you. There's nothing I wouldn't do for you. I gave up a modeling career for you."

Okay, that didn't ring true. "You once told me that models burn out early. That you'd already peaked."

This made her mother frown. "Well, I hadn't. I could have done any number of things if we hadn't moved here."

"Then why didn't you do those things?"

Mims sat there staring at her. "I... I just didn't."

Ella fell against the seat and stared back at her mother. "You ran away. You ran away from your life."

"I did not!" Mims said hotly.

"You got pregnant and you up and ran away. Why didn't I ever meet my father?"

Mims stiffened. "We've had this discussion before."

"It didn't work out and I have no idea where he is. That's a discussion?"

Mims set her fork down with enough force to break the table. "Really, Ella. What do you want from me?"

Ella slammed down her fork, too. "My life! And I don't want it to turn out like yours. I don't want to end up alone." Had that just come out of her mouth?

For a moment, she and her mother sat looking at each other in shocked silence. Finally Mims said, "There's nothing wrong with my life, and I'm not alone. I have you. We have each other. That man you were with, he was only going to bring you heartache."

"Like yours did?" Ella asked softly.

Mims squirmed in her seat. "I didn't need him, anyway. You don't need a man to be happy, baby, believe me."

"Are you all that happy, Mims?"

Her mother looked at her like she'd uttered some sort of blasphemy. "Of course I am!"

They fell into another strained silence as the waiter arrived to carry off their salad plates. As soon as he'd left, Ella asked, "Who *was* he?"

Mims rolled her eyes. "Oh, not this again. How many times have you asked me that question?"

About a million.

"What does it matter? The man's never been a part of your life."

"And why was that?"

"I've told you, we went our separate ways long before he even knew about you."

"Maybe he'd like to know about me."

Mims shook her head in disgust. "I doubt it."

"All you ever told me was that he was a model. Do you have any idea how many magazines I looked through growing up, studying each man, wondering if he could've been my father?" And wondering why, with two beautiful people as parents, she hadn't turned out more beautiful herself. Not that it had mattered after she met Jake.

"Ella, I'm not having this conversation."

Ella sighed. "I'm sorry he hurt you. Did he leave you for someone else?"

The expression on her mother's face said it all. "I told you, I'm done talking about this."

Some women told the whole world when a man left them, scattered their bitterness like so many seeds. Mims had put up a fence around her past and sown her bitterness inside, where it grew into mistrust. So was it really surprising that she'd been more than ready to believe Jake was cheating on her daughter? Her mother's mistrust, Ella's insecurity—what a deadly combination that had been!

It wasn't too late for Ella to recover from the ripple effect of her mother's long-ago liaison but maybe Mims never would. "Oh, Mims. I'm sorry. I'm sorry you were so badly hurt."

Now Mims looked like she was going to cry. She reached across the table and laid a hand over her daughter's. "I got the best part of him when I got you. And everything I've done has been for you, so you'd have a stable life."

"I did have a stable life," Ella assured her.

"And it hasn't been so bad, has it?"

"Of course not. But, Mims, I have to live my *own* life. You know yourself that eventually little girls grow up and leave home. You left home to be a model."

"And my mother never spoke to me again."

This was one story Ella had heard in plenty of detail. Sadly, her grandparents had died when she was young.

Maybe that was why Mims had clung to her so tightly. She was all her mother had. "I never left you, though," she said.

"He'd have been happy if you did," Mims said, and it didn't take a genius to figure out she was referring to Jake. "And he showed his true colors with that awful song."

The sounds of a guitar strumming intruded on their conversation. Ella looked up to see Jake approaching, his guitar strung over his shoulders.

"What's he doing here?" Mims said sourly.

Singing, obviously. "'This is just a thank-you to the women in my life,'" he crooned. "'To the mama who shared with me the beauty who's my wife.'"

A new song. He'd written a new song to make up for what he'd done! As Jake sang on, Ella stole a look across the table to see how Mims was receiving his peace offering. She was studying her salad plate, and wiping at a corner of her eye.

"'So here's a simple thank-you from a humble man, to the women in my life who make me who I am,'" Jake concluded.

The other diners applauded but he ignored them, keeping his gaze focused on Mims. "Lily, I know we haven't always gotten along, but I'd like to find a way to change that," he said. "I hope this song will be a beginning. I'm gonna sing it with my band and put it up on YouTube."

"Thank you," Mims said stiffly.

To Ella he said. "I have one more song. This one's for you." He began to strum and silence descended on the restaurant. Not a single fork clinked, not a glass was raised. Everyone, including the waitstaff, listened as Jake sang about the rough ride they'd had over the past year.

It had been, but maybe the ride had taken them to a new place, someplace more solid.

Now he was into the chorus, and every word held the promise of a better future.

By the time he'd finished, most of the women were blowing their noses or dabbing at their eyes, and that included Ella.

"I didn't get a chance to tell you, a talent manager from Nashville called me."

"A talent manager?" Ella smiled across the table. "He's going to make it, Mims."

Her mother grimaced, then—reluctantly—nodded.

"When you finish your dinner, how about you both come back to the house for dessert."

"We don't have any dessert," Ella said.

"Oh, yeah, we do. I called Cass and told her I had an emergency. She sold me a red velvet cake."

Ella's favorite, and the only dessert for which Mims had a weakness. Ella turned to her mother.

She was trying hard to look put upon. "I don't know. I have plans…"

"Well, if you do…" Jake began.

"I can change them."

Jake grinned. "Great. I'll see you girls back at the house."

He left and Ella turned to her mother. "I still love him, Mims. I tried not to but I can't seem to stop."

Her mother sighed. "Well, you could've done better. But I suppose you could've done worse. Time will tell."

Not exactly a movie ending, Ella thought, but a not a

bad new beginning, maybe for all of them. And the best Christmas present she could ask for.

It was Friday and the sign on the door of Gingerbread Haus read Closed for My Daughter's Wedding. Cass had taken the wedding cake home to decorate.

Late-afternoon shadows were stealing the light as she stepped away from the kitchen table to admire her magnum opus. It was a work of art, worthy of a baked-goods museum—a three-tiered pile of cake presents wrapped in fondant of white and red with silver frosting ribbon and dusted with delicate white snowflakes.

"Mom, it's beautiful," said Dani, who had joined her to admire the finished product.

The awe in her daughter's voice made the stiffness in Cass's back disappear. "I'm glad you like it."

"Like it? I love it!" Dani hugged her. "Now I'm glad you talked me out of cupcakes."

That was saying a lot.

Dani had just taken a picture with her cell phone when Mason entered the kitchen. "We're all ready to go to— Whoa, that is something else."

Cass smiled as she watched him approach the cake as though he was Indiana Jones moving toward lost Incan treasure. She'd come a long way from doll cakes and butterflies, and she couldn't help feeling gratified by his admiration of her art.

"And to think I used to make fun of your doll cakes," he said.

Now Babette joined them, with Cupcake trotting along behind. "Oh, that is gorgeous!"

Babette went up another notch in Cass's estimation.

A moment later Louise and Maddy were in the kitchen.

"We've been standing by the door forever," Maddy complained. "Are we leaving for the holiday lights parade or aren't we?"

"We were just looking at the cake," Dani said. "Isn't it beautiful?"

Louise studied it. "Hmm. Very nice."

Nice. Damning with faint praise. Cass felt a sudden desire to shove a pie in her former mother-in-law's face, but since there was no pie handy (probably just as well), she forced a smile and said, "We should get going."

"I didn't think you'd be able to come with us," Louise said.

Just one more day of her, Cass told herself. "I didn't, either," she said, pretending her unexpected presence was a pleasant surprise to Louise. "I thought this would take me longer." She'd figured she'd be decorating right up until the rehearsal, so the original plan had been to skip the parade and appetizers at Olivia's, finish the cake, then take it to the inn and set up before the rehearsal. Now she liked the idea of being able to join her family for all the festivities. Well, most of them.

"I don't understand why it took you so long to decorate," Louise said. "There isn't much to it."

Where was a good cream pie when you needed one?

"Fondant's very hard to work with," Dani said, springing to her mother's defense.

"Really?" Louise sounded like she didn't believe it.

"Let's go," Mason said. "We're all going to roast standing around here with our coats on."

Everyone trooped out of the kitchen, Cupcake dancing along with them and yapping. Willie and Amber had been waiting patiently on the couch—easy to do when you had a phone to play with—but now they both stood and the party was complete. Quite an impressive group.

We look like one, big, happy family, Cass thought. Boy, were looks deceiving.

At the door, Babette knelt and gave the furry little monster she called a dog a kiss on the head. "No, baby, you have to stay here and guard the house."

Mess up the house, more likely. Cass hoped Willie had shut his bedroom door. Otherwise, he'd be missing more shorts.

"The cake really is gorgeous," Maddy said to her as they paraded down the front walk.

"Thanks," Cass said. Maybe Maddy wasn't so bad, after all. Maybe this whole weekend wouldn't be so bad, after all. Life is good, she concluded with a smile.

Life is really good when you're a dog and you've discovered the world's biggest doggie treat sitting on the kitchen table.

The visiting exes had all been charmed by the parade, which consisted mostly of cars and horse-drawn sleighs decked out in lights and bearing various festival princesses and dignitaries and, of course, Santa. Now they all walked back to the house to get their cars for the drive to the lodge.

"The town looks like a giant snow globe," Babette said, taking in the twinkle lights everywhere. "I can see why you like living here," she said to Cass. Then to Mason, "I wouldn't mind having a condo up here."

Please God, no, Cass thought. She'd made her peace with Mason, but that didn't mean she wanted him and Babette living right around the corner.

Before she could speak, Mason said, "Cheaper to rent a condo once in a while."

Thank you, Mason.

"Anyway, I'm not sure Cass would want us here all the time."

Cass decided to change the subject.

A few minutes later they were back at the house. Louise said she needed to use the bathroom, Babette wanted to freshen her makeup and Mason offered to help Cass load the cake. It was too cold to wait outside, so everyone trooped into the house. Surprisingly, Cupcake wasn't at the door to greet them with her high-pitched bark. Or anything else, thank God.

"Where's Cupcake?" Babette wondered.

"Did you shut your bedroom doors?" Cass asked the kids.

"Uh, yeah," Willie said in a tone of voice that plainly stated he'd learned his lesson.

"Cupcake," Babette called, and walked through the dining room. "Cupcake." Now she headed for the kitchen. "Cup— Aaah!"

Cupcake…kitchen. Cass connected the dots and her heart dived to her feet. She rushed in past a stunned Babette and found Cupcake, destroyer of all, on the table and up to her furry face in frosting. She'd obviously used one of the kitchen chairs as a doggie stepstool to get to it. And get to it she had. There wasn't a layer of cake the little beast hadn't sampled.

With a shriek, Cass shooed the dog off the table. Cupcake yelped and scrammed, trailing cake and icing behind her, and the rest of the family entered the kitchen to see what was going on.

"Oh, Cupcake," Babette moaned. "Oh, Cass." That was as far as she got before bursting into tears.

Mason hesitated, torn between helping his distraught new wife and calming his former one.

There was no calming Cass. "That dog, that damned dog! Look what she's done. I'm going to kill her!"

"My cake," Dani wailed. Now she was crying, too.

"You shouldn't have left it on the table," Louise said. "You should've known that stupid dog would get it. In fact, I don't know why you brought it home."

Because, between waiting on customers and dealing with some family member calling her at the bakery every other minute with questions and needs, she'd thought it would be easier. Because she'd wanted to be where the family was. She'd wanted Dani to see her creation taking shape. She'd... Oh, she'd been stupid, that was all there was to it. She shoved her fist into a ruined layer and squeezed, pretending it was Cupcake's neck.

"Cass, I'm so sorry," Babette said in between sobs. "Your poor cake." Her eyes got big and she gasped. "Oh, no, and poor Cupcake. This is going to make her sick. Mason, we've got to find a vet." She whipped out her cell phone and strode from the kitchen past Willie and Amber.

"That cake is shit city," Willie observed.

"Shut up," Amber snapped at him. "It's okay, Mom," she said, hurrying over to Cass. "Maybe you can fix it."

"You'll never be able to fix that," Louise predicted. "The stupid animal has had its mouth all over the thing."

"Uh, let me know if you need me to do something," Mason said, and beat a hasty retreat.

Cass didn't blame him. She wished she could run away, too.

Accidents happened all the time, and she had mended

many a gingerbread house over the years and many a cake, too. But never one that had been practically bulldozed. She stood staring at her ruined work of art, her brain frozen.

"Do you have anything in stock at the bakery?" Maddy asked.

Two cakes that would feed twelve, six gingerbread houses and two dozen gingerbread boys, a dozen cream puff swans a-swimming... And a partridge in a pear tree. Cass began to laugh hysterically. She caught her former mother-and sister-in-law exchanging concerned glances. *The person responsible for the wedding cake has gone around the bend.* She fell onto a kitchen chair, willing her brain to cook up something.

Sheet cakes. She'd have to throw together some sheet cakes. Now, there was a memorable wedding present for her daughter.

Babette was back in the kitchen now. "Mason's taking Cupcake to the vet," she announced.

"Good for Cupcake," Cass muttered.

"Oh, my gosh, that's it!" Babette cried.

"What's it?" Louise demanded.

"Cupcakes. We could make cupcakes," Babette said gleefully.

"Oh, yes," Dani exclaimed.

Just what her daughter had wanted all along.

And Babette had been the one to suggest it—a bitter icing to top off this disaster. What made it even worse was that Cass didn't see how she could pull it off.

Dani was looking at her hopefully. Heck, everyone was looking at her.

"All right, cupcakes it is." They wouldn't be fancy

and she'd have to bake all through the night, but she'd get them done. Sleep was overrated, anyway.

Her daughter rushed to hug her. "Thank you, Mama. You're the best!"

Not the best at sharing, though. She still hated that it was Babette who'd promised to deliver Dani her heart's desire. But Babette was in her daughter's life to stay and *someone* needed to learn to share. There was no time like the present.

"We can all help," Babette said eagerly.

"I could use it," Cass admitted.

"Then let's get cracking." Louise rolled up her sleeves. "Tell us what to do, Cass."

"Okay," Cass said. "Dani, you take Amber and Willie and go on over to the lodge. Your father can join you there once he's dropped the dog off at the vet's."

"But the rehearsal dinner," Dani fretted.

"Will still happen," Cass assured her.

"Without you?"

"Never mind me," Cass said. "You've got your whole bridal party and Mike's family. You go and have fun."

"I can't leave you to bake all by yourself," Dani protested.

"You won't," Babette told her. "Remember, she'll have us."

"Absolutely," Maddy agreed.

"Family pulls together," Louise added, making Cass wonder if the woman's body had been taken over by aliens.

"I'm going to the bakery," Cass said. "I can bake more cupcakes more quickly over there. You all go to work here."

"I'll run to the store and get cake mixes." Babette started out of the kitchen.

"Don't forget butter and powdered sugar," Louise called after her, searching the cupboards.

"I've got plenty of both at the bakery," said Cass. "Stop by there on your way back."

"What should we do with this?" Maddy asked, pointing to the cake.

"Let's eat it," Willie said, and stuck a finger in the frosting.

"It's got dog drool all over it," Amber said in disgust.

Willie made a face, then said, "I'll eat around the drool."

"You don't have time," Amber told him. "We have to get to the rehearsal."

"I'll take a piece with me."

Cass didn't stick around to hear any more of the conversation. She had things to do.

She'd just put her first batch of cupcakes in the oven when she heard pounding on the bakery door. Thinking it was Babette coming by for frosting supplies, she hurried to answer.

It was, but she also had Samantha and Bailey with her.

"Sam, what are you doing here?" Cass asked.

"Kidnapping you," Samantha said.

"What?"

"I'm here to make sure you get to the rehearsal and the dinner."

Cass shook her head. "Maybe Babette didn't tell you, but we've got an emergency."

"She did and that's why we're here," Bailey said. "I'm taking over for you until after the dinner."

"Mom and Cecily are baking," said Samantha. "So are Ella and Charley. And Blake will be taking my cupcakes out of the oven in…" She checked the time on her cell phone. "Five minutes. Then I have to get a new batch in." She grinned. "Our secret chocolate cupcake recipe."

"How did you— I don't understand."

"Babette found me and I spread the word," Samantha said. "Half the women in town are busy baking even as we speak. So, come on. You have some mother-of-the-bride duties to perform."

Cass blinked back tears. "Thank you."

"Don't thank me, thank Babette," Samantha said. "She's the one who sounded the alarm."

Her beautiful cake was ruined and that made Cass sad. But her daughter's day *wasn't* ruined, thanks to friends and former in-laws pulling together. And that was amazing.

Even more amazing, she was becoming downright fond of Babette.

Twenty-One

Dani's wedding was one to remember and, happily, not because of any more wedding disasters but because everything was perfect. Sitting with Babette in the transformed big meeting room at Icicle Creek Lodge, Cass watched teary-eyed as Amber came down the aisle to Pachelbel's *Canon,* looking much older than the fifteen years she now was in a sophisticated red satin dress. Dani's friends Vanessa and Mikaila, both in gray satin, were next, two girls barely into their twenties and just beginning their lives.

Now, here came Dani, walking an indoor garden path lined with white roses, silver netting froth and greenery, carrying a bouquet of red and white tea roses. Her baby, all grown up, a snow princess, escorted by her beaming father. Cass was so glad her brother, Drew, was here, recording the whole thing.

"Who gives this woman to be wedded to this man?" asked Pastor Jim once they'd reached the front of the room.

"Her mother and I, with all our love," Mason said. His part in the ceremony over, he sat down between Cass and

Babette and, much to Cass's surprise, took her hand and gave it a squeeze. She smiled and squeezed back. It was so much better to be allies than enemies.

Pastor Jim made sure his talk was short and sweet. "I wish I could promise you that your life together will always be just like this day—perfect. But it won't, and I think you already know that. There are going to be times when you'll look at each other and ask, 'Why did I pick you?' So I want you to file away in your minds what you're thinking, what you're feeling, right now. Remember the good you see in each other right now. If you do that, you'll be fine."

Cass swallowed a lump. Maybe she and Mason would have been fine if she'd had a Pastor Jim to advise them when they first got together. Too late for those regrets now. She'd chosen the life she had and it wasn't so bad. In fact, it was pretty darned wonderful.

One of Dani's musical girlfriends played her guitar and sang the wedding song Jake had written for Ella as Dani and Mike poured colored sand—his silver, hers gold— into the tall crystal vase that had been Cass's mother's. Cass watched as the colors mingled and swirled. Two becoming one. Not just two people, she thought, looking to where Mike's mother, Delia, sat alongside her husband and mother, dabbing at her eyes with a tissue. Two families. No, make that three, she amended as Babette linked her arm through Mason's.

The couple exchanged vows and then Pastor Jim grinned. "And now, the moment we've all been waiting for. By the powers vested in me, I now proclaim you husband and wife. Mike, you may kiss your bride."

And kiss her he did, while his buddies hooted and everyone broke into applause. Then, to the surprise of everyone, including the mother of the bride, the bridal party danced their way down the aisle to a pumping rock song.

So, of course, as the ushers (including Willie, who'd decided he wasn't so averse to wearing a tux, after all) sent them on their way row by row, the guests did, too. It was a short walk to the huge dining room where the reception would be held. The room was lovely to begin with, but Heinrich and Kevin had turned it into something magical with white and silver floral arrangements and silver mercury-glass votive candles. Looking at all the flowers, greenery and netting, Cass knew they'd gone *way* beyond her budget. What a wedding gift!

With the help of Charley's waitstaff from Zelda's, Bailey had the food well in hand. And the cupcakes—every imaginable flavor—were to die for. Cass vowed to get the recipe for Janice Lind's banana cupcakes if it was the last thing she did.

"You'll never get it out of her," Dot predicted when Cass stopped by her table to visit with her and Tilda and some of her Chamber of Commerce pals.

"I'll just have to get my hands on some truth serum," Cass joked.

"Well," Louise said later as they all stood watching Dani and Mike feed each other cupcakes, "you did it."

"No," Cass corrected. "*We* did it. Thanks, Louise."

Her mother-in-law shrugged. "Anything for my granddaughter."

Cass couldn't help smiling.

Now Babette and Mason joined them. "What a lovely wedding," she told Cass. "Thanks for letting us stay with you. It was great to be a part of everything."

"I'm happy it worked out," Cass said, and realized she meant it.

"It's so lovely up here. I really have fallen in love with this place," Babette continued.

"I think we should all stay for Christmas," Louise said. "That'll give us a little more time with Dani and Mike before they leave for Spokane."

"Good idea," Maddy chimed in.

"Christmas?" Cass repeated weakly.

"But all our presents are back at the house," Babette protested.

"You don't want to miss out on those," Cass added, grabbing at straws.

"We can do presents anytime," Louise said. "Let's make a party out of this. Anyway, with all these cute shops, I'm sure we can find some small gifts to open."

"And that's why all my exes are still here," Cass told her friends at their chick-flick party the next evening.

They'd moved the festivities to Ella's house, figuring Cass would be beat. And she was. But she was also happy. Probably a sloppy sentiment hangover. Now she lounged on Ella's couch, Tiny keeping her company. She had no illusions about being his favorite, though. He was only there because she'd been slipping him bits of her cookie.

"Sounds like you're going to have some Christmas," Cecily said. "I don't envy you."

"Me, neither," Charley agreed.

"Speaking of Christmas, are you going to be okay?" Cecily asked her.

Charley nodded. "Absolutely. I'm off tomorrow to stay with my sister in Portland. I need a break anyway, otherwise I'm going to kill that Dan Masters."

Cass had heard from Cecily about the angry sparks that flew every time Charley had to deal with the tough-as-nails owner of Masters Construction who was going to be restoring Zelda's. Maybe those sparks were fueled by more than their disagreements. Cass hoped so. Charley was too young to spend the rest of her life without someone.

She's not that much younger than you, whispered a little voice. *Yeah,* Cass told it, *but I'm too set in my ways.* She didn't need a man. She had her business and her kids. *Who are growing up and leaving you,* the voice reminded her. Well, they wouldn't *all* leave. She hoped some of them would stay in town.

"I have some news," Ella said. The way she was beaming, it came as no surprise when she announced, "I just took an early pregnancy test. And I passed!"

"Oh, my gosh! Congratulations," Cecily cried, and jumped from her chair to hug her friend.

"Good," Charley said. "Another baby to play with."

"Not unless you want to come to Nashville." Ella smiled as she spoke. "That's the rest of my news. We're moving."

"Wow, that's fast," Cass said in astonishment.

"The house was already sold. Plus Jake's got a talent manager interested in him."

"Thanks to the YouTube song?" Cecily asked.

Ella nodded.

"How many views is that up to now?" Samantha asked, then let out a low whistle after Ella told her. "Looks like he's really got a hit on his hands."

"That *has* to have made your mom happy," Cecily said.

"She's okay with it. Sort of," Ella added with a grin. "Mainly because he wrote a nice one and put that up, too."

"So, what's your mom going to do?" Samantha asked.

"She says she'll come visit, but she's not moving down there. Too many rednecks."

"I kind of like rednecks," Charley said.

"Me, too," Ella said, making her friends smile. Then she turned serious. "We have one problem though. Tiny. We can't take him with us. We'll be living in an apartment. Plus he's a mountain dog. He needs cold, mountain air. It wouldn't be fair to make him swelter in the South."

"What are you going to do with him?" Cass asked, rubbing the dog's head.

"We need to find a good home, preferably here."

Cass remembered how Amber had fawned over Cupcake. The kids had been bugging her to get a dog for years. She'd always resisted, though, claiming that between them and the bakery she had enough to take care of.

Dani was moving. Cass needed to fill the hole in her home and her life.

She hadn't had a dog since she and Mason were first married. It would be nice to have one to come home to.

But did she have to start out with one the size of a horse?

Better that than a yippy, spoiled Pomeranian.

As if sensing a need to prove how lovable he was, he laid his head on Cass's lap and looked up at her with big, brown eyes. And drooled on her. Well, every male had his faults.

"He likes you," Samantha said.

"You want to come live with us?" Cass asked, and Tiny barked.

"Let me run it by the kids," she said to Ella.

"As if they're going to object," Samantha scoffed. "Just say yes. You know you want to."

"Okay, yes. But when Jake makes it big and comes to Seattle, you owe me concert tickets. Front row," Cass added with a smile.

"Front row," Ella agreed, beaming. "So, are you guys ready for my movie pick?"

"Let's have it," Charley said. "What are we watching?"

Ella's smile grew bigger as she pulled a DVD out of her purse. "The perfect movie. *It's a Wonderful Life.*"

"You know," Cass said with a smile. "You're right. It is."

She had to remind herself of that on Christmas Day when she tripped over Cupcake, lost her balance and dropped the red velvet cake she was bringing out to the dining room table for her open house.

"Oh, no," Babette wailed as she hurried to help clean up the mess. "Oh, Cass, I'm so—"

"Sorry," Cass finished with her. "Oh, well, we've still got cookies. And appetizers. And if you eat them you're dead," she informed the dog, who was now in the living room, seeking protection in Amber's lap.

"You hear that?" Babette said to Cupcake. "Bad dog!"

Of course, everyone who showed up for the party thought the little beast was adorable.

"Maybe you should bring Tiny over so they can get acquainted," Cass whispered to Ella.

Ella smiled. "You're evil."

"Thanks. I try."

"It's a great party," Ella said, looking around.

Indeed, it was. And it was made even better when her mother called from Florida. "Get the guest room ready. We'll be flying up in time for New Year's and I'll be setting off airport security all the way. So tell Dani not to leave before I get there."

"Don't worry. She'll still be here."

"Hopefully your other guests will be gone."

"They will," Cass said.

"I'm so proud of you," said her mother. "Not everyone could have pulled off hosting her exes the way you have."

She *had* pulled it off. Somehow, they'd all gotten through. Nearby Charley was laughing at something Cecily had said, and Jake and Ella had settled in on the couch and were acting as much like newlyweds as Dani and Mike. Louise had cornered poor Delia, and Maddy was showing off her engagement ring to Drew, who was looking for a way to escape.

As Cass surveyed the room she caught sight of Mason standing by the Christmas tree with Willie and Amber. He smiled at her and saluted her with his glass of eggnog.

She raised hers back. *Merry Ex-mas.*

Actually, it was.

* * * * *

RECIPES & BAKING HINTS FROM
CASS WILKES

We thought you might enjoy the recipes for some of our wedding cupcakes. These are so good you won't be able to eat just one. But before we get to the recipes, let me give you a few tips on baking cupcakes.

1. Use cupcake liners. They're not only pretty, but your cupcakes will rise higher and be easier to take from the pan.

2. When pouring your cupcakes, fill the liners two-thirds to three-quarters full. If you fill to the brim your cupcakes will overflow and you'll have a mess.

3. Most standard 2½ inch cupcakes are baked from 15 to 22 minutes. Don't overbake your cupcakes or they'll be dry.

4. When making a cake or cupcakes, add a package of plain gelatin to the mix. This will keep your cake from cracking.

Okay, now, you're ready to go.

Samantha Sterling's Chocolate Ganache-Marscarpone Cupcakes

(courtesy of New York Times *bestselling author Jill Barnett)*

MAKES 1 DOZEN

What you'll need in addition to the ingredients
Paper baking cups
1 cupcake holer or grapefruit spoon
muffin tin

Ingredients

For cake:
¼ lb. (1 stick) butter
1 cup sugar
1 cup all-purpose flour
4 extra-large eggs, room temperature
1 Tbsp. vanilla
16 oz. chocolate syrup such as Hershey's

For ganache:
⅓ cup heavy whipping cream
6 oz. high quality chocolate chips such as Ghirardelli (semisweet or milk chocolate)
½ tsp. instant espresso

For cream filling:
½ pint heavy whipping cream
1 small container mascarpone cheese or 4 oz. whipped cream cheese
1 tsp. vanilla
1-2 heaping Tbsp. sugar

Directions

For your cake, cream the butter, sugar and eggs and beat until fluffy. Add the chocolate syrup and vanilla and mix, then sift in flour and mix. Line muffin tin and pour the mix into each cupcake liner until ¼ inch away from the top of the liner. Bake at 350° for 13 to 18 minutes, until the tops of the cupcakes spring back. Cool.

For your ganache, heat chocolate chips and ⅓ cup heavy cream and espresso powder over boiling water, stirring constantly, until completely melted and glossy. Dip the top of your cooled cupcakes in the chocolate (twice if you want a thicker ganache layer). Let cool. Samantha (and Jill) usually make them the evening before a party and let them set overnight so the ganache is firm.

The next morning you can use your cupcake holer to take out a small part of the center of your cupcake, or you can simply use a melon baller or small grapefruit spoon.

For your mascarpone cream filling, mix in a bowl with a hand mixer, ½ pint whipping cream, 4 oz. mascarpone or whipped cream cheese, sugar and vanilla. Mix until very stiff. Then spoon into a quart-size plastic storage bag, cut off the tip and pipe into the center of the cupcakes, piping it up about an inch above the ganache.

Cupcakes don't have to be refrigerated unless it's hot out. (In fact, worrying about storing them is never a problem. These babies go in a hurry!)

CASS'S RED VELVET CUPCAKES

MAKES 2 DOZEN

Yes, they're everywhere now, but this particular recipe comes with Cass's top-secret frosting recipe. (She got it from Sheila Roberts, who kept both the frosting and the cake recipe a secret since she first got it from a Southern belle at the age of sixteen. We don't really know how many years ago that was, since Sheila has been lying about her age since she turned thirty, but we do know it's quite a long time.)

Ingredients

2 oz. red food coloring
3 Tbsp. powdered chocolate milk mix (such as Nestle's Quik)
½ cup shortening
2¼ cup cake flour
1 tsp. soda
1 Tbsp. vinegar
1 tsp. vanilla

2 eggs, beaten
1 cup buttermilk (Note: if you forgot to buy buttermilk, you can substitute milk with a small amount of vinegar added to it.)
1 tsp. (scant) salt

Directions

Mix food coloring and chocolate powder in a small bowl. Cream the shortening and sugar. Combine beaten eggs and food coloring mixture, then add it to the shortening mixture. Sift flour and salt together and add alternately with buttermilk. Add vanilla. Remove from mixer and add one at a time by hand, first the soda, then the vinegar.

Pour into muffin tins lined with paper baking cups and bake at 350° for 15 to 20 minutes, until the cake springs back when touched. As with the chocolate cupcakes (or any cake), don't overbake. Cool and then frost with Red Velvet Cake Frosting.

Frosting for Red Velvet Cake

Ingredients

¼ lb. (1 stick) butter
8 Tbsp. shortening
3 Tbsp. flour
1 cup sugar (Make sure you use pure cane sugar.)

⅔ cup milk, room temperature
1 tsp. vanilla

Directions

Combine, one at a time, the butter, shortening, sugar and flour, beating well after each addition. Add milk and vanilla and beat well. Will keep in refrigerator.

Note: Use pure cane sugar for this frosting. The cheaper beet sugar is coarser and will leave your frosting tasting grainy.

Cass's Wedding Cupcakes

Ingredients

2¼ cup sifted flour
2½ tsp. baking powder
1 tsp. salt
1½ cup sugar
½ cup butter, room
  temperature

1 Tbsp. oil (for added
  moistness)
1 cup milk
2 eggs
1 tsp. vanilla

Directions

Sift flour, salt and baking powder into a bowl. Then add sugar, butter, vanilla and two-thirds of the milk. Beat with mixer at medium speed for two minutes. Add remaining milk and unbeaten eggs and beat 2 minutes longer. Pour into muffin tins lined with paper cupcake liners and bake at 350° for 18 to 20 minutes. Cool. Frost with Rose Frosting.

Rose Frosting

Ingredients

2½ cups powdered sugar
3 Tbsp. butter, room
 temperature

3 Tbsp. milk, room
 temperature
⅛ tsp. rose water*

*Note: You can find rose water in the specialty section of a high quality grocery store. This is a powerful flavor so use sparingly. Remember, you can always add more, but if you add too much your guests will think they're eating soap.

Directions

Sift your powdered sugar, then mix in all your other ingredients. Sifting the powdered sugar and using room temperature butter and milk will help prevent lumps in your frosting. Add your favorite pastel food coloring.

Janice Lind's Banana Cupcakes

MAKES 2 DOZEN

Ingredients

2½ cups cake flour
2 cups sugar
2½ tsp. baking powder
1 tsp. salt
1 tsp. soda
1 Tbsp. oil (for added
  moistness)

1 tsp. banana extract
⅔ cup butter
2 eggs
1¼ cup mashed ripe
  bananas
1¼ cup coconut milk

Directions

Sift flour, soda, baking powder and salt into a mixing bowl. Add sugar, butter, bananas and half the coconut milk. Beat with mixer at medium speed for two minutes. Add eggs, banana extract and remaining coconut milk and beat for two more minutes. Pour batter into your cupcake liners and bake at 350° for 15 to 20 minutes, until cake springs back when you touch it. Cool. Frost with Red Velvet Cake Frosting. (Cream cheese frosting also works well with this recipe.)

Merry Christmas and happy baking!
—Cass

New York Times bestselling author

DEBBIE MACOMBER

National Bestselling Author

SHEILA ROBERTS

**Discover two heartwarming tales
in one stunning collection!**

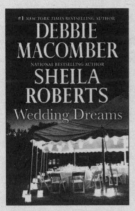

First Comes Marriage
by Debbie Macomber

Janine loves her grandfather but balks at his plan to choose her a husband. Zach, the intended groom, has recently merged his business with the family firm, and Grandfather insists it would be a perfect match. Zach and Janine agree on one thing—that Gramps is a stubborn, meddling old man. But... what if he's right?

Sweet Dreams on Center Street
by Sheila Roberts

Sweet Dreams Chocolate Company has been in the Sterling family for generations, but now it looks as if they're about to lose it to the bank. Unfortunately, the fate of Sweet Dreams is in the hands of Samantha's archenemy, Blake, the bank manager with the football-hero good looks. It's enough to drive her to chocolate.

Available now, wherever books are sold!

$1.⁰⁰ OFF

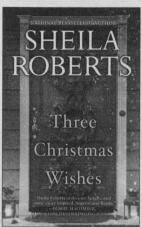

National Bestselling Author

SHEILA ROBERTS

Three women, three wishes—
one Christmas!

Three Christmas Wishes

MIRA®

Available October 18, 2016!

Pick up your copy today!

$7.99 U.S./$9.99 CAN.

$1.⁰⁰ OFF the purchase price of THREE CHRISTMAS WISHES by Sheila Roberts.

Offer valid from October 18, 2016, to November 30, 2016.
Redeemable at participating retail outlets, in-store only. Not redeemable at
Barnes & Noble. Limit one coupon per purchase. Valid in the U.S.A. and Canada only.

52614372

5 65373 00076 2   (8100)0 12226

® and ™ are trademarks owned and used by the trademark owner and/or its licensee.

© 2016 Harlequin Enterprises Limited

MCOUPSR1016

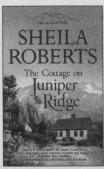
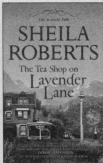
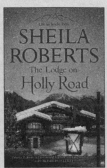
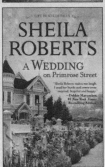
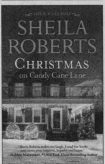
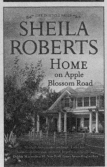

REQUEST YOUR FREE BOOKS!

2 FREE NOVELS
FROM THE ROMANCE COLLECTION,
PLUS 2 FREE GIFTS!

ROM15R

DEBBIE MACOMBER
SHEILA ROBERTS

31903 WEDDING DREAMS   ___ $7.99 U.S. ___ $9.99 CAN.

(limited quantities available)

TOTAL AMOUNT $ _____
POSTAGE & HANDLING $ _____
($1.00 for 1 book, 50¢ for each additional)
APPLICABLE TAXES* $ _____
TOTAL PAYABLE $ _____

(check or money order—please do not send cash)

To order, complete this form and send it, along with a check or money order for the total above, payable to MIRA Books, to: **In the U.S.:** 3010 Walden Avenue, P.O. Box 9077, Buffalo, NY 14269-9077; **In Canada:** P.O. Box 636, Fort Erie, Ontario, L2A 5X3.

Name: _____
Address: _____ City: _____
State/Prov.: _____ Zip/Postal Code: _____
Account Number (if applicable): _____
075 CSAS

*New York residents remit applicable sales taxes.
*Canadian residents remit applicable GST and provincial taxes.

MIRA®

www.MIRABooks.com

MDMSR1016BL